THE DUKE'S INDECENT SCANDAL

INDECENT DUKES
BOOK ONE

GOLDEN ANGEL

CONTENTS

To all the ladies who never knew they were a beautiful swan.

We are all tens.

PROLOGUE

G *regory*
The unlucky dukes. That's what we should call ourselves.
Eight of us down down to seven, in the blink of an eye.

Gregory Clarence, the Duke of Clarence, looked around the lavishly decorated private room at White's, the gentlemen's club where they'd congregated. The surrounds were such that they should have been completely comfortable. The furniture was heavy, masculine, the colors dark and rich, with every comfort provided.

Fit for a duke. Six of them, in fact, with a seventh on the way from the funeral services they'd all just attended together.

A funeral for their former eighth.

They had just come from the graveside of Sinclair Seymour, the Duke of Northumberland.

Perhaps fate thought that eight young, handsome, unmarried dukes in need of wives and heirs were too many at once and had thrown the storm in the path of his ship. Though Sinclair's heir was also unmarried, to call him 'handsome' would be stretching things too far. He'd been on the unlucky ship, though below decks, when

"

one of the sailors yelled, 'man, overboard'. Sinclair's body had floated away in the maelstrom, never to be recovered.

His heir, though now also a young and unmarried duke, would never truly be one of them.

They'd been bonded together by an explosion and fire at a hunting lodge that had taken their fathers' lives. All eight of them at once, leaving a plethora of them to be assailed by the marriage-minded ladies of the ton this upcoming Season, now that they were out of mourning for their fathers.

Now, Sinclair was gone as well, lost to nature's cruelty rather than man's conniving, but dead all the same. His grave held an empty coffin as his body had been lost at sea. Dead was dead, though, whether in the ground or at the bottom of the ocean.

Lifting the cut-crystal glass of brandy to his lips, his gut aching from the thought of what Sinclair must have gone through on his way to his watery grave, Gregory downed it in one go.

When his pater had died, Gregory had known he'd eventually need a wife and heir. They all had. Given their youth, compared to their fathers, none of them had felt in any rush. They had the expectation of years ahead of them.

Sinclair's death had thrown that cocky assurance into stark relief. Tomorrow was never a sure thing.

The burn of the alcohol down his throat did nothing to help with his grief and rage at the unfairness of it, though it provided a small distraction. Something for his overset mind to focus on.

Sebastian Graham, Duke of Bolton, came beside him, holding his own full glass of brandy. Sebastian was Gregory's closest friend among the group. They had met at school years ago and had been friends before the tragedy that brought the rest of the group together. It had often been remarked that they looked enough alike to be brothers, both with similarly dark hair and eyes, broad shoulders, and brooding gazes.

Normally Gregory was not the brooding sort, he much preferred being cheerful.

Not today, though. Today, he was as stalwart and grim as Sebastian.

Unlike Gregory, Sebastian did not seem inclined to drink his brandy. He merely held it in his hand, his dark gaze glinting as he stared at the painting above the fireplace. Gregory did not think his friend was actually seeing the painting of the hunting dog. Sebastian's eyes were unfocused, staring at nothing.

"What is taking Zachary so long?" Sebastian murmured after a long moment, his usually even tone full of consternation at being made to wait. They'd all agreed to come together to mourn on their own, away from the spectacle that Sinclair's death had created within greater society.

Sinclair's death had already created a hole in their company.

"He will stay as long as he feels Isabella needs him to." Gregory knew Sebastian's question was likely rhetorical, but he felt compelled to answer. Though Zachary was not known for his timeliness, in this case, it was understandable. Laudable even.

Sebastian sighed, his impatience stifled at the reminder of Sinclair's grieving fiancé. The pair had been a true love match, shocking Society. Gregory had found it more enviable than shocking, but he knew better than to expect such serendipity for himself. Love was rare, and even rarer among their set.

"All our fathers gone at once... will we go one by one?" Sebastian appeared deep in morbid thought, the line of which mirrored Gregory's own.

His stomach twisted.

"Sinclair was a tragic accident," he reminded Sebastian. "Not murder." Not like their fathers.

"We thought they were a tragic accident at first as well," Sebastian reminded him, finally turning away from the painting to look at Gregory. His dark eyes were full of sorrow that Gregory did not feel as he reached up with his free hand to rake his fingers through his dark hair.

Sebastian mourned his father. Gregory did not have the same reaction. The news of his father's death had come mostly as a relief.

But he was not sanguine about the loss of his father, either, if only because he worried it put himself and his mother in danger. They still did not know who had arranged the explosion at the hunting lodge that had ended their fathers' lives. They did not know what the motivation had been... though Gregory had found threatening letters hidden away when he'd been going through his father's things. Letters threatening his father's life.

He had not shared them with his fellow unlucky dukes yet. Not even Sebastian.

It had crossed his mind that it was entirely possible one of them desired an early inheritance, and the rest of the dukes had been unfortunate bystanders. It was also entirely possible they would think the same of him.

Unlike Sebastian, his relationship with his father had been cold. He was not the only one. While several of their group truly mourned their progenitors, there were just as many who did not.

The door to the room opened, and all of them turned from their quiet conversations to see the new arrival. Zachary strode into the room, stiffly upright as always, his collar points poking at his structured jawline and short brown hair still perfectly styled despite the windiness of the day. He was even more proper than Sebastian, sometimes annoyingly so, in Gregory's opinion. Both of them could be a damper to good fun, even if it had kept him out of trouble a time or two.

Today, however, he was far more sympathetic to Zachary's foibles. After all, if he'd been the one to lose Sebastian... he did not know if he would be able to keep the stiff upper lip the way Zachary had. Gregory was saddened by Sinclair's death but not devastated the way he would have been if he'd lost his closest friend.

"My apologies for my tardiness," Zachary said, stripping off his gloves and greatcoat to reveal his funeral dress. It felt odd to see Zachary in unrelieved black, as he normally preferred to have some touch of brightness about his personage. He appeared rather annoyed. "I was detained by Northumberland." He glowered at having to call someone other than Sinclair by the title. Especially a fawning upstart like William Seymour. Sinclair's heir had done his best to hide his glee at his good fortune in becoming a duke, but it had leaked through several times.

While his grief was sincere, the happiness at his sudden shift in position had made it hard not to resent him.

Christian, Duke of Montagu and the only light-haired duke among them, who had been standing by the drinking cart, now approached with a glass of brandy for Zachary. They looked like Gabriel and Lucifer standing next to each other—Christian's fair looks were often called heavenly, while Zachary's dark hair and eyes made him appear akin to a fallen angel. Together, they made quite a pair. Zachary took the offered drink and downed it in one go.

"What did he want?" Christian asked, frowning, his blue eyes cold and sharp, unlike his normal bored ennui. He'd taken a deep dislike to Sinclair's heir from the beginning, though he'd hidden it for Sinclair's sake. It was not as though they got to choose their heirs, after all. Something that had been very much on Gregory's mind from the moment he'd been informed of Sinclair's loss at sea.

"To reassure me that he would assist Isabella in the manner he knew Sinclair would have wanted and that he would safeguard the estate." Zachary made a face. "Also to toady up to me. He wanted to know where we were all gathering afterward."

Immediately, everyone frowned.

"He is not one of us." Sebastian shook his head, as if he could shake off the new Duke of Northumberland that easily. Being a young, new duke, William seemed to want to fit in with the rest of them, seeming not to understand that it was not only their youth that drew them together.

All of them had been trained to be dukes from the moment they were born, unlike him. All of them had lost their fathers, all together, unlike him. He might step into Sinclair's title by dint of birth, but he could not fill his shoes in every way.

"He is not, but we will have to deal with him at times, regardless," Zachary replied, though his deep frown indicated his own displeasure with the necessity. "He is Northumberland now, and there is nothing any of us can do about it."

"We could get lucky," Matthew replied. Not a surprising response from the Duke of St. Albans, who had been known to the *ton* as the Lord of Luck for years. He was legitimately the luckiest man Gregory had ever met. He wondered if Matthew considered the death of his father lucky... he'd had an even worse relationship with the man than Gregory had had with his.

"Lucky, how?" Christian asked cynically, shaking his head. "Another dead duke? At some point, it's going to seem as though we're cursed." The *ton's* acknowledged Adonis, blessed with the body and face of a Greek God, was rarely so serious. Sinclair's death had shaken all of them.

"Maybe we are," Gregory chimed in, rallying to the need he saw among his friends. "Cursed with good looks and good health." Sadly, those things were not enough to save a man who fell overboard in the middle of a storm at sea. Poor Sinclair. The jest fulfilled its purpose, though, making most of his friends chuckle or at least smile. Only Zachary was still somber, though the corners of his mouth did lift for a moment.

"Christian has certainly been cursed with good looks," Matthew said, making all of them laugh. All of them were handsome, but only Christian had the power to make the ladies swoon with a single wink. Literally swoon. Gregory had watched them fall into a faint with his own eyes, all because the *ton's* "most beautiful man" had noticed them.

"I would like to request to be cursed with riches," Nathanial joked.

"I believe you will be cursed when you find your riches," Gregory said with a wink to ease the sting of his jest. Nathanial would have to marry for money, and they all knew it. It was the only way to secure the funds he needed to build the estate back up again. None of the creditors were willing to look twice at him after the way his father had left them high and dry. Luckily for him, his position meant there were many wealthy daughters whose dowries would save the estate and who would happily become a duchess in exchange for said dowry.

All he had to do was choose one.

"I believe we're all going to be cursed soon unless we want a situation like Northumberland," Zachary pointed out. "My mother and uncle have already been prodding me."

The air seemed to go out of the room as they all looked at each other in dreary acknowledgment of the truth. Gregory had been doing his best not to think about it. They'd all known, of course, that a wife and heir were a requirement to carry on the family line. That fact had been drilled into them since birth.

But they'd all thought they'd have more time.

As much as Gregory had despised his father, the man had been a buffer between Gregory and his duties. He did not mind the running of the estate. One of the reasons he and his father had clashed was over how his father ran the estate, how he treated their people—and especially how he treated Gregory's mother. But Gregory had been in no hurry to marry.

Even after his father's death, he'd been in no rush. He was young, after all. Nearing thirty. Very young to inherit. There were things to do. The prescribed mourning to observe. Even if he was not mourning, Society demanded a certain ritual. Like the black armband tied just above his elbow to acknowledge the loss of Sinclair.

This upcoming Season was the first they were all out of mourning. Nathanial would not be the only one facing the marriage mart. If it were not for losing Sinclair, Gregory would be doing his best to hide himself away.

Sinclair's death had made him face his own mortality. He did not know his heir, a second cousin to his father, and had never met the man. He could not trust a stranger with his mother's care, not after all she'd suffered living with his father. He needed to ensure she was cared for. If his father's cousin was anything like his father, Gregory did not want the man anywhere near his mother.

That meant finding a wife and siring an heir.

"How hard can it be to find a bride?" Sebastian asked. "We are dukes. It is the first Season we'll be attending since being in mourning. We will likely be mobbed by debutantes and their mamas as soon as we step foot into the first ball. It is just a matter of choosing one of them."

"It is the choice that is difficult," Gregory replied, shaking his head. Sebastian had clearly not thought through the pitfalls. "It is not just a bride—it is a *wife*. The woman who will run your household, mother your children, and warm your bed. She'll know your secrets, at least some of them." Which was his largest concern.

"If she's awful, you can pack her off to the country and warm your mistress' bed," Christian said. Leaning back in his seat, he tugged his maroon waistcoat down into place, rolling his shoulders to settle the fabric of his black jacket.

"Not until you've sired your heir." Gregory had given it quite a bit of thought. "And if you do so, you risk someone else warming *her* bed."

Christian opened his mouth, then closed it again, frowning as if the thought had not occurred to him. It had occurred to Gregory. In large part because he'd warmed quite a few lonely *ton* wives' beds over the past decade. Fidelity was not an attribute the *ton* held in high regard.

One of the few points Gregory agreed with his father on was in wanting fidelity from his wife. He knew very well that his father had not considered himself beholden to the same standard, which was why Gregory had inherited the care of several younger half-sisters along with his estate. Whether or not he followed in his father's footsteps in that way... he was unsure.

It would likely depend on his wife. He did know that he would be discreet. He would not hurt his wife by rubbing her face in any mistresses or affairs.

More to the point, though, he knew firsthand how many women were willing to loosen more than their stays when taking a lover. They had loose tongues as well, spilling secrets of their households and husbands over pillow talk, things they would not tell their closest friend but which were revealed in the dark of night when they lay in a lover's arms.

No, he needed a wife to stay true to him, and he would ensure that he did not embarrass or distress her. How he would find such a woman was the dilemma.

"And yet we still need wives and heirs," Zachary muttered. "As quickly as possible." Or possibly end up like Sinclair, with a grieving fiancé, no heir, and a cousin taking his position. At least he did not have any dependents who the new Northumberland was now required to take care of.

The rest of them all did, in one manner or another.

"We can assist each other," Christian said, looking around the room and meeting all of their gazes. "We can use this Season to find appropriate wives for all of us."

"Speak for yourself." The Duke of Ormonde, and the quietest of their group, finally spoke up from where he was seated in the corner, lounging in an armchair. Drake was an even bigger rake than Gregory; he was also the only one of them who was engaged. However, he'd been putting off the wedding for three years now. "I am already spoken for. I'll be using this Season as a final run of merriment before I finally join the *blessed institution*." The sarcastic spin he put on the last two words made clear his real feelings of being betrothed to the daughter of his mother's best friend.

"We could trade situations," Matthew offered from across the room, lifting his glass of cognac by way of recognition. "I'll happily marry Lady Astrid rather than look for a bride."

Rather than decide on a bride was more likely what he meant. The Lord of Luck tended to make his decisions by flipping a coin—

and, strangely, following the coin always led to advantageous outcomes for himself.

"And you did not even flip a coin to choose her," Nathanial joked.

"Oh, I did." Matthew patted the breast pocket of his jacket, where he kept his lucky coin. "Just now. That's why I made the offer. It said to."

Drake scowled at him rather fiercely.

"Your coin cannot break the marriage contract, nor can it explain to my mother why said contract *should* be broken," he said darkly. "Find your own bride."

A rather vehement response, but then, the Duchess of Ormonde was formidable. If she had chosen Gregory's bride, he would not want to face her down, either. Especially on the flimsy basis of Matthew's lucky coin. The Lord of Luck's good fortune did not always extend to others.

"You can help us," he told Drake. "Since you do not need to look for your own bride. Especially when it comes to knowing which debutante to choose. Perhaps Lady Astrid will drop a word or two in your ear about our choices?"

"Did you not hear me when I said I was going to be enjoying myself this Season?" Drake turned his scowl Gregory's way, though it was not nearly as dark as when it had been directed at Matthew. "If I must be leg-shackled after it, I am going to enjoy myself during."

"Just get yourself a mistress or a lover if it bothers you that much," Christian told him with some exasperation. He'd warmed even more beds than Gregory. The ladies were happy to fall right into his arms when given the chance to claim the *ton's* Adonis as their lover for a night. "If Lady Astrid turns out to be a cold fish, you can find someone else to warm your bed."

"Right after he's married?" Sebastian frowned at him. "That seems unnecessarily cruel."

"I am not saying he should make an announcement, but one can be discreet," Christian retorted.

"Are you going to keep your current mistress?" Zachary asked him, sounding appalled. They all knew Christian had been playing bed games with an actress at the Royal Theater for the past few months. Zachary was the only other one of them with a regular lover; he'd been sharing his nights with the stunningly beautiful Dowager Baroness Ashfield.

"Of course." Christian tilted his head curiously at Zachary. "Are you not?"

"Of course not! I will be courting a debutante for marriage. It would not be proper to have a mistress at the same time." Zachary frowned at him.

"Why not marry the baroness, then?" Nathanial asked, causing Zachary to look at him, aghast.

Zachary made a face.

"My mother would have a conniption. Delilah is no virginal debutante. Even if she and my mother did get along…" Zachary shook his head. "Mother is most insistent that I not marry Delilah. She still has not taken off the black since Father's death. I do not want to add to her pain. Besides, you know what people would say." He looked distinctly uncomfortable with the admission.

It was true, there would be whispers that Zachary could not possibly know if his children were truly his if he married an experienced widow rather than an innocent. Taking the baroness as his lover before he was married or returning to her after he was married would be seen as perfectly acceptable, but actually marrying her?

Still, from what Gregory had seen, there were true feelings between the two of them. He was almost sorry that Zachary was going to bow to Society's scripts rather than forging his own path with the baroness. But that was Zachary's decision to make.

He also could not blame Zachary for being so sensitive to his mother's opinions. Gregory's mother had worn the black for his father's death, but neither of them had truly mourned him. Zachary's mother was still struggling with her grief, unfashionably long after her official mourning period had ended. She was fragile, more than physically. As protective as Gregory was of his own mother, he could only imagine how much worse it was for Zachary.

"Making a debutante a duchess is the proper thing to do," Matthew agreed with Zachary. His hand rubbed at the pocket where his coin was, as if he was uncomfortable making such a definitive statement without flipping it first.

"You could still keep your baroness until you have your duchess," Christian said. Then rolled his eyes when his statement was met with a round of head shaking from the others. "Well, I am going to keep my actress until I find my duchess. Perhaps even beyond."

Hardly an uncommon occurrence, though Gregory hoped the man would be discreet. Though, with so many other dukes to bring up to scratch, it was possible he would find that it was not so easy to secure a bride this Season with a mistress in tow. Only time would tell.

"Well, then." Drake unfolded his long frame from the chair, getting to his feet and raising his glass. "A toast. To everyone finding their duchess."

"Hear, hear!"

There were only a few drops of brandy left in the bottom of Gregory's glass, but he lifted it to his lips and let them slide onto his tongue. He needed to find a woman worth making his duchess this Season. One who would be faithful, keep his secrets, run his household, and make a good mother to his children. Being a pleasant bedwarmer would be a bonus. To ask that she tolerate his... preferences was probably too much to hope for, so a mistress was likely in his future regardless, though he would hold off until his wife was with child so as not to distress her.

It was not going to be an easy hill to climb. Perhaps he should spend more time with Matthew, because he was going to need all the luck he could collect.

CHAPTER
ONE

G*regory*

"You do not know how lucky you are to be able to avoid the events of the little Season," Sebastian complained with a dark scowl. He'd escaped a supper party with his mother and sister that evening when Gregory had sent him a letter asking him to come over for a private evening. After they'd eaten their meal, they'd retired to the library, where they could indulge in some brandy and talk.

Gregory, as yet, had not made an appearance at any of the small events. He was waiting until the official opening of the Season, the Duchess of Richmond's ball.

He still was unsure how to go about procuring a bride, to be truthful. Seducing a woman to bed was one thing; wooing a woman to marry him was quite another. As a rake, he'd made it a habit to avoid debutantes, not seek them out.

Truthfully, it was not so much the courting that worried him. He was a duke, after all. Even if he blundered it, the matchmaking mamas would throw their daughters at him. It was the choosing that concerned him the most.

"Perhaps I should join you," he said thoughtfully. Waiting for the Season proper might be a mistake. "The little events may be more conducive to getting to know the young ladies than the larger balls."

"Yes, so much more conducive, as you are mobbed for being the only duke in attendance." Sebastian snorted. "Not that any of them have anything worth saying. They all repeat each other. The only difference is what instrument they've learned to play or which is their favorite accomplishment. What embroidery has to do with making a good wife, I have yet to learn."

"Well, you are escorting your sister so she can gain some polish before the Season, so perhaps the other young ladies are doing the same with you," Gregory suggested. "Maybe I will wait until they're spruced up a bit more, with better conversation. How is your sister's polishing going, by the way?"

It was Tiffany's first Season. Gregory had yet to see her. The last time he'd encountered her had been years ago, and he had not paid much attention, if he was being truthful. He remembered a scrawny young thing with mousy brown hair in braids and spots all over her complexion. She'd been rather forgettable, poor thing, and from what Sebastian had said, her situation had not improved much.

"She's still practically silent in any group." Sebastian shrugged. "She seems comfortable enough with me, but any time Mother introduces her to someone, it's as though she loses her tongue completely. If she cannot even speak to someone other than her family, I do not know how she is supposed to secure a husband, sister of a duke or not."

"Some men would probably prefer a quiet wife," Gregory said thoughtfully as an idea suddenly occurred to him. "What if I married her?"

The incredulous look Sebastian gave him did not deter his thoughts in that direction.

"Marry my sister?"

Well, he did not need to sound so scandalized.

"Yes, she would likely make a good wife for me. She is your sister, so I assume she's been trained on how to run a ducal household. She's obviously from a good family with good connections. She understands our Society and the pressures of our station. I do not mind if she does not want to talk to anyone but you or your mother." In fact, he'd encourage it. If she were not talking to anyone but her immediate family, she would not be flirting with them, either. That and her plainness could prove a boon. He could always darken the bedroom for himself, and a plain wife would not constantly have the rakes of the ton looking to warm her bed.

"What makes you think you would be a good husband for her?" Sebastian scoffed.

"I am a duke, after all. It's not as though she could aim much higher," Gregory argued without any heat. He was not truly invested in the idea, but he did enjoy tweaking his friend, and if Sebastian said yes, it would make Gregory's Season much easier. "She would be able to live as she pleased, do as she pleased, and enjoy all the privileges of being my duchess."

"What of fidelity?" Sebastian turned a gimlet eye on Gregory, who made a face.

"I would be discreet." He had no desire to cause his wife any pain, especially if she was Sebastian's sister.

"Absolutely not. My sister does not deserve to have her heart broken while you carry on your affairs just because she is too plain and dull to keep your interest." Sebastian shook his head. "She's too sweet for the likes of you."

"Breaking her heart would be taking things a bit far. She does not expect a love match, does she?" At their station, such things were highly irregular. Sinclair and Isabella were a singular exception, and look how that had ended—him dead and her grieving like a widow, even though they'd never made it to the altar.

"She is sensitive." Sebastian glowered at him. "I will not allow her to be hurt."

"Ah, well. You might have a point if she is sensitive." Gregory sighed. On the surface, it had appeared to be a perfect solution.

Though, it did not seem reasonable that she be plain and dull, yet still expected to keep her husband's interest. Perhaps Sebastian would be able to find her an equally plain and dull husband who would be happy with the prestige of being married to a duke's sister and who he could intimidate into fidelity if not love.

Not sensitive was another factor to add to his own list of attributes he was searching for. Though, it might be difficult to find a wife who was understanding of how such affairs worked while remaining uninterested in embarking on her own.

But the notion of taking a plain wife was a good one. A shy, quiet one. Who was not too sensitive. One who wanted to be a mother more than a lover, so she would focus on her children and find her satisfaction there.

Yes. This was good.

Not his best friend's sister, either, but a family who would not protest his... activities if they became known. He would do his best to be discreet, of course, but the only certainty in life was death. Perhaps a baron or viscount's daughter.

The door to the library opened, cutting off their conversation. Gregory and Sebastian got to their feet as Gregory's mother came into the room. As always, she was smiling widely. Most of his memories of his mother included her smile, and the few that did not made him want to ensure that she always had something to smile about.

The household's steward, Arthur Montblanc, stood by the door, waiting for the duchess. Stiffly holding himself upright, the older man looked at her with worshipful eyes, waiting patiently for however long she would take.

"Mother," Gregory said by way of greeting, dutifully stepping forward and giving her a kiss on each cheek. She was much shorter than him, with a plump, rounded figure that made her look like a small cake when she wore the ruffles she adored.

"Your Grace," Sebastian said, stepping forward to take her hand and bow over it, making her titter with amusement.

"Oh, stop, Sebastian. You know you are supposed to call me

Marguerite," she said, waving her hand and beaming warmly at him. "You will not stand on ceremony here, not with me." It was the same thing she told him every time he visited.

"Yes, Your Grace," he replied, as he always did, making her laugh again.

"One day, you will do so, I hope. You are too tied to proprieties, Sebastian," Mother said, shaking her head, making the feathers atop it bounce and flutter with the movement. "It is not good to live your life under such strictures."

As someone who had lived with his father's strictures for far too long, his mother would know. She had blossomed since his father's death and was enjoying her first Season back in London since her wedding to the man. Gregory enjoyed seeing it, even though he had begged off on accompanying her to any of the engagements.

She wanted to see him wed and thought herself a marvelous matchmaker, but he did not want to be set up with any of her friends' daughters or granddaughters. Like Sebastian, it was too close a connection. Also, his mother's idea of a suitable bride and his were rather misaligned, going by the ladies she'd tried to introduce him to when they were in the country.

Over Christmas, another of his old school friends had visited with a woman who was obviously his lover, and Gregory's mother had still thought she should be considered. Lady Catherine, formerly the Dowager Countess of Cross and now Mrs. Samuel North, had been a delightful woman and obviously in love with Samuel. His mother had liked her, though, and that was enough for her to recommend the woman as a potential bride.

As his mother liked just about everyone she met, it did cause a bit of a conundrum for him.

"How was your party?" he asked her, drawing her attention away from Sebastian.

"Lovely." She yawned. "But tiring. I wanted to say goodnight before I go to bed and see how your evening went."

"Very quiet. Other than Sebastian's complaints, of course."

"He is a whinger when he wants to be."

"I am right here," Sebastian complained. "I can hear you."

"See? Whinging again." Gregory shook his head, then bent it to give his mother another buss on the cheek. "Goodnight, Mother."

"Goodnight, boys." She smiled at both of them, then went back to the doorway, where Montblanc was waiting for her. The steward bowed his head as she passed, then closed the door behind them.

"She is enjoying her Season, then?" Sebastian asked.

"She is. Though she also considers it her duty to find me a wife, much to my dismay." Gregory sighed, turning back to his seat in the plush armchair by the fireside. He paused before sitting down. His mother's appearance had made him think of his father again, which led his mind to the letters to his father that he'd found at their estate. Threatening letters.

Letters that he still had not told Sebastian about and the true reason for him inviting Sebastian over for the evening, though he had avoided bringing it up.

It was time.

Gregory cleared his throat, leaning against the side of the chair rather than sitting on it. Raising his eyebrows in curiosity, Sebastian lowered himself into his former seat.

"Have you found anything in your father's papers since his passing?"

Frowning, Sebastian leaned back in the chair, the firelight flickering over his expression.

"I have found a great many things. What do you mean?"

"Wait here." Gregory straightened and strode to the door, yanking it open and going down the hall to his study. Picking up the box where he'd stashed the letters, he tucked it under his arm and walked back to the library, passing his mother's lady's maid on the way. Montblanc was just coming down the stairs to lock the front door after escorting the duchess to her room. "Sebastian and I will be occupied for a while, Montblanc, do not wait up for us."

The older man hesitated a moment, like he thought he should protest, before bowing.

"Thank you, Your Grace."

Of all the staff Gregory had inherited from his father, Montblanc had to be among the most capable. He'd been invaluable in teaching Gregory the ins and outs of the estate, all the foibles that his father had either kept from him or considered unimportant. Though Montblanc had originally protested coming to London, he'd eventually given way to the duchess' pleading that she wanted to be surrounded by familiar faces.

Satisfied that the older man would not attempt to keep the same late hours that he and Sebastian were likely to, Gregory reentered the library and closed the door behind him. Sebastian was no longer lounging in his chair but sitting forward, elbows on his knees, with his hands dangling between them. The frown on his face had deepened.

Gregory took a deep breath. He did not think that Sebastian had anything to do with his father's death. And he did not think Sebastian would blame him if it turned out that the target had been Gregory's father, and Sebastian had lost his in the process. But sometimes, people reacted unpredictably.

It was best to just say the words and get them over with.

"My father received threatening letters, including several threatening his life." Gregory walked back to his chair and placed the wooden box on his lap. It felt heavier than ever against his legs as Sebastian stared at him. "With the evidence that the explosion was not an accident, it seems that there were plenty of people who would have the motivation to kill *my* father, at least."

Which was less surprising than it should have been. The hardest part of admitting it was wondering if the others' fathers had been killed by accident while his father had been murdered.

"You think someone killed seven other dukes in order to kill your father?" Sebastian blinked, taking in the information. "What, exactly, is in these letters?"

Opening the box, Gregory picked up the pile of papers, which he'd tied with a black ribbon, and handed them over to Sebastian. He watched, at first, in silence as Sebastian began to read his way through the letters, then finally looked away into the fire as Sebastian's expression did not change.

The crackling heat and the flickering flames helped to calm some of his nerves far more than the brandy did. As he stared into them, he wondered which was the more dire plight this Season—his need for a wife or finding out who had murdered his father.

CHAPTER

TWO

T*iffany*
The library was cold, the hearth dark, but slipping into the room still felt like finding sanctuary. As a child, she'd rarely seen her father except at night when he was in the library, reading. She'd sneak out of bed and join him there. He'd look up and smile, then pointedly look down again and pretend he did not see her rather than sending her back to her bed.

She would pick out a book and hide under the table closest to him, using the same light to read. At some point, she would fall asleep, and when she woke again, she would be back in her room, tucked safely into her bed. As she'd gotten older, the library had often been unoccupied at night. Then her mother had found her sneaking out of her room one night and boxed her ears, and that had been that.

It was not worth the risk when there was no guarantee of her father being there.

After his death, she'd found herself returning to the library in the dark. She was now old enough that if her mother found her out of bed, she could claim an inability to sleep, fetch a book, and return to her room with very little consequence. Perhaps some grumbling from her mother about how she read too much.

Her mother was distracted with other things right now, anyway, like the start of the Season. The Duchess of Richmond's ball was almost upon them, and she was still not satisfied with how Tiffany comported herself in company. Not that Tiffany understood what her mother wanted her to do.

She was trying; she really was.

Sighing, she made her way over to the shelves and ran her fingers along the spines of the books, inhaling the rich scent of leather and paper. If only there were some pipe smoke in the air and a fire to warm the room, it would take her right back to her childhood with her father. But just like the fire in the hearth, her father was gone.

If only he were here... He had just begun to take an interest in her again when he'd realized she was only a couple of years away from her debut, then, just as suddenly, he was gone. Killed in a tragic, horrific accident involving gunpowder and some kind of carousing at a hunting lodge. Tiffany did not know the details. She assumed everyone thought she was too delicate to know. That or that they were not suited to a young lady's ears.

As if she did not know that her father had had a mistress, her mother a lover, and her brother was bedding married ladies across the length and breadth of the *ton*. And she knew exactly what all of that meant and what they were doing. Her mother and her mother's friends had very loose tongues when they were gossiping with each other over tea, and very few of them noticed when a young lady might be within earshot.

What she had not been able to glean from her mother's conversation, she'd learned through the lessons of animal husbandry that she'd been given while they were trapped out in the country during their mourning period. In a bid for freedom from her mother's attention, Tiffany had pointed out that many gentlemen among the *ton* had an interest in dogs and horses and that learning about them could help her land a suitor.

Her mother, always eager to find attributes to help make up for Tiffany's lack of beauty, had given permission for her to learn from their Master of the Hunt. Her feigned interest eventually led to a true interest rather than an escape to the stables or kennels.

Though, of course, the rest from her mother's incessant critiques was also welcome. She'd found peace and affection with the animals and learned quite a bit more about breeding than either her mother or brother likely intended. A few etchings, hidden away on the top shelves of her father's library, had completed her education.

Tiffany wandered over to the window overlooking the front of the house and peered out. Her brother was still at Clarence House with his friend, the Duke of Clarence. He was only supposed to be there for a meal, which had left her alone with her mother at Lady Teasingdale's supper party. It had been an interminable evening. She had not been able to say anything right, as evidenced by the number of bruises her mother had left on her thigh from pinching her every time she said something her mother found objectionable.

Thankfully, her shorter and shorter answers had finally ceased the questions directed to her and the pinching had stopped. Though she'd had to listen to a lecture on the way home about how she would never find a husband if she could not form a coherent sentence, she preferred that over the pinches.

Her hand drifted down to rub her sore thigh, and she sighed.

Then stiffened as the door behind her creaked, pushing all the way open, and she turned to see her mother in the doorway. The light from the candle she'd left on the table was not very bright, but certainly bright enough that her mother could see her as well. The moonlight coming in from the window outlined her silhouette in case the candle was not enough.

"Tiffany." Her mother's sharp, high tone made her hunch inward, ducking slightly, even though her mother was not beside her. "What are you doing?"

"I could not sleep, so I came to find a book. I thought I heard a noise outside and wondered if Sebastian was home." Tiffany kept her voice as meekly unobjectionable as possible while also raising it enough that her mother would be able to hear her from across the room. Her mother detested mumbling.

"He is not." Her mother's tone seemed sharper than usual as she pulled the sides of her wrapper together in front of her body, as if she were cold. "You need to be abed. We have a busy day tomorrow, and you need as much sleep as you can to rid yourself of those dark circles under your eyes. We will start tomorrow with some cold compresses to keep you from being too puffy. No man wants a puffy wife with a marred complexion."

"Yes, Mother." Tiffany turned and quickly reached out to snatch a book off the shelf, holding it to her chest as she hurried to the table to pick up her candle and retreat from the room. At least with the open flame in hand, her mother would not pinch or slap at her as she passed.

Shoulders hunched, she hurried out of the door, past her mother. Just in case.

Moving as quickly as she could, she was up the stairs and just into the hall when she heard the front door open. She paused. Was that Sebastian? There was a masculine voice, then her mother's voice answering, though her tone was no longer sharp but a melodic coo.

Not her brother, just her mother's lover.

Wrinkling her nose, Tiffany hurried back to her room. She was not supposed to know about her mother's lover, and she did not like to think how her mother would react if she knew Tiffany was still about.

Perhaps she would see Sebastian in the morning. Her mother was always in a better temper when he was present.

GREGORY

Waiting for Sebastian to get through the letters meant being patient, which was not one of Gregory's strong suits. He'd known that about himself for a while and accepted it, but it did not make the waiting any easier. Eventually, rather than sitting still, he got up and started pacing the room, aware of Sebastian's gaze flicking to him, then back to the letters.

Finally, Sebastian finished. Rather than saying anything, he sat back in the chair, staring into the fire, much the same way Gregory had. Pausing in his pacing, Gregory watched his friend looking at the fire.

It took less than a minute before he could not stand the silence anymore.

"Well?" he asked. "What do you think?"

Sebastian turned his head toward Gregory, a thoughtful expression on his face.

"I think several people were very angry at your father, but one in particular."

"One?" Gregory frowned. "The handwriting is all different."

"Mostly." Sebastian shuffled through the letters, pulling out several as Gregory came over and sat down again to look at them. "See here? The very distinctive loop and slant on the capital P. They realize their handwriting is recognizable and take pains to change it, to make every letter look different, but when they become particularly emotional, they forget themselves."

"Damn." Gregory stared down at the letters. Some of the capital Ps were different, but several were the same throughout the letters. "I have stared at these letters almost every day since I found them, and I never noticed that." Though, to be fair, he had been looking at the content, not at the handwriting. It was different enough at a glance that he had not thought to look more closely.

That and it had been easy enough to believe that so many different people would threaten his father.

He flipped through the letters, though he practically had the contents memorized, just to make sure he was seeing what he thought he was seeing.

"They are all the ones about my half-sisters."

The ones that accused his father of neglecting his bastard daughters, of not providing for them and their mothers, and of rape. Considering the first two were true, Gregory had no problem believing the last.

"Yes. What do you know about them?" Sebastian asked seriously.

Not a topic that Gregory liked to dwell on, but considering someone might have killed Sebastian's father to get to Gregory's... he felt as though he owed his friend. Hell, he felt as though he was lucky Sebastian had not gone storming out the door. It was not normally in Sebastian's nature to blame one person for another's misdeeds, but the fear had still been there.

It was his father, and, unlike Gregory, Sebastian had been close with his.

"Quite a bit, but very little that is pertinent to this. Clara is the oldest at six, Priscilla the youngest at two. Elizabeth is five, and her fondness for peppermints reaches unholy heights. Loretta is three and, so far, the most serious of the four." Gregory sighed. None of that was particularly helpful, and he knew it. "All of their mothers were on my father's estates in some capacity. Loretta's mother has a husband, and he's very protective of her, so I do not know her well. Agatha, Clara's mother, and Maggie, Elizabeth's mother, both married after... well, after. They seem happy enough with their husbands. I have barely heard Priscilla's mother put two words together. She's the youngest." As was her daughter.

Of all of them, Betty, Priscilla's mother, was the most skittish around him. She was also the only unmarried of the mothers. Though she did not try to keep Priscilla from playing with him, she always held back in a way the others did not. He hoped, eventually, she realized that he was not anything like his father and that her duties to the lord of the manor were done with.

"If only the letters were dated..." Sebastian muttered, reaching out to take them from Gregory so he could look through them again. "I wish I knew when they were received."

"You think one of the mothers..."

"I think a family member of one of the mothers. The handwriting seems masculine to me." Sebastian looked up at Gregory and raised his eyebrow. "You said three of them are married, and one of them has a very protective husband?"

"Yes, but John would not..." Gregory's voice trailed off. John *was* very protective of Rose and Loretta. He'd taken Loretta in as one of his own. A widower with two older children, they'd come together to make a happy family, and Loretta was currently pregnant with their first child. Bloody hell. He liked John, but if his father had threatened Loretta or Rose or any of John's family... no, John would not have taken it well. "He would have targeted my father and just my father, not an entire cadre of dukes."

"Are you sure?"

Gregory shook his head. "I can never be sure, but that's not what I would expect from John. He is slow to anger, but once he is, it's fast and furious. When someone insulted Loretta in front of him, he immediately punched the other man in the face and left him lying there in the street. If we'd found my father with his head bashed in, I would be more suspicious of John, but a long plot to kill my father that also risked hurting others? I cannot see it."

"Very well," Sebastian said, nodding slowly. It was a relief to know he still trusted Gregory's judgment despite missing a clue. Even if it was not an obvious clue. "We should make a list, though, of who might have sent the letters about your sisters. There are some others here as well that stand out. Some of the handwriting seems very familiar, though I cannot place it."

"I did not know you were such an expert on handwriting," Gregory joked.

"I notice small details," Sebastian said. "It is not exactly an accomplishment that one boasts of."

"Well, you should. It is most impressive."

That made Sebastian laugh, despite the topic of discussion.

"Thank you. I shall keep that in mind." He handed the rest of the letters back to Gregory. "Perhaps we should see if any of the other dukes are secretly experts in handwriting or have received similar letters."

Closing his fingers around the stack of papers, Gregory paused, grimacing.

"I..." His voice trailed off. It was hard to state a fear aloud, even to his closest friend.

"What?" Sebastian frowned at him. "They could help."

"And what if we discover that my father is the reason for all of their father's deaths?" he asked. A few of them, like Nathanial, might thank him. Sebastian had handled the revelation easily enough, but others, like Christian, might not.

"What makes you think your father is the only one with a grudge against him?" Sebastian leaned back in his chair, lifting his foot to rest the ankle of his boot on the opposite knee, his hands curved over his leg. "Nathanial, for instance. If his father was not receiving threats about his debts, I will eat that whole stack of letters."

Which was a good point. Gregory snorted at the visual.

"Was your father receiving threats?" he asked.

"Other than from my mother?" Sebastian asked dryly, making Gregory laugh. The fights between the duchess and the deceased Duke of Bolton were legendary. "Not to my knowledge, but..."

"But?" Gregory prompted.

"I found a secret passageway from the library to the stable in the manor home," Sebastian admitted. "My father never showed it to me. I never knew it was there. So, it makes me wonder what else I did not know about him."

A secret passageway?

"I want to see it."

Sebastian laughed. "Next time you visit the estate... which will require you actually visiting."

"For a secret passageway, I will make the trip."

"But not to visit me, of course." Sebastian rolled his eyes. "Very well, if that's what it takes to get you to travel to someone else's home."

Gregory shrugged. He preferred the comforts of his own space. Who did not? Besides, the fights between Sebastian's parents had made him uncomfortable. He had not liked the shouting. Now, of course, that would not be a concern.

Though, if Sebastian did not get his sister married off this Season, he would have to watch himself while he was there. Sebastian had rejected his offer of marriage for her, but that did not mean that he and her mother would agree. He did not want to anger Sebastian if Sebastian's mother and sister thought to make a match between him and Tiffany.

THREE

T*iffany*

The Duchess of Richmond's ball was an absolute crush. Tiffany felt like she could not breathe, and not just because her mother had insisted on a set of ill-fitting stays to help flatten Tiffany's obscenely large bosom. There were so many people. Far more than the smaller events she'd been attending with her mother.

A dizzying array of jewels, silks, satins, feathers, and ribbons swirled in eddies within the crowd. There were a few dressed in darker colors, mostly the gentlemen, but they were small dots among the more decadent displays of sartorial splendor. Despite her own beautiful gown, she felt like she did not quite measure up to those around her.

Perhaps because of her bosom. All the other ladies had their waists neatly nipped in, their figures like the hourglass in her father's library. She resembled more of a square. At least the pale yellow of her dress was of a similar hue to several other young ladies, so she did not stand out in that way.

It was also the prettiest dress she'd ever worn and certainly the most fashionable. She fingered the silky fabric of her skirt, sighing inwardly at how soft it was. She'd actually felt pretty when she put it on, though she knew it was the dress and not *her*. With her hair piled on her head, a few ringlets curling down, and her mother's borrowed jewels around her throat, she hoped that she would at least fit in with the other debutantes. So far, she did not stand out, and that was probably the best she could hope for.

"Sebastian, would you be a dear and fetch us some punch?" her mother asked, smiling up at her brother. He was looking particularly handsome this evening in a dark green jacket over a mint green waistcoat with silver edging. His white shirt was immaculate, the points of his collar high at his chin, and his cravat tied in a complicated knot.

Tiffany sighed inwardly. It was unfair of him to be so beautiful. Sometimes, she wondered if being born first meant that he had taken all the good looks from their parents and if that was why she was so plain.

"Of course, Mother," Sebastian said with a smile and a small bow. He turned and headed toward what must be the punch table. Tiffany could not see it, but she could only assume he knew where he was going.

As soon as he'd left them, her mother pulled Tiffany to the side.

"Stand straighter. No, do not thrust your chest at me." Her mother rolled her eyes at Tiffany's inability to follow her direction. She was trying her best, but sometimes, her mother's instructions seemed contradictory. This was one of those times. "I did not say to hunch your shoulders. Now, where is your dance card?"

Tiffany held her hand up in front of her, a dance card and pencil dangling from her wrist.

"Good. I have a list of gentlemen I want you introduced to. Hopefully, a few of them will be agreeable to dancing with you. We do not want to start this Season on the wrong foot." Her mother eyed her. "Are you listening, Tiffany?"

"Yes, Mama." She'd practiced the dance lessons with her instructor until she'd nearly dropped, her mother always pushing her to be more perfect in her steps and form. It still was not good enough for her mother, but hopefully, she did not make too much a fool of herself.

"Smile, girl. You are already plain. You cannot be dour as well. Ah, your brother is returning." Her mother straightened, beaming at him. Despite the pang in her chest, Tiffany forced a smile on her face.

Once, just once, she wished her mother would tell her that she looked pretty or even passing. At least Sebastian had told her she looked nice this evening, though he had done so in a rather absent-minded way.

"Thank you, Sebastian," her mother said sweetly smiling as she took the glass of punch from Sebastian. "Now, you must put yourself on your sister's dance card. The first dance, of course, then a second. I have some gentlemen to introduce her to, but can you find some of your friends to dance with her at least once as a favor to you? If she dances with a few dukes, she may be able to attract more attention."

"Of course, whatever I can do to help with your Season," Sebastian said to Tiffany, smiling fondly at her. She took the punch with one hand and lifted her wrist with her dance card for him to take and write his name down, smiling back at him. Quickly, he scrawled his name in the first spot and another for later in the evening. "I am certain it will be no trouble filling your dance card. You are the sister of a duke, after all."

She was, and from what she understood, that was likely to be her saving grace when it came to marriage. Though she had no beauty and often fumbled her way through conversations, her connections would ensure she not only married but married well. At least she had that. Her mother had often remarked that if she'd been born to a baron, her case would be hopeless.

"Thank you, Sebastian."

Her brother smiled again, nodding as he let the card drop, then looked around. "As it happens, I see a few of my friends right now."

Jerking his chin up at someone in the crowd—it must be easier to see everything at his height; Tiffany felt like all she could see were shoulders—Sebastian summoned several gentlemen to them. A moment later, Tiffany felt like the breath had been knocked out of her by the sheer amount of male beauty surrounding her.

By the way her mother tittered and fanned herself as each of the dukes greeted her, bending over her hand, she agreed with Tiffany's assessment. Unlike Tiffany, she had clearly met them all before, as she did not require an introduction.

"Tiffany, this is the Duke of Ormonde, the Duke of Hereford, and the Duke of St. Albans. Gentlemen, my sister, Lady Tiffany." Sebastian's smile stayed on his face, but he watched closely as each of his friends greeted her. She was not sure why.

"Lady Tiffany, a delight to make your acquaintance," Ormonde said, bowing over her hand. His dark good looks rivaled her brother's, and his easy confidence and charm surpassed Sebastian's. Just having him hold her hand, his dark gaze meeting hers and holding it effortlessly, made her feel rather weak in the knees.

"I am even more delighted," Hereford said, stealing her hand from Ormonde and making her giggle. He was very handsome as well, with wavy brown hair, only a shade or two darker than hers, a strong Roman nose, and dark eyes that were thankfully not as penetrating as Ormonde's. She knew they were not truly fighting over her attention, but even the jest was exciting. Hereford kissed the back of her hand, and she blushed a hot red.

"Not *too* delighted," Sebastian murmured in a kind of warning, glaring at his friend. Tiffany frowned at him in confusion, but Hereford backed away, allowing St. Albans to take her hand and kiss the back of it. She could feel the press of his lips through the thin fabric of her glove and thought she might faint.

"I believe that leaves me to be the most delighted," he declared with a wink as he straightened.

Tiffany rather thought *she* was the most delighted, but she held her tongue rather than saying the wrong thing in front of the dukes. She could only imagine how her mother would react.

"Thank you, Your Grace. Your Graces," she quickly amended so as not to leave the other two out. "It is a pleasure to meet you."

"You are all so kind," her mother said, stepping forward. "We have a favor to ask of you. It is Tiffany's first Season, and we were hoping some of Sebastian's friends might help fill out her dance card. If the gentlemen see you dancing with her, surely some of them might have their interest piqued."

"More than some," Hereford said, quickly stepping forward to be the first to take her card. Tiffany lifted her wrist.

"No waltzes," her mother said quickly when she saw where Hereford had the pencil poised. "She has not been given permission yet. We will be going to Almack's on Wednesday."

One of the requirements for a debutante before she could waltz —receiving permission for the Season from one of the hostesses at Almack's. That was the dance Tiffany had practiced the most, usually when her mother was not around. Waltzes used to be forbidden; they were so risqué, and she did not want to embarrass herself.

There was also a part of her that dreamed...

A man who was so taken by her dancing that he did not mind her plain face and excessive bosom or that she never said the right thing. A man who offered to marry her, who would love her, and preferably lived far, far away from her mother. A thought that instantly swamped her in guilt for not wanting to be near her mother or her brother, but sometimes, they made her feel so...

"I would like to talk to you later, Bolton," Hereford said to her brother, still smiling at her.

Her brother frowned but then nodded. "We can meet later."

The Dukes of Ormonde and St. Albans also signed her card. St. Albans went last, and, oddly, she could have sworn she saw him flip a coin while the Duke of Ormonde picked his dance. When he stepped up to put his name down for a dance, his smile was still charming but not the same as he'd smiled at her before.

Or perhaps she was imagining things. As her mother said, she always had her head in the clouds. It was likely her own fault for reading too many of the romantic Gothic novels her maid would sometimes sneak to her. As if any of her brother's contemporaries would ever have an interest in marrying her.

They did not need the prestige of marrying a duke's sister, plain or otherwise. They *were* dukes. They could marry anyone they chose.

"There." St. Albans dropped her card and pencil. "I look forward to our dance, Lady Tiffany."

"Thank you, Your Grace," she replied immediately. Those four words she knew her mother would never be able to criticize, so they were completely safe.

"All of you are too good," her mother said, beaming around up at them. "We appreciate your efforts on our behalf."

"Believe me, it is our pleasure." The way Hereford looked at her, almost admiringly, made Tiffany feel warm from the inside out. Would it be so bad to pretend that perhaps he was truly interested in her? If only for a moment, to dream a little?

"Unfortunately, we must take our leave of you and make our rounds," her mother said, gripping Tiffany's arm tightly, so she did not protest. She was enjoying being surrounded by her brother's handsome friends, especially because they were being so kind, but it was not worth upsetting her mother over. "Come along, Tiffany."

"I will see you for our dance," Hereford said, smiling widely at her again as the others nodded their farewells. Tiffany glanced over her shoulder as her mother dragged her away. The dukes had already closed ranks, bending their heads together in some kind of discussion while also glancing surreptitiously around the room. She also spotted several determined-looking mamas—very reminiscent of her own mother—pulling their daughters along behind them, headed toward her brother and the others.

Then the crowd swallowed them up, and she could not see them anymore, leaving her surrounded by strangers once again.

"Why were you so quiet?" her mother demanded to know in a hushed undertone that, hopefully, only Tiffany could hear. "You must make interesting conversation to engage the gentlemen. Your brother's friends would have made perfect practice, as there is no need to actually impress any of them."

"I should not try to impress dukes?" She was confused because she did not think her mother would be calm if she had said something or done something incorrectly in front of them, her brother's friends or not.

Her mother gave her arm a hard pinch, and Tiffany bit her lip against a squeal as tears sprang to her eyes.

"Do not be glib," her mother said sharply. "You cannot make a fool of yourself, of course, but a duke is hardly going to marry you. Did you not see all the beauties converging on them? They have their choice among the crowd. They are perfect for practice because if you make a fool of yourself, it will not matter since you could never win one of them, regardless."

The stabbing sensation in her chest came from knowing that even her mother did not believe she could marry a duke. She knew that. She knew that her brother likely agreed with her, but it still hurt to hear her mother state it so baldly.

"Yes, Mother," she said quietly.

"They likely think you a dullard for not being able to speak a word." Her mother sighed heavily. "At least it does not truly matter, as I said. But do not just stand there like a stump when I introduce you to this next gentleman. Now, smile." Her mother pinched her again to accentuate her order, and Tiffany's smile felt more like a grimace, but she did her best.

They stopped in front of a rather startled-looking gentleman, who did not appear to have expected her mother. He was not as handsome as her brother's friends, but he was certainly not plain. Tall, broad-shouldered, with blond hair that waved back from his face and pale blue eyes that looked like a cloudless sky, she would have thought him far beyond her reach by looks alone. Tiffany felt her trepidation rise.

"Baron Grimaldi, may I introduce you to my daughter, Lady

Tiffany," her mother said, stepping back with a sincerely pleased smile on her face.

"Lady Tiffany." Baron Grimaldi smiled so kindly and took her hand the same way the dukes had, bending over it. "A pleasure to meet you. You know, my favorite great-aunt's name was Tiffany, so I have always liked it as a name."

The kind way he looked at her combined with her mother's admonition to speak more, made her feel bolder than she might have been otherwise.

"Did you know that it comes from the Greek name 'Theophania'?" she asked because it was the first thing she thought of to say.

"I did." His smile widened. "Dare I guess that your birthday is January sixth?"

"It is!" She was delighted, not just because he clearly knew the roots of her name and its connection to Epiphany and the naming tradition of children born on that day, but because he seemed happy with her response.

"It was also my great-aunt's birthday," he confessed. "She was also proud of her name, though she liked to harken back to Empress Theodora rather than Theophania."

"I was always fascinated by Empress Theodora!" Tiffany was delighted to find a commonality between them.

Unfortunately, before she could say anything more or ask him about his own interest in the Roman empress, her mother interrupted. The smile on her face had disappeared at some point while Tiffany and Baron Grimaldi had been talking, and she had not even noticed. Her heart sank. What had she done wrong this time?

"My apologies, Baron Grimaldi, but Lady Jersey is summoning us. You must excuse us."

"Of course. May I put my name on your card for a dance?" Baron Grimaldi asked.

"Yes, please." Tiffany held up her hand with the card, despite being extremely aware of her mother's impatience. Anyone else in the ballroom, at a glance, would not realize that her mother was simmering, but Tiffany knew the signs.

Still, she did not think her mother would approve of her passing up a dance with a nobleman once he'd asked, and it would have been extremely rude to tell him no.

"Thank you," she said to him before her mother pulled her away. This time, her grip pressed on the spots she'd already pinched, and the pain of her fingers digging into Tiffany's flesh stung up the length of her arm, from elbow to shoulder.

Her mother did not say anything right away, which did not bode well for her. When her mother pulled her into a small alcove rather than to Lady Jersey, her heart sank even further. She truly did not know what she had done to displease her mother this time. She should have been watching her more closely to gauge her reactions, but she'd been so pleased and excited when Baron Grimaldi had been interested in what she had to say that she had forgotten herself.

"What were you doing?" her mother demanded to know as soon as they were tucked away from the main ballroom. The alcove had two sconces on the wall providing light, drapes at the columns that made up the entrance, and a bench with cushions for people to sit and talk, but Tiffany did not dare try to do something so audacious as sit while her mother was upset with her.

"I... I was trying to talk to him."

Her mother rolled her eyes, putting her hands on her hips.

"About your own name? He is likely to think you incredibly self-centered. And if you must talk to a gentleman about history or anything so unladylike, you must ask him questions. Do not present yourself as some sort of expert. Gentlemen do not find overly knowledgeable ladies attractive, and they certainly do not enjoy being educated by them." Her mother shook her head, sighing heavily for the second time since they'd arrived at the ball, causing the little bit of confidence Tiffany had managed to garner to shrivel back to nothing.

"You are lucky he was mannerly enough to ask you to dance

despite that. When you do so, you must repair the damage you have done. Ask him questions, listen to what he has to say, and, for goodness sake, keep any of your own conversation to appropriate topics. How well you can sew, your music lessons, that you are trained to run a household. Now, come along. There are more gentlemen to introduce you to. Next time, do as I have told you."

Shaking her head, her mother swept out of the alcove, and Tiffany meekly followed behind her, hoping that no one had been able to hear the set down she'd been given. Yet she could not look up to see if anyone was watching them emerge because she was too busy trying to push away the tears that had gathered in her eyes.

CHAPTER

FOUR

G<u>regory</u>

A duke in need of a wife was a precarious position to be in, Gregory had quickly discovered after arriving at the ball. He should have come with some of his friends instead of alone, but he'd had the grand idea of arriving unfashionably early so he could see more of the guests arriving. Instead, he'd made himself a target as the highest-ranking and earliest-arriving nobleman. He also quickly realized that such an unusual move for a man such as himself signaled to the mamas that he was in search of a wife this Season.

They'd practically trampled each other in a bid to shove their daughters in front of him.

All of them smiling, all of them staring at him with hopeful stars in their eyes, all of them ready to do whatever he asked in order to win the desired proposal.

Drake's appearance at the ball had not given them any pause. It was well known that the Duke of Ormonde was betrothed to Lady Astrid Blackwood. Thankfully, he'd brought Nathanial with him. About half of the young ladies—all with very large dowries—peeled

40

away from the group that had cornered Gregory. Hereford was an easier target for them, as his need of funds made him more desperate to marry faster, whereas Gregory did not have such a pressing deadline. He'd done a good job of shining himself up, but when next to the others, it was clear that his clothing was a touch shabbier, and his dusky rose waistcoat was at least two Seasons out of fashion in style.

The slight lessening of the crowd had allowed Gregory to make an escape to the library, where he'd stubbornly stayed for the past hour and a quarter. Venturing back to the ballroom held no appeal, even though plenty of other guests were here now. He would likely blend in better.

And yet...

Gregory had always been the hunter when it came to the pursuit of ladies. He enjoyed the chase. While he'd occasionally allowed himself to be caught by a particularly eager potential lover, it was the challenge he'd relished the most.

There was no challenge to this. It was like going on a hunt only to be mobbed by the prey—how could a man get a shot off when he could not see? Yes, he would hit something if he did, but who knew what... and Gregory was not willing to take the risk.

Clearly, he was going to need to come up with another plan of attack for his mission. One that never again involved arriving early at a ball.

The door to the library opened a crack, and Gregory froze, hunching down in the large armchair he'd seated himself in. Had the mamas found him? The armchair was currently tucked away in the shadows, so even if someone was looking for him, hopefully, they would not see him.

But it was not a mama and debutante, nor was it a couple looking for a spot of privacy, but a young woman. The light in the room came from the moonlight trickling in from the windows, so he did not get a very good look at her until she stepped past the first set of shelves and into the light.

Very pretty, was his first thought.

Her dress was a trifle old-fashioned, though it might just be that her figure was naturally boxy, and this was the most flattering style for her. She did not have the same silhouette as the other women. That did not detract from how pretty she was, though. Her hair was pulled back in a fashionable coiffure, tendrils curling against her face and the sides of her neck. The lighting made it hard to see the particular color, though it appeared to be more dark than light.

She appeared sad by her expression.

With a soft sigh, she walked over to the shelves and began to run her fingers over the spines of the books. Gregory watched with interest, sitting up. He still did not make his presence known. He was not sure what she was doing in here or where her chaperone was.

Who let a pretty young debutante wander alone at a ball?

Whoever her guardian was, they were not properly watching over her.

That or someone does know I am in here, and this is a trap.

That thought nearly made him stand to flee or perhaps find a good hiding spot, but she did not seem to be looking for anyone. Instead, she leaned her forehead against the books and sighed again, fingers clinging to the bookshelf like it was the only thing holding her upright.

Her first ball must not be going very well.

Sympathy welled up inside him as neither was his. Still, comforting her was out of the question. If someone did come in and found them here together, her reputation would be ruined, and he would be obliged to marry her. The thought appealed momentarily, as she truly was rather pretty, and that would mean his hunt for a bride was over, but then common sense reasserted herself.

He did not know her, did not know why she had come into the library, and so had no idea if she'd be suitable as a bride, much less whether or not she fit his personal criteria. Besides, he was still pondering the merits of a plain wife, and she was far too pretty.

However, he was curious about what she was doing, so he

watched as she took several deep breaths, then lifted her head again. Running her fingers over the spines of the books seemed to soothe her as she walked back and forth along the shelves of the same row.

Gregory was so intrigued watching her, he jumped when the door opened again.

Good lord, the library was turning into a bloody meeting room.

He hunched in his chair again and watched as the young lady tucked herself back against a curtain. Not that either of them needed to worry about hiding away with each other. The couple who came stumbling into the room were far too wrapped up to notice their surroundings.

They closed the door and kissed passionately, the man's hands sliding over the woman's body. When they turned and the man lifted his head, Gregory did not recognize either of them. They were very young. He wondered why they had snuck away for their rendezvous.

"David, David… you must lock the door," the young woman whispered.

The young man frowned down at her. "If the door is locked, people will wonder why, and if they discover us on the other side, they will think I have ruined you."

"We have already snuck away without a chaperone. I am as good as ruined whether we do anything or not," she retorted.

Gregory admired her brazenness. He wondered what her name was. Once she married and gave her husband an heir, she was the type to be ripe for the plucking.

And therefore not the wife for me, but perhaps David feels differently.

David stiffened, seeming displeased.

"Is that why you begged me to sneak away for a kiss? So you could trap me into marriage?" He shook his head. "I told you, Penelope, I am not ready for marriage yet."

"I told you, I have to marry this Season, or I will not have another!"

Gregory did not know who he felt sorrier for, David or Penelope. David was quickly realizing the danger he was in with his manipulative minx, and Penelope was clearly in dire straits. He wondered why she was having trouble bringing a husband up to scratch... unless, of course, there were too many gentlemen who did not appreciate her boldness.

That seemed very likely.

"This is not well done, Penelope." David stepped away and quickly opened the door, walking out with Penelope scurrying after him, calling his name.

Unable to help himself, watching the drama of the pair, Gregory chuckled.

"Who is there?" The low, feminine voice made him curse inwardly. He'd gotten so caught up in the couple, he'd forgotten the other young woman was there.

Sighing, he unfolded himself from the chair and stood, looking over to where she was still standing by the curtain she'd been ready to hide behind.

"My lady, my apologies for startling you," he said. "I was looking for some peace, and when you entered, I did not say anything because... well, I did not wish to be disturbed."

Her eyes had gone very wide, but she stared silently at him. She did not jump forward. Did not immediately curtsy or 'Your Grace' him. Was it possible she did not know who he was? That she did not recognize him?

She must have arrived after he'd retreated from the ballroom, or surely her mama would have pointed him out to her.

As Gregory moved toward her, his sense of relief that she was not excited to find herself ensconced by herself with a duke was accompanied by another emotion, though he could not quite put his finger on what it was. Her lack of excitement over his person had stirred a kind of unexpected interest in him. Eventually, she would discover his identity, but for now, the ability to flirt with her rather than having her throw herself at him was too appealing to ignore.

"Is there anything I can do for you, my lady?" he asked, coming to a halt in front of her, standing closer than was perhaps polite. It gave him a much better view of her face.

Her hair was caught somewhere between brown and blonde, and her eyes were a dark brown that looked nearly black in the dim light. The perfect bow of her pink lips looked ripe for kissing—if only she was not a debutante, but she was too young to be anything else. The dress she was wearing had a rather high neckline, higher than was fashionable, covering her boxy frame very modestly.

Despite knowing she was an innocent, he had the oddest desire to tug the front of her dress down and reveal more of her body to him. Definitely not his usual reaction to debutantes.

"I... I was also looking for peace," she said after a long moment, still staring up at him in wonderment. Perhaps she was over-whelmed at the idea of speaking to any gentleman. "It is a crush, and, well, I do not believe I was comporting myself very well."

He smiled rakishly at her, enjoying being able to relax into his preferred manner of interacting with ladies. Staring up at him, she appeared almost entranced by his attention on her.

"I am sure you were doing much better than you think. Did you receive any offers to dance?"

"Several, but... I believe they were doing so out of pity."

"Pity?" He raised his eyebrow at her, and she stared back at him.

"Yes... I am no great beauty, after all. Especially compared to some of the other debutantes."

Ah, poor girl. Someone must have said something nasty to her. Society could be cruel. That dress, as unflattering as it was, would garner some looks and remarks, he was sure.

"There are some very beautiful debutantes," he agreed. "But you are very pretty. Certainly too pretty to only receive offers out of pity." Some gentlemen might be put off by her bluntness, but not all of them. Some, like himself, would enjoy it.

She frowned at him. Gregory shook his head at her obvious disbelief, wondering if he should be insulted that she clearly thought him dishonest.

"I can honestly say that I am not flirting with you out of pity," he told her, just to see her reaction.

Her dark eyes widened.

"You are flirting with me?"

Damn. He must be losing his touch if she had to ask the question. Or perhaps she had so little experience with Society, she did not know a flirtation when she tripped over it. Well, he was happy to educate her. This private moment was turning into the most enjoyable part of his evening.

"I am flirting with you," he confirmed with his best rakish grin. It did his heart good to see her quick intake of breath and the change in her expression as she reacted to him. Less than an hour with debutantes who cared for nothing but his title and his need for a wife made her reactions to him particularly satisfying.

Eventually, once she returned to the ballroom or perhaps at another event, she would discover his identity. Perhaps he should give her a fond memory to take with her through the Season and a thrill for when she did realize who he was. There was no danger of her spreading the word about; it would only damage her reputation if anyone even believed her.

He was not known for dallying with debutantes.

But something about her was irresistible. Perhaps the novelty. Perhaps because she did not know who he was.

Yes, he should definitely give her something pleasurable to remember him by.

"I am flirting with you," he repeated. "And now I'm going to kiss you."

Her eyes widened, but she did not move away as he lowered his head.

When their lips touched, an unexpected thrill went through him, then she shifted, kissing him back, and Gregory put his arms around her. He had not meant to; it just happened. He had not realized she would kiss him back, and he had not anticipated it would affect him so much. That he would want to deepen the kiss, to hold her closer, and his cock start to rise.

~

<u>*TIFFANY*</u>

He does not know who I am.

At first, she had not quite believed that her brother's friend, now the Duke of Clarence, did not recognize her. Though the light in here was not good. The dark navy blue he was wearing helped him blend into the shadows, even with his starched white shirt. But she had recognized him the moment he'd revealed himself. How could she not? He was the most handsome man she'd ever seen, with his dark wavy hair, dark eyes, and charming smile.

She'd thought he was jesting with her, mocking her even.

She still remembered the last time she'd seen him, when she'd been still in the schoolroom and he'd visited. Not that she had seen very much of him. He and Sebastian had spent most of their time together, away from the house, and even when they'd been there, she had been too shy to approach. And the one night they *had* eaten with her family, her mother had sent Tiffany to bed without supper for reading when she was supposed to be practicing her needlepoint.

So, she should not have expected him to recognize her, yet part of her had wanted him to.

But if he had, he might not have flirted with her.

If he had, he might not have bent his head to kiss her.

She felt like she was dreaming, but his lips pressing against hers were so very real. Her first kiss. From the most handsome man she'd ever met. From a duke, the very kind of man her mother had told her to have no expectations of. From a man who did not know who she was and was not kissing her because she was a duke's sister.

From a man who was kissing her for no other reason than she was pretty.

So, she kissed him back, knowing she would likely never have *this* again.

She did not expect him to marry her, of course. This was a secret kiss in the dark, something to hold on to. He would marry some other debutante. One far more beautiful, more accomplished than her.

But this moment, this one moment, was hers and all hers to remember for the rest of her life.

A loud bang interrupted her moment, and she jumped in shock, causing the duke's arms to tighten around her. They both went toppling over, falling away from where they'd been nearly invisible against the shelves. The duke twisted so he did not land atop her— she landed atop him, cushioned against him—onto the floor right in front of the group streaming into the room from the door that had just been thrown open.

She did not recognize any of them.

"That's not Penelope," the woman in front said, frowning down at them.

"And that is not David," the woman beside her said triumphantly.

"No, that is the Duke of Clarence!" Lady Jersey pushed her way through the two women, staring down at Tiffany, who looked back up at her with absolute horror. Of all the people to come into the room. Lady Jersey put her hand to her bosom. "Oh my goodness... and the Lady Tiffany! She's been ruined!"

"Lady Tiffany?" Clarence whispered, sounding just as horrified as Lady Jersey.

"Tiffany!" Her brother shouted her name from behind the ever-growing crowd of people as he elbowed his way through them.

Tiffany closed her eyes and wished with all her might to completely disappear.

FIVE

Tiffany.

The moment her brother reached her, he plucked her from where she was still lying atop the Duke of Clarence. She hid her face behind her hands, her cheeks hot against her palms.

"How dare you?" Her brother roared. "I told you to stay away from my sister!"

He had?

The Duke of Clarence had talked to her brother about her?

Tiffany peeked through her fingers. The Duke of Clarence was getting to his feet, brushing himself off, while more people crowded around them, leaving them in the center. It was a circle of Society that cut off any avenue of escape.

"You also told me she was plain," Clarence said, shaking his head and giving her brother a scornful look. "If you had told me not to kiss any pretty girl who looked nothing like they did when I met them, I might have been more careful."

Even though she knew it was true, hearing that her brother had spoken so of her sent a pang through Tiffany's heart, which was immediately followed by shock and warmth as what Clarence had said pushed through that hurt.

He thinks I'm pretty?

She did not have time to ponder any of this because as soon as Clarence was on his feet, her brother surged forward and punched him in the face, knocking him right into the people behind him. They caught him as he fell backward, keeping him half upright.

"Sebastian!" Tiffany jumped forward, grabbing onto his arm and pulling him back so he could not do it again, as he appeared to be ready to do. "Stop!"

"He ruined you!"

"He... we... it was just a kiss!" Even as she said the words, Tiffany knew it was hopeless. Alone in a library with a rake? Kissing a rake? And then being caught by an entire multitude of witnesses. She was thoroughly compromised.

The ruining had been rather nice, if she was being honest about it. It was the aftermath that she did not enjoy so much. If half the *ton* and her brother had not come bursting through the door, she would have thoroughly enjoyed being ruined.

And now she was having to keep her brother from punching his best friend for a second time because of her.

Clarence got to his feet with the help of those who had caught him, his expression darker than before. He rubbed his jaw where Sebastian's punch had landed.

"One," he said in the most dangerously serious voice she'd ever heard. "You get one because she is your sister, but I will have you remember that I did not know she was your sister, and your description of her was wholly inadequate."

"I..." Sebastian's voice trailed off, and he turned his head to look at her. Bafflement suffused his expression as he stared at her, almost like he'd never seen her before.

"She need not remain ruined." Hereford pushed his way through the crowd and gave Clarence a stern frown. "Remember, Bolton, I wanted to speak with you about her before. This has changed nothing about my offer."

He had? He'd said he wanted to speak with her brother, but Tiffany had not realized that *she* would be the topic of conversation. The Duke of Hereford had been going to ask her brother for her hand? After one short meeting? When he could have any beauty with a dowry?

Clarence said I was pretty.

"You are not marrying her," Clarence said irritably, tugging at the sleeves of his jacket as he glared at Hereford. "I compromised her. I'm marrying her."

They both want to marry me?

There was no gossip about Clarence's finances. He certainly had no need of her dowry. So, why was he suddenly set on marrying her? Except... was it sudden? She was so confused and was starting to feel lightheaded from all the shocks.

Her first ball and she had been compromised, caused a physical altercation, and received two offers of marriage. What on earth could happen next?

Caterwauling in the hallway happened next before any of the gentlemen could say another word. Tiffany winced, her grip on her brother's arms tightening—she recognized her mother's shrieks.

"Oh, dear," the Countess of Spencer said from her position by the door in a drawling tone, turning away from the hallway to continue watching what was happening in the library. "It seems the Duchess of Bolton is having hysterics. Someone should probably attend her." The Countess did not make a move to do so herself. She smiled and looked around, as if she were enjoying the entertainment immensely.

Thankfully, several other older ladies moved quickly, including Lady Jersey, who shook her head at the Countess of Spencer as she passed. The Countess beamed at her. Tiffany had heard the woman was an eccentric, but goodness.

"Go, see to Mother, and take her home," Sebastian said to her, interrupting her thoughts. His voice was cold, but she could tell that coolness was directed at his friends, not at her. "I need to speak to Clarence. And Hereford, you might as well come, too, just in case."

Casting one last glance around—still baffled by the way Clarence was glaring at Hereford and the way Hereford was glaring back at him—Tiffany went to collect her mother. It was going to be a Herculean task and one she did not look forward to, but at least she would no longer be *here* in front of all the gleeful watchers.

She'd sparked enough gossip for one night.

GREGORY

Why on earth was he insisting he marry Sebastian's sister?

Especially when she had another offer that would salvage her reputation just as much as marrying *him* would? Not only that, but marrying her would solve Hereford's money problems. It was a sensible solution for everyone involved.

Except the moment Nathanial had stepped forward with his offer, every part of Gregory's body had rebelled at the idea of anyone else marrying her. He was the one she'd kissed. The kiss that had set him aflame.

While she was not as plain as Sebastian had described, it was true that she was not as fashionable or as glorious a beauty as some of the other debutantes. She was still trained to run a household. She was still very shy, though she had spoken to him easily enough once he'd revealed himself. And she was passionate.

A wife who would be faithful, was not so beautiful that all the rakes would be chasing her relentlessly, but still passionate in bed... Tiffany was perfect. And pretty enough that he would not need to darken the bedroom. He was very attracted to her. What on earth had her brother been thinking?

Plain.

Ha.

The Duchess of Richmond, having clearly been informed that there was some drama in her library, had come to clear away the onlookers, and she gave permission for them to stay there to have their conversation. Tiffany and her mother were already gone, her mother wailing the whole way about the ignominy of having a ruined daughter.

He wished she and Sebastian would stop using that word.

Tiffany had not been ruined. She'd been compromised. If she'd been ruined, this tedium would be far more worth it, and he would not have to put up with Nathanial attempting to poach his bride.

"What on earth were you thinking?" Sebastian exploded as soon as the door was shut behind the Duchess of Richmond.

Gregory glared right back at him, still rubbing his jaw. It was a fair shot. He would have given the same to any man who caught Gregory kissing his virgin sister. But it was not as though Gregory had known she was Sebastian's sister.

"I was thinking there was a pretty girl alone here in the library, one who did not know who I was and therefore was not attempting to leg-shackle me and that it might be fun to flirt and steal a kiss." He shook his head. "If I had known she was your sister, obviously, I would not have done any of that. If anything, this is all your fault for your uncomplimentary and inaccurate description of her!"

"If you told him she was plain, he does have a point," Hereford said reluctantly, frowning at Sebastian. "She is not at all plain."

"Plain and dull was how he described her," Gregory told him before Sebastian could reply. "He was lamenting how difficult it would be to find her a husband, despite her rank."

Nathanial stared in astonishment at Sebastian, who now appeared decidedly uncomfortable that both his friends were in obvious disagreement with his assessment of his sister's charms.

"Plain? Dull? She's very pretty, and I found her quite charming, though your mother is a bit overbearing."

"My mother..." Sebastian's voice trailed off, and he sighed, dropping the defensiveness. "My mother can be a bit difficult at times, it is true, but she is still my mother."

Holding up both hands in a gesture of surrender, Nathanial nodded. "We all have difficult family members. I do not mind adding another one to my own family, and I truly did intend to talk to you about offering for her."

"I know." Sebastian looked over at Gregory, still frowning. "He does have a prior claim."

"Yet, I am the one who ruined her," Gregory retorted. While he might not agree with Sebastian's use of the more dire term, in this instance, it served his cause. "It is *my* honor at stake if I do not make it right. Besides, I offered for her before him, and you rejected my suit for reasons that are now moot, as I am the one who kissed her. She is not going to get a love match either way. I promise I will be a good husband and endeavor never to hurt her in any way."

All the wind went out of Sebastian's sails, and he sagged where he stood. Leaning back against the bookshelves, he ran his hand over his face, looking rather distraught.

"I wish my father were here to deal with this," he admitted. "He would know what to do. He was the one who was supposed to oversee Tiffany's debut and find her a husband. I am mucking it all up."

"I think I might be the one mucking it up for you," Gregory admitted, his heart going out to the other man as he moved to stand by his side. He slung his arm around Sebastian's shoulders. Nathanial came up to Sebastian's other side, leaning against the shelves with them. None of them had been ready to take up this mantle, and with a debutante sister, Sebastian surely had the roughest lot of all. "Let me make it right. I will marry her. I will try to make her happy. I will do my best not to hurt her. That is about all a man can hope for when finding a husband for his sister."

Eventually, he would have to do the same for his half-sisters. An endeavor he was not looking forward to but one which he hoped he met with as much care as Sebastian was trying to.

"I let her be compromised at her first ball." Sebastian covered his face with his hands. "I should have been watching her more closely. I thought my mother had things under control. I was not paying attention."

"Gregory is right," Nathanial said gently. "He is the one best suited to make it right. Though if he were not, I would happily marry her, and not just for her dowry. None of us were ready for this. We are all doing the best we can."

Sebastian took a deep breath and slowly let it out, leaning his head back against Gregory's arm.

"Very well," he said after a long moment, turning his head to look at Gregory. "You will marry my sister. You will do your best to ensure her happiness. And if you ever hurt her, I will punch you again."

"Fair enough." Gregory looked back at him. "I have to ask though... she's plain?"

"Are you blind?" Nathanial chimed in from Sebastian's other side.

Straightening, Sebastian threw his hands in the air in resignation. "Apparently! She was plain, and then, at some point, she grew out of it, and I suppose I did not notice. I am her brother, after all. I was not paying particular attention."

"Well, I am getting a pretty wife out of it, so I suppose I cannot complain," Gregory teased. It felt very odd to say 'wife', yet he was pleased to be able to do so.

Married. And he found his wife at the first ball of the Season. It was truly quite an accomplishment. Now, all he had to do was get through the wedding, ensure his bride was happy enough with being married to him—and why would she not be?—and beget an heir.

Considering how easily the first step had fallen into his lap, there was no reason the rest should be any more difficult. Though, he did wonder how Tiffany was dealing with her mother. Hopefully, his soon-to-be mother-in-law would be satisfied that her daughter was marrying a duke and her son's friend and not hold the manner of how the proposal happened against him.

CHAPTER

SIX

Tiffany.

Her mother's screeching grated on her ears and did not stop the entire carriage ride home.

"How could you do this to me? The shame of it! What will people think of you? Of me? What were you thinking? You were not; of course, you were not. Oh, the shame! It will follow me to my grave!"

The diatribe went nonstop all the way back to Bolton House, by which time any excitement or enjoyment from Clarence's kiss and the knowledge that two dukes thought she was pretty had been entirely erased. Now, she felt drained and like hiding under her bed, but that was not an option as her mother had to be physically assisted from the carriage. If she did not tend to her mother, it would make everything worse.

Thomas Coachman gave her a sympathetic look as he helped her down from the carriage, though he was wise enough to hold his tongue. Her mother was leaning on the two footmen who had come to greet them, and her ladies' maid, Harleen, was hurrying down the stairs from the front door. The same age as Tiffany's mother, Harleen was a stalwart presence in Bolton House, a master at deferring to Tiffany's mother on some matters and guiding her on others.

She was a rock upon which the rest of the staff leaned when the duchess was in one of her many moods and often their shield as well. Her age and skills made her invaluable to the household, and even Tiffany's mother did not push her too far. It was clear she'd been preparing for bed, her dressing gown flapping over her long, pale nightdress as she hurried down the stairs, a sleeping bonnet over her greying brown hair.

The expression on her face was one of extreme concern, as it should be. Tiffany's mother had never made such a scene publicly before. She was far too cognizant of keeping up appearances. To be wailing and crying on the street was unprecedented behavior on her part. That it had begun at Richmond House was even more worrying. Tiffany did not like to think about what consequences her mother was going to devise for her once she was no longer hysterical.

"Oh, I am faint," her mother wailed, falling upon Harleen and throwing her arms around the woman's neck, much to Harleen's shock. Tiffany's, too. Her mother was not prone to speaking to the servants, much less touching them, and while her own ladies' maid was one of the few her mother spoke to, it was not normally like this. "My own daughter... the disgrace... I cannot bear it."

"What happened? Your Grace," Harleen quickly tacked on, so surprised that she almost addressed Tiffany's mother without the honorific. Tiffany came up on the other side of her mother, quietly helping support her toward the front door.

"I cannot speak of it." Her mother let out another sob. "It is too awful. My own daughter, ruined! And at her very first ball! What will everyone say?"

"Ruined?" Harleen mouthed the word at Tiffany, and Tiffany shook her head as they made their way into the house. The front door closed behind them. Harleen raked her sharp gaze over Tiffany's personage, taking in her immaculate dress. The skirt was not even creased. Harleen frowned.

"How will we ever find a husband for you now?" her mother wailed, even louder than she had when they were out of doors, or perhaps it was because her voice now echoed off the tiled floor and high ceiling of the foyer. Tiffany blinked in surprise before she realized her mother must not have heard everything that went on while she was in the hall—she had never made it all the way into the library. Whoever had told her that Tiffany was compromised had not seen the entirety of the aftermath.

Relief flooded her that she would be able to set her mother's mind at ease.

"The Duke of Clarence and the Duke of Hereford both offered for me," she said quickly. "That is why Sebastian did not depart with us. He is speaking with them." Her heart fluttered at the reminder. Two dukes fighting over her! And Clarence one of them... For a moment, her lips tingled at the memory of his against hers.

Immediately, her mother straightened, eyes flashing.

"They what?" The screech was nearly as loud as her wailing had been, and for a moment, Tiffany thought her mother appeared angry, though she could not imagine why.

"That is wonderful!" Harleen said at the same time, beaming at Tiffany. "Is... did one of them..." She darted a look at Tiffany's mother, quickly realizing how counter her reaction was to the duchess', which was always a dangerous place to stand.

"Clarence," Tiffany confirmed. "Hereford offered, though, saying he had already asked to speak to Sebastian about it." Which made her feel... she did not know. Like floating on air. Though, if she were being truthful about the whole situation, it was Clarence who stuck in her mind.

She knew enough of men to understand that he had been rakishly flirting and that he had probably not meant a word of what he'd said, but if she married Hereford, she also knew she would never forget tonight or the way that Clarence had made her feel.

"I cannot think," her mother said, reaching up to press her fingertips against her temples. It hid the expression on her face, and she pulled away from both Harleen and Tiffany. "It is all too much. I have a *megrim,* and I need to be alone. Harleen, you will attend me."

Tiffany stood in shock as her mother rushed up the stairs, suddenly completely capable of moving on her own and moving quite quickly. Shooting her a glance Tiffany could not interpret, Harleen followed the duchess.

Well, then.

Looking down at her pretty dress, which had made her feel so wonderful, Tiffany stared at it for a long moment as the full implications of the evening all came crashing down at once now that she was alone.

She'd been kissed.

She was to be married.

She did not know either of her suitors.

Tiffany closed her eyes and took a deep breath, counting down from ten in her head, the way she'd done as a child when she was particularly anxious. Sometimes, it had been the only way to remain calm in the face of her mother's emotions. Now, her mother had retreated, and her own concerns were bubbling up.

Married to a stranger, either way. Though, she trusted her brother to make the right choice for her. God, she hoped he made the right choice for her.

Hereford or Clarence? Which would be better? Or would it not matter at all?

Pressing her hand to her stomach, she wandered into the drawing room and over to the window seat. Perhaps any minute, she would wake and find that this entire evening had been a dream, that she had yet to attend the Duchess of Richmond's ball... yet, despite how surreal everything felt, she knew it was not a dream.

Sitting down among the cushions, she pressed her forehead to the cool glass, staring out at the street. There would be no sleep for her tonight. Not until her brother came home and she learned her fate.

GREGORY

Married.

On the carriage ride to Bolton House, which was not far from his own home in Mayfair, the reality seemed to hit Gregory, and his hands went rather clammy. It was not the idea of marriage that caused such consternation, as such, because he had gone into the Season prepared to marry, but somehow, there were so many things he had not thought of when it was a mere idea.

Like a wedding.

Like how to make a woman happy for more than a night.

He was not the type to keep a mistress; he'd always preferred lovers.

Perhaps he should ask Christian and Zachary how they kept their mistresses happy.

No, wait... he could not treat his wife as a mistress, could he? But then, all women liked jewelry. He was sure Christian and Zachary had spoken of how expensive their gifts of jewelry were. His own mother loved jewelry.

Damnation.

Mother.

He nearly groaned aloud at the thought of her reaction.

Not that she would be disappointed that he was to be married, but she was certainly going to scold him for the circumstances. And he was going to have to tell her, if she did not already know. She would likely scold him about the fact she'd had to find out from the gossip that he was sure had spread through the ballroom like the plague the moment the Duchess of Richmond had emptied the library.

He and Sebastian had decided *not* to walk through the ballroom but rather to slip away more discreetly while Nathanial returned to the throng to make their excuses. Under the circumstances, they felt their fellow duke would understand. Though it was not in Nathanial's nature to enjoy being surrounded by a mob eager for gossip, it could only help him on his quest for a wife.

He might even be the one to tell Gregory's mother that her son was now engaged in an utterly scandalous fashion.

Hopefully, Nathanial *was* the first to reach her so he could inform her of the story they'd contrived. How the hell had Gregory forgotten about his mother at the ball when they'd been coming up with it?

Because I am not used to her being in London.

Because I was distracted.

Bollocks.

Tomorrow morning was going to be bloody horrific. Not tonight, because he was going to go home as late as possible to avoid his mother for as long as possible.

"You had better not be having second thoughts," Sebastian said darkly from across the carriage, proving that his friend knew him all too well. "By now, Hereford has already told everyone that you and Tiffany are engaged and that it was all a misunderstanding."

"I know. It is a good story. I am not having second thoughts." Gregory clenched his jaw against saying anything else. Sebastian was not the appropriate party to spill his trepidation to. His closest friend was already upset with him. He did not want to provoke him further.

"Good. Because my sister's happiness is in your hands, and I will not take it lightly if you do anything to cause her any more distress than you already have."

The longer this carriage ride continued, the broodier Sebastian was becoming, and he was already a broody fellow. Gregory let out a long, slow breath. He was normally the cheerful one, but it was feeling rather difficult in the face of such monumental events and the growing knowledge that his friendship with the other man was at risk. Sebastian might not have realized his sister had turned out rather pretty, but he was still a protective big brother.

"I was thinking about my mother's reaction," he admitted.

"What do you think are the chances that she left the ball before Hereford returned?"

Sebastian barked with sudden laughter as Gregory's problem came to the fore.

"Very, very slim, my friend." Sebastian's grin flashed white in the dark confines of the carriage. "You are going to have a reckoning to face at home."

"Truer words were never spoken," Gregory muttered, relieved when Sebastian chuckled again. It felt like perhaps their friendship was righting itself through a few jokes, the kind they often exchanged. Yet, it felt like something had irrevocably changed as well.

There was a weight on their friendship that had not been there before.

The carriage came to a halt, and Gregory felt that weight settle into his chest. Would he be facing his bride and his future mother-in-law? He and Sebastian had agreed to work out the marriage contract tonight, to get it into place immediately. Also, Sebastian wanted him to propose properly to Tiffany. And they needed to ensure Tiffany and her mother were fully informed of the explanation he and Sebastian had devised.

Sebastian got out of the carriage first, and Gregory followed, looking up at the house. The windows in the foyer were brightly lit, the rest of the house dark, but there was just enough light from the streetlamps and the moon for him to see a figure in the front window stand up.

Tiffany.

He recognized her immediately. Not a maid. Not her mother.

My wife.

Waiting for him.

It was time to face the music.

CHAPTER
SEVEN

There he was. Her future husband.

The Duke of Clarence. Looking up at the window where she stood as if he could see her, despite the dark and the distance from the street. Her brother was already walking toward the door, and after a moment, the Duke of Clarence followed him.

Closing her eyes, Tiffany took a deep breath. She'd been preparing for marriage her entire life. She'd been training for it. Every lesson her mother had put her through, every critique that had been leveled at her, had all been pointed at the final goal of marrying and marrying well.

She was going to do that.

She had succeeded, despite her looks, despite her inability to satisfy her mother with her conversation. She was going to marry, and she was going to marry a duke. It was beyond her wildest dreams and certainly any of her mother's expectations for her.

So, why was there a hard pit in the center of her stomach, surrounded by rabid butterflies?

Part of her wanted to rush into the foyer to meet her brother at the door and demand to know everything. If the Duke of Clarence had not been with him, that was exactly what she would have done. Instead, she hung back, moving to the doorway of the drawing room, watching as their butler Paulson opened the door and greeted the two dukes.

"Thank you, Paulson," her brother said as he passed him, Clarence right on his heels.

The two of them were certainly striking beside each other, both dark-haired, broad-shouldered, and handsome enough to make every lady of the *ton* sigh. Clarence's navy-blue jacket hugged him as neatly as her brother's green one did him, emphasizing a long, lean figure. The biggest difference between them was the bruise that was beginning to bloom on Clarence's jaw.

Sebastian looked around.

"Where are my mother and sister?"

"Your mother has gone to bed, Your Grace, with a *megrim*," Paulson informed him, taking the men's gloves. "Your sister…" He turned, and Tiffany stifled the urge to duck back into the drawing room and pretend she was not there.

Both Clarence and her brother turned to look with Paulson, and her gaze met Sebastian's for only a fleeting second before it was drawn to Clarence. Her breath hitched as he looked back at her, just like he had in the library earlier this evening.

Like she was beautiful.

Like she mattered.

"Good, well." Her brother huffed. "I will have to speak with Mother in the morning. Thank you, Paulson. Please have someone bring some brandy to the drawing room and something for my sister. We will need the room lit as well."

"Yes, Your Grace." Paulson bowed and took himself off, but not before glancing over at Tiffany and giving her a supportive smile. She smiled weakly back at him. An older man, he often acted something like a secondary father, as much as he was able to be, considering the difference in their stations, and she'd always been grateful to him for that. Especially after losing her own father so unexpectedly.

Knowing that he was supportive helped.

"Right, well." Her brother stared at her and sighed. "Let us go into the drawing room so we can talk."

It only took a few minutes for the gas lamps to be lit, brightening the room. Tiffany sat on the couch and tried not to startle when the Duke of Clarence seated himself beside her. Her brother took one of the armchairs, glowering at the other duke the entire time.

As impatient to demand answers as she was, Tiffany held her tongue as Polly, the maid, brightened the room. When she was just finishing, Jane from the kitchens came in with a tray of brandy, tea, and Tiffany's favorite biscuits. She thanked Jane with relief, even as impatience gripped her, but she knew better than anyone not to treat the servants as if they did not exist.

It always startled her the number of people who forgot that their maids and footmen were just people, and they liked to gossip as much as the *ton* did. While she trusted her brother's staff, she did not want to give them any more cause for wagging tongues than she already had.

When Jane quit the room, closing the door behind her, Tiffany gave her brother a look as she leaned forward to pour herself some tea. He cleared his throat, tugging at the cravat around his neck to loosen it, waiting for her to sit back before he picked up one of the brandies.

Beside her, the Duke of Clarence did not move. He sat perfectly still, watching her, his hands on his knees with one finger tapping against his right knee. It was rather unnerving.

"You pour tea very well," he said after a moment.

Tiffany blinked, nonplussed by the unusual and unexpected compliment. "Thank you, Your Grace."

It came out as more of a question than a statement, due to her confusion.

"Right, well." Her brother cleared his throat again. It occurred to Tiffany that both men were as unnerved as she was, though her brother did finally take the reins of conversation. "As I am sure you have guessed, Gregory has made an offer for your hand. I do encourage you to accept it due to… well, circumstances. If you would like to speak with me privately, I can send him out of the room." He frowned. "I should probably have done so, anyway."

"There is no need. I understand what is necessary," Tiffany said quickly. Anything to shorten this drawn-out torture of awkwardness between them all.

Sebastian gave Clarence a look.

Immediately, Clarence slid from the couch, startling her so that she nearly spilled her tea as he went down on one knee beside her. Hot liquid splashed against her fingertips on the saucer, but she managed to keep her grip despite that.

"Lady Tiffany," he said, reaching for her hand and then halting when he realized they were full. He frowned, then took the cup and saucer from her, turning slightly to put it back on the tray before returning his attention to her and taking one of her hands to hold in his. He cleared his throat again, and Tiffany had to stifle a giggle.

Perhaps she was tired, perhaps she was becoming hysterical, but there was something so farcical about all of this that she had the mad urge to burst into laughter.

"Lady Tiffany, would you do me the great honor of agreeing to be my wife?"

"Yes," she replied, practically choking on the word in her endeavor not to laugh. She could barely hold it back, and the only thing that could make this moment worse would be to laugh at a duke's proposal of marriage.

"Good. Right then." He cleared his throat again, and she coughed to cover the sound that bubbled up. "That's done."

Her amusement was wiped away with those two words. Farcical, yes, and yet this was her life. Her reputation at stake. Her reflection back on her family. She was going to marry a duke because she had to, and he was going to marry her because his honor demanded it and no other reason. There were worse reasons to marry, she supposed, and yet...

And yet.

She did not have the heart to admit to herself now what she had truly hoped for.

The duke resumed his place on the couch beside her, but he did not let go of her hand. Her fingers felt so small against his, his hand rougher than her soft skin, and he held it very gently but firmly, as though he did not want to let her go... Tiffany's stomach did an odd flip. She did not want to let go, either.

Her brother frowned at them both and dropped his gaze to where Tiffany's hand now rested in Clarence's, the back of her hand against his thigh. Tiffany pretended not to see the frown. Clarence turned his head away from her brother to focus on her.

"We have come up with a plan to make this evening appear less scandalous," Clarence said, putting his other hand overtop hers. Her brother made a disgruntled sound, but the duke did not look away from her, his dark eyes wholly focused. "We are going to put it about that you and I met and became engaged before the Season began but had an agreement with your brother that you were not to be deprived of a Season, so you could meet other gentlemen and be sure of your choice."

"Because no one in their right mind would agree to marry you if they had a choice," Sebastian muttered, not very quietly. Tiffany shot him a look, but the Duke of Clarence just grinned as if Sebastian had complimented rather than insulted him. He squeezed Tiffany's hand, and she looked back at him. It was probably best to ignore her brother, as he seemed determined to be surly.

"Then, tonight..." She let her voice trail off. How did they explain tonight if she was supposed to be meeting other possible suitors? And would anyone truly believe that the Duke of Clarence *wanted* to marry her?

"Tonight, we were overcome with our passion for one another."

Clarence winked at her, and she blushed. There was some truth to that, on her side at least. "We snuck off to the library together for a private moment and to complain about your overbearing brother insisting we remain apart for the whole Season. You will be the Juliet to my Romeo, and everyone will be so overcome by the romance of it that any hint of scandal will be quickly squashed."

"We are pretending to be a love match?" Tiffany stared at him. He could not actually think anyone would believe that someone like *him* was in love with someone like *her*.

"A love match being tested by your brother," the Duke of Clarence replied cheerfully. "Tongues will wag, but the focus will be on the romance of it all. As long as we play our parts until the wedding, no one will think twice of it."

"And what of after the wedding?"

He shrugged. "No one pays attention to what anyone does after the wedding."

"I mean, how will we behave?" Regardless of his answer, she was rather trapped in the situation, but she wanted to steel herself for whatever the future might hold. She could easily imagine herself being overcome by his charm, his pretense of love, which was likely a recipe for disaster.

The man was a rake, after all.

He tilted his head at her, as if confused.

"Well, I imagine we will settle into our marriage. I would like children. I prefer to live in London most of the year, though I do go to the country for a few months in the summer. My mother will be delighted to have a daughter-in-law to keep her company... and... ah, I should warn you, I have four half-sisters. They're all very young and very sweet, and they live in the manor house, though they have their own wing." He smiled again, a kind of bashful, hopeful smile.

Tiffany did not know if he was purposefully neglecting the topic of mistresses and lovers or if he truly did not understand what she was attempting to ask. She supposed it was an awkward subject with her brother's presence.

It did not matter, after all. She would marry him, regardless. And while they were pretending to be in love, she would hold her heart apart to protect it.

The idea of a second mother nearly made her quail, but then she remembered that she would no longer be living with her own. At least she would only have to deal with one mother at a time.

"I would like children, too. And to meet your mother and half-sisters." That seemed to be the appropriate response to make, and Clarence beamed at her, patting her hand.

"You will like his mother," Sebastian said. "Everyone does."

Everyone liked her mother, too. She had a great many friends. That did not make her criticism any easier to bear. Tiffany smiled placidly. She would make the best of the situation, just like she was now.

"Tomorrow, Gregory will join us in the afternoon. We will take a turn around Hyde Park before opening the house to visitors." Sebastian sighed. "I expect we will have a great many. Being seen in Hyde Park will make it clear that we are not hanging our heads in shame and that, indeed, you have done nothing to be ashamed of."

"And you and I will play star-crossed lovers now allowed to reunite." The duke winked at her. "Your brother will be your growling guardian, displeased with being thwarted, a task I am sure he will find most difficult."

Tiffany could not help but giggle, glancing at her brother, who was scowling at his friend again. He cleared his expression when he realized she was looking at him and smiled at her. It was a pained smile but a smile, nonetheless.

"Do not worry, Tiff. I do not blame you for this evening's events. This ploy will keep any tarnish from your reputation and the family's name—"

"And *my* reputation, such that it is," Clarence murmured, ignoring the way her brother glared at him again.

"By the time the Season is over, no one will even remember that your marriage started with a scandal." Sebastian rubbed his hand against his knee. "It will be well, I promise. This scoundrel has promised to do his best to make you happy, or he will answer to me."

That last sentence was a definitive threat, and the smile dropped from Clarence's face, all remnants of teasing gone. She almost wanted to scold her brother because it was akin to watching a puppy being kicked.

"I am sure we will be happy," she said reassuringly, even though she was not sure of it at all. She also could not be sure they would be unhappy.

Her brother nodded and got to his feet.

"We need to talk through the marriage contract and write the announcement. You should go to bed, Tiffany. It is going to be a long day tomorrow, and we still have to explain our plan to Mother."

What her mother would think of it, Tiffany had no idea. She was very concerned with the family's reputation, though, so likely, she would be agreeable to any plan that helped keep it unblemished. But then, she'd thought her mother would be pleased to hear that two dukes had offered for her to save her reputation, and instead, she'd come down with a *megrim*.

Nonetheless, Tiffany still got to her feet, her hand still in Clarence's. She found herself rather reluctant to let go.

Do not be naïve. He is already pretending, probably. Practicing. He does not want to keep holding your hand. It is part of the pretense.

"Thank you, Your Grace," she said. "I wish you a good night."

She attempted to pull her fingers away from his, but he held on to them.

"Call me Gregory, please," he said, smiling at her. "We are to be married, after all, Tiffany."

Hearing him call her by her name with no honorific near took her breath away, especially with the way he was looking at her, as though he could see into her very soul.

"Of course," she said faintly.

He raised his eyebrow at her. "Of course, Gregory."

"Of course, Gregory," she parroted, though it felt incredibly wrong to use his Christian name.

Thankfully, her brother came barging in, shouldering the duke aside and back, pulling their hands apart.

"Goodnight, Tiffany," Sebastian said, bending down to give her cheek a kiss. "Do not worry. Everything will be all right."

She hoped he was correct.

EIGHT

Gregory

Utterly wrung out by the evening's events and then wrangling with Sebastian over the marriage contract terms, Gregory slipped quietly into his house. He'd had the coachman take him around back to the mews, where he let himself out, then crept in the back. The house was quiet and dark, giving him hope.

He might be safe.

Tiptoeing through the hall, he pushed open the door to the kitchen... and froze.

His mother was waiting for him there, perched atop a stool, a steaming mug of tea beside a plate of biscuits she'd apparently been nibbling on. As soon as he walked in, she brightened and turned to their housekeeper, Mrs. Bryant, who was beside her. Both were dressed for bed, wrappers over their nightclothes and bonnets over their hair. While Mrs. Bryant's wrapper was a dark, earthy brown, his mother's was a burst of color patterned with red, orange, and yellow flowers, as though they'd matched their personalities to their attire.

Mrs. Bryant gave him a stern look as he walked in, silently admonishing him for keeping his mother up later than she should have been.

"There he is," his mother said, holding a biscuit aloft in the air as if she was brandishing... well, as if brandishing something with far more pomp and circumstance than a chocolate biscuit. "My son returns, through the back... just as I told you he would, Joy."

"Yes, you did, Your Grace." Mrs. Bryant was still glaring at him. His mother was the only one who called her by her Christian name; Gregory would not dare. She'd changed his nappies, as she liked to remind him, and had been a second mother to him in many ways. "I thought he would have the courage to come through the front rather than attempting to sneak into the house, but apparently, I am to be disappointed."

"I was trying to be respectful and not wake up the household," Gregory protested, even though he was doing exactly what Mrs. Bryant accused him of. Excuse him for wanting to postpone the inquisition until he'd gotten some sleep.

"So, is what I heard at the ball correct?" His mother asked, lowering her cookie. "You ruined a duke's sister and will be dueling to the death on the morrow?" Despite the direness of her question, she sounded more curious than concerned.

"No!" Gregory shook his head. Good lord. This was why they were going to make a public outing to Hyde Park tomorrow, to quell such nonsense.

"Oh, good. I was a bit worried for a while, especially when you did not come home immediately."

"Yes, well..." He cleared his throat. "I did not ruin anyone, but I did accidentally compromise a young lady. Bolton's sister, in point of fact. That is why I am late. We had to work out the marriage contract and also a plan for dealing with the *ton*."

"You are getting married!" His mother clapped her hands together, sending cookie crumbs scattering across the floor, not that she noticed as she jumped up to throw herself at him in glee. Gregory caught her, hugging her tightly. Anything that brought his mother joy was a good thing as far as he was concerned.

Even Mrs. Bryant did not look so upset with him anymore.

"Yes, I am getting married." To a woman he was finding more and more remarkable by the minute. She had handled this entire evening with grace and aplomb, and he'd very much enjoyed kissing her. Sebastian seemed to have come around to the idea, though with some grumbling, and neither of their families' reputations would come to any harm. "Did you say anything to anyone tonight about it?"

"Of course not." His mother pulled away from him, shaking her head. "The moment I knew you were the source of the contretemps, I deserted the field, as anyone with common sense would, until I could speak with you."

"You have always been blessed with an abundance of common sense," he said gratefully. Sitting her back down, he quickly outlined the plan he and Sebastian had devised. His mother's quick departure from the ball could easily be explained by her own confusion. After all, if he and Tiffany had a secret engagement, she would not have divulged that information without knowing what had happened.

When he finished, his mother and Mrs. Bryant looked at each other, and his mother nodded thoughtfully.

"It is certainly an interesting plan." His mother turned back to him. "Do you believe you will be able to carry it off?"

"I do not see why not."

His mother stared at him, unblinking.

"Gregory, in order to be a believable love match, you are going to have to cleave to her and only to her. It is going to take weeks for the bans to be read and to plan the wedding. Are you sure..." Her voice trailed off, and she wrinkled her nose, obviously trying to come up with the appropriate words.

"What your mother is trying to say is that if you do not remain celibate throughout the engagement, it is unlikely anyone will believe any declarations of love you make," Mrs. Bryant said baldly.

"Yes." His mother beamed at her. "That."

Lord help him, he was having to discuss his lovers with his mother and his housekeeper. What had his life come to?

"I can be celibate until my wedding," he said indignantly. They both exchanged a look, and he scowled. Did no one believe he could behave himself for a few weeks? "I would not disrespect my bride in such a manner." Besides, if he did and Sebastian found out, that would likely be the end of their friendship. Even if he had been willing to hurt his bride by taking a lover during their engagement period—which he was not—he would certainly not risk his friendship.

"And after?" His mother asked.

"I would rather think you want grandchildren."

"You know what I am talking about." She stabbed another biscuit in his direction. "You are going to be playacting a love match. How do you know real feelings will not become involved?"

"We both agreed to the pretense. She is hardly going to fall in love with me over a false courtship." He shook his head. They had just met this evening, after all. The brief glimpses he'd had of her when she was still in the schoolroom hardly counted. Love? No. She seemed far too sensible for such a thing. Attraction? Certainly. There was plenty of that between them.

The period of celibacy would just ensure anticipation of the wedding night, not that he thought that would be a problem. She truly was very pretty, and her kiss had been eager and passionate. Educating her on bedroom activities would likely prove very enjoyable. Sebastian's glaring face popped up in his head for even daring to think about bedroom activities with his sister.

But his sister was going to be Gregory's wife.

His mother huffed and exchanged a look with Mrs. Bryant.

Gregory took the opportunity to steal a biscuit.

"We should all go to bed," he said, offering his mother his arm. "Tomorrow is going to be a very long day."

Sighing, she took his arm and allowed him to escort her upstairs while Mrs. Bryant cleaned up the kitchen and went to her own bed. While they walked, his mother told him all about everything he had missed while hiding and then creating a scandal in the library.

"The Marquess of Camden was out with his new wife for the first time... married his nurse, you know! The whole family was there in support, so no one dared say a thing crosswise. Your friend Mr. North was there with Mrs. North, looking pleased as punch with themselves, taking congratulations for their recent nuptials." She sighed. "Eloping to Gretna Green, can you imagine?"

"Not particularly, no," Gregory murmured. If he and Tiffany had truly needed to marry in a hurry, as a duke, it would be far less effort to procure a special license than to take the North Road to Scotland. His mother elbowed him in the side as they went up the stairs, and he let out a small grunt.

"Did you hear the Earl of Stilton's youngest is back in London this Season? And with an Indian wife and a son and daughter."

Gregory cast his mind about.

"I do not think I am familiar with the family."

"No, you likely are not... *very* stuffy lot." His mother shook her head. "They gave Mr. Little and his family the cut direct when they met. Broke his heart, right in front of everyone. The wife and daughter are beauties, and the daughter is dowried to the hilt if the rumors are true, but no one talked to them after that. They persevered despite that. Even the wife had a stiff upper lip. They were still there when I left."

Gregory raised his eyebrow at her.

"*No one* talked to them?"

His mother smiled. "I might have introduced myself. If you had not caused such a scandal this evening, I would have introduced you to the daughter. Marrying a duke would make it impossible for the Stilton clan to ignore them."

"Well, they are in luck, as there is certainly no shortage of dukes in search of brides this Season. Perhaps we can introduce Sebastian to her since I have already secured my own bride." He could not help but feel a bit chuffed at that. Despite the very real knowledge that he was unsure of how to make a good husband—other than to be nothing like his own father—he was pleased to be the first duke to fulfill their mutual goal.

"Now, there is a thought." His mother's voice was full of amusement. "Truly, any of your friends would do. Which reminds me, what on earth happened between the Dowager Baroness of Ashfield and your friend Grafton? He was following her around like a puppy dog all night while she ignored him, then he turned into a mastiff any time another man approached her."

Snorting a laugh, Gregory shook his head. He was sorry he'd missed seeing that for himself. Stopping in front of his mother's door, he grinned down at her.

"He gave the baroness her *congé*."

His mother stared at him.

"Why did he not ask *her* to marry him? She is still young, certainly young enough to bear children."

"Because he feels he should marry a debutante. That is the done thing." He shrugged. Zachary's reasoning had not surprised him, but his mother had always been a romantic—as she'd proven when she'd questioned him about falling in love with Tiffany because they were pretending to be in love. "Christian is keeping his mistress while he looks for a bride."

His mother rolled her eyes. "I do not think I wanted to know that. Men," she said disgustedly. "A bunch of nitwits, all of you."

"Not me, surely."

"Especially you." She sniffed and then pulled him down for a kiss on the cheek. "But you are a good boy, even if you are foolish."

Bemused, Gregory stood as she went into her room and closed the door. He was not sure why she was calling him foolish, but then, his mother's reasoning did not always make sense to him. Making his way to his wing of the house, his mind wandered back to the events of the evening and to Tiffany.

He truly did not understand how her brother had thought her plain. The dress she'd been wearing could have been a good deal more flattering, and she was not an exceptional beauty, it was true, but she was pretty enough, and there had certainly been a spark between them. Especially when they'd kissed.

The press of her lips against his had taken him off guard in an entirely unexpected manner, which was how they'd ended up in the position they had. Granted, they might have ended up married anyway, just by dint of her being alone in a room with him for an untold amount of time, but at least they would not have ended up on the floor in front of everyone.

Though, she'd felt very nice atop him, all soft feminine flesh and plump curves.

No, he did not think he would have difficulties when it came to bedding her. In fact, he was very much looking forward to it.

Letting himself into his room, he found his valet, Redding, there waiting for him. Thankfully, Redding read his mood—as he always did—and helped him out of his clothes and into his nightshirt in silence. He also shook his head over the cravat that Gregory had mangled by pulling on it several times throughout the evening but did not bother to admonish him. Gregory knew the next time he saw the piece of fabric, it would be perfectly starched.

"Thank you, Redding, that will be all," he said, dismissing the other man. Redding bowed and left, carrying the clothing with him, and Gregory went to flop down on his bed.

Bloody hell.

What a night.

Perhaps he should be worried about his marriage, but the more he thought about Tiffany, the more he was looking forward to having a wife. He'd never had a virgin before. That part was a bit daunting...

but there was something rather exciting thinking about being able to introduce her to the pleasures of the bedroom.

Showing her the joy that could be found there.

He loved pleasuring a woman, but the women he dallied with knew exactly what to expect from him.

His wife would not. He'd be able to demonstrate everything, make her feel everything, see her reactions to everything.

Her lips had tasted sweet when they'd kissed... he'd wager her nether lips would as well. Gregory could just picture how she would look the first time he spread her legs and put his mouth on her pussy, licking and sucking. He could picture the way her eyes would widen in shock, then pleasure, the way she would blush at the intimacy of it... then cry out from the ecstasy.

Groaning as his cock stiffened, he rolled over to take a handkerchief from his nightstand, wrapping it around the hard length and beginning to pump his fist.

Would she even know what a climax was? Would she understand what was happening? Some ladies touched themselves... but even if she did, it was an entirely different thing to be touched by someone else. Especially someone who knew exactly what they were doing.

He could be her first climax.

The first mouth to taste her.

The first cock to slide inside her.

The first man to hear her cries of pleasure.

His own pleasure was growing at the thought, and he fisted himself harder, moving his hand up and down on his cock.

His would be the first cock she held... would she balk at the idea of using her mouth the same way he loved to use his? He could imagine her on her knees before him, cheeks pink with embarrassment, pouting lips opening to receive his cock. She would not know what to do, but he could teach her.

Imagining sliding his cock between her lips was what finally did it for him, and he cried out as his climax spurted from his cock. The length of it throbbed against his hand, waves of pleasure pulsing through him until he was completely spent.

Bloody hell.

For a moment, he felt just a twinge of guilt—it was his closest friend's sister he was imagining defiling... but wife trumped sibling relationship. Once his ring was on her finger, she would be all his.

He felt an unexpected amount of satisfaction in that.

Tiffany

Sitting in the dining room, empty stomach clenched too tight with anxiety to eat, Tiffany jumped at every small sound outside the dining room doors. The footmen eyed her warily, and she sent them a small, apologetic smile. Her nerves were affecting them.

Though she'd wanted to retreat to the library, she was not sure she would find the same peace there she normally did. Instead, she'd come to the dining room, waiting for her mother and brother to emerge. She had come down so early, though, because she'd had such difficulty sleeping.

When the doors at the end of the room finally opened to reveal her brother, Tiffany let out a long sigh of relief. She had not realized how much she hoped he would precede her mother into the dining room until she saw him.

Coming in, her brother glanced around.

"Mother is still abed?" he asked, and Tiffany nodded, even though she did not think he required an answer. He was looking at her rather oddly, frowning as he came closer, studying her. Stopping beside the table, several feet away, he stared at her face.

The close scrutiny made her stomach start to tighten again.

"You really are very pretty," he said after a long moment.

Tiffany blinked.

"Thank you." She had not dressed particularly carefully this morning, as she assumed her mother would have her own opinion on what Tiffany should wear for their ride around Hyde Park. That her brother still thought she was pretty, despite her plain dress, was rather nice.

"I am not sure that color is the most flattering on you, nor the style, but you really are very pretty." He sounded rather astonished, but his astonishment could not match her own.

When she looked in the mirror this morning, she had not seen anything different about her. She was not sure what he meant by the color. The beige of her dress was a neutral color, one that made her hair appear brighter, according to her mother. The dullness of the dress helped her hair seem more colorful by contrast. At least, that's what she thought it was supposed to do, but her brother disagreed... And she did not know what he meant by the style being unflattering. Though, she supposed, it might be due to her excessive bosom.

"Thank you?" This time, it came out as more of a question, and he shook his head.

"My apologies, Tiffany. I do not mean to sound so surprised. It is just that I have gotten used to thinking of you a certain way and having my friends not only fight over your hand but also ask me if I'm blind..." His smile was apologetic. "I'm afraid I *have* been blind and not a very good brother."

Tiffany jumped to her feet. She was not about to take any of this negativity from him.

"You are the best brother," she said adamantly, reaching out to take his hands and squeeze them as she stared intently up into his face. "You stepped into Father's shoes long before you were ready, you supported Mother and me through our grief, and you have secured me a marriage... and at my very first ball."

"I am not, though I am glad you see me as such. I am going to start making up for it now and give you no reason to ever doubt your belief in me." Pulling her toward him, he let go of her hands so he could put his arms around her, hugging her close.

Tiffany felt tears spring to her eyes as she leaned against his supportive weight, hugging him back. Something they had not done since the official end of mourning for their father.

"You deserve the very best. Unfortunately, you are going to have to settle for marrying Gregory instead, but I will do everything in my power to ensure your happiness despite that."

"I am sorry I put you in such a position last night," Tiffany said, breaking away. "I do not mind marrying... marrying Clarence." She could not quite bring herself to call him Gregory. Not yet. "It was my own fault. I was struggling some making conversation and just needed a few minutes to myself. I told Mother I needed the retiring room, and instead, I asked a servant the way to the library. I did not think anyone would be there. If I had realized he was in there, I would have left immediately. I let you down. I let the whole family down."

"No, I should have watched you closer, and so should mother."

"She wanted to speak with her friends, and, truthfully, it was probably a relief not to have to make up for my own shortcomings in conversation for a little while." Tiffany wrinkled her nose. She had not been able to say a single thing right last night. Which was not that unusual, but it was lowering. "I should not have lied about where I was going. She would have never let me go to the library if I had told her the truth."

As if speaking about her had summoned her, the door to the dining room opened and their mother stood there wearing her black mourning dress. Seeing her so dressed made Tiffany's heart stutter as the memories of grief came crowding back. Sebastian stepped away, though he kept one hand at Tiffany's back for support.

"Sebastian! You are here... I mean, you are awake." Her mother walked in, clutching something to her chest. Tiffany thought it might be a handkerchief, though she could not tell. "I did not think you would have arisen so early after such a late night." She shot an accusing glance at Tiffany, as the dramatics had been her doing and the late night necessitated by her actions.

Tiffany dropped her head down, feeling the shame wash over her. She truly had disrupted everything.

"I wanted to be awake early to make sure we were able to discuss today while we break our fast," her brother said. He gave her another pat before stepping away to greet their mother. "Did you choose that particular dress for a reason, Mother?"

He asked the question with some trepidation, but he did ask it. Tiffany would have tried to avoid the topic, though she did not doubt it would come out eventually, and she was sure it would have something to do with her and last night's events.

Mother sniffled, reaching up to dab at her face and confirming Tiffany's supposition that she was holding a handkerchief. One of her father's, if she was seeing the monogram correctly. Which was another direct hit to her heart.

"I woke up this morning missing your father and mourning the loss of our family's reputation," Mother replied, dabbing at her eyes. "Though... Tiffany did say she thought you might have salvaged the situation? One of your friends?"

Relief flooded Tiffany. With her brother there to explain things, her mother would have to believe him, which meant she might escape the lecture Mother had surely planned.

"Two of my friends, though it was Clarence's offer I accepted," her brother said. "Let us get our food, then I will tell you everything."

Now that her brother was there, supporting her, Tiffany found that she could eat after all. Her stomach had unknotted. The worst was over with.

Once they were sitting down, her brother explained everything to their mother.

"A love match?" She laughed. "You think the *ton* will believe such a thing?"

"It explains most everything," Sebastian said. "Which is why I agreed with Gregory when he explained the idea to me. Even his reaction to Hereford's offer for Tiffany's hand can be explained if they're in love. Some might even suspect that he compromised her on purpose rather than having to watch her flirt with and be courted by other gentlemen during the Season."

Her mother sniffed, but she did not contradict Sebastian. She never did once he stated something outright.

"Very well then, I suppose there is no harm in attempting to salvage our family's reputation by such means." Though, her tone indicated she did not have much faith in the success of such a deception. She shot a sharp glance at Tiffany, her gaze full of censure for putting their reputation at stake.

Tiffany looked down at her plate, heart heavy in her chest. If only her mother would support her and overlook her mistakes in the same way Sebastian had... but she did not think her mother ever would.

Mother glanced at the clock on the mantle. "If we are going to be ready in time for a ride with Clarence, we must start now. There is a great deal of work to do."

"Yes... and..." Her brother hesitated, looking at their mother's crepe mourning dress.

"Do not worry. I will change into something appropriate," her mother said, getting to her feet. Walking around the table to where her brother sat, she cupped Sebastian's face in her hands. "You are a credit to your father with how you lead the family."

Sebastian's eyes shone up at her, and Tiffany was both happy for him and also wished that one day her mother would say something so uplifting to her. She tried so hard, yet she failed over and over again. Perhaps by marrying a duke, she would finally get the recognition from her mother that she craved.

Bending down, her mother gave Sebastian a kiss on the cheek

before straightening and turning to Tiffany, casting a critical eye over her. Tiffany sat straight in her chair, practically quivering, wondering if her mother might have some kind word for her.

It was a vain hope.

"Come along, Tiffany," she said. "We have a lot of work to do if you are going to look presentable enough to ride alongside the Duke of Clarence in front of the entirety of the *ton* and convince them you are a love match."

Her brother smiled at her encouragingly.

"Do not worry, Tiff, everything will be fine."

Tiffany sighed inwardly but nodded, getting up from her seat at the table and following her mother up to her room, where she endured an arduous hour of her mother hemming and hawing over what she would wear for the drive. Harleen quietly did Tiffany's hair, and her quiet made Tiffany even more nervous. If she was being quiet, then Tiffany wanted to be *silent*.

Even when her mother decided she would wear the apricot day dress with the citrine trim. It was Tiffany's least favorite of her dresses, but she did not dare protest. Not when her mother was in such a mood. Even that did not seem to please her mother.

With Tiffany fully outfitted, kid gloves covering her hands and hair in the matching apricot bonnet decorated with cascading citrine ribbons, her mother's mouth was pursed. She ran a critical eye over Tiffany and shook her head, muttering something under her breath.

"If Your Grace is displeased, perhaps the mint instead?" Harleen suggested, pulling the article in question from the wardrobe. It also happened to be Tiffany's favorite day dress, as she felt it was the prettiest color of all her day dresses. She looked over at her mother pleadingly, but her mother was ignoring her, staring at the mint and frowning before finally giving her head a shake.

"No. We need her to stand out. The mint is too dull, and it will only emphasize how plain she is." Her mother waved at Harleen, who pressed her lips together and shot an apologetic look at Tiffany.

Strangely, though, Tiffany did not mind. Her mother might still think her plain, but the Duke of Clarence thought she was pretty.

The love match would be a pretense, but he had kissed her because he thought she was pretty.

Her brother had confirmed this morning that she was pretty.

As much as Tiffany wanted to hear her mother say it, Clarence and her brother's opinions had already bolstered her so much, she felt no sting to her mother's words. Perhaps one day, even her mother would look at her anew and say that she was pretty...

"Harleen, attend me. We have spent enough time on Tiffany." Her mother gestured at the ladies' maid. "Tiffany, go... sit somewhere. We do not want you mussing yourself before the drive."

"Yes, Mother."

Tiffany heaved a sigh of relief as her mother sashayed out of the room, Harleen right behind her, leaving her alone. Somehow, it was always easier to breathe when her mother was not in the room.

Walking over to the mirror, she stared into it. She looked the same as ever.

Pretty?

She was not entirely sure.

But she wanted to believe it.

If only for a day.

CHAPTER

TEN

G*regory*
The greys he had hitched to his curricle tossed their heads as he pulled them to a halt in front of Bolton House. They were high steppers, a matched pair, and incredibly well trained. Though they loved to run, they responded to the reins docilely enough, which was important for a jaunt around Hyde Park. At this time of day, they were hardly going to be able to do any racing.

"How do I look?" his mother asked from beside him, reaching up to test her hat and assure herself that it had not changed position from where she'd pinned it before leaving.

"Perfect," he replied, handing his reins over to a footman who approached from the side. Then he stepped out of the curricle and came around to help his mother down from her spot. She beamed at him. Before she could say anything else, the front door of Bolton House opened and a scowling Sebastian stepped out, followed by an awestruck—and very brightly dressed—Tiffany.

"What is that?" Sebastian called out, still scowling, as he came down the stairs.

"My curricle," Gregory said cheerfully once Sebastian was close enough to hear him without having to raise his voice. He quickly realized that Sebastian meant for them all to drive around in the Bolton landau together, but this would be far more effective in portraying the story they were trying to sell. Plus, it would give him and his future wife a chance to get to know each other better without raising any eyebrows. "Tiffany and I will ride in here, so we can... talk. After all, we are very much in love and have a great deal to talk about."

He raised his eyebrows at Sebastian, whose scowl deepened as he tried to muster an argument against the idea. Tiffany came up beside her brother, standing silently and staring at the curricle and the greys before she finally focused her gaze on him.

It was when she looked at him that her attractiveness came through. Today's dress was even less flattering than yesterday's had been, but the features of her face could not be hidden away. Why she favored the yellows and oranges that made her complexion appear rather sickly, he had no idea, but perhaps it would work in his favor. After all, the rakes and *roués* of the *ton* tended to chase beauty, wit, and a certain open-mindedness. He should know, being one of them. The less other men were interested in his wife, the happier a husband he would be.

"My lady," he said, holding out his hand to take hers. Even through the fabric of their gloves, he could feel the heat of her fingers as he bowed over her hand. At the last moment, he turned her hand so he could drop a kiss on the inside of her wrist, and she let out a little gasp.

Sebastian growled. Actually growled.

This was more fun than he'd expected, but Gregory was also very aware that he did not want to push his friend too far. They were to be brothers, regardless, but he did not want to lose his friend in the transition.

Straightening up, he gave Tiffany a wink.

The door to Bolton House opened again, and because he was

watching her, he saw Tiffany flinch before she tugged her fingers away from his. Frowning, he turned to see what caused such a reaction, but it was only her mother coming toward them. A wide smile was on her face as her gaze flitted between himself and his mother.

He had met the Duchess of Bolton several times before, though it had been years.

"Your Grace," he said, holding out his hand in much the same way he had for Tiffany when she reached them. She put her hand in his, and he bowed over it, eschewing the kiss that he'd given her daughter. "It is lovely to see you again. May I introduce my own mother, the Duchess of Clarence."

"Soon-to-be dowager duchess, much to my delight," his mother said, beaming at Tiffany before turning her attention to Tiffany's mother.

Oh, bollocks. He'd made a hash of things again. He'd been so distracted by Sebastian's ire, he'd forgotten to introduce his mother to his fiancé. This whole courtship thing was damnably difficult. Hopefully, things would be easier after today.

"Yes." The Duchess of Bolton's smile thinned and then broadened again. "Lovely to meet you as well." They exchanged their greetings, then Gregory introduced Tiffany to his mother. She was quiet, as she had been before, folding her hands in front of her and listening as the two mothers talked.

His mother complimented her bonnet, which he almost wished she had not. He would rather throw the frowsy thing in a fireplace, but the compliment did brighten the look in Tiffany's eyes. Which was when he remembered that her brother had described her as quite plain—and she had been surprised when he'd called her pretty in the library.

At the time, he'd thought her adorably modest. Now, he wondered if it was more due to her brother's attitude. Her reaction to any compliment was striking, which meant she did not hear them often enough. He wondered if perhaps her mother had also not realized that her daughter had grown into a beauty.

Well, he was certainly not going to say anything remotely negative about her clothing or appearance. Even if he could not bring himself to compliment her dress or hat, he would not denigrate them either. Not in front of her. Perhaps once they were married, he could attempt to influence her style... discreetly. Or perhaps not. Especially if it were off-putting to other rakes.

But he was very much going to enjoy taking the clothes *off* of her.

Perhaps they could spend the majority of their time together in the nude. That might be for the best.

"Clarence," Sebastian growled again, elbowing him in the side, which was when he realized that he was staring at Tiffany, who was staring back at him with some concern. He had been picturing what she might look like naked, in front of her brother, her mother, and his own mother.

Bloody hell.

He gave himself a shake and smiled to cover his discomfiture.

"My apologies. Shall we go then?" he asked, stepping forward to take Tiffany's hand and wrap it around his forearm.

"Wait, where are you taking my daughter?" Tiffany's mother asked, her voice going higher and shriller as Gregory stepped away.

"To my curricle with me." He winked at her. "Do not fret, Your Grace. I shall return her to you in nothing less than perfect condition."

"This will give us a chance to talk about the happy couple and the upcoming wedding," his mother said when the Duchess of Bolton frowned, looking rather unhappy at the idea of being separated from her daughter. No doubt, feeling protective, especially after she'd already been compromised, but they were going on a ride through Hyde Park.

Having Tiffany at his side in the curricle while the two mothers followed with her brother the duke would only benefit all of them, and especially the picture they were trying to paint.

Besides, he wanted his soon-to-be bride to himself for a little while.

~

Tiffany

Seated beside a rakish duke as he drove her into Hyde Park with two high steppers pulling his curricle was like something out of a fairy tale. Except that she was no princess. Still, for a moment, she was able to pretend.

"Which is how I ended up with these two," the duke finished, nodding his head at the two greys prancing in front of them. They preened as they moved, as if aware of the attention the curricle was drawing and assuming it was all due to them. Tiffany rather wished. She was all too aware of the wide eyes turning toward her and Clarence—no, Gregory. She needed to start at least trying to think of him as Gregory.

"They are lovely. Did you train them yourself?" she asked.

"Not at all. But I worked with the trainer I hired." He eyed her. "Have you ever driven a curricle?"

"I... ah... no." She had not been expecting a question in return. Her fingers twitched as she looked at the greys, then moved her gaze over to his hands on the reins. Though she actually did know how to, her mother had pounded it into her head that admitting to such a thing was not ladylike. She was very specific about the things Tiffany was to learn, and handling the reins was not one of the items on her exhaustive list. But Tiffany liked to learn. "How did you assist the trainer?"

Rather than answering, Gregory glanced over at her, raising his eyebrow.

"Do you ever talk about yourself?"

"Myself?" she stared up at him, her attention jerked away from both the horses and the numerous passersby watching them. "I... my mother always told me it was forward to talk about myself and that I should encourage gentlemen to talk about themselves instead."

"Well, that might be true when catching a gentleman, but I am already caught." He grinned, winking at her. "Therefore, I would like to know more about you. Especially seeing as we are deeply, madly in love. I propose that for every question I answer, you must answer one as well."

"Oh... I suppose that makes sense." Though, the idea felt very uncomfortable. She ignored the way he spoke of being deeply, madly in love, though when he'd said the words, her stomach had turned over in a very particular manner. He was only teasing. "What would you like to know?"

"Well, as you are a duke's sister, I presume that you are well trained in running a household, watercolors, embroidery, dancing, and some kind of instrument." Though he did not ask it as a question, he paused as if prodding her to provide the kind of instrument. Tiffany could not help but smile since he was getting an answer without truly asking a question.

"Pianoforte, harp, and flute," she replied. When he blinked in astonishment, turning his head to shoot her a glance of pure surprise, she blushed and looked away—which meant that her gaze went right to the row of *ton* ladies in their landaus, all staring at her and Gregory with sharp eyes. Hardly an improvement. She looked back down at the greys. They, at least, were delightful to watch. "I enjoyed my music lessons and wanted to learn different kinds."

Ladies were only supposed to learn one, but Tiffany liked learning new things. Especially things that required practice that allowed her to be shut away in the music room for hours.

"You are certainly more accomplished than I," he admitted. "I can sing, but I cannot play a single instrument. I never had the patience for it."

"You, impatient?" she quipped, startling a laugh from him, which made her smile in delight. He had laughed at one of her jests! Some of the tension in her shoulders lessened, and she relaxed, realizing how tight her muscles had been until this very moment.

Not that they knew each other very well, but from everything she had observed over the past day, he was not a particularly patient fellow. Very much the opposite of both her and her brother.

Still chuckling, he nodded at another man in a curricle, who was coming toward them with a matched pair of bays pulling him. The gentleman came to a halt. Tiffany leaned toward Gregory to look at the crest on the other man's curricle, and her eyes widened. The Duke of Montagu. Another rake. Another duke who inherited his title after the explosion that had taken her father. Also friends with her brother, of course, but she had not met him before.

"Clarence." The Duke of Montagu nodded at him, his amused blue gaze going back and forth between her and Gregory, then to behind them, where her brother and the mothers were sitting in the Bolton landau. Tiffany almost wanted to turn to look at them, but she knew her mother would disapprove if she caught Tiffany looking.

Ladies did not turn about in carriages to see behind them.

"Montagu. Have you met my fiancé, Lady Tiffany Bolton?" Gregory grinned widely. "Lady Tiffany, my friend, the Duke of Montagu."

"Lady Tiffany, a pleasure to meet your acquaintance." Montagu half bowed in his seat, pressing his hand to his heart. His blond locks were tucked neatly under his hat, his grin sparkling with as much charm as Gregory, and yet she did not feel the same tug toward him that she did toward the man at her side.

"Thank you, Your Grace," she nodded her head at him as low as she could. Obviously, she could not curtsy. Somehow, her mother had never drilled her on what to do when meeting a duke while sitting in a carriage, so she did her best. "It is a pleasure to meet you."

"Shall I congratulate you on your engagement, then?" He raised a questioning eyebrow at Gregory, asking for more information, waiting for a lead to follow.

Clearly, the camaraderie and support that she had witnessed between her brother and Gregory went beyond the two of them and to the other dukes. It was more than several of his friends being willing to ask his sister to dance—Montagu was very perceptively waiting for the line that Gregory wanted to feed to the *ton* and ensuring he did not say anything out of turn before he knew where to go.

"Her brother is very put out that we could not wait till the end of the Season to make our announcement," Gregory said, leaning forward as though he was imparting some sort of secret, though he actually raised his voice to ensure that those nearby could hear. It did not escape Tiffany's notice that they were hardly the only carriages who had stopped. Yes, it was causing a blockage along the path, but no one was complaining, likely because they were all eavesdropping. "I did promise her a proper Season, after all, but love cannot be denied."

He shrugged as a gasp went along the row. Quite a few of those who had heard him say the word 'love' were suddenly dashing off, in a hurry to be the first to spread the word to those too far away to hear. Tiffany's jaw nearly dropped in shock at the reaction—it was so very *blatant*. Not everyone dashed away, of course, though many appeared as though they wanted to, but they seemed to realize the conversation was not over yet.

Montagu's smile widened.

"Yes, well, how lucky for you that you do not have to hide your feelings any longer." There was a slight question at the end of his sentence, as though he wanted reassurance that he'd followed the right hint.

Gregory nodded, reaching out to take Tiffany's hand in his.

"It was going to be a trial, attempting to hide our feelings for one another for an entire Season." He lifted her gloved fingers to his lips, kissing the soft kid leather rather than her wrist this time, to her relief. "Though I did not mean to cause a scandal, of course."

"Of course," Montagu replied, nodding, his lips quirking with amusement. Tiffany was realizing that he and Gregory were a great deal alike, both far less serious than her brother. "You would not want to damage your bride's reputation."

"No, but now, at least I do not have to wait. You know how I hate waiting." He winked at Tiffany again, lowering their hands back down and giving her fingers a squeeze before releasing them. She found herself smiling back at him in a rather giddy manner.

He is only pretending.

She knew he was. Yet she could not help but be charmed.

Well, there was no harm in being charmed by a charming fellow, was there? The charm was real enough, even if the love was a pretense.

"Very good," Montagu said with a nod. "I will pass the word on to our friends. We will see you this evening?"

"Yes, I will see you at White's." Gregory nodded back to him, and it seemed that more passed with their mutual recognition than mere acknowledgment. Tiffany was curious about the interaction, but she did not dare ask, in case she was imagining things.

Despite their pretense, she did not know the man beside her very well at all.

But she was starting to want to.

CHAPTER
ELEVEN

iffany

Riding around Hyde Park with Gregory turned out to be far more pleasant than Tiffany had expected and not only because he had such a lovely pair of greys. They had stopped several times to speak to others, including the Duchess of Richmond, to apologize for disrupting her ball, and each time, Gregory had dropped more hints about how he and Tiffany had planned to announce their engagement... at the end of the Season. The *ton* was agog. The gossip had only heightened interest in them, and Tiffany had been painfully aware of all the eyes on her. Watching her. Weighing her. Judging her.

Wondering what she had done to make a duke fall in love with her.

She was sure they were full of skepticism rather than belief.

She would have been as stiff as a poker if not for Gregory's charm as he joked with her, prying answers to his questions from her one at a time. It became easier and easier to talk to him, and she even made him laugh several more times. Perhaps the difference truly was

98

whether she was trying to catch a gentleman or if she had already caught him.

A small, selfish part of her was relieved that they were not in the landau with her mother, where she would have to see her mother's responses to everything she said. Perhaps her mother would not have disapproved, as Gregory was already engaged to her, but Tiffany was glad she did not have to find out.

When they left the park, she let out a sigh of relief, even though she knew there would only be a short reprieve before this afternoon's at-home. At the very least, she was sure her mother's friends would come calling, and from the reactions of the *ton* in the park, they would likely not be alone.

"That was not so bad, was it?" Gregory asked as they tooled along the street. Tiffany shot him a look of frank disbelief, which had him throwing his head back and laughing again. "It could have been far worse. And we got to know one another a bit better, which is very good as we are to be married."

"That is true enough," she admitted, though she still did not feel as though she knew him *well*. But she knew more about him than she had the day before when she'd kissed him. "I will be happier when all the attention turns elsewhere."

"You are not interested in being the center of the *ton*'s interest?" he teased, seeming rather pleased.

"Not at all." She stated it very firmly, and he nodded in approval.

"Good girl."

The two words did something very odd to her insides, making her stomach flutter, but it was very low in her stomach. Tiffany pressed her thighs together at the sudden ache in her lower belly. Her skin felt odd, as though it was tingling, especially along her chest. What caused such a reaction, she had no idea, but pure warmth had flooded her body.

She opened her lips to say something, but her head had gone blank, and she found she did not have the breath to murmur a word, even if she could think of one.

"Here we are, then," Gregory said cheerfully as he pulled the curricle to a stop in front of Bolton House. Thankfully, he did not seem to notice that she had been suddenly struck mute. He handed the reins over to their footman, Archie, then hopped down to help her down.

The landau had come up behind them, and Sebastian was doing the same with the mothers.

When she stepped down, Gregory did not immediately let go of her hand, and she looked up at him in surprise. He brought her hand to his lips again, his gaze holding hers, and her whole body flushed through, the same way it had when he'd called her a good girl. Everything felt like it tightened and loosened, and her head went dizzy.

"Perhaps tomorrow we can take another ride?" he asked.

"Oh, no, I'm so sorry, Your Grace," Tiffany's mother said, coming up alongside them and giving him a sweet smile. "There is so much to do to prepare for the wedding, you see. Your mother and I have been talking, of course, but we need to start immediately if we are to have a wedding in a month. It is possible that another scandal will take precedence, of course, but the sooner we can move to salvage everyone's reputation, the better."

Tiffany sighed quietly in disappointment, but her mother was likely correct. The Duchess of Clarence came to join them, smiling and nodding in a way that made Tiffany feel rather uneasy. Her own mother had never smiled at her like that, so she could not understand what she had done to earn such instant approval from Gregory's.

"We will return for this afternoon's at-home," the Duchess of Clarence said, giving Tiffany's mother a nod before turning to Tiffany and beaming up at her. Though she was very petite, she was somehow the most intimidating person Tiffany had ever met. The duchess reached out her hands, and Tiffany held out her own for the duchess to take in a surprisingly strong grip. "I am so looking forward to getting to know you, my dear."

Terror. Utter and complete terror was what Tiffany felt, but she nodded and made herself smile because she knew that was the expected thing to do.

"Thank you, Your Grace," she said, bobbing awkwardly into a curtsy—awkward because the duchess still had not let go of her hands.

"Come along, Mother, we will have plenty of time for that in the weeks to come," Gregory said, putting a gentle arm around his mother's shoulders. She gave Tiffany's hands another squeeze and released them.

"Toodle-loo! We will return soon!" The duchess gave them a wave and allowed her son to escort her away.

"Gaudy creature," Tiffany's mother muttered under her breath, where only Tiffany could hear her. "If she were not a duchess..."

Sensing her mother's disapproval, Tiffany knew better than to speak up. She did not know what to think of her mother's description of the Duchess of Clarence as 'gaudy'. She had not been decked in jewels, though her clothing had been rather bright—but so were the clothes Tiffany's mother insisted she wear.

Perhaps because the Duchess of Clarence was her mother's age? Tiffany's mother did not wear the brighter colors Tiffany did. She was partial to deep greens and blues. Perhaps she felt the Duchess of Clarence should be more muted?

If her mother was in a better mood, Tiffany might have dared to ask.

"Come. We have much work to do to make you presentable," her mother said irritably, gesturing sharply. "A mere ride in a park is hardly going to convince anyone that you two are in love."

Tiffany nodded meekly, following her mother to the front door where Sebastian was waiting for them. Their butler, Graves, stood beside the open door, bowing as they entered. Tiffany smiled and quietly thanked him after her mother and Sebastian had passed, and he gave her a quick smile in return, breaking his customary formality for a mere moment.

"That was a good first outing, I think," Sebastian said, pulling off his gloves as he walked toward the stairs, their mother beside him. Tiffany trailed behind them. "I would have liked to have shared the ride, but I think Gregory had the right idea. The two of you on your own made a far better impression than if we had all been together. I think everyone we spoke with believed there was an understanding between the two of you before the Season began. Well, everyone but Lady Tremaine."

Lady Tremaine was a marchioness and their mother's closest confidant. She had a daughter who was also debuting this year, Lady Louisa, who detested when she and Tiffany were forced to spend time together because of their mother's friendship. Tiffany did not much enjoy it, either.

"That is because Alice knows I tell her everything, and if my daughter was going to marry a duke at the end of the Season, she would know about it." Their mother sighed, putting her hand on the banister of the stairwell to assist her ascent. "This is why this will not work."

Tiffany's stomach turned over. Her mother had a point. The servants knew the truth, though they were very protective of the family. She thought most of them liked her well enough and would not speak out of turn.

"Yes, it will." Sebastian gave their mother a look. "You can tell her you had agreed not to say anything as it was not going to be announced 'til the end of the Season. She will understand that you did not want to look foolish if Gregory and Tiffany's... romance... did not last."

"That might do." Their mother reached up to pat at her hair, which was still pinned neatly in place. They'd hardly been moving fast enough for it to become windswept, even in the streets. "Yes, Alice will understand that I did not expect Tiffany to be able to keep the attention of the Duke of Clarence throughout the Season."

"He does have a bit of a reputation as a rake," Sebastian agreed.

"But reformed rakes make the best husbands… that is the saying, is it not?"

"It is, but the reformation is necessary." Tiffany's mother sniffed. "Come, Tiffany, we must get you dressed."

"In a different color," Sebastian said, frowning as Tiffany walked past him. "I think Lady Tremaine was correct. This is certainly not the most flattering dress for her."

The look Tiffany shot him was one of pure relief. If he could convince her mother not to force her into the apricot again, she would be most grateful.

"Yes, yes," her mother waved her hand. "I had already come to that conclusion myself. She will wear the mint this afternoon."

"Fashion is hardly one of my interests, so I will leave you to it," Sebastian responded with a wink at Tiffany as they reached the juncture where his wing separated from the one where her room was. Part of her wished he could come and advise on fashion since her mother was far more likely to listen to his opinion.

"Come, Tiffany," her mother said sharply as she watched Sebastian saunter down the hall to his suite. "Do not dawdle. Just because you are to be a duchess does not mean you can keep everyone waiting."

She almost opened her mouth to protest when she thought the better of it. Meekly, she followed her mother down the hall. At least she was to wear the mint dress for the at-home. If she were truly lucky, she would never have to wear the apricot again. It was the first time in her life that she felt grateful to Lady Tremaine.

∼

GREGORY

Bolton House had been mobbed. The drawing room was packed, not only with young ladies and their mothers all looking for gossip but with some young gentlemen as well. His friends—other than the noticeably absent Drake—were also there, which was causing a bit of a tizzy among the ladies who had come to call. Five eligible dukes in one small gathering were enough to send all of them into a confused flutter, trying to decide where to focus their attention.

Christian rather looked to be enjoying himself, with a small crowd of young ladies all gazing at him with stars in their eyes, struck dumb by his beauty. Sebastian and Nathanial had been cornered near the front windows by a bevy of beauties, and he could see the strain in their smiles as their eyes flitted back and forth, looking for escape. Zachary and Matthew were hardly better off, though they managed to commandeer a position beside the tea cart, where drink and food were plentiful. Matthew did not have enough elbow room to flip his coin, which was likely paining him, and Gregory was amused to see that he had his hand pressed against the chest pocket where he kept it.

Gregory searched the room for the bright apricot dress Tiffany had been wearing earlier and was surprised when he finally found her wearing a pale green one instead, seated in the center of the room. Perhaps she had not wanted to be seen in the same dress twice in one day. Her mother was on one side of her, speaking with Lady Tremaine, a dragon of the *ton* he recognized immediately. Lady Louisa, the daughter of Lady Tremaine, was on Tiffany's other side.

Seeing them together gave him pause.

Lady Louisa had already been acknowledged as a Diamond of the First Water upon her debut this Season. She had curling blonde hair, dark brown eyes, delicate features, an oval face, and was the very definition of an English rose. Gentlemen had already begun writing poems to her beauty, and it was agreed that she would have her pick of the gentlemen this Season. Everyone expected her to marry one of the dukes, in fact, though the lower ranks were vying for her attention in hopes of drawing her beauty—and her large dowry—to themselves.

Yet, despite her great beauty, his eye was immediately drawn to the young lady beside her. The pale green dress Tiffany now wore was much more flattering to both her complexion and her hair, though it did not benefit either very much; at least, it did not detract from her. Still, next to Louisa, most gentlemen would not pay attention to Tiffany... but his was arrested.

He had no interest in Louisa, despite the way the chit suddenly sat to attention and beamed at him when he approached them.

"Tiffany," he said, deliberately leaving off the honorific of 'lady' to emphasize their situation for all those listening ears. Two young ladies on the other side of the couch began to fan themselves as they watched and listened with wide eyes. He held his hand out, taking hers in his, and dropped a kiss to the back of her hand—this time, he did not take improprieties with her wrist.

"Your Grace," she replied, a heated blush flushing her cheeks despite the chaste kiss. "I mean, Gregory." He winked at her. She cleared her throat when he did not let go of her hand, turning slightly to her side. "Have you met Lady Louisa Tremaine?"

"I have not had the pleasure," he said, reluctantly letting go of Tiffany's fingers to take Lady Louisa's. He bowed over them, eschewing the kiss, and immediately let go of the young beauty's hand as she simpered up at him.

Sadly, he could not take Tiffany's hand again, according to good manners. Instead, he had to step to the side of the sofa, which meant he was on the other side of Louisa and not at all close to Tiffany.

"Lady Louisa is my maid of honor," Tiffany explained, though she did not seem very enthused by the prospect. Neither did Lady Louisa when he glanced at her. Interesting. He looked over at their mothers, who were so deep in conversation, he was not sure Tiffany's mother even realized he'd arrived.

Perhaps Tiffany had been forced to have Louisa as her maid of honor because of her mother's friendship with Lady Tremaine?

Should she not have a friend of her own fill the position?

She only wants to speak with me and my mother. Sebastian's words echoed in his head. At the time, he'd liked the idea of a wife who only wanted to speak with her immediate family, but...

It was not as though he wanted her gallivanting around the *ton* flirting with all the rakes and *roués*, but...

She should have a friend.

TWELVE

*G*regory

Trying to speak with Tiffany while Lady Louisa was beside her was an exercise in frustration. Tiffany was quiet, while Lady Louisa was exuberant, loud, and flirtatious. Considering he was now affianced to the woman sitting beside her and she was in the wedding party, he found her demeanor particularly grating.

Not that he could show such a thing, of course. It would be bad manners, and, on top of that, it could make things harder for Tiffany.

The best he could do was wait for the conversation to die down, then ask Tiffany to accompany him on a turnabout the room.

"Oh, ah, yes," she said, stumbling over her words and blushing as she got to her feet. While it was not the most graceful acceptance, several of the ladies watching did sigh, then start to whisper to each other.

The fact that he was pointedly leaving Lady Louisa off his invitation, as well as Tiffany's hot blush, would seem confirmation that he was in love with his bride. Gregory grinned, pulling her hand over his arm, then putting his own hand atop her fingers to keep it there, as though he could not bear to be parted from her.

Truth be told, she was the only person in the room he wanted to talk to other than his fellow dukes.

He leaned in.

"It appears as though you are the Season's sensation," he murmured, chuckling when she snorted, then lifted her hand to cover her mouth and nose, pretending to cough to cover the noise as she realized how indelicate she'd sounded.

"So it appears." She sighed and looked around at the crowd of people gathered in the drawing room. Some of them were watching the two of them walk; most were now involved in their own conversations. Sebastian glanced at them, narrowing his eyes in warning, though Tiffany did not seem to notice. "Mother seems happy, at least."

"You are not?"

"I am... content." It took her a moment to find the word. Gregory's stomach stirred uneasily.

"Is there anything I can do to make you happier? Do you have a friend you would prefer stand up beside you in the wedding?" He was making a guess based on what he'd observed between her and Lady Louisa, but he hoped that her lack of happiness did not come from knowing she had to marry him.

He was a catch, after all. And he was looking forward to marrying her. It would be rather lowering to find she did not return his regard in the least.

"I do not have another friend who could," she admitted, shrugging. Whether she was truly indifferent to her lack of friends or pretending indifference, he could not tell. "And it makes Mother happy."

"What would make Tiffany happy?" he asked gently, still guiding her on their promenade. Their constant movement made it easier for them to speak frankly since they were not standing in one place for too long, so no one could overhear more than a few words of what they were saying.

"I..." Once again, she seemed at a loss for words. She looked around the drawing room. "More time in the country?"

It sounded more a question than a statement, as if she was unsure. As if she did not know what made her happy. Well. His first duty as a husband would be to help her find things that made her happy. And he would enlist her brother for support. Surely, Sebastian would have some ideas.

"I certainly enjoy being in the country," he said, smiling down at her. "Though, of course, we will have to be in London for the Season. This will likely be the most frenzied drawing room you will have to oversee... at least until our daughter is of age to debut." He winked at her, enjoying the way she blushed again, this time the mottled pink heating her entire face, down her neck, and into the top of her dress.

He would very much like to see exactly how far down that blush went.

Soon. I can explore that mystery on our wedding night.

Which he was very much looking forward to.

"What do you enjoy doing in the country?" he asked.

"Rising earlier and spending the morning doing absolutely nothing," she said immediately. "Mother always sleeps late, even in the country, so I am able to do whatever I please."

"And what do you please?"

"Oh... whatever strikes my fancy on the day. Reading. Painting. Music. Riding." She seemed almost as though she was about to say more, but she cut herself off short, which intrigued him.

Perhaps whatever she was going to say was unladylike. Did she ride astride? Or sometimes race? She'd been very interested in his matched set earlier today. Perhaps she did some driving?

They did not know each other well enough, so he did not pursue the question for the moment. There would be time enough to delve into her small secrets.

"That does not sound like 'nothing,'" he teased. She smiled up at him, the hint of mischief in her eyes making his chest do a flip.

"I suppose not, but it does not feel like very much either." She shrugged, but again, Gregory got the distinct feeling she was hiding something from him. He was looking forward to finding out what it was.

In the meantime, they'd circled the room twice and needed to return to socializing with her guests. However, he did not take her back to the couch where Lady Louisa was still sitting, now speaking with several other young ladies who had come to take Tiffany's place. Instead, he moved her over to the group of young ladies who were speaking with Sebastian and Nathanial.

As he'd expected, the ladies latched onto Tiffany's presence as a way to gather more information about her brother, including her in their conversation. Slowly, she relaxed as both he and she focused on Sebastian, who seemed torn between pleasure that Tiffany was included in the conversation and annoyance at Gregory for the stories being told.

An hour later, when the other dukes were ready to depart, Gregory went with them, well pleased with himself. Tiffany might not be able to replace Lady Louisa, but at least he'd put her in the way of more pleasant company, which meant he could retreat from the field with a clear conscience.

TIFFANY

Watching Gregory, Sebastian, and the other dukes leave the room, Tiffany sighed. She was not the only one. The drawing room was suddenly quite gusty with feminine sighs.

Although she knew plenty of their guests had come to see if the rumors about her and the Duke of Clarence were true, just as many were there to sight a duke... and be sighted by one. Three out of the four who had been present were still in the market for wives, after all.

She knew that was why most of the young ladies were willing to talk to her, which was proven by how quickly they all disappeared from her side as soon as the dukes left. Even though she'd expected it, the proof still hurt. Especially when Lady Louisa sent her a triumphant look from across the room as many of them moved to join her coterie instead.

Why Louisa always felt the need to compete with Tiffany, Tiffany had no idea. Louisa was *always* the winner under such circumstances. Tiffany's mother had often bemoaned how she wished Tiffany was more like Louisa—effortlessly beautiful, an expert conversationalist, popular...

But that was not Tiffany's lot in life.

Sitting in the window seat, Tiffany stared out at the street as if she did not mind being abandoned by everyone and needed a moment to rest and collect herself. Another carriage pulled up as she watched, a young woman and her mother exiting. Tiffany recognized her immediately, of course, as would any young lady of the *ton*.

Lady Astrid Blackstone, the betrothed of the Duke of Ormonde. Though she was the daughter of a Marquess in her own right, it was the assurance of her future as a duchess that gave her so much stature among the debutantes. She was an eccentric and an Original, which was immediately apparent upon viewing her as she was wearing an unfashionably colored dress of burnt orange trimmed with coppery brown. It was a far brighter and deeper color than any other debutante wore, though it looked wonderful with her creamy skin and the red hair peeking out from beneath her matching bonnet.

"Oh my goodness, is that Lady Astrid?" A young lady at the other window facing the front street said loudly, causing an immediate stampede to the windows. The older ladies stayed where they were, of course, but Tiffany suddenly found herself surrounded by the other debutantes once again.

And, once again, they were oblivious to her presence.

She supposed it was not merely Lady Astrid's betrothal to a duke that made her so sought after and admired. It was the confident way she held herself. The manner in which she turned up her nose at fashions, forging her own way instead. She was everything a duchess should be—like Lady Louisa.

Tiffany, on the other hand, was plain, awkward, and far better at managing a household than managing Society.

No wonder no one wanted to be her friend.

She stared down at the street, watching as Lady Astrid and her mother approached the house, ignoring the whispers flying above her head.

"Ladies, please, remember yourselves," Tiffany's mother said sharply, sending everyone back to their previous places, many of them giggling. "Tiffany, do not gawk at Lady Astrid. For goodness sake, show some decorum."

Tears sparked in Tiffany's eyes as she turned away from the window, biting her lip against protesting the unfairness of it all. *She* had already been at the window when Lady Astrid arrived; she had not rushed to it. She had not even been the one to announce the lady's arrival. Dropping her gaze down to her hands in her lap, she took in a deep breath, determined not to show her upset.

She did not need more gossip about her, especially when everyone was supposed to be focused on her and Gregory's 'love match'.

Thankfully, no one was going to notice her when Lady Blackstone and Lady Astrid entered the room.

Immediately, Tiffany's mother stood to greet the two—and several of the bolder debutantes stepped forward to draw Lady Astrid into their company, including Lady Louisa. Drawing in another deep breath, Tiffany turned toward the window again, watching the carriages and horses go by on the street, focusing on them to help regain her equilibrium.

"Tiffany, do you have your head in the clouds again?" Louisa's snide amusement punctured Tiffany's attempt at quiet, and she turned to look at the other woman. Seeing Lady Astrid beside her, watching the two of them with an inscrutable expression on her beautiful face, Tiffany immediately jumped to her feet.

It was intimidating, to say the least, to be facing off with two such widely acknowledged beauties, knowing she did not hold a candle to either of them alone. Put them together, and she might as well have been a potted plant. One that was wilting.

"Lady Astrid. I... um... welcome." As expected, she stumbled over her words and blushed hotly as the other ladies around them tittered.

Louisa rolled her eyes, and Tiffany hunched her shoulders inward, wishing she could disappear. Bad enough to appear at such a disadvantage with Louisa watching, but Lady Astrid...

"Thank you. You have a lovely home," Lady Astrid replied, as if Tiffany's response had been perfectly acceptable. Her green eyes were full of... sympathy? Kind. She looked kind. Which Tiffany had not been expecting at all. "I would love a tour of your conservatory."

"You would? I mean, of course, I would be happy to give you one." Good lord, she was acting a twit. If she could sink into the floor, she would. She had expected Lady Astrid to be polite and move on, at best.

"We can all go," Lady Louisa interjected, her gaze suddenly much more sharp and less smug. "I spend a great deal of time here, after all."

"No, Lady Tiffany and I will go alone," Lady Astrid said, smiling as she stepped to Tiffany's side and slid her arm through Tiffany's, joining them together. Tiffany locked her jaw against dropping, which it felt like it was going to do at any moment. Lady Astrid wanted to walk with her alone? It was an unheard-of show of her favor. "We are both future duchesses, after all, and we must get to know each other."

Lady Louisa's expression was such that Tiffany almost felt sorry for her, despite the way Louisa had treated Tiffany in the past. The rejection was kindly toned, but it was a definitive setdown, the likes of which Louisa had likely never experienced before.

"Yes, of course," Louisa said faintly. "I just..."

Whatever she was about to say trailed off as Lady Astrid ignored her and began to walk forward. With her arm interlocked with Tiffany's, Tiffany moved as well. She was aware of her mother's head coming up, looking at the two of them with a frown, but then something the Duchess of Clarence said drew her back into the conversation with the other mothers.

Tiffany's heart soared as she and Lady Astrid walked out of the drawing room together, the envy of every other young lady in there. It was one thing to draw a duke, especially when there were so many currently available—each young lady could imagine herself also being in Tiffany's position—but to have Lady Astrid's undivided and interested attention?

That was a coup she could have never expected. Even if Lady Astrid turned into a total harridan once they were alone, she would remember this brief and shining moment forever.

THIRTEEN

Tiffany.

Rather than becoming cruel out of sight of the others, Lady Astrid seemed happy to chat about the house and the weather as Tiffany led her down the hall to the conservatory. It was Tiffany's second favorite place in the house after the library. Her mother did not approve of her digging in the dirt, so she had to be very careful about when and how often she did so, but she still loved being surrounded by the plants.

"How very lovely," Lady Astrid said, craning her head to look around. "You have quite an array of flowers."

"We do. I enjoy breeding the roses," Tiffany admitted. What she truly enjoyed was that her mother did not mind the results of the new rose colors that came from Tiffany's efforts, even if she thought their head gardener, Masters, was responsible for them. "Here, I think you might like this one in particular."

The dark orange color would look very well with Lady Astrid's day gown. As soon as Tiffany escorted her down the path and the orange rose bush came into sight, Lady Astrid's face lit up.

"Gorgeous." She grinned widely. "Orange is my favorite color. Was it that obvious?"

"Just a bit." Tiffany smiled back at her, finding Lady Astrid's bold way of speaking to be inspiring. "You are certainly the most daringly colored bird in the flock."

The jest made Lady Astrid laugh as she released Tiffany's arm, moving to bend her head over the roses and inhale.

"Lovely," she said, straightening up again. "Well, as I have gone to the trouble of gaining us some privacy, we should take advantage of it to talk before the others join us."

Tiffany blinked.

"The others will join us?"

"You think they will not?" Lady Astrid snorted as she took a seat on the wrought-iron bench across the aisle from the roses. She tilted her head at Tiffany. "Then again, you have not been out in Society as much as I. Yes, where one leads, others will follow. I am a leader, and you shall be, too."

"I will?" Tiffany could not imagine others following her. Lady Astrid frowned, looking at Tiffany as if she thought her daft.

"Of course. You are to be a duchess. They will follow."

Though Tiffany did not want to contradict Lady Astrid, not when she was being so kind, she could not help but wonder if the lady's attitude was biased toward her own experiences. She herself had been noting how merely being engaged to Gregory did not garner her the same kind of reaction that Lady Astrid had received.

She must not have done a good job of hiding her emotions, though, because Lady Astrid raised one delicate eyebrow at her.

"I have been a duke's sister all my life, and no one has ever followed me before," Tiffany said. Not that anyone had been given much opportunity, but even at home on their country estate, she'd been nearly invisible at her mother's side. She'd had no friends outside the maids and certainly no suitors.

"Well. We shall see." Lady Astrid shook her head, appearing amused. "Either way, we shall be duchesses together and to two of the tragic dukes. That is if Drake ever slows down his bedhopping long enough to find his way to the altar with me." She snorted indelicately, as if deriding the idea that her betrothed might change his ways long enough to complete the wedding ceremony.

"The tragic dukes?" Tiffany echoed, more focused on the nickname than Lady Astrid's commentary on her betrothed's rakish ways.

"That is what the *ton* is calling them. Of course, you might not have heard, seeing as your father was one of the victims." Lady Astrid sighed. "My condolences, by the way. It cannot be easy losing your father in such a manner, especially when justice seems to be unlikely."

"Justice?" It felt as though they were having two completely different conversations. Lady Astrid was speaking as though surely Tiffany would understand her, and all Tiffany could do was echo her words because she did not.

Lady Astrid blinked. "Justice for their murders... you did not know."

"I... murder? Sebastian... my brother told me it was an accident. A tragic one, to be sure, but..." Her voice trailed off again as Lady Astrid shook her head. Suddenly feeling wobbly, Tiffany stepped forward to the bench where Lady Astrid was seated, sitting down hard and with very little grace beside her.

The other lady wrapped a comforting arm around Tiffany's shoulders.

"Of course, he did. I apologize. I should not have assumed he told you the truth." Lady Astrid shook her head.

"My father was murdered?" Even as she asked the question, Tiffany felt the truth of it in her heart.

"That is what I think, and I do believe my betrothed and your brother agree with me." Lady Astrid made a face. "I believe, in part, that is why Drake is dragging his feet about marrying me. Not that he particularly wants to be married, but he's the protective sort. He does not want to inadvertently put me in danger. Or perhaps I am giving him too much credence. He knows he needs to marry soon, yet he keeps postponing any sort of discussion on the topic."

As she thought about it, it explained so much of her brother's behavior. Yes, she could easily see how Sebastian might believe that their father had been murdered but kept that belief from her and their mother.

"Why would he keep it a secret?" she asked, more to herself, though Lady Astrid answered.

"He likely thought he was protecting you," Lady Astrid replied, rolling her eyes. She reached out and took Tiffany's hand, which felt very cold in the other lady's warm one. "I am sorry. I should not have been so abrupt. I am used to being blunt to the point of shocking, it amuses me, but I should have been more circumspect in this instance."

"It is all right." A thread of anger was rising in Tiffany's chest, but it was not directed at Lady Astrid. "Sebastian should have told me." They had not been close in years, but the murder of one's father should supersede that. She huffed in annoyance.

"Why is no one speaking of this?"

"For protection, again." Lady Astrid shook her head. "From what I've observed, they are keeping their suppositions to themselves as a group. I've been wondering if they have even decided to ignore the possibility, but for my own safety, I am not so sanguine."

"Your safety?" Blast, she was back to echoing Lady Astrid again.

"Of course. And now yours." Turning toward Tiffany, Lady Astrid reached out and took Tiffany's other hand in hers as well, so she was now holding both of them. Her green eyes were somber. "It was one thing as a duke's sister, but now you are going to be marrying a duke and bearing him an heir. If the reasons the dukes were killed had anything to do with the lineage or the inheritance..."

"We could be in danger, too..." Tiffany breathed out the words as they struck her. "But if that were the motive, why kill so many of them?"

"Perhaps as cover for the misdeed? With so many killed, who is to say who the true target was?" Astrid scowled. "It would take a black heart, indeed, to carry out such a plan, but it is not out of the realm of possibility. The point is we do not know, and therefore, we cannot be assured of our own safety."

Tiffany felt the pronouncement like a blow to the gut.

Marrying Gregory might be putting her own life in danger. Of course, she knew that bearing children was dangerous, but that was a threat every woman faced. This was different.

Did he know? Did he suspect? Had he thought that through?

Yet, what other honorable choice did he have once he'd ruined her? What honorable choice did she have? None at all.

"What are we going to do?" she asked, again more to herself than to Lady Astrid, but the lady had an answer for that as well.

"We are going to find out why the dukes were killed and by whom," she said matter-of-factly. "That's the only way to be assured of our safety and that of our future children."

She made it sound so much easier than it was likely going to be.

Tiffany did not get a chance to process the idea, much less protest, because Lady Astrid proved right on another front. The sound of the door to the conservatory opening was swiftly followed by the chattering of the ladies they'd left behind.

Their moment of privacy was over.

GREGORY

What would a group of dukes be called?

A group of birds was a flock, and he'd called a group of debutantes the same thing on occasion. A flock of crows was a murder. What would a group of dukes be? Especially this group of dukes?

"Perhaps an Indecency," he joked softly to himself, causing Sebastian to give him an odd look. Gregory was not sure his friend had heard what he'd said, though, since he did not inquire further.

They were gathered at Whites in one of the private rooms with their fellow dukes for a meeting of the minds and to discuss the deaths of their fathers. Again. Whether or not he would admit to the letters he'd found threatening his father and the fact that Sebastian thought that several of them had been written by the same hand, he did not know. He wanted to trust his friends, he did... but that did not mean it was the wisest decision.

What if one of them *had* decided to hasten his inheritance?

Though, even with that prospect, Gregory had a truly difficult time seeing any of them deciding to both hasten their inheritance and do away with so many others simultaneously. Then again, anyone who would murder their own father... He had no reason to regret his father's death, yet he could not imagine actually committing patricide.

It was a quandary.

"Gregory! Congratulations on your unexpected engagement," Drake said as soon as he entered the room, spotting Gregory across it and grinning widely with amusement. Since he was usually so dour, it was almost an odd expression to see on his face. "It is the most exciting start to the Season I can remember."

"Happy to entertain," Gregory replied, edging slightly away from Sebastian, who was suddenly scowling again. He'd pushed his friend far enough for today, in his estimation, which was really a pity.

Unfortunately, Christian either did not have as good a read on Sebastian's emotions, or he did not care. He'd been keeping watch at the window, watching the various passersby and keeping up a running commentary on who was out and about for anyone who cared to listen. It had been rather amusing commentary, which Gregory had been half paying attention to.

"Do not forget to congratulate Sebastian, too, for having his sister properly taken care of," he joked. "Managed to land her a duke and without any effort on his part!"

Sebastian's scowl deepened as Christian laughed, several of the others chuckling.

"She could have landed a duke, anyway," Nathanial chimed in

from where he was sitting at a table with Matthew, playing a half-hearted game of poker. They were not playing for money, as Nathanial had none, and because no one with any sense of self-preservation for his wallet ever gambled with the Lord of Luck. They were merely playing to pass the time. "I was already thinking about offering for her."

"I would not have necessarily said yes," Sebastian retorted with a scowl. "I hope you all know that none of you are good enough for her."

"If not a duke, then who?" Gregory asked, trying not to show how Sebastian's words stung. Yes, he'd heard Sebastian's opinion before, but he did not need to hear it over and over again, especially now that the deed was done.

Sebastian's lips tightened, the muscle in his cheek popping as he clenched his jaw.

"Do not take it personally," Nathanial advised before Sebastian could answer, looking up from his cards. "I have sisters who are approaching their debuts far too rapidly, so I understand. The answer is no one. Absolutely no one is good enough for her."

Ah. Well, that did actually make it better. Especially when Gregory looked at Sebastian for confirmation and Sebastian looked away, unwilling to face the truth in Nathanial's statement.

As long as his friend did not have some paragon of manhood in mind for Tiffany, and no one was ever going to be to his satisfaction, Gregory could live with that.

The door to the room opened again, admitting the final member of their quorum. Zachary, with a black scowl on his face, stormed into the room. His boots stomped across the floor in a manner that even the thick rug could not entirely muffle the noise.

"All right there, chap?" Matthew asked benignly, raising his eyebrows as Zachary practically threw himself into one of the empty seats at the table.

"Fine." Zachary's head swiveled around. "I need a drink. What do we have?"

As if he'd anticipated Zachary's need, Christian appeared at his side, brandy in hand. Zachary took the crystal snifter from Christian and put it to his lips, throwing his head back and downing it in one go.

"Here now," Christian objected. "That's no way to treat a good brandy."

"I'll drink the next one slower," Zachary replied irritably.

"What's the matter?" Nathanial asked, looking at Zachary, then looking around at the others, trying to find the answer. "What happened?"

"Zachary did not follow my advice and gave his baroness her *congé* now," Christian replied, shaking his head ruefully.

"You think it would have been better if I'd waited 'til I had a bride?" Zachary scoffed. "She'd be even angrier that I strung her along, and she's already mad enough about that now. She's flirting with Conyngham—Conyngham!—and Boringdon! Sunderland is circling, too, and you know none of them are serious."

"Neither were you, apparently," Drake murmured, taking a sip of his own drink and not blinking when Zachary turned his furious gaze upon him.

"They are *rakes*. They are likely competing over her attention. They would not offer her any sort of arrangement like I did."

He did have a point. Those three were part of the same crowd, thick as thieves, and seemed to have no intention of marrying any time soon. Neither did they take long-term lovers, the way Zachary and the baroness had been. They were very like Gregory, in fact.

"If you have ended things with her, you have to let her go," Christian advised, shaking his head. "You are supposed to be looking for a bride."

"But she is encouraging the advances of the wrong kind of gentlemen for her!"

"And what do you care?" Christian shook his head. "If you wanted to stay in her bed, you should not have ended the affair."

Zachary's face was turning very red, and Christian was not

helping in the least. Though they were the only two with long-term mistresses, it was clearly very different arrangements. Christian's emotions had never been engaged by his actress… Zachary's obviously were, but Christian was unable to empathize.

Still.

"Christian is right in one regard," Gregory said, stepping in. "You are supposed to be finding a bride right now. Otherwise, you gave the baroness her *congé* for naught. Go ask her for her hand if you cannot stand to see her with another."

"But… she's a widow." Zachary's expression was pained.

"You are going to have to make a decision… if you want a virgin, you need to let the widow go," Sebastian admonished, shaking his head.

Slumping in his chair, Zachary crossed his arms over his chest rather than answering, moodily staring at the window, even though it was too far away from him to see anything out of it. Clearly, he was not in a state of mind to listen to sense.

Nathanial cleared his throat, placing his cards down on the table in front of him and folding his hands atop them. The nervous energy he was putting off seemed to double as Gregory watched.

"As fascinating as Zachary's self-induced dilemma is," Nathanial started to say, ignoring the inappropriate gesture Zachary sent his way, "I asked if we could meet today because I have a confession to make. About my father."

There was an immediate and stark change in the room as everyone turned their focus on him. Gregory felt his chest tighten. Even before Nathanial spoke, Gregory felt something coming, like a foreboding that hovered around him.

"I have found some letters that were sent to my father," Nathanial said. He kept his gaze lowered, focused on the table in front of him, unable to look up at any of his friends. Guilt weighed down his voice. Guilt Gregory understood all too well. "Threatening letters. It is very possible that my father is the reason our fathers were killed."

The very air seemed as though it had been sucked out of the room. Everyone stared at him.

Everyone except Sebastian. He looked at Gregory. Their gazes met, and Sebastian nodded his head.

It is time.

Gregory stepped forward, and everyone looked at him, which was highly unnerving. He reached up to adjust his cravat, moving to sit at the table across from Nathanial.

"Your father was not the only one to receive threatening letters," he confessed. "I have found some among my father's effects as well."

The silence broke as the others all started shouting at once.

FOURTEEN

G*regory*
"Why did you not tell us before?"
"Who was sending the letters?"
"What was the threat?"
"When did you find them?"

Everyone was shouting, it seemed, except himself, Nathanial, and Sebastian. When Sebastian did begin to shout, it was to quell the others.

"Stop! We cannot talk to everyone at once." Sebastian held up his hands, managing to be heard over the others loudly enough that they subsided, though Christian continued to grumble. Nathanial was staring across the table at Gregory in relief, and he understood the emotion. He felt a bit ashamed that he had not had Nathanial's courage in coming forward.

Yet, he also could not help but wonder... had Nathanial considered that one of them might be the culprit? Was he just more trusting than Gregory? Or had he considered the possibility and discarded it? If so, what had convinced him to trust them all?

Now that no one was shouting, Sebastian turned toward the

table where Gregory, Nathanial, Zachary, and Matthew were sitting. Matthew was rubbing his pocket where his coin was, his expression extremely blank, as if he was trying to figure out a way to make his luck work for him under these circumstances... but there was nothing to flip for.

Zachary had gone from red in the face over the topic of his baroness to very pale as he looked back and forth between Nathanial and Gregory. He'd truly mourned the passing of his father, if Gregory was any judge.

In some ways, the topics of a bride and women were a good distraction from the harsh reality of the mystery of their fathers' deaths.

"What kind of threats was your father receiving?" Sebastian asked Nathanial, with a glance at Gregory so he would know it was his turn next. Sebastian already had seen the letters to Gregory's father, of course, but he was right... the contents needed to be shared with everyone.

"He was not paying his gambling debts." Nathanial shrugged, turning up his hands helplessly. "We did not have the money. Not that it stopped him from gambling. He had letters from several hells and from gentlemen of our set for personal loans. I also found a small stack of debts from others who did not send him a letter."

"But if he is dead, he cannot pay them," Matthew pointed out. Though his luck always ran true—or turned true at some point—he was the most familiar of them all with the hells and the ways gentlemen worked out their debts. He had enough of them who owed him.

"Several of the letters intimated that perhaps his heir would be more likely to pay what he owed," Nathanial said grimly. "I have not heard from any of them... yet. It is possible they are waiting to see if I find a wife with a dowry before they approach."

Which would be the most sensible tack. Poor Nathanial.

"If you would just—" Matthew started to say, but Nathanial cut him off with a sharp gesture.

"It is my estate and my inheritance, and I will fix it myself," he snapped. Matthew sighed, a sound echoed by several of them around the room. "But you have my gratitude for wanting to help. I promise I will come to you before allowing my sisters to be thrown into the streets, but you must allow me to fix this my way."

His way, which would mean marriage to a lady with a massive dowry that she—or, more to the point, her father—was willing to trade for the title.

"I still have time," Nathanial muttered. He took a deep breath.

"You still have time." Drake walked around to the back of Nathanial and dropped a comforting hand on his shoulder. "But we are here if you need us."

Nathanial was doing his best to clean up a mess that was not his. All of them wanted to help him. All of them knew they'd be likely to react the same way in his position. It might not be his mess, but it was his father's mess, and he'd inherited it along with his title. Allowing the others to help him without doing everything in his power to fix things himself would be massively damaging to his pride... which was about the only thing he had left. Gregory did not envy him.

"My father's letters were all vague, though I suspect that at least several have to do with my half-sisters," Gregory said grimly, taking charge of his part of the conversation rather than being pressed into it. He glanced at Sebastian. "Sebastian has looked them over and we think there might be a few written by the same hand, though efforts were taken to disguise the handwriting."

"You knew about his letters, too?" Christian scowled at Sebastian. "Why did no one say anything? Why did you keep them to yourself?"

"Think about it, man. Would you want to admit that your father might be the reason all your friends' fathers are dead?" Matthew retorted, shaking his head. "I would not want to admit to such a thing."

"You must also have wondered if sharing the letters with the possible murderer was wise," Drake commented. Everyone looked at him, but he was unperturbed by the implication he'd made. "If none of you have at least had the thought that all of us have motive, you are not the men I took you to be."

The truth was hard to hear, but it was necessary to face it. They all looked at each other with similarly drawn faces, nodding in acknowledgment of the truth that they had all had the thought.

"It is hard to trust, but I feel as though I have gotten to know all of you well enough to measure your character," Sebastian said, breaking the uncomfortable silence. "While there are a few of you that might have occasionally thought about killing your father, I do not believe any of you capable of doing so... and certainly not of doing so in a manner that might injure, much less kill, others around him."

A few chuckles, despite the darkness of the jest, escaped. Gregory was one of those because Sebastian spoke truly.

There were certainly times he'd thought about killing his father, especially when his father was mistreating his mother. Now, knowing what he did about his half-sisters and the way his father had treated them and their mothers, there were times when he wished he'd had the stones to carry out the thought.

"I thought about it more than occasionally once I understood what my father was doing to our family," Nathanial admitted. "There have even been times I have felt relief. Things are bad now, but they could have been even worse if he'd lived longer." He grimaced. "I am sure that makes me sound even guiltier."

"You are not the only one," Gregory reassured him. "I have felt the same."

"And I," Matthew said. "I admit, I thought about it when I was younger and rasher."

"The coin never told you to do it?" Christian joked, going for a spot of levity amidst the admitted dark discussion.

"I never flipped for it," Matthew laughed, though there was no amusement in the sound. "I was too afraid of what it might say."

Gregory could not blame him. It was one thing to choose an evening's entertainment with the flip of a coin, or even what funds to invest in, whether or not to bet on a certain horse... patricide was something altogether different.

"We should gather again and compare the notes," Sebastian said, looking between them.

"Yes, because we all have so much time with the social demands pressing down on us," Christian replied with a grimace. "I was lucky to get away for *this* meeting, and I have to leave soon to escort my mother to the Colfax ball."

"If you give your actress her *congé,* you'll have more time, even with your mother's demands," Zachary replied, a bit snidely, causing Christian to glare at him.

"Should we consider bringing... Seymour in on this discovery?" Nathanial grimaced as he referenced the current Duke of Northumberland. Eventually, they would all have to move past Sinclair's death, but at the moment, it still felt wrong to use the title when referring to William Seymour. "At the very least, ask him if he's discovered any letters."

From the reluctance in every single expression, no one liked the idea very much.

"We should," Drake finally declared with an air of supreme resignation. "At least I will try to discover if he's found any threatening letters toward Sinclair or his father." He made a face. "Since I already have a fiancé, I suppose I have more time than the rest of you."

"Gregory has one now, too," Matthew pointed out.

"Yes, which means all the planning that goes into a wedding and even more events where I escort her around," Gregory replied. "Unlike Drake, I intend to marry quickly rather than continuing to dance around the parson's trap."

Drake waved his hand, dismissing Gregory's words. "Time enough for that at the end of the Season. As I said, I intend to enjoy myself before I'm leg-shackled. And since it gives me the advantage of having more time to do things like speak with... Seymour, you should all be grateful for me. Unless someone else wishes to take on the duty of approaching him."

"No, no, I am sure you have it well in hand," Gregory said hastily. "I was just pointing out how busy I am in comparison."

Sebastian snorted but did not comment. He was going to be even busier than Gregory, helping with the wedding plans while also looking for his own bride. And on top of that, the mystery of their fathers' deaths lurked in the background.

Bloody hell, what a Season.

At least he'd managed the task of finding his own bride already. A pretty, biddable one. Once he was leg-shackled, he could focus more of his efforts on the mystery of the dead dukes and leave his new wife to tend to the household.

~

TIFFANY

Consternation stirred in Tiffany's breast as she struggled to recover from Lady Astrid's revelations, all while facing down the onslaught of debutantes and their mothers now crowding into the conservatory with them. Her own mother was among them, frowning at Tiffany as she often did. Likely, she would disapprove of Tiffany leaving the drawing room and all the guests assembled there, even though none of them had been speaking with Tiffany. At least she would have the excuse that Lady Astrid had specifically asked her for a tour and to speak with her alone. Her mother could not blame Tiffany for another lady's request.

She raised her hand to her temple as her head began to throb.

Did her mother suspect that her late husband's death had been anything but an accident?

If she did, she certainly had not confided in Tiffany. But then, would she? Or would she speak with Sebastian about it? Were the two of them speaking of it and leaving Tiffany out?

Lady Astrid seemed sure that Sebastian suspected. Tiffany

thought it likely, when she thought about her brother's behavior. But she was unsure of her mother.

"There you are, Tiffany," Lady Tremaine said, sailing up to her and Lady Astrid. She beamed down at Tiffany. They had not actually spoken since Tiffany greeted her. Lady Louisa and Tiffany's mother followed along in Lady Tremaine's wake. "I did not have the opportunity to tell you earlier how lovely you look in mint. You are turning into quite the beauty, is she not, Susan?"

Lady Tremaine turned back toward Tiffany's mother, who smiled widely at her, making Tiffany stare in shock as her mother nodded in agreement.

"Oh, yes, the mint is much better for her coloring. You were right, Alice." Tiffany's mother laughed lightly. "But young ladies always have their own opinions about what looks best on them."

"Of course, but that is why you must listen to your mother for guidance, my dear," Lady Tremaine said, turning back to Tiffany, who stared back at her, uncertain of what was happening. Was her mother implying that *she* was the one who wanted to wear that awful apricot? Tiffany always wore what her mother told her to, today included. "Though, you did catch a duke despite your preference for that awful orange-y color."

She laughed and turned to Lady Astrid, who was smiling cooly beside Tiffany.

"No insult to you, Lady Astrid. Orange is a color that suits you down to the ground, but I am afraid it is rather unfortunate on dear Tiffany here." Lady Tremaine winked. "The mint is much more flattering. You know, dear, you should really try to wear more greens and perhaps some blues or violets."

"I... thank you for your advice, Lady Tremaine," Tiffany responded faintly. Then, bolstered by the opportunity she saw, her voice strengthened. Surely, her mother would not force her into more apricot dresses if her own closest friend had publicly advised Tiffany not to wear them, and Tiffany agreed. "I will certainly take your advice for the rest of the Season."

"Good girl," Lady Tremaine said approvingly. "Listen to your mother. She'll steer you right." Reaching up, she patted the underside of her curls as she turned back to Tiffany's mother, whose smile now appeared a trifle strained.

Tiffany quailed to see it, but… she was only agreeing with Lady Tremaine.

"You must be so proud, Susan, your dear girl landing a duke and before the Season even began."

"Very proud," Tiffany's mother said, echoing Lady Tremaine's words. It sounded correct, yet something about the way she said it still made Tiffany want to shrink out of view.

"My own Louisa is going to be Tiffany's maid of honor," Lady Tremaine told Lady Astrid, gesturing at her daughter, who currently looked as though she was sucking on a lemon.

Tiffany finally understood what was going on. Lady Astrid had shown Tiffany favor, and now Lady Tremaine was hoping that her own daughter would be able to benefit from the connection. Yet… Lady Tremaine had sounded completely sincere in her compliments toward Tiffany.

"I am sure she is very honored," Lady Astrid said, smiling. The way she made it sound like a jest seemed to take Lady Tremaine aback, yet there was nothing wrong with Lady Astrid's statement. As if to take the sting out of the ambiguity of her statement, she turned to smile at Tiffany. "I agree with Lady Tremaine. I think blue would suit you perfectly. You should make it your signature color."

Glancing at her mother, whose expression was still placid, but the look in her eyes was growing fiercer by the moment, Tiffany shrugged helplessly.

"I do not believe I have any blue… perhaps for my wedding trousseau…" She had an entire wardrobe of gowns made up for the Season, and not a one was blue.

"Of course," Lady Tremaine said triumphantly, turning to Tiffany's mother. "Susan, you must see to it that she has new gowns in blue for her trousseau. We must not let our young ladies run over our advice with their own preferences." She laughed again, and Tiffany's mother laughed with her.

"Yes, you are right, of course," Tiffany's mother said. She shook her head, leaning into Lady Tremaine. "If only Tiffany was as obedient as Louisa." She shrugged helplessly, spreading her hands in front of her as a shocking flash of rage bolted through Tiffany.

She sat straight up, hands clenched in her lap. She was *always* obedient. She *always* did what her mother asked of her. But her mother was making it sound as if the apricot gown had been at Tiffany's insistence. As if Tiffany had not wanted gowns that were less brightly colored. As if Tiffany was some wayward spoiled chit who only wore what she wanted and eschewed her mother's advice.

"Well, she did land a duke without that," Lady Tremaine pointed out again. "I am always telling Louisa that she needs to take her lead from Tiffany, and I am proven correct again."

She *what?*

Tiffany could not help but stare at Louisa, who had suddenly averted her gaze to examine the bush beside her. The very green bush with nary a flower in sight. Lady Tremaine was giving the back of her daughter's head a hard look, and she sniffed in a manner very reminiscent of Tiffany's own mother.

Did Lady Tremaine constantly compare Louisa to Tiffany the way her own mother compared her to Louisa? The thought had never occurred to Tiffany. Louisa was so obviously everything a young lady ought to be, as well as possessing uncommon beauty. Yet she was quite sure she saw the sparkle of tears in Louisa's eyes, as if her mother's words cut her the same way Tiffany's mother's criticisms did her.

For the first time in her life, Tiffany wondered if perhaps she and Louisa had more in common than she'd realized.

As Lady Tremaine continued to expound on Tiffany's virtues, something Tiffany would have very much liked to listen to under other circumstances, Lady Astrid leaned over.

"Send me a note when you go to the dressmakers for your

trousseau, and I will come join you." She winked at Tiffany, who looked at her with astonishment, then a surge of gratitude.

Tiffany did not trust her own judgment, and she now realized that she should not trust her mother's, either. Perhaps she could trust Lady Astrid's. Yes, she knew the only reason Lady Astrid was being helpful was because they were both to be duchesses and because Lady Astrid felt they might both be in danger, but it was still the closest thing to a gesture of friendship that she'd ever received.

FIFTEEN

Tiffany

When the at-home concluded, Tiffany's mother announced that she had a headache and would be retiring. They would have to miss the Colfax ball this evening. Tiffany was beginning to worry about her mother's health. This many headaches so close together? And bad enough, her mother sequestered herself away?

At the same time, she was relieved to be alone.

Not that her mother would have brooked any argument from her, anyway. Tiffany was almost sorry to miss the Colfax ball, though. The at-home had been rather enjoyable, and she'd hoped to see Lady Astrid again this evening. Maybe even to see Louisa, to try to talk to her about... well, about their mothers.

Sitting in the window seat, she watched and waited for her brother's return. If he returned. She did not know what his plans were for this evening. He could very well stay out to all hours of the night with the other dukes. Men sometimes did that. Though her stomach clenched at the idea of Gregory gallivanting with other women...

She pushed her thoughts away from the idea. There was no point in torturing herself when she had no idea what they were doing. The dukes might all be gathered to ponder the mystery of their fathers' deaths. Their fathers and hers. She huffed at knowing she had been left out.

A carriage stopped in front of the house, and Tiffany sat up straight as her brother exited the conveyance. Hurrying out of the drawing room, she rushed to the front door to greet him, much to the displeasure of their butler. Riggs huffed as she darted in front of him, drawing back so he did not run into her.

"My apologies, Riggs," she said, looking over her shoulder. "I need to speak with my brother. Immediately. Can you have Mrs. Mays send a tray to the library for us?"

She was already opening the door as she made her request, which meant Sebastian overheard it as he stopped just in the doorway, frowning.

"A tray?" he asked. "Why are you not dressed? Where is Mother? We are going to be late to the Colfaxes."

"We are not going to the Colfaxes," she informed him, reaching out to catch his coat sleeve and tug him inside, shutting the door behind him. Riggs had already disappeared to go find Mrs. Mays, though he'd left a lingering aura of disapproval behind. She was going to have to find him and apologize to him later. "Mother has a *megrim,* and I have already sent our apologies. I need to talk to you."

"So I heard," he replied with some bemusement, allowing her to pull him along through the house. "Badly enough to risk upsetting Riggs. You know how stuffy he gets about the proprieties."

"I will apologize to him later," Tiffany said with a sigh, Sebastian's thoughts reflecting her own.

"What is so important?" he asked.

"I will tell you after we are in the library," she replied in a hushed voice. As much as she trusted their staff, she did not want to hinder whatever her brother was doing, and if he did believe their father had been murdered, he was keeping it a secret for a reason. She cleared her throat. "Was there any lady that caught your attention today?"

"You are lucky that is not the matter of importance," he muttered before answering her. "None that caught my eye."

Tiffany blinked, surprised. Not because she had noticed Sebastian looking at any of the ladies with particular attention but because she assumed that someone must have at some point. There had been so many of them, and he'd been surrounded.

"*None?*"

"I do have rather exacting standards," he said with a chuckle. "And I can afford to take some time to find the right duchess. Do you have any suggestions as to who I should be paying attention to?"

"Anyone but Lady Louisa." The words popped out of her mouth before she could stop them, and Sebastian laughed uproariously as they entered the library. Tiffany hunched her shoulders.

"I mean... if you fell in love with her..."

"Love is the last thing I am looking for," he managed to say as he laughed even harder.

Tiffany sighed inwardly. She should have known. In her family, she was the only romantic. Yet, the love in her engagement was pure pretense. She could hardly blame Sebastian for his reaction.

"What are you looking for in a wife?" she asked as they moved to the armchairs. One of the maids had already been in to light the candles; she could only assume Riggs had sent one running so the room would be prepared for them. He was very efficient, even when annoyed with her. "Perhaps I can help you narrow the list."

"That you and she get along is high on the list, which automatically removes Lady Louisa from it." He winked, sitting down across from her.

"That is appreciated." The fact that he put her comfort so high on his list made her beam at him, her chest filling with warmth that he cared. She had not realized. "What else?"

"That she be of our set, of course, so that she understands her duties and Society. Daughter of an earl or higher. I want her to be able to run the household like Mother does. Attractive. Intelligent. Even-tempered. Accomplished but not boastful. A generous hostess. Able to run the staff. I would like her to be interested in our children, though, of course, she will have plenty of assistance in raising them." He waved his hand as Tiffany did her best to keep a straight face.

Part of her knew these were all logical, considered points that many of their set would agree with, yet it sounded so cold when he spoke it out loud. Gregory likely had a similar mental list, and she knew she would fulfill most of it. She'd been trained to check the boxes of such a list.

"A pleasant voice to listen to and not given to screeching."

Tiffany pressed her lips together to keep from making an unkind comment about their mother.

"I see," she murmured.

Sebastian looked at her, tilting his head, his expression changing like he was seeing her anew. He kept looking at her in such a manner lately, and she found it unnerving to have his focus so attuned to her.

"What did you have on your list at the beginning of this Season?"

She hesitated for a moment. She knew he would scoff at her list, but he had spoken honestly, and she should do no less. She began with the attributes he would understand the best.

"One of our set. With a country house and who would not mind me spending most of my time there. Intelligence and attractiveness, yes. Someone who is... generous and kind. Someone who appreciates me. Who does not mind that I am quiet. Who allows me to choose my own fashion. Who listens to me." Someone who cared for her, even if it was not love.

"It is a good thing I was in charge of finding you a husband," Sebastian said, shaking his head. He held up his hand to stop her protest. "It is not that those things are not important, but they should not be at the top of the list. A husband who can provide for you and your children—"

"I did say he should be of our set."

"—at least a Marquess, Tiffany. An honorable man who will

protect you. One with standing in Society and deep pockets to ensure your future. One who will *not* just let you disappear into the country." He sent her an admonishing look, and Tiffany stuck her tongue out at him, as though she was a child, startling a laugh from him. "And one who will tolerate occasional disrespect."

Now it was her turn to giggle, and he grinned at her.

"Strangely, though I disapprove of the manner in which you and Gregory became affianced, I do think he will fulfill both our lists," Sebastian admitted. "I will do everything in my power to ensure he does."

"Thank you, Sebastian." She smiled at him, though she hid a pang in her heart because there was one thing she'd left off the list. The most important thing.

Love.

She wanted her husband to love her. The way Gregory was pretending to.

But if she could not have love from her husband, perhaps she would from their children together. She would be a good mother. She... she did not want to criticize her own mother, but there were many, many things she wanted to do differently from her mother.

The door to the library opened, and one of the maids came in with a cart containing tea and a supper tray.

"Thank you, Ivy. Please leave the tray here," Tiffany said, gesturing beside her and Sebastian. "We will be dining very informally."

"Yes, miss," Ivy said, putting the tray in place and bobbing a curtsy before swiftly departing.

Leaning forward to inspect the offerings, Tiffany looked up to find her brother looking at her oddly again.

"How did you know her name?" he asked, the edges of his lips turned down into a frown, not as if he disapproved, but as if he was puzzled.

"I know all of our staff's names." She was not surprised he did not. Neither did their mother. They mostly interacted with Riggs and Mrs. Mays and relied upon them to handle everything.

"You do?"

"I do." She hid her smile as she picked up a scone to nibble on. "So often they were the only ones I could speak with at the manor, without mother hovering over my every word."

Their names, their families, their woes, their happiness... she knew it all, but she doubted Sebastian would understand. He had never had their mother critiquing every sentence out of his mouth. Their mother had left him to their father to train, and he had done so well, he never said a word out of turn or disappointed her, unlike Tiffany.

Sebastian was still frowning, but she did not want to speak of her friendships with the staff. In part because she was unsure he would approve, and she had no intention of changing her ways. She knew their mother would not approve, so she had always assumed he would not, either. Now, she wondered if perhaps she was incorrect, but she was not sure enough to elaborate further.

"Now that we are alone, I must ask you... do you think father was murdered?" She asked it baldly, outright, rather than hedging around the subject because she wanted to see his sincere, unadulterated reaction.

He did not protest.

He did not shake his head.

He did not immediately denounce such a ridiculous notion.

Instead, he froze.

Tiffany's mouth went dry, and she gasped.

"You do! You think Father was murdered, and you kept it from me!"

"Hush!" Sebastian gestured for her to lower her voice, looking around as if someone might have overheard her.

"No one can hear me," she said furiously. "How could you keep this from me?"

"What could you do?" he asked in return, fresh grief blooming on his face. "What could you have done if you had known, other than suffer more? What good would it have done?"

It felt like a blow, not just his words, but seeing his emotions bubbling up, his anger, his sorrow. Sebastian had been stalwart after their father's death. He'd held both her and their mother as they'd cried. Coaxed her mother off their father's coffin when she'd become hysterical and thrown herself upon it in a fit of passion. He'd arranged the entire funeral with Riggs and Mrs. Mays' assistance because Tiffany had had to attend to their mother.

If he'd cried, he'd done it alone.

Seeing the tears spark in his eyes now, the way his mouth firmed as he clenched his jaw against the tumult of emotions, she felt a surge of guilt for ambushing him in such a manner. It did not entirely wash out her anger, but it did blunt it.

"I am sorry, Sebastian." She reached out her hand to put it atop his. He turned his own hand over so that he could hold hers. "You are correct. I could not have done anything." And she might not have been able to hide the truth from her mother in her own distress, which would have only made things worse.

"What... how did you know?" he asked.

She hesitated. The desire to tell him the full truth was strong, but she had already decided upon a small deflection for Lady Astrid's sake. After all, he had not been completely honest with her, so she need not feel any guilt about protecting her new friend.

"Someone at the at-home today, after you left, said there was some gossip that the fire was no accident. I did not want to believe it, but it made me think... if it was not an accident, and someone intentionally killed our father and the other dukes, could we be in danger? You and I? Or Gregory? Could marrying Gregory put me in more danger?" The words came out in a rush because she did not want him to question who had been spreading the gossip but focused on the ramifications of the truth.

Sebastian stilled.

"No matter what happens, I will protect you," he said sternly.

"I know you will. But I also want to know the truth. You knew... do the other dukes? Does Gregory? If the reason they were killed was for inheritance reasons... do you suspect the current Northumberland of doing the same with the previous? Is that why you do not like him? Because you think he killed your friend's father and then your friend, all of our fathers being unlucky bystanders, all to inherit?" All the questions tumbled out, one after another.

Her brother looked aghast.

"No! Zounds, Tiffany, that had not actually occurred to me. I do not like... Northumberland because he is a toady." Sebastian stumbled over the man's title. No wonder when the previous duke had been his friend. "He could never have expected to actually inherit."

"Then what reason could anyone have to kill eight dukes?" Because if they knew the who, they would know the why.

Sighing, Sebastian released her hand.

"We should eat to garner our strength, and while we do, I will tell you everything."

Taking a plate, Tiffany did as he said and listened wide-eyed as he told her all about the threatening letters Gregory's father had received, the revelation that Nathan's father had received some as well, and everything that Sebastian had managed to put together so far.

It was not enough to identify a culprit, of course, but it was enough to satisfy her for now.

CHAPTER

SIXTEEN

Gregory

Planning a wedding with speed was enough to make any man's head spin. Having to do so while attempting to solve a murder—multiple murders—during the social Season was madness. And throughout all of it, he also had to convince the entirety of Society that he was marrying for love, which meant dancing attendance on his fiancé far more often than if it were a known arrangement.

Arriving at Bolton House for a day of wedding planning, he was braced to be bored and hopeful that perhaps he could spend some more time speaking with Tiffany. Or with Sebastian. At least his friend's presence would also be required. Not that they would likely be any help in the planning, but a show must be made.

He helped his mother out of the carriage, escorting her up to the door where the butler let them in and showed them into the drawing room. It was empty, unlike during the at-home, and the space appeared far larger than it had on that day.

"The duchess will be with you momentarily," Riggs said with a touch of butlerish hauteur.

143

"Thank you, Riggs," Gregory said with a grin for the stuffy man. He had not changed a bit in all the years Gregory and Sebastian had been friends. The butler nodded stiffly, closing the door behind him, though it did not take more than a few moments for them to open again and a maid to enter with the tea cart.

Gregory got his mother settled on the couch while the maid set out the tea tray and sandwiches on the table in front of them. She was just finishing setting up when Sebastian and his mother walked in.

Immediately, the Duchess of Bolton frowned when she looked around the room.

"Where is Tiffany?" she asked.

"Probably in the music room," Sebastian replied, shaking his head with a slight smile. "I will fetch her."

"No, I will. I should as her fiancé," Gregory said, jumping to his feet. He wanted just a few brief moments alone with her, if possible, and this seemed like the perfect opportunity.

"Thank you, Your Grace," the duchess replied, then, tugging on her son's arm, pulled him forward to greet Gregory's mother. "Marguerite, you look lovely today."

It was kind of her to say so. Since his father's death, his mother had a penchant for wearing so many brightly colored ruffles on her dresses that she ended up resembling an exotic confection. Being a duchess meant she could indulge in eccentric fashion if she wished and be complimented on it.

"Thank you, Susan, you do as well. I am so delighted to embark on our planning today. What did you have in mind to start?"

His mother's voice faded as he let himself out of the drawing room, smirking a bit at the pained expression he glimpsed on Sebastian's face before he managed his own escape. Of course, he would be returning soon enough, but any reprieve Sebastian did not receive was a kind of victory.

He knew his way to the music room from past visits, though it had been a while. It did not matter. Even if he had never been to the music room, he would have found it.

As he walked down the hallway, the melodious sound of a harp danced through the air to greet him, the waterfall of notes reaching out to draw him forward like a siren's song. Young ladies were encouraged to learn an instrument, for what reason Gregory had never understood, though supposedly it was a skill required to be deemed marriageable.

He did not think such a skill had ever made it onto any gentleman's list of attributes used to search for a wife. Especially because very few of the young ladies ever managed anything but bare proficiency.

Not so Tiffany.

Beyond proficiency, beyond skill, she was a master.

He felt almost drunk as he stepped through the doorway into the music room.

Her back was to him, the great harp resting against her shoulder, sunlight streaming in from the window she was facing. It glinted over her hair, showing off highlights of gold and rose in what he'd formally thought of as mousy brown. In this light, the canary yellow dress she was wearing did not seem so gauche. Despite the small size of her hands, she managed the huge instrument as if it fit on her lap rather than needing to be cradled against her entire body.

The quickness of her fingers moving over the strings with such a delicate touch was breathtaking. He could have watched her all day. All night.

Bloody hell.

His groin tightened.

He had never, *never*, had such a reaction to any sort of musical display.

Not until today.

He felt as though he could not breathe, did not dare breathe, because it might break the spell.

She came to the end of the notes, the musical resolution settling something inside him. Her hands gracefully lifted like bird wings as the final harmony vibrated through the room, then came back to rest on the strings to still them. Gregory's lungs were seized in that shining moment when the music ended, the beauty of it hanging in the silence, before he stepped forward, clapping his hands together as if it were a concert.

Because, indeed, she was more than concert qualified.

"Bravo!"

Tiffany startled, her head whipping around, jerking in shock, and Gregory bound forward as the balance of her harp wavered. At her side, a firm grip on the wooden frame, he smiled down at her, all too aware of how close her body was to his and how her seat on the bench put her face—and therefore her mouth—perilously close to his groin.

"My apologies," he said, trying to ignore his body's reaction to their positioning and the lingering effects her playing had on him. "I did not mean to startle you."

She let out a sigh of relief as the harp was settled back into place.

"My apologies as well. I lost track of the time." She rubbed her hands on her lap, and Gregory frowned, reaching down to pick her hand up and turn it over so he could see her palms.

The redness on the tips of her fingers looked like they would be sore.

"Does this happen every time you play?"

"Yes. I have a special lotion to keep my hands soft, but if I play too often, I begin to callus." Tiffany got to her feet, ducking her head. "Mother gets very upset."

Personally, Gregory would rather that she have calluses than be in pain, but he knew the unspoken expectations of the *ton*. Young ladies should always have soft hands.

"Well, you are very good." He cradled her hands in his, examining them. "I never would have guessed these hands held such incredible talent."

She laughed.

"You are too kind, good sir," she replied teasingly, as if he were joking. He raised his eyebrow at her.

"I am entirely serious. I have never heard such talented playing outside of a concert hall."

Tiffany blinked, her doe eyes full of startled wonder as she realized he was serious, her lips parting in surprise... and as if she was begging for a kiss. Which... they were alone, after all.

Taking advantage of her stunned silence, Gregory used her hands to pull her toward him, lowering his head for the kiss he desired. Felt her gasp rather than heard it as she was pulled against him, and he took the opportunity to slide his tongue between her lips, exploring her mouth.

No need to rein in his passion this time. She was no mysterious debutante at a ball, with a reputation that needed to be carefully handled. She was his fiancé. He was going to marry her.

It was almost expected that he take some liberties when the opportunity arose.

So, he kissed her the way he'd been wanting to kiss her ever since that night in the library, and after a brief moment of hesitation, she met him with equal passion. Their tongues stroked together, his hands sliding up her arms and then down her back while her fingers gripped the front of his coat. He felt every shudder, every quiver of her body, as she reacted to him with shocking intensity.

His fingers had just found the buttons on the back of her dress when there was a hard knock of fist against wood from the doorway, and Sebastian's voice cut through Gregory's haze of desire. Nothing like his best friend and his bride's older brother to dampen the mood.

"Gregory." That was all Sebastian said, but there were layers of meaning piled onto Gregory's name.

Tiffany tried to pull away, but he tightened his hold on her, keeping her in his arms, though he lifted his head from the kiss, lazily turning to face Sebastian. His friend was glaring at them, but Gregory refused to be cowed. He *was* marrying her, after all.

"Sebastian." His own response had the same levels of reproach, resignation, and threat as Sebastian's had, but with a touch of mockery as well.

The other man scowled.

"Do not make me wallop you again."

"No one is walloping anyone," Tiffany said firmly, pulling away from Gregory again, and this time, he let her—mostly. He kept his hand on the small of her back, sighing internally at the sudden lack of soft, warm female in his arms. Finding more ways to sneak away and kiss her, touch her, was definitely at the top of his list.

No one would blame him.

It was a 'love match' after all. Doing so would only bolster their trick.

"The mothers are waiting for us," Sebastian said, giving Gregory another baleful look that promised retribution for daring to lay his hands on Sebastian's sister.

"Oh dear, yes, I forgot the time. I am sorry." Tiffany hurried forward, away from Gregory's supportive hand, and now it was his turn to scowl. He moved quickly to catch up to her, catching her hand with his just before she reached Sebastian and slowing her.

"They know I came to fetch you," he said, pulling her hand over his arm and trapping it there so she could not rush away without him again. "I do not know why they sent this lout along as well."

"Because you were taking too long."

"We were taking too long, or you could not tolerate being alone while the hens are chirping?"

"Both," Sebastian replied stoutly, and Gregory laughed.

Deep breaths.

Not just because her wits were flustered from being kissed sense-less by the duke, but because she knew her mother was going to be highly displeased at her lateness. Hurrying would do no good, yet the impulse was still there. At least her mother would probably not chide her in front of Gregory.

She took the time during the short walk to the drawing room to settle herself, as much as she could while her body was still humming from Gregory's touch, her lips still tingling from his kiss. Lord, the effect he had on her...

Me and probably countless other women.

But for now, his focus was on her.

Perhaps she should just let herself enjoy it while it lasted, even if some of it was nothing more than flummery.

We were alone. There was no audience. No one waiting upon us but our mothers and Sebastian. There was no need to advance the pretense.

What if he kissed me because he wanted to?

He wanted to kiss me in the library.

It was thoughts such as these that had hounded her this morning and how she'd ended up at her harp in the first place, drowning herself in music to escape both her concerns over her upcoming marriage as well as the revelations about her father's death. Her mind batted back and forth between the two subjects, like a birdie on the badminton court, and there had been no escape until she'd sat down at the harp.

Playing music had always been an escape. The harp required more concentration than some of the other instruments she played, which was why she'd chosen it, though the stinging in her fingertips said she would be paying for that choice for the next few days. It was unladylike to have calluses, but she wished that no one cared because she would have loved to play the harp every day. But at the slightest hint of a callus, her mother's disapprobation would come down upon her with harsh weight, and she would be banned from playing for at least two months.

It was better to only play once a week or so and deal with the pain in her fingers than to be barred for months.

"There you are," her mother said, though her remonstrance was less sharp than usual, when Tiffany entered the room on Gregory's arm, Sebastian bringing up the rear. "Did you forget that we have guests this morning?"

"No, Mother, I am sorry. I lost track of time," Tiffany said, blushing hotly as she faced Gregory's mother, hoping the women would forgive her for such an error and not take it as a personal slight. She dipped down in a curtsy, awkwardly positioned as Gregory did not let go of her arm as she did so. "My apologies, Your Grace."

"You should hear her play the harp, Mother. She is incredible," Gregory enthused as Tiffany straightened, making her blush even harder. She saw the frown on her mother's face before it was replaced by a slight social smile.

Her mother did not approve of braggery or boastfulness, especially in young ladies. It was one thing for a man to act a popinjay, but young ladies should be modest and not excessively prideful.

"I am badly out of practice," she said, shaking her head, which was very true. Of course, she had been playing a more difficult piece as a means to distract herself.

"That only makes your talent even more astonishing," Gregory continued, seating her in one of the chairs before taking the seat beside hers, leaving Sebastian to join their mothers on the couch.

"I would love to hear you play," the Duchess of Clarence said, beaming at her. The constant show of approval was very discomforting, especially now that it was just the family and there was hardly a need for it. Everyone in this room knew that she and Gregory were not actually a love match. "I have always been partial to the harp. What piece were you playing?"

Tiffany glanced at her mother, whose smile was becoming rather stilted, but Tiffany could hardly avoid answering such a simple question. Besides, just naming the piece was hardly boasting, was it?

"Sonata in G by Bach," she replied, folding her hands on her lap, missing the warmth of Gregory's arm beneath her palm.

The Duchess of Clarence gasped, putting her hand to her chest.

"That is one of my favorites! And it is so difficult."

"She played it like a maestro," Gregory said, reaching over to put his hand atop hers on her lap.

Warmth flooded her cheeks and chest again, basking a bit in his compliments, even if he was being overly effusive.

Sebastian was giving her that look again, the one like he was seeing her for the first time. Wondering. Assessing.

She risked a peek at her mother, whose pinched lips said she disapproved, but she did not scold Gregory the way she did Tiffany. Perhaps because she expected his own mother to take him to task if necessary. Or perhaps because he was a duke.

Or perhaps because it did not count as boasting if she was not saying the words herself.

But for one shining moment, she allowed herself to enjoy the admiration and believe that, perhaps, she was everything he said she was.

SEVENTEEN

regory!

Over the next week, Sebastian proved far too deft at playing chaperone, guarding the hen house after the fox had already gotten in. Gregory felt sure his friend was doing so for no other reason than to frustrate him as a kind of torment for kissing Tiffany in the library in the first place. He could grin and bear it.

Besides, he'd never minded a challenge. He hoped he could find some time to pull Tiffany away from the others this evening. He'd even enlisted his mother's help to keep the Duchess of Bolton occupied. She had agreed, although she had not seemed entirely thrilled by the request. The two mothers had been getting along when it came to wedding plans, but Gregory had noticed that the Duchess of Bolton had a tendency to talk over Tiffany. Even when a question was asked directly to her.

His mother wanted to get to know his bride, and it was difficult when his bride's mother was constantly speaking for her. But his mother also acknowledged that it was more important that *he* have the time with Tiffany than her. Besides, there would be plenty of time after the wedding for the two to bond.

While the wedding plans moved ahead apace, unfortunately, their attempts to discover who murdered their fathers did not. Nathan provided the letters he'd found to Sebastian, who had examined each of them carefully and found no sign that any attempt had been made to disguise their hands, unlike the letters Gregory had found. All the letters were signed, in fact, which made sense as the creditors would want their identities known so they could receive repayment.

Even the less-than-savory debt holders signed their notes.

None of them had even been close to the same handwriting as any of the notes Gregory's father had received.

Though the notes indicated anger at both of their fathers, as far as clues went, it was a disappointing dead end.

Gregory even gathered some handwriting samples from his half-sister's mothers and their husbands. It was easy to cross all of them off as suspects unless they'd had someone else write the letters for them. The best handwriting came from Maggie, the worst from Agatha's husband, John, who could barely do more than scrawl his name.

It did make him realize one important fact. Whoever had written the letters and been accomplished enough to disguise their handwriting while doing so was educated. Well educated. All the letters —including the ones that did not have disguised handwriting— were not only legible, but the handwriting was also well structured and practiced.

The letters Nathan's father had received ran the gamut in terms of skill, but not Gregory's. Perhaps it narrowed the pool... a bit. He hoped. At some point, he was going to need to interview the staff to see if any of them had any idea who might have sent the notes. He was not looking forward to the interviews. He liked most of them a good deal better than he had his father.

Lifting his chin, he gave his valet more room to tie his cravat. Redding was frowning in focused concentration, intent on doing one of the more complicated knots. Gregory wanted to look his best as the Boltons were coming over for a private, soon-to-be family dinner. It was the first time Tiffany would see the house she would soon be mistress of. His mother was already having the dowager house prepared, gleeful at handing off the duties she'd never enjoyed to her new daughter-in-law and decorating the smaller house to suit her own tastes without having to worry about anyone else's preferences.

Gregory expected an explosion of color and textures that would make his eyes water.

"That should do it, Your Grace." Redding nodded, stepping back so Gregory could look at himself in the mirror. He grinned.

Yes, he was dressed a tad formally for a family dinner, but he wanted to show how seriously he was taking this union. And... perhaps... because he wanted to impress Tiffany. Though she was attracted to him—of that much, he was certain—he did not have any particular talents that he was bringing to their marriage.

Granted, he had never before considered playing a musical instrument to be one of the attributes he would like in a bride, but hearing her play had changed his mind. For the first time, he'd understood why one might include such talent on a list. She'd been breathtaking.

Enough so that he'd had a rather delightful dream last night of her playing the harp while she was seated on his cock, his hands full of her breasts. He very much hoped it was a prophetic dream.

His navy coat was trimmed with gold, the sapphire blue jacket he was wearing boasted gold buttons, and he had a matching sapphire pin in his cravat. Redding had done a fine job with Gregory's hair, so it waved back away from his face, neatly framing his square jawline. He turned his head this way and that, the stiff points of his collar poking at said jawline as he admired himself.

"Thank you, Redding," he said, running his hand over his stomach, unnecessarily tugging at the jacket to straighten the fabric out, even though it was already perfectly smooth. His valet gave a satisfied bow and was about to turn away when Gregory's next words stopped him. "Redding... you have had some time to get to know my father's staff by now... have you heard from anyone who held particular rancor toward him?"

The other man hesitated. He was only a bit older than Gregory, and they had been together since Gregory left his father's household. He'd hired Redding after realizing that his former valet, provided by his father, was reporting Gregory's activities back to the duke. Redding had proven to be a devoted valet, accomplished in his skills and completely loyal to Gregory. He also tended to stand on ceremony more than Gregory did.

"I do not wish to speak ill of the dead, Your Grace," he said finally, "but it would be easier to give you a list of those who did not."

Wonderful.

His father had left behind an entire staff of people who may wish to do him harm. Gregory did not think it was any of the staff—most of them were not educated enough to produce the letters that had been sent to his father—but it had occurred to him that perhaps someone could have been convinced to act on behalf of the letter sender.

He was hoping Redding would be able to point him in a particular direction to start his questioning, but if his father had been that unpopular...

Gregory sighed. "A list of those who did not hold a grudge against my father would be appreciated."

At the very least, he could probably save them for last. Unless perhaps they would have a better idea of who held the most ill will toward his father. Good grief, why could this not be easier?

"Yes, Your Grace," Redding said with a bow, just as there was a knock at the door. Redding went to answer it to find a footman on the other side.

"Your guests have arrived, Your Grace," he said.

"Thank you." Gregory gave himself one last look in the mirror before leaving his room. The problem of his father's murder would have to wait. His wedding was the more pressing issue.

~

TIFFANY

Trying to be discreet, Tiffany looked all around her as Gregory's butler led them to a sitting room. Unfortunately, her mother caught her at it and reached out, pinching the soft skin on her upper arm, where it was covered by her sleeve.

"Do not gawk!" her mother hissed. "And try not to show your avarice so plainly."

What avarice?

Tiffany felt a kernel of anger like a pit in her belly. She had just been looking at the house she would soon be living in, and her mother assumed the worst of her. It was starting to feel like her mother always assumed the worst of her.

Her brother looked over his shoulder at them and smiled. She did not think he'd heard what their mother had said. Tiffany smiled back, thankful he was there with her. It felt as if ever since her engagement, she made more and more mistakes—at least in her mother's eyes. Sebastian had not seemed to notice her gaffes, or if he did, he did not think her missteps were as disgraceful as their mother did.

Last night, her mother had kept her up hours past when Tiffany usually went to sleep, lecturing her on the long list of things she had done wrong at the Manchester ball. Tiffany could not even remember what half of them were, and thankfully, they had been too busy today for her mother to quiz her on them.

At least tonight, it was no one but family. Surely, she could not commit too many horrible blunders.

The Duchess of Clarence was waiting for them in the sitting room. She straightened up with a smile on her face the moment they walked in, getting to her feet from the chaise where she had been sitting. It did not appear as if she had been doing anything other than waiting for them. Tonight, she wore a patterned damask dress, three feathers bobbing above her head to match the bright violet, sky blue, and bronze of her gown, and only one ruffle along the hem.

"Tiffany! And Susan and Sebastian, of course," the duchess said, rushing over to take Tiffany's hands and pull her down to kiss her cheeks. The duchess was a good deal shorter than Tiffany. She laughed as she turned to Tiffany's mother, who was standing stiffly beside Tiffany. "You must forgive me for not standing on ceremony, Susan, but as we are all to be family…"

"Of course," Tiffany's mother said, though her smile was strained as she took the duchess' hands and exchanged cheek kisses with her as well. Tiffany winced inwardly. Family or not, she could tell her mother was displeased at the Duchess of Clarence ignoring the proprieties of rank.

As Tiffany's mother and the current Duchess of Bolton, she should have been greeted before Tiffany.

"Come, come, please sit. Gregory should be joining us any moment." The Duchess of Clarence gestured at them after giving Sebastian a kiss on his cheek as well. He grinned down at her. Turning back to Tiffany, the duchess beamed. "Tiffany, I was hoping that perhaps you might play the harp for us after dinner. Things have been so hectic, I am afraid if I do not take advantage of you this evening, I may not get the chance again for weeks!"

"I will be happy to play for you any time," Tiffany responded truthfully, despite the disapproving look her mother shot her. She could almost hear her mother's voice in her head, accusing her of showing off. But she was not! The duchess, her soon-to-be mother-in-law, had made a request.

Likely, her mother would say that she should have found a way to politely decline so as not to appear too eager to draw attention to herself.

Right now, Tiffany did not care.

Except that she did, and a curl of fear was making her belly ache, but she remained resolute. Any time Gregory's mother wanted Tiffany to play for her, she would. She did not want to disrespect her own mother, but soon, she would be part of Gregory's household, and his mother's desires would take precedence.

And my mother will hardly be able to stand over me before I go to sleep, lecturing me on all my faults once I am part of Gregory's household.

Even if she had no kind of tender feelings toward him, that one benefit alone would have her eager to marry.

"Do you have a particular song you would like to hear?" she asked, feeling rather rebellious, avoiding her mother's gaze and focusing on Gregory's mother. If she did not see her mother glaring at her, she could pretend she did not know her mother disapproved. Her stomach dipped uneasily. Despite her pretense, she was all too aware of her mother's censure.

Her mother tittered, the sound sharp to Tiffany's ear.

"Tiffany does not mean to make it sound as though she could play *any* song anyone might request," her mother said.

Tiffany opened her mouth, then closed it. The truth was, there was not a song anyone could request that she could not at least make an attempt at. Including songs that were not originally meant for the harp. She liked to challenge herself by trying to learn them.

But her mother did not know that because her mother had never approved of how much time she spent practicing, even though she was the one who insisted Tiffany learn to play in the first place. Since she did not have the looks to set her apart from other young ladies, once her mother had realized she was accomplished at pianoforte and violin, she'd hired a flute and harp instructor as well to ensure that Tiffany had something the average debutante did not.

Tiffany loved to play any of her instruments, but the harp was her particular favorite because of how versatile it was.

"Oh, I am happy to listen to anything, though if you are of a mood to play the Bach again that Gregory heard..." The Duchess of Clarence let her voice trail off, smiling hopefully.

"I would like to hear that, too," Sebastian chimed in. "I missed it when I went to fetch you, and it has been ages since I heard you play."

"It would be my pleasure." Tiffany smiled back at Gregory's mother before sharing that smile with Sebastian. She was becoming used to the way the Duchess of Clarence was always looking at her with approval and warmth. It was just how the duchess was.

She wished her own mother was just a bit more like the Duchess of Clarence, even though it felt like a horrible betrayal to think such a thing. But she could feel the glare in her mother's eyes even as there was a smile upon her lips. Her mother was displeased with her.

Again.

"Good evening." Gregory strode into the room, and a knot in Tiffany's shoulders loosened as he walked toward her immediately, as if no one else was in the room. She smiled up at him, feeling better now that he was here. Strange, but true. "You look lovely tonight, my sweet."

"Thank you, Your Grace," she said, blushing hotly. She was wearing the mint dress. Again. Because he seemed to have liked that one.

Her mother sighed.

"It is just family this evening, Gregory. You do not need to keep up the pretense for us."

"Who says it is pretense?" he asked, and Tiffany blinked because it seemed like there was an edge to his voice. Had he just admonished her mother? "Tiffany, can I steal you away for a few minutes? I have something I would like to show you."

"Oh... I... yes." Tiffany got to her feet as her brother scowled.

"Perhaps I should come," Sebastian said, moving to stand.

"Oh, no, I have some particulars I would love your opinion on," Gregory's mother said. "You and your mother's. I promise you, they will not be left entirely to their own devices."

"Ah, yes, well then." Sebastian settled back into his chair with a peculiar expression on his face, obviously not having expected to be thwarted. Her mother's face was completely void of an expression, but she was sitting very stiffly.

Tiffany was happy to escape the room on Gregory's arm. If she was not near her mother then her mother could not comment on her behavior or her conversation.

EIGHTEEN

T*iffany*

Part of her wondered if Gregory might whisk her away to some private room to continue their activities from when he'd caught her off guard in her music room, but instead, he took her to the back of the house where light spilled out of a doorway, the sound of children's laughter traveling down the hall to where they approached. She glanced at him in curiosity.

"My half-sisters," he explained as they drew closer. "I wanted you to meet them before the wedding, and I do not know if there will be another chance, but... I was unsure if your mother would approve. And Sebastian can be a bit intimidating."

"Half-sisters... Oh... *oh!*" Of course. His half-sisters, born to his father's mistress. Mistresses?

Gentlemen of their rank were still expected to take care of any progeny they might produce outside of their marriage, but upon his father's death, Gregory would have inherited that duty along with his title. Though, not everyone took that duty seriously.

She was well aware of Gregory watching her, waiting for her reaction, and she smiled at him.

"I am delighted to be introduced to them," she said. After all, their birth was not their fault, and they sounded like bright, happy children. Tiffany loved children. Visiting the nearby village to the manor, she often took the opportunity to play with them when her mother was not with her.

Gregory relaxed, smiling back at her. "They will be delighted to meet you."

A statement that held true a few minutes later when Gregory brought her into the room. It was a large room filled with all sorts of things that might entertain young children, four little girls, four young women, and three men who were seated on the other side of the room. Tiffany blinked in surprise when she saw how young Gregory's half-sisters were.

Not only were they young, but their mothers were, too. The former duke had certainly not let his own age deter him from pursuing young women not much older than Tiffany. There was an air of tension that filled the room the moment she and Gregory appeared, though the children seemed unaffected. All of them turned to see Gregory, and their expressions lit up with happiness at seeing him.

The men got to their feet, going to stand with a young woman as she and Gregory walked in. The only young woman without a man beside her hung back, her head ducked down.

The duke had apparently preferred young women of the lower classes. Tiffany's gut clenched. She had spoken with their maids enough to know that working for nobility was not always a safe occupation for a woman. Sebastian did not harass the maids, and neither had Tiffany's father, but that was not always true.

And the maids often did not feel as though they could deny their employers advances.

Not just pursue… but had Gregory's father taken advantage of these young women?

That could be a reason for murder, a little voice whispered in her head, and she made a mental note to tell Astrid the next time she had the opportunity.

"These are my half-sisters," Gregory said, grinning as the youngest of them toddled over to him, lifting her arms up to be picked up. Dressed in a gown of pale yellow, she had a head of golden curls and big brown eyes that were currently full of demand. "This little imp is Priscilla."

"Gweg. Pwetty." She reached for his sapphire cravat pin.

"Uh-uh," he replied gently, putting his hand between her chubby fingers and the pin. "I have to look nice for dinner, Priss."

She huffed, making Tiffany giggle at her adorable scowl. Clearly, she did not enjoy being denied.

"Here, Priscilla, you should not bother the duke," one of the young women whispered, stepping forward to take the tot from Gregory's arms. He gave her over willingly.

"This is Betty, Priscilla's mother," he said, his voice gentling. Betty ducked her head. Tiffany could not have said what her eye color was because she never lifted her face high enough for Tiffany to be able to see, keeping her gaze cast downward, her own blonde hair falling forward to cover her face even more. She was afraid, Tiffany realized. A fact that obviously bothered Gregory, but he did not know what to do about it.

"It is a pleasure to meet you both," Tiffany said gently. She did not want to unnerve the poor woman any more than she already was.

Another little girl was already coming up to them, also lifting up her hands to be picked up. Another young woman came forward, clearly the mother, with the gentleman at her side. A big, burly fellow, he was the tallest in the room, and though he smiled, he also watched Gregory very closely.

Her fiancé did not seem at all perturbed by the man's scrutiny. Either he was used to it, he did not care, or some combination therein.

"Hello, Loretta," he said seriously to the very serious-looking child. She was not much older than Priscilla, by Tiffany's estimation, nor was she sunny or importuning. She studied Gregory closely before leaning forward to give him a tiny kiss on the cheek that just about melted Tiffany's heart.

"Hewwo, Gweg."

The combination of the inability to pronounce the 'r' in his name or the 'l' in 'hello' was going to be Tiffany's undoing. The way he clearly knew his sisters, adjusting his approach to both their personalities and their mothers' comfort, showed how much he cared.

He was going to be an amazing father.

Tiffany was introduced to Loretta and her mother, Rose, and her stepfather, John. The older two were Clara and Elizabeth, both adorable brunettes, a couple of years older than Loretta and Priscilla.

Clara's mother was introduced as Agatha; her stepfather was Peter. Elizabeth's mother was Maggie, and her stepfather was Andrew.

John was the gruffest of the three men, though he saved his suspicion and wariness for Gregory. Tiffany was greeted with a respectful bow.

Wondering if one of them could have been involved in her father's murder did put the damper on meeting them, but the little girls more than made up for it.

"Unfortunately, we do not have much time," Gregory said after the introductions. "But I wanted you all to meet Tiffany now, and I am sure we will find more time to spend together after the wedding." Tiffany felt a tug on her skirt and looked down to see that Priscilla had escaped her mother's arms and was now at Tiffany's side, lifting her arms to be picked up. She looked at Betty, and the young woman finally met her gaze with the same big brown eyes that her daughter had, though hers were fearful while Priscilla's were fearless.

Tiffany nodded her head down at Priscilla, and Betty nodded before ducking her head again. Smiling, heart heavy for the young mother, Tiffany bent down to pick up the little girl. She was a soft, warm weight in Tiffany's arms, her sunny smile widening as she was lifted up the way she wanted to be.

Putting one hand on either side of Tiffany's face, she looked intently into Tiffany's eyes.

"Pwetty," she said definitively.

"Yes, she is very pretty, is she not?" Gregory said, turning and grinning at his little sister.

Heaven help her, she was starting to believe it, though she did not know how to handle such a change in her life.

"Thank you," she said faintly. Priscilla giggled.

"Down." The tot made the demand with as much self-assurance as the queen. Tiffany was starting to wonder if perhaps she could learn a thing or two from Priscilla. She put the girl down, and she toddled off.

Straightening back up, Tiffany smiled around the room. Betty looked up long enough for their gazes to meet again before she ducked her head again. Everyone smiled back at her, even John.

"I am so glad I was able to meet all of you this evening." She was able to make that statement with absolute sincerity. In part because she felt like Gregory had shown that he truly trusted her and in part because she had enjoyed meeting them for themselves.

The girls were adorable. The ladies held themselves back, unsure of their position and how she might react to them, but they were now smiling with more assurance as well. Well, everyone but poor Betty. Tiffany was going to make it a special project to try to help the poor young woman get past the fear that was obviously burdening her. The gentlemen all bowed, and the ladies and the two older girls curtsied.

Gregory made an exasperated noise.

"How many times must I order you *not* to do that?"

"At least once more, Your Grace," Agatha said, with more than a hint of sass in her voice.

He shook his head but was grinning as he led Tiffany out of the room.

"Thank you for introducing them to me," she said as they walked back down the hall.

"Thank you for treating them as family," he replied.

She was glad to have met them and happy to treat them as family because they were, but she did have to wonder... would the son take after the father? One day, would her own son be introducing his bride to a collection of half-sisters?

The thought made her stomach hurt. She could not imagine how Gregory's mother must have felt... and she did not like to think that might one day be her fate.

~

Gregory

If he'd had any qualms about marrying Tiffany, tonight would have eradicated them. She'd been wonderful with his sisters and their parents. Betty had even looked up at her, and John had relaxed with her even faster than he had with Gregory's mother.

In some ways, introducing her to them tonight had been a kind of test. From his reading of her character, he'd thought it likely she would not turn up her nose at them like some of their set might, but now he knew for certain. Not only that, but he'd seen how quickly and easily she'd dealt with the surprise. Which was not a necessary attribute for a duchess to have, but things did arise unexpectedly.

Surprising her had also given him the true measure of her reaction, which had been nothing but welcoming and sweet. When she'd picked Priscilla up, for a shining moment, he'd seen a vision of her holding her own child in her arms... his child. Not something he would have ever thought he'd be eager to see, but that had all changed since becoming engaged to Tiffany.

When they returned to the others, it was clear to him that his mother was relieved to no longer be entertaining Sebastian and the Duchess of Bolton on her own. They decamped to the dining room immediately. As they were informal, Gregory kept Tiffany on his arm while Sebastian escorted the mothers.

"What did Gregory want to show you?" Sebastian asked Tiffany as they sat down. Gregory helped her into her seat as Sebastian did the Duchess of Bolton, then Gregory turned to assist his own mother.

"Some family matters," she replied serenely. "Did we miss anything important for the wedding planning?" Neatly answering the question, then turning the topic of conversation.

It made Sebastian scowl and Gregory grin. His mother brightened and immediately began recounting everything they had discussed, cutting off Sebastian's line of questioning completely.

Tiffany did not seem to have any objection to the plans the mothers were making—they had everything well handled from what Gregory knew. Though, admittedly, he had never been in charge of planning any large event, so he did not know much.

"You still need your dress, and Gregory has not mentioned where you will be honeymooning..." His mother turned to look at him over the fish course.

"We will be postponing the honeymoon 'til the end of the Season," Gregory said hastily. "I would not want to part Tiffany from Sebastian when he is in dire need of assistance."

"Assistance with what?" The Duchess of Bolton sat up straight.

"With finding a bride, of course." He smiled to take any sting out of his words since he had noticed how prickly the duchess could be. The truth was, he would have been happy to whisk Tiffany away, and Sebastian's needs be damned, but there was still the mystery of their fathers to solve. Abandoning his fellow dukes in the middle of such a mess, when his father was one of the only two who had received any threatening letters, would not do. "As a new duchess and so recently a debutante herself, they will reveal themselves to her in ways that they would not to a gentleman nor to ladies who are not of their generation."

The duchess sniffed, pressing her lips together. Gregory had the impression that she wanted to object but could not find a flaw in his logic since it was completely true. Tiffany was in the best position to help Sebastian.

His friend glanced at him from across the table, a silent message passing between them. Sebastian knew what he was on about.

"I appreciate you making the sacrifice," Sebastian said dryly.

"Oh, not to worry, old chap, we will still be off at the end of the Season. I was thinking France or Germany. Depending on what my lovely bride prefers."

"Either sounds wonderful," she replied, brightening.

"Tiffany will be happy to go wherever her husband desires, like a good duchess," Tiffany's mother said, giving her daughter a pointed look, even though Tiffany had already said as much.

His own mother stiffened, dropping her gaze down to her plate. Gregory's father had desired her to be in the country and stay there. He moved her around like a pawn on a chessboard. Gregory knew that was not what the Duchess of Bolton meant, but his chest tightened in reaction, the old anger flaring up again. It did not help that there was something in the duchess' voice that reminded him of the way his father had spoken to his mother when admonishing her in front of company.

"Her husband would like to hear her preferences as well," he said rather sharply. The duchess widened her eyes, immediately making him feel guilty. He had not meant to snap at her. "My apologies, Your Grace. I do not like to think of myself as a tyrant in our marriage."

"My apologies as well, Your Grace," she replied just as formally, appearing chagrined. "I certainly did not mean any insult toward you."

"I truly am happy with either location," Tiffany said earnestly, turning to him and putting her fingers on the back of his hand to draw his attention to her. "I have always wanted to travel."

"Then perhaps we shall do both."

The awkward moment passed, along with the rest of the dinner, with far more lively conversation. Tiffany invited his mother to come to the modiste for her wedding gown, which made his mother so happy, he was almost surprised she did not jump up and hug Tiffany right then and there. Although his bride-to-be was rather shy with his mother, more so than she was with him, she was making the effort, and he knew his mother would reward that heftily.

As their dinner finished, there was a knock on the dining room door, and Montblanc let himself in, a folio in his hands and an apologetic expression on his face. The steward looked almost pained as he entered the room. He glanced around, paling when he saw the caliber of guests seated at the table he had dared intrude upon.

"I apologize for the interruption, Your Grace, but I need to speak with you immediately. I will be on my way immediately after."

"Oh no, Montblanc, we are going to listen to Lady Tiffany play the harp after dinner. I know how you enjoy harp music. You must join us," Gregory's mother said, interjecting.

Montblanc blinked rapidly. "I, ah..."

"Yes, you can round out our numbers," Gregory said as he got to his feet. "Unless what you are bringing me means that you must rush off?"

"Well... no." Montblanc appeared flummoxed. "But... Your Grace... I am hardly..."

He was hardly of a rank to join two dukes, two duchesses, and one soon-to-be duchess in musical entertainment, but Gregory saw no harm in it since they were being informal this evening. Indeed, it would mean that Montblanc could escort Gregory's mother rather than leave Sebastian with double duty. And Montblanc and his mother always got along well.

Obviously, he would not have Montblanc escort the Duchess of Bolton—she was far too much of a high stickler to take that as anything but an insult.

"You can escort my mother, so I can tend properly to my fiancé," he said with a smile.

Montblanc rallied, straightening.

"Thank you, Your Grace, any way that I can be of assistance."

They stepped outside so Montblanc could show Gregory some of the discrepancies he'd found in a bill that needed to be settled on the morrow, which explained his desire for haste. Montblanc abhorred being late with anything.

Then, they returned to the others and escorted them to the music room. His mother was happy to have Montblanc's arm, Gregory was able to focus on Tiffany and her glorious music, and if Tiffany's mother was a bit stiff about having a mere steward join their part, well, that was Sebastian's problem.

NINETEEN

Tiffany

Despite what Lady Tremaine had said about blues and greens and Tiffany's coloring, Tiffany's mother seemed determined that everything about her wedding should be yellow, cream, and gold. As the Duchess of Clarence had been thrilled at the idea of such 'bright' spring colors, Tiffany could hardly gainsay her mother.

Not that she would have dared, anyway.

Arriving at Bruton Street, she went into the dressmakers with the two mothers, already resigned to wearing whatever her own mother might choose for her. Lady Tremaine and Lady Louisa were there waiting for them so they could choose the fabric for Lady Louisa's gown as well.

Luckily for Louisa, she looked rather well in multiple shades of yellow.

"Madame Allard will be with you momentarily," the modiste's assistant said after greeting their little crowd.

"Ooh, mama, what about this one?" Louisa asked, tapping her

finger against one of the bolts of fabric on display. It was a gauzy pastel yellow, decorated with embroidery. Immediately, Lady Tremaine and Tiffany's mother converged on her, cooing over how pretty she would look.

"Have you thought about what color you would like to wear?" The Duchess of Clarence nearly made Tiffany jump out of her skin. She had not realized the petite woman was beside her. The older woman moved very quietly when she wanted to, not drawing attention to herself, despite the brightness of her pink and green striped dress with the panels of ruffles in the same fabric going down either side of her skirt.

"White, I presume," she said with a bit of trepidation. It was hard enough not to spill anything on a gown with color on it; white was going to be a particular trial.

"Ah, yes, the queen did set a bit of a fashion, did she not?" The duchess shook her head, leaning in to whisper to Tiffany as if revealing a dire secret. "I must confess, I miss the days when one could be more colorful at their wedding ceremony."

Tiffany could not help but laugh, because she rather thought the duchess would be happy if all the fashions tended toward bright colors. Unfortunately, her laughter drew her mother's attention back to her, away from Lady Louisa. She felt the sharp glare, the hint of a downturned lip, like a cut against her amusement.

Too loud. Too boisterous. Too something.

Whatever it was, she knew she would hear the lecture later.

Thankfully, her mother did not have the opportunity to begin such a lecture now, as the curtain to the back of the shop was pulled back, and Madame Allard escorted a beautiful woman with mahogany brown hair and startlingly light amber eyes out from the room there. Now, there was a woman who looked well in yellow. She was older than Tiffany, perhaps in her late twenties, and had an enviable amount of confidence in her stance. Her dress was a deep, rich yellow, like the leaves in the fall, trimmed with black. A large yellow topaz pin set in gold decorated her hat, holding a length of shimmering yellow ribbon in place against the black headpiece.

The woman's golden gaze swept around the room, taking in all of them, and she gave the mothers a deferential nod. Tiffany's mother barely nodded back, though Gregory's mother smiled and nodded at her. Lady Tremaine's acknowledgment fell somewhere in between the two.

"*Merci*, Baroness," Madame Allard said, escorting the woman to the door. "The gown will be ready for you in three days."

"Perfect. Thank you, Madame Allard." The baroness had a throaty voice, the kind that Tiffany had always wanted. Just hearing her made Tiffany feel positively squeaky.

Louisa sidled up to Tiffany's side, surprising her by leaning in to whisper in Tiffany's ear as the baroness went out the door.

"Did you hear? She was the Duke of Grafton's mistress, but now that he is looking for a bride, they have parted ways. They say she is looking for a new lover and that instead of properly searching for a wife, he's been glaring at any man who dares speak to her." Lady Louisa sounded thrilled, and she was not looking at Tiffany, thankfully, because Tiffany did not know how to respond.

She'd overheard gossip at several of the events she'd been to this Season, but she'd never had any come to her to share gossip. Responding to gossip was certainly not a conversational skill her mother had ever tested her on.

"The duke is friends with your brother, is he not?" Louisa turned to look at Tiffany now, an eager expression on her face. "Do you know if it is true that Grafton is in love with her?"

"I... do not know." It was the truth. "Sebastian would not talk about his friend's mistress with me."

"Oh." Louisa sighed with disappointment.

"Louisa, come here and speak with Madame." Lady Tremaine called her daughter over to where Madame Allard had now joined the mothers, leaving Tiffany alone.

Her chest felt strangely tight again. It was true—Sebastian

would not talk about his friend's mistresses with her. It would be wildly inappropriate. Though Tiffany understood that gentlemen had mistresses, women they sought love and pleasure from outside of their marriages, no one was supposed to actually speak of such things to a debutante.

Which meant if Gregory had a recent mistress or if he had one right now, Sebastian would not tell her.

Her stomach flipped over before she remembered that Lady Louisa likely would take great pleasure in telling Tiffany if Gregory currently had a mistress. She had not been gossiping with Tiffany to be friendly; she had been doing so because she hoped Tiffany knew something.

The hard knot in Tiffany's stomach relaxed a bit.

Why the idea bothered her, she could not say. Plenty of gentlemen had mistresses. It was a way of life for their set. And Gregory was a rake. She could hardly expect to keep him to herself.

Putting her hand on her stomach, she breathed through the unhappiness that swirled in her belly, a technique she'd perfected over the years. Pushing down the emotions, she took one deep breath after another until she was calm again, the uneasiness in her center squashed into insignificance.

"Tiffany, stop daydreaming and come here," her mother called out, beckoning to her as Lady Tremaine and Lady Louisa went into the backroom with Madame Allard, carrying the fabric that Louisa had picked. Her mother held up a creamy bolt of fabric. "I want to see how this would look on you."

"Yes, mother." Tiffany sighed inwardly and dutifully moved across the room to let her mother hold the fabric up to her. Beside her mother, the Duchess of Clarence frowned.

"That might work," Tiffany's mother said.

"It is nice," the Duchess of Clarence agreed, though her tone of voice did not entirely match her words. "Perhaps something whiter instead of cream?"

"Perhaps." Tiffany's mother bristled, looking down her nose at

Gregory's mother. "I *have* been dressing my daughter her entire life. I think a cream will be best."

Thus began the most uncomfortable half hour of Tiffany's life as her mother and Gregory's mother disagreed again and again. The worst part was hoping that Gregory's mother would win. Despite her own clear preference for reds and rusts and oranges and yellows, the Duchess of Clarence suggested blues, greens, and purples for Tiffany.

Her own mother dug in her heels on all of them, in the politest manner possible.

By the time Lady Tremaine and Lady Louisa emerged from the back room, the duchesses were glaring at each other and speaking through gritted teeth. Tiffany had no idea what to do and was reduced to silently wringing her hands. To take her mother's side was to alienate her future mother-in-law; to take the Duchess of Clarence's side was to betray her mother.

"I will get her the blue as a gift," the Duchess of Clarence said, lifting her chin up. "It need not be part of her trousseau."

"Well." Tiffany's mother seemed at a loss for words as she was outmaneuvered by her fellow duchess.

"Thank you," Tiffany said quietly to the duchess, hoping to break some of the tension. "That is very thoughtful of you."

"Oh, yes, that is a beautiful blue," Lady Tremaine said, coming forward to inspect the bolt the Duchess of Clarence had chosen. "It will be lovely on you, Tiffany. Such a wonderful gift, Marguerite."

"Then that is what I will do," the duchess said, shooting a look of challenge at Tiffany's mother, who had suddenly become very interested in the array of bronze fabrics beside her. She missed the look entirely, though Lady Tremaine caught it and appeared confused.

There was no explanation, however, as Tiffany was hustled into the back room along with the two mothers. She was rather disappointed that Lady Tremaine and Lady Louisa opted to go to the milliner next door rather than staying for her fitting. Of course, it would have been a very tight squeeze to have all the women in the back room, but she had hoped that Lady Tremaine might lend the Duchess of Clarence some support.

Up on the pedestal, fabrics were draped and hung around Tiffany. As usual, Madame Allard and Tiffany's mother carried on the discussion. Despite what Tiffany's mother had said to Lady Tremaine previously, the fabrics that she was having the assistant fetch for Tiffany's trousseau were all her usual colors and shades.

"Mother," Tiffany said hesitantly after the fifth dress had been added to the tally. "You said I could have some blues and greens, too." The blue bolt the Duchess of Clarence had chosen was stunning, but Tiffany had seen another that she hoped to look at...

The duchess' insistence on a blue and Lady Tremaine's comments had given her unusual courage.

"Do not be greedy, Tiffany," her mother said sharply. Beside her, the Duchess of Clarence stirred. Her mother sighed, putting her fingers to her temple as if signaling yet another megrim. "I suppose we can add one or two... yes, one of each. One green and one blue."

It was more than Tiffany could have hoped for.

"Come, Bridgit," Tiffany's mother said, gesturing at the assistant. "I will show you the ones I want."

Bridgit drew back the curtain for her and Tiffany's mother to return to the front just as the shop's door opened, and Lady Tremaine and Lady Louisa returned, followed by Lady Astrid and a maid.

"Susan! You must come next door; they have the perfect hat for you, but I saw Lady Greywood eyeing it. You must come at once."

"Oh, well..." Tiffany's mother halted. "We are still working on Tiffany's trousseau..." But from her voice, it was clear she wanted to go see the hat Lady Tremaine was so excited about.

"You must be almost finished. Duchess Clarence can help her. Would you mind, Marguerite?" Lady Tremaine asked.

"I would be delighted," Gregory's mother replied, jumping to her feet from where she'd been sitting and coming forward. "Having no daughter of my own, I am thoroughly enjoying assisting Tiffany."

"Well… she still needs to try on her gown for the engagement ball tonight…" Tiffany's mother was hedging, obviously not wanting to leave the modistes before their trip had finished.

"If Lady Greywood purchases the hat, you will be devastated when you see her wearing it, I promise you." Lady Tremaine shook her head.

"I am happy to assist as well," Lady Astrid said. "As Tiffany and I will be duchesses together, I should like to get to know her better. Do go on, Duchess Bolton. I am sure you do not want to miss this hat. It truly is quite splendid."

There was something sardonic to the way she said the words, and it was a clear order… yet Tiffany's mother did not protest. Instead, she allowed Lady Tremaine and her daughter to usher her out of the modiste, though she did not seem entirely happy about it.

"My goodness," Lady Astrid said, walking into the backroom after pointing her maid to a seat in the front. She frowned as she looked at the fabrics around them. "What is all this?"

"My trousseau," Tiffany said with a sigh. She gestured at the cream-colored bolt that had been set off to the side. "And my wedding gown."

"Absolutely not." Lady Astrid turned to Madame Allard, hands on her hips. "I am shocked you allowed this. You assured me that you never allow a woman to purchase a gown that will not flatter her. Did you do all of Lady Tiffany's gowns for this Season?"

The modiste had a slight look of panic on her face as she waved her hands in front of her.

"Lady Astrid… I could not deny a duchess. Duchess Bolton was very specific in her requirements for Lady Tiffany's gowns."

Her frown deepening, Lady Astrid stepped forward and tugged at the fabric draped over Tiffany's form and took her first good look at her undergarments.

"What is that?"

"I was wondering that as well," Gregory's mother admitted.

"The Duchess of Bolton was very specific—" Madame Allard

started to say tremulously before Lady Astrid whirled around and pinned her with a look.

"I am now going to be very specific because Lady Tiffany is going to be the Duchess of Clarence, and if you do not do exactly as I say, you are going to experience the displeasure of three duchesses, not one."

The flurry of activity that Lady Astrid's barking orders propelled was a rush of fabrics, ribbons, and obsequious compliments from Madame Allard. The fabrics Tiffany's mother had picked out were discarded, including the cream for Tiffany's wedding gown. There was no hemming and hawing by Lady Astrid.

She asked Tiffany a single question.

"You need a signature color. Blue or green?"

"Blue," Tiffany replied faintly.

And that was enough. Within ten minutes, all the fabrics Tiffany's mother had chosen had been replaced at Lady Astrid's direction, with the Duchess of Clarence's rather gleeful encouragement. New bolts were chosen, new designs picked out of a book, and new undergarments ordered.

Tiffany was unsure, nervy over her mother's likely reaction, but she knew that she was tired of yellow. She was tired of orange. She liked blue. She wanted blue. And by the time her mother saw the gowns, she would hopefully already be in Clarence House.

So, when Lady Astrid picked out an icy blue, so light in hue it was nearly white, for her wedding gown, Tiffany nodded.

Her heart was pounding near out of her chest, but things moved so quickly—including trying on her engagement ball gown and the demands Lady Astrid made for changes to it—she did not have time to grow fearful or change her mind.

Neither did she have time to consider the implications of Madame Allard's words until after they'd left the shop.

Her mother had given the modiste particular direction on how to dress Tiffany. The style, the colors... and the modiste had not denied Lady Astrid's accusation that Tiffany's gowns had not been flattering on her. Yet they had been created to her mother's strict specifications.

Which begged the question... had her mother purposefully chosen the styles and colors to be unflattering on her?

If she had, why had she done that to her own daughter?

And did Tiffany really want to know the answer?

TWENTY

Gregory

Delicately questioning his staff was an exercise in frustration. He did not want to cause turmoil among them, which meant he could hardly go around demanding they inform him of anyone who might have had ill will against his father. It would cause an uproar within the household.

But, of course, discreetly questioning them when he was a duke was rather difficult since he did not normally interact with any of them. Certainly not for casual conversation.

Finally, he summoned Montblanc, Paulson, and Mrs. Bryant to him. Assistance was required, and they were his intermediaries to the understairs staff. More Paulson and Mrs. Bryant, of course, but Montblanc had worked with his father for the past five years and knew those outside the house his father interacted with as well as some of the understairs staff.

Truthfully, he should have gone to them initially, but his inclination had been to keep things close. Just as how he had not admitted anything to the other dukes at first.

Still, all of them were loyal to him; he was certain of that.

All three were horrified by the revelation that the previous duke had been murdered, however they personally felt about him. Mrs. Bryant audibly gasped while both Montblanc and Paulson went pale. Thankfully, Paulson was quick thinking enough to hastily pull a chair over for Mrs. Bryant to sit in as her stance wavered. She looked up at him with a weak smile of gratitude.

"I cannot question each member of the household, not without raising alarms I would rather not have raised," he explained. He looked at Montblanc. The other man had taken out a handkerchief and was dabbing at his hairline where droplets of sweat had gathered. "And you can speak with others in my father's employ. I am sure you have all heard complaints about him at one time or another."

The three glanced at each other, then away.

Mrs. Bryant's lips tightened.

"One should not speak ill of the dead," she murmured.

"One should not have so much ill to speak of," Paulson muttered back, then coughed, looking ashamed as the others in the room all focused on him. He met Gregory's gaze. "My apologies, Your Grace. I..." He floundered, and Gregory took pity on him.

"Thank you, Paulson. I am well aware of my father's shortcomings." Gregory grimaced. "There is quite a bit of ill that I could speak of myself, but my concern is for the living. As Lady Tiffany and I will shortly be married, I would like to reassure myself that neither myself, she, nor any children we have are in danger from whoever was willing to cause the death of eight dukes. Possibly nine."

"Northumberland," Montblanc whispered, putting his hand to his heart. "Surely not..."

"I cannot ignore that he died shortly after his father. In which case, it could be that his heir was involved... but it could also be a horrible coincidence, and only our fathers were targets. As we said, there was much ill about my father to speak of." Gregory sighed. "But murder is murder, and he was not the only one lost. Until we know why the dukes were targeted, none of us can feel assured of our safety or the safety of our families. Discovering the 'why' requires discovering the 'who'."

"Goodness," Mrs. Bryant muttered, fanning herself with her hand. "To think... No, it is too horrible to think. We must do everything to protect Your Grace, as well as Lady Tiffany and your future children."

"Your Grace, I do not mean to be indelicate, but who *is* your heir?" Paulson asked anxiously. "What should I do if he comes to the door?" Ah, his butler was concerned about letting a possible murderer into the house. Very understandable.

"I have to ask Mother." Gregory winced as they all looked at him in surprise. Yes, he likely should have known, but he had been a bit busy, taking over the duchy long before he'd anticipated the need to, setting up his half-sisters to make up for his father's neglect, Sinclair's death and funeral, then needing to find a bride, and all while trying to run the damn duchy that he'd inherited. "The family tree is rather sparse. It will be some cousin or such. I am sure Mother will know."

After all, she'd been going through the family tree to send out wedding invitations.

"Does she know..." Montblanc started to ask, his voice trailing off.

"She believes my father died in a tragic accident, and I would not like to disillusion her," Gregory said firmly. All three of them nodded, appearing relieved. "That it was murder should be kept as quiet as possible. Thus far, the murderer likely thinks he has gotten away with it. I do not want to alert him to the fact that we are aware of his crime, much less investigating."

Gregory said 'he', though he supposed it could be a 'she', but the sheer violence of the way the dukes had died made him think it must be a man.

"Very good, Your Grace," Paulson said with a bow. Mrs. Bryant and Montblanc echoed the sentiment as Mrs. Bryant got to her feet. "We will help assure you and your duchess of your safety."

"Thank you. Anything you find at all suspicious, report back to me immediately. Or as soon as possible," he amended. "After all, I am in the middle of planning a wedding." An event that was quickly approaching, yet not quick enough for him.

He found that he was rather impatient to have Tiffany under his roof and to himself. Parading about in front of the *ton* was an exercise in patience. He was very much looking forward to spending more time with her, both in and out of bed, which was a rather surprising revelation to have. In the bedroom would not have been surprising once he found out that she was passably pretty, but out of it?

Sebastian had been as blind to her charm and her intellect as much as he had been to her beauty. Gregory was sure he was not only going to tolerate his bride, but he actually liked her. He certainly felt protective of her.

He looked at the steward.

"Montblanc, can you stay for a moment longer? I wanted to speak to you about my sisters—" The steward had been the one to help him set his sisters up and had spent the most time with them and their families, but his conversation with Montblanc was going to have to wait because a commotion out in the hall had all of them turning their heads in alarm.

"Gregory!" The door burst open, and his mother came to an abrupt halt as Mrs. Bryant dropped into a curtsy, and the two men bowed, her cheeks coloring as she realized that he was not alone and that she was making a scene. She immediately dropped the volume of her voice to a speaking tone. "Gregory, I need to speak with you."

"Of course." He looked at the others. "Montblanc, we'll speak tomorrow."

"Yes, Your Grace." He dabbed at his brow again, turning to follow the others out the door, dipping his head in acknowledgment as he passed by the duchess. Turning, he shut the door behind them to give Gregory and his mother some privacy.

"What is wrong, Mother?" he asked, bewildered as to what could have put her in such a tizzy as the dressmaker's.

"That woman!" She actually stomped her foot as she said it, her hands clenching and unclenching by her sides. "That poor girl… I do not know how she has turned out as well as she has with that harridan for a mother!"

Gregory blinked, as his mother was speaking without any context, though it did not take him more than a moment to come to the proper conclusion. Part of his confusion was because he had never heard his mother speak so about anyone.

"The Duchess of Bolton?" he asked, just to be sure he understood.

"Yes." His mother shook her head, starting to pace as if to rid herself of excess energy. Gregory had never seen her like this before, not even when dealing with his father. "That woman is a bully! She did not let Tiffany pick one thing for her trousseau. The poor child looks terrible in those colors she insists on dressing her in. I had to offer to buy her a blue dress, which is a color she actually likes!"

"Who likes blue?" He was losing the thread of his mother's rant again.

"Tiffany! And she looks much better in blue than those oranges or yellows her shrew of a mother insists on."

"Mother!" Gregory was both aghast and slightly amused at his mother's vehemence.

"Well, she is a shrew," she huffed, coming to a halt and crossing her arms over her chest.

It must have been quite a scene at the shop to set his mother off like this. After living with his father for so many years, she could be very sensitive to anyone telling another person how to dress. Tiffany's mother was a very different kind of person than his own, so perhaps he should not be so surprised they were not getting along. The Duchess of Bolton had very strong opinions, which she obviously used to make the choices for her daughter's life, as was her right.

"As her mother, I am sure she is just choosing the colors she thinks are best," he said soothingly, walking forward to wrap his mother in a reassuring hug. Perhaps he should not have been surprised that something like clothing would make his mother react so badly. "Once she's my wife, Tiffany can choose whatever color dresses she likes, and I will replace her entire trousseau if necessary."

"Well, thankfully, it will not be necessary." His mother sniffed, breaking apart from him, her dander obviously still up. "Her mother departed to look at a hat... *a hat* of all things. If I were not so grateful that it gave Lady Astrid and me the opportunity to set things right, I would have been incensed over her choosing a hat over her own daughter, for goodness' sake."

"Lady Astrid was there?" Drake's fiancé and his coming together in friendship. Gregory was rather pleased to hear it. Lady Astrid would be a good influence on Tiffany, he was sure. After all, she had been raised to be Drake's duchess.

"Yes, and she agreed with me wholeheartedly." His mother shot him a narrow-eyed look, and he held up his hands in a gesture of surrender. Far be it from him to get involved in any kind of fashion debate between the females. "Thankfully, while Tiffany's mother was buying her *hat*, we were able to talk the modiste into some sense, and Tiffany will have a trousseau and wedding gown worthy of her."

"Then I look forward to seeing it," he said placatingly. Something about his tone must have alerted his mother that he was not taking this as seriously as she wanted him to.

"You *will* see," she muttered, turning on her heel and stalking out of the room. If nothing else, having a daughter-in-law to focus on was certainly giving his mother something to invest her energy in, which he was glad to see. Hopefully, that would continue to keep her occupied while he hunted down whoever had murdered his father.

TIFFANY

Smoothing her hands over her engagement ball dress, which had been delivered a mere hour before, Tiffany stared at herself in the mirror.

It had been too late to change the style, much to Lady Astrid's displeasure, or the main color, which was a rather sickly looking yellowish-green, but the trim had been replaced with blue lace in several layers so that the chartreuse was not directly against Tiffany's skin. A matching lace ruffle was wrapped around her throat, like a necklace, the fabric hugging her skin.

She'd never had a dress that she liked so much. Though she would have preferred a less bold color of green, less bright, less yellow, it was at least green. And the blue ruffle made all the difference. Her skin looked creamier. Not so sallow. Her brown eyes appeared darker, richer. Her hair even looked better somehow, though Tiffany could not pinpoint the difference.

She looked almost pretty.

Reaching up, she pressed her fingertips against her cheek. The figure in the mirror did the same.

It was really her.

"The blue really sets you off, my lady," Sarah, the maid assigned to assist Tiffany this evening, said. Harleen was helping Tiffany's mother. Originally, Tiffany had thought Harleen would help her as well, but her mother had claimed she needed Harleen to herself exclusively. She'd been in such a temperament since the modiste, Tiffany had not dared request that Harleen attend her if there was time. Especially knowing how upset her mother was likely to be when she realized that all the instructions she had given for Tiffany's trousseau and wedding gown had been countermanded by the Duchess of Clarence and Lady Astrid.

Her mother did not like to be opposed.

"Do you think so?" Tiffany asked, twisting in front of the mirror to try to see her back as well. She wanted to look nice for the engagement ball.

"I do. Suits you much better than... well." Sarah coughed to cover the criticism she was about to utter, though Tiffany did not mind. "I never understood why her grace insisted on the colors she put you in. They dinna do anything for your complexion, always made you look a mite sickly, I thought. This green is bright too, but the blue... the blue makes it work."

"I think so, too." Tiffany stared at herself in the mirror. Astrid had said she needed a signature color.

Blue it was.

The knock at the door had her stiffening up, then relaxing when it was revealed to be Sebastian rather than her mother. The idea of facing her mother in the altered dress, even though they had done nothing more than add a few ruffles, nearly made her want to run and hide in the attic.

"Bloody hell..." Sebastian stared at her from the doorway. The green of his coat was much darker than her dress, but it gave her some consolation that they were dressed in the same color, if not the same shade. "Tiffany, you look..."

Her nerves rose up again.

"Bad? Good? Presentable?" She smoothed her hands down over her skirts, trying not to squirm in place as Sebastian continued to stare at her.

"Lovely," he replied firmly. "I really was blind to how pretty you have grown. I think you should wear blue more often. It looks quite well on you."

Relief flooded through her. If even Sebastian thought the difference was enough to comment on, she knew that she had made the correct decision in allowing Lady Astrid to alter the dress.

Stepping back through the door, Sebastian turned, offering up his arm.

"Come along, sister. Your fiancé and his mother await."

"And our mother?" she asked, moving to take his arm.

"Overseeing some last-minute touches on the ballroom, though it is very likely she will beat us to meet Gregory and the duchess in the foyer." He grinned down at her. "It should be quite the gathering."

Tiffany dug in her heels, grinding them to a halt in the middle of the hallway. Sebastian stopped with her, obviously startled.

"Sebastian... I... does Gregory have a mistress?" She blurted the words out before she could lose her courage.

"What? Tiffany, that is not an appropriate—" Sebastian was hissing the words at her, his face turning bright red in embarrassment.

Turning toward him, she put her other hand on his arm, digging her fingers in as she looked up at him imploringly.

"I do not care if it is not an appropriate topic of conversation, Sebastian. I am going to be marrying him. I just want to know what to prepare myself for. He... he introduced me to his half-sisters. That was why he whisked me away from the rest of you at Clarence House."

Sebastian let out a long, slow breath.

"I see." He said shortly. Then he sighed. "To my knowledge, Gregory has never had a mistress."

"But... he is a rake."

Sebastian scrubbed his hand over his face, obviously unhappy with the entirety of this conversation.

"A mistress is long term. Gregory's... partners are not." The pained expression on Sebastian's face would have been amusing under other circumstances.

"Does he have a lover right now?"

"Tiffany!"

"Sebastian!" She glared at him, and he huffed.

"No. And I told him that he is to make you happy. That means discretion. If he does ever embarrass you, I will pound him." Sebastian groaned. "Can we please stop talking about this now?"

Though she did not feel all that much better, Tiffany nodded. At least she knew that Gregory did not have some long-time love he was pining for. From what Sebastian was saying, Gregory had rakish conquests. Not lovers.

She did not know if that made it better or worse, but at least now she knew.

"Yes, let us go and meet them."

They walked in silence the last bit of the way to the top of the staircase. Voices drifted up from the foyer. Her mother speaking with Gregory and his mother. They were all down there.

Tiffany and Sebastian stepped up to the top of the staircase, and she looked down, instinctively looking to Gregory for his reaction to seeing her. Dressed in a navy superfine jacket with a gold and blue patterned waistcoat, his hair brushed back from his head, he looked almost unbearably handsome. His mouth parted slightly as he stared up at her in wonderment, blinking rapidly before refocusing, as if he were having trouble believing it was her that he was seeing. Warmth, interest, and delight filled his eyes and his expression, his lips curving up in appreciation.

Butterflies burst into flight in her stomach, but in a good way. A way that made her feel tingly and excited. Her heart pattered faster in her chest.

Her own smile lifted in response.

Then she looked at her mother and saw nothing but rage on her mother's face.

CHAPTER
TWENTY-ONE

Tiffany

"See?" Sebastian whispered in her ear, pulling Tiffany's attention away from her mother. She dropped her gaze, shifting it as he spoke to Gregory. "You look wonderful. Gregory looks like a carp just pulled from the water."

With the way his mouth was partway open, Gregory did indeed resemble a fish on land. He moved to the bottom of the staircase to meet them as Sebastian led her down. She was nearly at the bottom step when she risked a peek at her mother again. The rage she'd seen before was so completely absent, she began to question whether she'd seen it at all.

But there was still a fierce frown of disapproval on her mother's lips.

"That is not the dress I ordered," she said, her tone cold and unhappy as Tiffany and Sebastian reached the bottom of the stairs. Recognizing the tone, Tiffany immediately moved to placate her mother.

"It is, but Lady Astrid suggested a blue ruffle be added earlier today, and Madame Allard assured us that adding the decoration would be of no concern," Tiffany said earnestly. Her mother had told her at the beginning of the Season that Lady Astrid was the epitome of fashion. Surely, knowing it had been Lady Astrid's idea would help reconcile her mother to the change.

"It is inspired," Sebastian said, smiling approvingly at Tiffany, which took some of the sting out of her mother's obvious disapproval. He shot their mother a curious look. "With me in green and Gregory in blue this evening, we could not have planned our attire better. You represent a mix of both households."

He spoke true, though the mothers were not in either color. Her mother was wearing a very dark burgundy, while the Duchess of Clarence wore a very similar apricot color to the dress Tiffany had worn for her ride through Hyde Park with Gregory.

"I am very happy with how the blue looks," the Duchess of Clarence said, stepping forward and holding out her hands for Tiffany to take. She released Sebastian's arm to do so and exchanged air kisses with the duchess. The older woman gave her hands a brief squeeze before she released them, which heartened Tiffany. "I funded the alteration if that is the concern."

Now, Tiffany was sure she saw a flash of fury on her mother's face before she hid it, obviously outraged at the implication that perhaps the Bolton household could not afford a mere ruffle.

"It is of no concern," her mother said with a wave of her hand. "I was merely startled. I know what I ordered, after all, and since I was not informed of any alterations, the result was unexpected."

"Delightfully unexpected," Gregory said, finally stepping forward to claim her hand. He bowed over it, giving her a kiss on the back of her gloved hand but also a wink as he straightened. "You look beautiful."

As always, he sounded as though he meant it.

Such attention would turn any young lady's head.

It certainly did hers. They were with family, though. Not in public. There was no need for pretense. They were not a true love match. Which meant this was what Gregory was like with any young lady. Charming. Flirtatious. Sigh-inducing. She needed to remember he had kissed her in the library without even knowing who she was, merely because he thought her pretty.

Tiffany smiled at him, steeling herself against her natural reaction to him. She needed to remember that she could be any woman to him, and he would treat her the same.

"I am especially glad for the blue, because I have an engagement present for you." He slid his hand into his coat and pulled out a box. "Mother and I went through the family jewels this afternoon, and she helped me pick this to bring for you to wear tonight... now I understand why."

Curious, Tiffany took the box from him. She gasped when she opened it and saw the dazzling blue and white stones set in gold and arranged on the velvet lining inside. *Sapphires and diamonds*, her mind provided dizzily. A king's ransom worth.

She was utterly dazzled and utterly intimidated. She had never worn such an array of jewels before. Though the Boltons had their own family jewels, those were reserved for her mother to wear.

Not Tiffany.

Yet here was Gregory's mother, sharing the family jewels with her when they were not even married yet. The gesture of welcome was so moving, tears sparked in her eyes. She pushed them back so as not to ruin her complexion if she started weeping.

"They're beautiful."

"Put them on her, dear. I want to see how they look." The Duchess of Clarence appeared almost giddy. From the way she was standing and how Sebastian had crowded around her other side to see, Tiffany was unable to look at her mother to see her reaction, to see if her mother approved... and the inability brought her both relief and consternation.

It also meant she had nothing to distract her as Gregory stepped behind her, so close to her that his legs brushed her skirts as he replaced the ruffle around her throat with the sapphire necklace, heavy and cool against her skin, unlike his warm breath which wafted over the same area. The combination made her feel rather faint before he finally stepped away to retrieve the rest of the jewelry. There were matching earrings, a bracelet, and a pin. While she managed the earrings and pin on her own, he was the one to attach the bracelet to her wrist.

With her hand still in his, he closed the clasp, then looked up at her, and her breath caught in her throat. There was something about the way that he looked at her as he closed the bracelet around her arm, as if by wearing his jewels, he had now claimed her as his own.

More likely, that was her own overly romantic imagination... yet she could swear there was something possessive in his gaze.

"We did not bring the tiara for this evening, but I hope you will wear it for your wedding," Gregory's mother said, her eyes shining brightly as she looked up at Tiffany. "Did you already have jewelry picked out?"

"I did not," Tiffany replied, her fingers lifting to trace the heavy stones now lying on her collarbone. "I would be honored to wear the set. Thank you for letting me borrow it."

"Oh, my dear, these will be yours to wear from now." The duchess smiled, patting Tiffany's hand. "I never wore them. Not my style, but they suit you admirably."

"They do." Gregory lifted her hand to his lips again, this time turning it to kiss the inside of her wrist, right where her pulse was fluttering. Tiffany felt a similar flutter in her core as her whole body heated in response.

Sebastian cleared his throat, the sound not entirely condemning but certainly not approving either. More like a warning that Gregory was sailing too close to the line.

As Gregory stepped back, Tiffany looked at her mother, and, for the first time, she was able to see her without obstruction. But there was nothing to see. Her mother's expression was entirely blank.

The lack of expression did not bode well for her once the others were not around, but she could not help but be bolstered by the others' admiration. For the first time in her life, she was able to ignore her mother.

Mostly.

~

GREGORY

For all that this was their engagement party, his bride-to-be's head seemed in the clouds. Perhaps because of the way her mother had reacted to her altering her dress for the evening? Truthfully, though he was not a man who normally noticed ruffles, he thought the addition of the blue was a boon to her.

Understanding the vagaries of ladies' fashion might not be a strength of his, but even he could see that the shade of green of the dress was not as flattering to her as the blue of the ruffle. And he did rather enjoy that they were wearing matched colors, the dark blue of her trim complementing the navy of his coat. He was known for wearing blue regularly.

The family sapphires looked perfect around Tiffany's throat, shimmering all over her body. From the moment he'd seen her fully decorated, he'd had a vision of her in his bed wearing nothing but the jewels.

It felt as though every time he saw her, she became more beautiful. Because he was becoming more familiar with her? More intimate? Because he knew he was going to be marrying her soon, and he was increasingly viewing her as his—his to protect, his to claim? Or did the clothing she was wearing truly make such a difference?

Perhaps it was a combination of all of it.

Regardless, he was feeling very proprietary, especially as his fellow dukes came to congratulate them. Even though Nathanial had withdrawn his offer and not one of them would think to poach, they were all single dukes themselves. Only Drake did not aggravate his senses, likely because he was the only one officially off the marriage mart.

During the receiving line, there was one small moment of near awkwardness. His mother had taken it upon herself to invite the Littles, and he saw the Duchess of Bolton stiffen as she realized who was approaching the line. Gregory did not mind being introduced to the slightly scandalous family—he was happy to support his mother's *cause célèbre*. After having been kept away from Society by his father for so long, he knew she was outraged by the idea that a family would not accept their son, his wife, and their grandchildren because he had married outside of their preferences.

Mr. Little was a proper English gentleman in every degree other than his family. Being vaguely acquainted with the Earl of Stilton and his heir, Mr. Little's father and eldest brother, Gregory could see the resemblance in features. As his mother had stated, the wife and daughter were beautiful, though, of course, not the usual sort of beauty that graced the *ton*. Miss Kalina Little would turn heads with her dark skin set against the rose-pink dress she was wearing, her black hair coiled into a fashionable coiffure... but whether she would actually garner suitors with her father in disgrace with his family was another question entirely. The son, Ashwin Little, was a stripling youth, similar enough in age to his sister that Gregory could not tell which was the elder, though he suspected it was Miss Little.

Despite getting her back up in a snobbish tizzy, the Duchess of Bolton did her duty. Gregory was beginning to look forward to his wedding for more reasons than Tiffany. While Duchess Bolton would be his mother-in-law, once Tiffany joined his household, there would be less reason for her mother's constant company. She would be Sebastian's problem to deal with... him and his wife's, and Gregory did not envy the poor woman who took that position and found herself dealing with the prickly dowager.

He had thought to introduce Miss Little to Sebastian and encourage his friend in that direction, which would make his own mother happy, but perhaps for Miss Little's sake he should steer her toward a different friend. Nathanial, perhaps, if the rumors about her being dowered to the hilt were true. His mother was certainly correct that a daughter marrying a duke would ensure the Stilton clan could not turn up their nose at their youngest son completely.

Once the guests had been received, Gregory and Tiffany waited until their mothers and Sebastian had been announced before making their own triumphant entrance. With Tiffany on his arm, Gregory ignored the rest of the room, smiling at her and putting his hand over hers before they entered.

It was not all that hard to pretend to be in love with her, truthfully.

She shone as they walked into the room. No, she was no Diamond of the First Water, but he truly did think she looked beautiful tonight. The dress or the jewels, or the combination thereof, were far more flattering than anything he'd seen her in before. Her skin was creamier, her hair seemed to have more color, and there was a brightness in her eyes that drew him in like a moth to the flame.

He wanted to see that brightness more often.

Moving to the center of the floor, they turned to each other, and she looked up at him. There was trepidation in her eyes as she met his hand for their waltz, and he felt her fingers tremble against his as she placed her hand in his.

"Are you all right?" he murmured.

"Everyone is staring," she whispered back. She looked up at him, her expression almost pleading. For all the attention that had been poured on them since that initial scandal and announcing their engagement, this was the first time they'd been at the center of an entire room.

"Just look at me," he whispered, tightening his grip on her as the strings began the first notes of the song. He kept his gaze steady on hers, holding her to him with more than his hands. "Just look at me and no one else. No one else matters."

∾

TIFFANY

Heart pounding in her chest, both from the number of eyes on her and from Gregory's nearness, Tiffany stared at her future husband.

No one else matters.

It was the opposite of what her mother had always told her. She'd been trained her whole life to hold up under societal pressure, knowing she had to perform perfectly to make up for her lack of beauty. Now, the moment she was before the *ton's* scrutinizing gaze, she felt like she could barely breathe.

But it did not matter.

No one else mattered.

The music began, then Gregory's leg was stepping forward, his body moving forward, pushing her back, and she responded automatically. The hours that she had spent training came to her rescue as she moved with him. His powerful lead certainly assisted as she did not need to do anything but follow, still staring up into his dark eyes, acutely aware of the way he held her, his hard body against hers, his leg moving between hers with every step.

They whirled around the floor until there was a smattering of applause from their audience, then Sebastian led her mother out to join them. A moment later, the Duchess of Clarence took to the floor led by the Duke of Hereford. Then, another couple and another, and finally, she felt like she could breathe again as the other dancers crowded in around them, so they were no longer the sole focus.

"There, you see?" Gregory smiled down at her. "You performed admirably."

"Thanks to you," she whispered.

Raising his eyebrow at her, he seemed to consider something, then he raised his head to peer around. His gaze dropped back to her.

"No one is looking at us now," he murmured. He shifted the direction of their bodies, moving them to the side of the ballroom, near the doors that led to the hallway. "Let us go somewhere that you can thank me properly."

Now, she could not breathe again for an entirely different reason.

TWENTY-TWO

Tiffany

"The library?" she asked as Gregory pulled her into the room, somewhat bemused to find herself in the room where she felt most comfortable. She had not been sure where he would take her.

"Some of my favorite memories are in libraries," he said with a wink, closing the door behind them and frowning as he inspected the handle. "Why does no one bother to install a lock on their libraries?"

"Does your library have a lock?" she asked, amused.

"No." He sighed and looked around. Then, reaching out, he took hold of her hand and began to lead her to the other side of the room where the light was more shadowed. "Over here."

It was very reminiscent of the shadowed corner where he'd first kissed her. Something she was sure he realized as he suddenly turned, pulling her up against him. Her hands went to his chest, bracing against the soft fabric of his jacket.

"As much as I would like to take my time, I fear we do not have much of it," he murmured just before he lowered his head for a kiss.

Likely, they only had until her brother noticed she was missing. That was the last fleeting thought that passed through Tiffany's mind before their lips met, and all subsequent thoughts flew out of her head. This kiss was not forbidden. It was not a light touch, it was not meant to gently seduce… it was a kiss that claimed her.

His tongue slid between her parted lips when she gasped, his hands moving along her back as he pulled her closer to him, crushing her breasts against his chest as her fingers curled around the lapels of his jacket. Every part of her body flamed with heat as he touched her, his hands roaming over her in a flagrantly possessive manner that claimed he had every right to touch her as he wished…

And she had absolutely no desire to stop him.

More.

She wanted more.

When his hand slid up to cup her breast over her dress, she gasped again, moaning as the heady sensation, the pleasure, surged through her. Never had she experienced anything like his touch in her entire life, and he was not even touching her skin.

"Shh," he murmured as he lifted his lips from hers, moving them down over her throat, making her whimper. "Stay quiet for me, my little swan."

"Swan?" She managed to keep her voice low as she gasped out the word.

His hand massaged her breast, making her knees weaken, and she might have fallen had he not pressed her up against the shelves behind her. The wood dug into her back, and she reached out with one arm to brace herself, the back of her hand touching the leather-bound books that she'd so often run her fingertips over to soothe herself.

There was no soothing herself now. He had lit a fire inside her, and she had no idea how to put it out.

"Graceful. Beautiful. With a lovely long neck." He ran kisses up the side of her neck as he spoke, and she shuddered at the hot path of passion he left along her sensitive skin. "On our wedding night, I want you to wear these jewels and nothing else."

"Oh!" Tiffany gasped.

"Quiet, little swan."

She clamped her mouth shut, closing her eyes as she tried to focus on what was happening inside her. But it was all for naught, as he suddenly dropped away from her, and her eyes flew open again, just in time to see him lifting the hem of her skirt to disappear underneath.

"Gregory!"

"Hush." Broad shoulders pushed between her thighs, and Tiffany found herself leaning back against the shelves, both hands now clutching at them to hold herself upright as Gregory pushed between her legs. She felt the split in her drawers open, then his fingers sliding against the soft skin between her thighs as he pushed her back against the shelves, making it easier for him to part her legs.

Hot air wafted over her most sensitive parts, then he touched her... there... where no man had *ever* touched her.

She suddenly understood why young ladies were not to be left alone with rakes.

Because this was *sinful.*

Utterly wicked.

Totally indecent.

And from the moment he touched her there, she wanted—no, *needed*—more. Like a compulsion.

Her body ached. Throbbed. Demanded.

Holding onto the shelves for dear life, she found herself going up on her toes as her back arched, her head falling back against the heavy wood as pure pleasure shot through her. He was kissing her again, using his tongue for depravity, and she was lifting one of her legs... it ended up over his shoulder, opening herself more to him, letting him touch what she was supposed to guard.

She wanted to say something. To beg for more. To plea for him to stop so she could catch her breath. To cry out from the overload of sensations running rampant through her body.

But he had told her to be quiet.

Covering her mouth with her hand, she felt her body shudder as he ran his tongue along the seam of her cleft before finding a spot at the apex that was tingling even more than the rest of her. When he found that spot, his tongue circled, her knees going weak, then he suckled.

Tiffany shattered. His hands and his shoulders held her up against the shelves, supporting her weight as she fell to pieces all around him. The rush of ecstasy, the explosion of passion, had her squirming against his mouth, gasping as she tried to hold back her cries.

Wave after pulsating wave of pleasure rippled through her until they finally ebbed, leaving her boneless and spent against the shelves.

A moment later, Gregory pulled her skirts back over his head, his face flushed as he panted for breath. Tiffany stared back at him with glazed eyes, her breasts heaving as the aftereffects of whatever he had done to her quivered through her.

On his knees, he smoothed down her skirts, patting them into place, and got to his feet with a smug smile on his face. Tiffany shuddered, blinking, as her body attempted to right itself.

"What did you do to me?" she whispered, her voice husky.

Gregory raised his eyebrow at her.

"Have you never had an orgasm before?" he asked. "*La petite mort?*" His French translated to 'the little death', and while she had heard the term before, she had never understood what it meant.

Now, she did. She felt as though she had died and gone to heaven, then risen again. Sacrilegious. Not something she would ever admit aloud to anyone. But it was still the truth.

She shook her head. The smug smile on Gregory's face widened, and she could not find it within herself to be annoyed. Not when he'd made her feel like that.

Helping her straighten up, he took some of her weight on his arm.

"We have to return to the ballroom." He leaned in, his lips brushing her ear and sending a tremor down her spine as he spoke. "I am looking forward to being married to you, my little swan."

She felt like a swan, gliding down the hall on his arm, utterly content. Confident in a manner that she'd never experienced before. On Gregory's arm, she could face anything.

Including her brother, who was coming down the hall toward them with thunderclouds on his face.

"Clarence." Her brother growled Gregory's title rather than calling him by his Christian name, which did not bode well.

"Bolton." Gregory's responding tone was much lighter than her brother's, almost amused. He glanced at her and sighed. "I told you we had to return to the ballroom."

She blinked at him, nonplussed. Sebastian came to a halt before them, his arms crossed over his chest.

"You are blaming my sister for your disappearance from your own engagement ball?"

"Blame? No, not at all. I was being a conscientious fiancé. My bride-to-be was a trifle overwhelmed by all the attention and needed some air. We took a walk to the library, and now, feeling much fortified by our brief sojourn, we are returning." It was all the truth, and it would have been very convincing if Gregory had not looked quite so much like the cat who had nipped the cream.

Sebastian looked to her for confirmation, and she nodded because what else could she do?

The suspicion on his face did not entirely clear, but he moved to the side.

"Do not leave the room again without me," he commanded.

"Of course, old chap." Gregory smirked as he led her past Sebastian. "Wouldn't think of it."

Tiffany pressed her lips together at the expression on her brother's face. Suspicion. Annoyance. He was sure he was having the wool pulled over his eyes, yet there was nothing he could say about it.

There was something satisfying in that.

They reentered the ballroom, drawing the attention of their guests by the door. Tiffany lifted her chin, doing her best to ignore the looks and whispers that followed them through the room, assisted by Gregory's steady presence at her side. They began to circulate, her on his arm, with Sebastian gloweringly keeping watch from the sidelines.

Gregory did not seem inclined to whisk her away again. She almost wished he would. She was sure there was more to discover, more he could show her... teach her... She finally understood what it was between a man and a woman that everyone found so fascinating. Her body still hummed from it. She felt as though she'd been changed, even though no one could see it.

It was a secret between her and Gregory.

And how many other women does he have secrets with?

She banished the thought from her mind. At least, she attempted to. It was there, under all her other thoughts, though.

"Tiffany? Are you thirsty? Can I fetch you something to drink?" Gregory was looking at her with concern, and Tiffany started as she realized he'd been talking to her, and she had no idea how long.

"Ah, yes, please. Some ratafia or lemonade." Flustered, she gave herself a shake as he smiled, still watching her closely.

"Perhaps both," he quipped, releasing her hand from his arm and giving her a short bow before turning to walk away. Almost as soon as he'd taken two steps from her side, Sebastian joined him, both of them bending their heads together to converse as they moved to the refreshments.

Tiffany took a deep breath, putting her hand on her stomach, just under her bosom. She needed to get her head out of the clouds. She could not wish that Gregory had not taken her to the library, but she did wish that she could overcome the aftereffects more easily. Did one become used to such pleasures? He certainly did not seem as overcome as she was.

Blast. She was back to thinking about that.

"Well done," said a low voice beside her, and Tiffany startled again as Lady Astrid suddenly appeared at her side, taking Gregory's place.

The lady was resplendent in a bronze and burnt orange striped dress with amber trim. Dark orange jewels set in gold made a shining ring around her delicate throat, dripped from her ears, and were set throughout her dark red curls where they were piled on her head. Tiffany recognized the popular Cairngorm crystals, a particular favorite of the queen's, making her wonder about Lady Astrid's ties to Scotland. But she had a more important question first.

"What was well done?" she asked.

Seeing Lady Astrid by her side, several young ladies started toward them, then suddenly stopped and turned away. Tiffany glanced at the young woman beside her and realized the lady was glaring at anyone who dared to look like they might approach.

"I heard a few ladies whispering during your waltz that your love match was a sham," Lady Astrid murmured. The general feeling of happy calm Tiffany had been feeling vanished in an instant. "It will not matter once you are married, but it gives the *ton* another *on dit* to pick over. Once everyone realized you had disappeared, and now, with your smiling reappearance, that rumor was squashed before it could truly begin."

The sudden panic in Tiffany's chest relaxed. Her reputation would be salvaged by Gregory marrying her regardless, but she would be lying if she said she did not care what the rest of the *ton* thought. Moreso, she knew her mother would be appalled if the ton thought she'd been compromised—or, more likely, that she'd trapped Gregory into the position of having to marry her or face dishonor and her brother's retaliation.

It did make her wonder, though, if Gregory had somehow heard the whispers. If they had started before tonight. Was that why he'd whisked her away? To keep up appearances for their love match?

The panic that had been rising was now replaced by a cold feeling in her chest. The warmth of his kisses, his body against hers, the pleasure he'd wrought, was gone. She'd wished for a clear head, and now that she had it, she regretted the wish wholeheartedly.

"Do not worry," Lady Astrid said reassuringly, misconstruing the look on Tiffany's face. "It was only a few older ladies. Likely, jealous mamas, upset that another duke is off the market and not because of one of their daughters. There have been all manner of rumors about why Drake and I have not yet stepped before the altar."

Tiffany found herself looking around, wondering who the ladies had been. Wondering where and why the rumor had started. Had she done something wrong? Had it shown? Perhaps Lady Astrid was right, and it was mere jealousy fueling the rumor… but considering the truth of it, Tiffany could not help but wonder if someone knew something.

Her eye caught on her mother, as she scanned the ballroom, speaking rather closely with a tall, handsome older gentleman. He had salt and pepper hair and was dressed dashingly, and the way he was speaking so familiarly with her mother set bells ringing in Tiffany's head. She'd known for a long time that her mother had a lover, though she had never set eyes on him. Until now, perhaps?

The way they looked at each other… Tiffany could not help her curiosity.

"Lady Astrid," she said quietly, leaning toward the other woman. "Do you recognize the gentleman my mother is speaking to?"

The redhead turned to look.

"That is the Marquess of Selter."

"Marquess," Tiffany murmured. That was certainly high enough a rank that perhaps she could see her mother with such a man.

"An honorary title while he is the Duke of Grafton's heir," Lady Astrid clarified. "He's the current duke's uncle, the younger brother of the previous duke."

Oh yes, of course. Tiffany should have known that. Her mother had been determined to have her memorize Debrett's handbook, which listed all the titles of every nobleman of rank, but Tiffany had been a constant disappointment in that area. While her mother was often disappointed with Tiffany's efforts, she had disappointed herself in her inability to retain the information. It just would not stick in her head.

Presumably, Lady Astrid did not have such problems. Or, perhaps, it was because she had actually interacted with the person in question, having been active in Society for more than a few weeks. It was certainly easier for Tiffany to remember people she had met or seen. Tiffany did not think she would forget about the Marquess of Selter again now that she had seen him—and, more importantly, seen the way he interacted with her mother.

The way he and her mother looked at each other was very reminiscent of the way she and Gregory looked at each other. She wondered if her mother had ever... oh, dear. No. *No.* She did not want to think about that. She could not imagine her mother allowing such... liberties. Neither did she want to imagine it. Although at least now she could better understand why her mother would want a lover.

She turned away and saw Gregory and Sebastian returning to them. Gregory held two glasses in his hand, as did Sebastian.

"Lemonade and ratafia, as promised," Gregory said with a slight bow, holding the drinks out in front of him as an offering. "Which would you prefer?"

Tiffany laughed and took the lemonade as Sebastian made the same offer to Lady Astrid, who took the drink with a smile.

It did not escape Tiffany's notice that a few moments later, the Duke of Ormonde joined their coterie. He did not dance attendance on his fiancé, did not even stand beside her, but he did keep a very close eye on Sebastian for the remainder of the evening.

She also noted that the bronze waistcoat he wore perfectly

matched the bronze on Lady Astrid's dress, and a Cairngorm pin held his cravat in place. All of which she found very interesting.

TWENTY-THREE

regory

The morning after his engagement ball, Gregory woke from a wildly tantalizing dream about his bride-to-be, the phantom taste of her lingering on his lips. God, he loved the taste of a woman, of bringing her to pleasure with his tongue over and over, and it had been far too long since he'd supped on ambrosia. It had also been too brief. Too quiet. He wanted to hear her gasps, her moans, her cries of passion. Both the quickness and the silence had been necessary evils. He wished he'd been able to watch her climax for the first time, though part of him was also appalled that it was the first time. If he'd known...

This was why he did not seduce debutantes. He'd always preferred experienced women. Women who knew what they wanted. Women who knew what was possible and were looking to achieve it. Women who would not demand anything more from him than that price of pleasure.

But with Tiffany... her inexperience did not feel as much of a barrier. Perhaps because she was so responsive to him despite her lack of knowledge. The attraction between them had only grown stronger over the days since he'd first seen her in the library, as had his desire to protect her, to claim her. He'd been amused at her brother's protectiveness last night and far less amused at the way some of the wolves of the *ton* had started eyeing her.

Once they were married, once she'd produced an heir, those wolves would descend. Some of them liked to plan far in advance, apparently. Gregory would need to be on his guard to keep the wolves from hunting his sweet swan.

Fidelity.

That was what he had wanted from his wife from the beginning. To his relief, Tiffany did not seem inclined to give her attention to anyone but him, and he was determined to keep it that way. What surprised him was his disinterest in anyone but *her*. Was it the novelty? Was it the enforced wait until he could have his fill of her?

He was not sure. He had the uneasy feeling that even after their wedding night, his fascination with her would continue. What she would make of some of his proclivities... that he did not know. Not that his desires were as extreme as some of his brethren, but she did not have any experience to draw upon, much less knowledge of some of the more indecent activities a couple could engage in.

On the other hand, perhaps that could be a boon.

She would not know that the things he wanted to do to her, the activities he wanted to initiate her in, were considered perversions because she did not know anything about any such activities.

Which was certainly an interesting thought that put a smile on his face first thing in the morning.

Unfortunately, his smile only lasted through breakfast, at the end of which, his mother came barreling into the dining room in a fluster, waving a piece of paper in her hand.

"He's gone! He's gone! I do not understand!" She looked ready to burst into tears.

Gregory did not understand either. He'd jumped to his feet when his mother had barged through the door, and now he hurried to her, holding his hand out for the paper she was waving about.

"Who is gone?"

"Montblanc! He says it is his fault. I do not understand!" His mother wailed out the words, and Gregory took a moment to wrap her in his arms, propping his chin on her head while she sobbed into his chest so he could still read the note he held in one hand.

It was written in Montblanc's hand, the penmanship scrawled over the page in a far less fluid manner than Gregory normally saw from him.

My dearest Duchess,

I must apologize.

You deserve so much more than a humble man like myself, yet also so much more than the manner in which a duke treated you. I never wanted to cause you a moment's distress, yet I fear that is what I must do.

It has been my honor to watch you enjoy life again, no longer buried in the country under the mandate of your late husband. I wish you nothing but joy going forward in the future.

But I must still apologize.

I did not know what I was becoming involved in or where all of my actions would lead. Indeed, had I known, I do not think I would have changed my course.

My Betty deserved justice, and so did you, and no court in the land would have granted it... not when the perpetrator was a duke. Taking matters into my own hands had unintended consequences, but I cannot regret them.

I regret only whatever pain I have caused you.

Please show this note to your son and assure him that I have no ill intention toward either him or his bride. As far as I know, neither do any of the others. But now, for my own safety, I cannot remain.

Tell him to cease his investigation, or my reassurances may no longer hold true.

Your devoted servant,

Arthur

Staring at the note, Gregory felt his heart thudding in his chest where his mother had her cheek pressed against it. His jaw felt locked into place as his mind whirled at the implications.

"He is saying what I think he is... is he not?" she whispered. "He is responsible for your father's death... and for the others."

At least partially responsible from what it looked like. And now that he was paying particular attention to the handwriting, or perhaps because Montblanc's normally elegant hand had been so hasty, he could see the markers that Sebastian had caught in the threatening notes. Montblanc had been the one to send them to Gregory's father, he was almost sure of it, though he'd want Sebastian to look them over as well. A secondary opinion to confirm the supposition.

"I think so, yes," Gregory replied grimly. "What is this about 'his' Betty? Did they... were they..." His voice trailed off as he tried to think of a way to delicately state his suspicion to his mother. There was a vast difference in years between Montblanc and Betty after all. From the letter, he also was now wondering if Montblanc had hidden a *tendre* for the duchess. Which also made him more confused about a connection between him and Betty.

"I do not know." His mother stepped back, her eyes red-rimmed from crying. "I... I do not know what to think. I thought I knew him, but now I feel as if I did not know him at all."

"I did not either, apparently." Gregory stared at the note. He had trusted Montblanc. Been sure that he *could* trust Montblanc.

In some ways, he supposed that remained true. Montblanc had fled rather than trying to do Gregory or anyone else in the household harm.

Blast... had he taken Betty and Priscilla with him?

Fear clutched at Gregory's heart, in large part for his half-sister and her mother. They had already been dealt a rum hand, and the responsibility he felt for them would not disappear even if they did. If anything, he would feel obliged to find them again to ensure they were cared for.

Thankfully, now that the initial outburst was over with, his mother was amenable to sitting down, and he called upon Mrs. Bryant to come and tend to her. The housekeeper would be better at soothing her rattled nerves than him. He quickly ordered one of the footmen to fetch Betty, if she could be found, and dashed off a note summoning Sebastian, telling him to come immediately as one of the culprits had been revealed but also escaped.

He did not reach out to the other dukes. Not yet. Not until he could talk things over with Sebastian.

Setting the hounds on Montblanc did not quite sit right with him. He wanted to know what the man had meant about Gregory's mother and Betty needing justice. He wanted to talk with Sebastian about the alleged conspiracy that he was sure Montblanc was referring to. The man was not the only guilty party if Gregory was reading between the lines correctly.

Whatever he had done, he seemed to have felt justified in doing it.

Betty and Priscilla were located, and Gregory had the young mother sent to his study so that he could question her once he reclaimed his equanimity. It would not do to appear before her in an upset state of mind. He would likely frighten her, then questioning her for information would be impossible. She had enough difficulty speaking to him when everyone around her was calm.

Before he could go talk with her, Sebastian arrived... with his sister in tow.

Gregory stared at his fiancé, dumbfounded. She was wearing the mint green dress again, which he was beginning to think must be a particular favorite of hers.

"Ah..." He looked at Sebastian.

"Tiffany knows everything." Sebastian appeared annoyed at the fact rather than smug, which helped Gregory feel a bit better about his own consternation. "Lady Astrid told her, then Tiffany came to me, and I felt obliged to inform her of everything I knew so she had all the information."

"I see." Gregory did not see. Why did Sebastian feel obliged to tell her? Then again, a sibling relationship had always been a mystery to him. Even now that he had sisters, the difference in their ages was far greater than between Sebastian and Tiffany. "This is not a conversation for the foyer. Let us go to the back parlor." The parlor beside his study, where Betty was waiting for him, so she did not have to wait much longer.

Once there, he shared the note from Montblanc with the siblings, and both of them read it quickly, then sat back. He also handed Sebastian the original notes so he could compare the handwriting.

"I think they are the same," Sebastian said, inspecting it, holding Montblanc's note to the duchess in one hand and a threatening note to Gregory's father in the other. "The only question is why? What does Betty have to do with anything?" He raised his eyebrow at Gregory. "And were you aware of his feelings for your mother?"

"Of course not." Not that he would have stood in the way if his mother had returned the steward's feelings. His rank was of no importance to Gregory if it was not to his mother. "I do not know why he mentions Betty. She's in my study, waiting for me so I can ask her, but you two arrived before I could."

"Your study is next door, correct?" Tiffany asked, looking up at him. She inclined her head in the direction of his study.

"Yes."

Getting to her feet, she brushed off her skirts. Both he and Sebastian jumped up as well, their manners far too entrenched for them to remain seated when a lady stood.

"I will go speak with Betty," Tiffany declared. "She seemed more comfortable around other ladies than other men, and as Montblanc's actions were more directed toward your family than mine, she might be more amenable to speaking with me than you."

About to automatically protest, Gregory managed to hold himself back when he realized she made sense. Betty was already acutely uncomfortable around him. If she did know anything, she was likely braced against an interrogation. Tiffany's appearance would throw her off, and she would probably be more comfortable being questioned by another woman, as Tiffany had noted.

Besides, it would give him the time to ask Sebastian what the devil he was thinking, telling his sister everything.

"That sounds like the best course of action," he agreed.

Letting herself into Gregory's study, Tiffany looked around the room. It was strictly masculine, though richly furnished. Heavy mahogany furniture rested on a navy rug that featured a forest green, burgundy, and cream pattern. The curtains, drawn back from the window, were navy and cream brocade, held in place with golden ties that ended in large tassels. Not a room she would have felt comfortable sitting in by herself for very long.

Which was why her heart went out to poor Betty, who was hunched over in one of the large armchairs, making her appear even more slight than she had when Tiffany had first met her in the nursery.

"Good morning," she said gently. Betty's head swung up, her eyes widening in surprise when she saw Tiffany rather than Gregory or someone else. Tiffany smiled at her, hoping to put the young woman at ease, and was rewarded when Betty's shoulders relaxed minutely. Then, remembering herself, Betty sprang to her feet and curtsied deeply.

"Your Grace," she whispered.

"Not yet," Tiffany replied, making a joke of it. "Not until after I marry his grace, that is. Right now, I am still 'my lady'."

"Yes, my lady." Betty kept her head down.

"Please, sit." Tiffany gestured to the chair Betty had just leapt up from and moved to the one beside it rather than taking Gregory's usual seat behind his desk. Betty wavered on her feet as Tiffany sat down, and Tiffany nodded her head at the chair behind her. The young woman sank down as if her knees would no longer hold her up. Her head dropped down at the same time, fingers fidgeting together in her lap.

Leaning forward, Tiffany took Betty's hand in hers, and the young woman froze.

"Betty, do you know why his grace wished to speak with you?" She kept her voice as low and gentle as she could. She felt very much like she was coaxing a wild bird to her hand, and to startle it would mean watching it flutter away.

"No, my lady," Betty whispered, shaking her head.

"Do you know Arthur Montblanc?"

Betty nodded, pressing her lips together.

"Do you know where he went?"

"Where he went?" Betty repeated, lifting her gaze to meet Tiffany's, fear filling her eyes. "He's gone?"

"He left sometime in the night. And he left a note for the duchess, apologizing for... for an action which he said he took on your behalf and her behalf."

"Uncle Arthur is gone," Betty said quietly, more to herself than Tiffany, then she burst into tears.

Tiffany moved beside her to comfort her, putting her arm around the poor girl. It did not take her long to gently elicit the entire story from her. Montblanc was her uncle, and they had hidden the family connection because he'd been the one to get her a job in the household as a maid.

Which was why he blamed himself when she caught the eye of Gregory's father, who forced himself on her. It had been Montblanc who had helped her and her daughter once she'd been discovered to be *enceinte,* and the duke had dismissed her from his household. From what Betty said, the other young mothers of Gregory's half-sisters had found themselves in similar circumstances—pressured into the duke's bed, then dismissed as soon as they were pregnant.

If it had not been for Montblanc, Betty and Priscilla would have been on the street before Gregory inherited and went searching for his half-sisters.

Tiffany's jaw was set. By-blows were not unusual, but even she knew that they were supposed to be taken care of, regardless of their mother's station. Apparently, Gregory's father had felt he was above all that. And hearing Betty cry as she talked about how he'd held her down...

While she'd known, in a general sort of way, that being ruined involved touching a man, she was now far more aware of exactly what kind of touch that would be. She could extrapolate from her own experience how it might be to have a man who she did not like nor trust to touch her where Gregory had, in the manner he had. The very idea was revolting.

If the duke was not already dead, she might want to kill him herself.

The bloodthirsty track of her thoughts was nearly as distressing as Betty's tears, but she could not help it. While she mourned her own father's death, part of her could not help but feel relief that there would be no more victims of the former Duke of Clarence.

Montblanc had put a stop to it. Justice had been served.

But he killed my father, too.

She let out a long breath. No wonder she was feeling conflicted.

Once Betty got herself more under control, Tiffany released her. All Betty wanted to do was return to her daughter, and Tiffany was not going to detain her any further. She certainly was not going to make Betty repeat herself to two dukes. No wonder the poor girl was terrified of Gregory.

Well.

If she did nothing else as Gregory's duchess, Tiffany would ensure that all the mothers of his half-sisters felt safe.

Head held high, she sailed back into the parlor to inform the men of what she'd learned. Watched as Sebastian's expression turned to grim horror, and Gregory's head dropped down with the weight of his father's sins. She reached out to take his hand, giving it a squeeze. Felt him try to tug his hand away and held on even tighter.

His dark eyes lifted to hers, full of grief and shame.

"You are not responsible for his actions," she told him quietly. "You are an honorable man."

"You are," Sebastian agreed, giving himself a shake as he realized how low the revelations had brought his friend. "Even Montblanc thinks so." The jest should have fallen flat, but something about the gallows humor actually startled a laugh from Gregory, even as Tiffany shot her brother a reproving look.

She squeezed Gregory's hand again, and this time, he squeezed her fingers back.

"Now, what do we do?" she asked.

Sebastian and Gregory exchanged a look.

"*We*," Sebastian inclined his head at Gregory, "will inform the other dukes of this new development, then see where things lead from there."

Tiffany pursed her lips but did not argue. If the gentlemen were going to leave her out of their plans, then she did not feel bound to tell them hers. They could speak to the other dukes. *She* would find an opportunity to speak with Lady Astrid.

Finding Montblanc would also be of utmost importance. Obviously, there was more he would be able to tell them, like who else had been involved and what the lingering danger was if they continued to investigate. She could not search herself, but everyone always forgot about the staff. They would be more than willing to help keep an eye out for Montblanc if she told them who he was and described him.

It might come to naught, but she could not sit back and do nothing as her brother and fiancé obviously expected her to.

CHAPTER

TWENTY-FOUR

regory.

The days until his wedding passed by in a blink. He and Sebastian spoke to the dukes, showing them the letters. They all agreed that it appeared Montblanc had been part of a larger group effort, which made sense, considering all it would have taken to organize such a massive project. It did not sound as though he was the mastermind behind the murders, but clearly, he did not want to be made to turn on his co-conspirators, or else he would not have fled.

Discovering his own father's culpability, what he had done to Betty... it turned Gregory's stomach. He had been unable to visit the nursery for days until Priscilla escaped from the room when her mother was distracted and came looking for him. It had thrown the entire household into a tizzy before she'd been found. Holding her, faced with her unwavering affection for him, had healed something inside him. And when he'd handed her back to her mother, Betty had actually smiled at him in relief.

She did not blame him for not knowing. Neither did any of his sisters' mothers.

219

To save his own mother some distress, he'd given her only the bare bones of the matter. Betty was Montblanc's niece. Since his mother had been the force behind ensuring her husband's by-blows were located and returned to the fold to be cared for, he let her think that had been the only reason for Montblanc's revenge.

He did probe gently to discern whether his father's abuse of her had ever turned physical. Realizing his direction, his mother reassured him that he had not. Though she'd been shut away in the country, she had relatives who would have come rushing to her aid if she'd been able to make some kind of physical complaint. They were already unhappy with how she was kept from Society, though there had been nothing they could do about it. His father had not needed to lift a finger to make her miserable; he used his words and his power to grind her down. Something Montblanc had obviously realized.

All he could do now was try to repair what his father had done and ensure that they were all cared for and safe within his household.

If it had only been his own father who had died in the explosion and subsequent fire, Gregory might have been tempted to let the matter drop and allow Montblanc's disappearance to be the end of things. But there were seven other dukes to consider. Seven other sons—and some daughters—left fatherless.

Justice might have been served on his father, but there was yet justice to be served for the deaths of the other dukes. Gregory could not believe all of them guilty of such crimes.

The threat that Montblanc mentioned, the idea that there were those who would not want them to investigate, did not stymy any of them. For now, they could hide it behind a search for Montblanc himself, which was what they did. Two Bow Street runners were hired, as well as a private investigator Drake said he had used in the past.

Without knowing who else might have been involved with Montblanc, it was important to project the proper image to keep everyone safe and suspicions low. No one wanted to ignore Mont-blanc's warning against continuing the investigation, but of course, they could not stop, either... they just had to be discreet.

In the meantime, Gregory had been caught up in the social whirl that was required of a man of his status when preparing for a wedding. That was the best way to throw anyone off the scent of the investigation. The purported love match between him and the sister of the Duke of Bolton had caught the *ton*'s interest, and that interest had solidified during the engagement ball.

The waltz, their brief disappearance, then Tiffany's pink cheeks when they'd reappeared had set tongues wagging. It appeared to Gregory that it was his lot to be a distraction... which would have been far more enjoyable without Sebastian hovering over his every move.

Despite Gregory's desire to get his fiancé alone again, neither Sebastian nor his mother seemed to appreciate the brief sojourn they'd been missing during the engagement ball. His own mother seemed to have taken it upon herself to keep the Duchess of Bolton preoccupied, but there was nothing he could do about Sebastian but grin and bear it.

Now, today, at least he was going to be able to have Tiffany all to himself. He just had to get through the ceremony and the wedding breakfast, then the first order of married business was to lock himself and his new wife in her bedroom and spend the remainder of the day in bed.

He met his mother in the front hall, elegantly turned out in a navy-blue silk dress that matched his waistcoat and pocket square. Gregory frowned as he recognized the box that held the sapphires Tiffany had worn for their engagement ball.

"Is that what I think it is?" he asked, nodding at the box, finishing tugging on his gloves as he did so.

"If you mean Tiffany's sapphires, yes," his mother replied serenely. She smiled, but there was a sharpness to her gaze. "She returned them to me the morning after your engagement ball and asked that I hold on to them until today. She said she did not want to risk losing them."

"How could she lose them?" He frowned. Nothing about Tiffany had ever made him think that she was so flighty that she would accidentally misplace something as important as the Clarence sapphire set.

"Perhaps she was less concerned with losing them than with having *someone* take them from her." His mother sniffed, a tic that he was becoming accustomed to seeing whenever the topic of the Duchess of Bolton arose. Who the 'someone' might be was very clear.

Bemused, Gregory stared at his mother.

"Are you insinuating that the duchess would take the jewels from her own daughter? For what purpose? They are hardly in the weeds. The Bolton accounts are as flush as our own."

"For what purpose indeed," his mother muttered darkly.

He understood that she had taken a dislike to Tiffany's mother, but this was taking it a bit far. On the other hand, if Tiffany had given them back to his mother, doing so must have set her mind at ease for some reason.

"That is why we must hurry over, though. I want her to have time to put them on and set the tiara perfectly in her hair before the wedding."

"Very well." Gregory held out his arm. It was not as if he had anything better to do. They would make a stop at Bolton House so his mother could pass off the jewels, then it would be on to St. George's Cathedral, where he would wait for his bride's arrival.

The excitement he felt surge in his chest was not entirely unexpected, but the force of it was rather unanticipated. A month ago, he would have bet his entire fortune that his wedding day would be pure duty and not particularly exciting. Yet, here he was, about to become a married man, and rather than needing to be dragged to the altar, he was more inclined to hurry.

Fate was fickle that way.

TIFFANY

She did not recognize the woman in the mirror.

If the blue ruffle had made a difference before... this... this was... Tiffany inhaled, staring at herself. The new undergarments Astrid had ordered be made to go with the altered design of the wedding dress and her trousseau were so much more comfortable than what she'd been wearing. She had grown so accustomed to the discomfort that she had not realized how uncomfortable she had been until now.

She'd thought it had to be that way.

But it did not.

The neckline of the dress was broad, dipping down to give just a hint of her cleavage, the size of her breasts emphasized by the flounce of Honiton lace that draped across from shoulder to shoulder. It hung down from her bosom, revealing a narrowed waist beneath, the streamlined corset nipping in, the bottom of it coming to a sharp point in the center of her body. The bottom of the corset was decorated with a narrow band of cord that matched the color of her dress exactly.

More lace fell from the bottom of her puffed sleeve, covering her elbows and adding another touch of decoration to the dress, which was otherwise all Spitalfields silk.

Her skirt puffed out from her narrowed waist, emphasizing her hips, the pleats in the fabric drawing attention to her hips, then spreading wider farther down the length of her skirt.

The cool, icy white of her wedding gown with just a hint of blue in its tone made her skin appear brighter, creamier. Her cheeks looked pinker. Even the color of her hair was much improved, appearing richer and brighter. Harleen had done it before Tiffany dressed this morning, before rushing off to assist Tiffany's mother, and she had done a lovely job. Combined with the dress, Tiffany looked like a fashion plate.

She could not stop looking at herself.

At least she was alone, so that she did not have to listen to her mother scold her over vanity. She was also nervous about her mother's reaction to seeing her today of all days. Her mother had immediately gone downstairs this morning to oversee the preparations for the wedding breakfast. She still did not know about the changes to Tiffany's dress. Ever since the engagement ball, she had mostly ignored Tiffany in favor of focusing on planning, as though now that the ball was past, she had relinquished responsibility for guiding Tiffany in her dress, conversation, and behavior.

Part of Tiffany had felt adrift without her mother's constant supervision. Another part of her had felt relief. Especially as someone else had always been there to support her at the various soirees, balls, and musicales, whether it was Sebastian, Gregory, or Gregory's mother. A few times, it had been Lady Astrid, and she'd managed to pass along the news about Montblanc's note, his reasonings, and subsequent disappearance.

Astrid had not known what to make of that any more than Tiffany and the others had.

A knock at the door made Tiffany jump, her heart fluttering up to her chest. Was it her mother?

She hoped it was Sebastian.

"Lady Tiffany, the Duchess of Clarence, Lady Tremaine, and Lady Louisa are here to see you." She recognized Polly's voice. The maid must have been sent to guide them since the rest of the household was preparing for the day.

Relief poured through her, so strong that it made her sag in place. It was not her mother. The thought did occur to her that she should not feel so relieved it was not her own mother at the door, but she did not have time to contemplate the fact.

"Yes, of course, let them in, please," she replied, turning away from the mirror to face the doorway.

The door opened to reveal the maid and the three other women, and the expressions of astonishment on their faces matched the way Tiffany felt.

"Oh my goodness, my dear." Gregory's mother rushed forward, holding her hands out in front of her to take Tiffany's. Tears sparked in her kind eyes. "You are a vision."

"Truly, an incredible change," Lady Tremaine agreed, stepping into the room. Louisa followed her, the slack-jawed shock on her face now hidden as she looked away. "I did not realize..." Her voice trailed off, then she gave her head a shake. "You look stunning, Tiffany."

"You do, but you are missing something." Duchess Clarence turned and gestured to Polly, who hurried forward to give her the velvet box she was holding for her. Polly beamed as the duchess opened it, revealing the full set.

"Yes, perfection," Lady Tremaine said. Louisa, as pretty as ever, stood off to the side, appearing sulky as her mother cooed over Tiffany. Despite everything, Tiffany could not help but feel bad for her. She knew what it was like to desire her mother's attention and approval.

"You look lovely as well, Lady Louisa," she said, smiling at her. Louisa's head jerked up, her startled gaze meeting Tiffany's. "The gown you chose suits you."

"Thank you." Lady Louisa's smile was small but appeared sincere. "You look beautiful."

"Thank you." The acknowledgment from her sometimes rival made Tiffany's chest warm in a manner that even the duchess' and Lady Tremaine's had not.

"You will have to crouch down a bit, dear, so I can fasten the necklace," the Duchess of Clarence said, gesturing.

Tiffany did as she bade. The heavy coolness of the necklace took her immediately back to the night of her engagement ball when she truly had felt like the belle of the ball. She remembered the look in Gregory's eyes when he'd seen her. She could not wait to see how he looked at her today.

The earrings went on and the bracelet, then the duchess and

Lady Tremaine combined forces to affix the tiara to Tiffany's head when there was another knock at the door.

"Tiffany, are you ready?" Her mother's sharp tones made Tiffany hunch for a moment before she quickly straightened. The Duchess of Clarence gave her a sympathetic look, though Lady Tremaine appeared not to notice.

"She is, Susan. You must come see," Lady Tremaine replied, obvious pride in her voice, though she had not done much more than assist with the tiara. Though Tiffany supposed, she might think to be taking credit for the dress as well, since she had been the one to initially suggest to Tiffany's mother that she should wear more blues and greens.

There was a very brief pause, and Tiffany wondered if her mother knew that the other ladies had arrived and joined her. Perhaps she did not. Though she had not ventured downstairs, she could only imagine it was rather chaotic as the house was prepared for the important event.

Then the door opened, revealing her mother on the other side.

Her jaw dropped as she stared at Tiffany, something flashing through her eyes that Tiffany could not define but she instinctively started to hunch in again.

"Does she not look lovely, Susan?" Lady Tremaine asked fondly. She had already turned toward Tiffany again and reached up to smooth some of the hair over where the tiara rested on her head. "Like a princess."

"I..." Tiffany's mother struggled with what she wanted to say.

"Just like a princess," Duchess Clarence agreed, patting Tiffany's hand encouragingly. "The dress is perfect on you. The style, the color... Lady Astrid's influence was inspired."

"Oh, I almost forgot Lady Astrid was there to tender her opinion," Lady Tremaine said. "No wonder it turned out so well. She never misses a trick, that one. Sheer genius when it comes to fashion. And look at how well Tiffany turned out! Such a credit to you and the Bolton family." Lady Tremaine turned back toward Tiffany's mother, who was still staring at Tiffany with an oddly blank look in her eyes.

Tiffany did not dare say a word since she was not sure which way the chips were about to fall. Her heart was pounding in her chest like a racing horse, nothing like the excited flutter she'd felt earlier. The urge to hunch down was growing ever stronger, even though she knew that her mother would order her to straighten up again.

"Yes... yes, she is a credit to the family," her mother repeated slowly. Her chin lifted, and she gave a nod of approval. "I daresay this will be the wedding of the year, and Tiffany acknowledged as the most beautiful bride of the Season."

"You are certainly setting the bar intimidatingly high," Lady Tremaine said approvingly.

"As are you," Duchess Clarence murmured to Tiffany, giving her a final pat on the hand. "I must return to Gregory. He is waiting, very impatiently, in the carriage. I will see you at the church, dear." Tiffany leaned down so the duchess could give her another cheek kiss, then she fluttered off through the door.

Watching her go would have given Tiffany a sinking feeling at being left alone with only her mother, Lady Tremaine, and Louisa, but as the duchess exited Tiffany's room, she was greeted by a masculine voice on the other side. Sebastian had arrived at her door. Her mother frowned, turning her head, obviously aware of his presence as well, though Tiffany was surprised because she had never seen her mother unhappy over Sebastian appearing.

"Is that Sebastian?" Lady Tremaine asked, her face lighting up. She turned to address her daughter. "Louisa, go let him in."

Tiffany's lips twitched at the way Louisa jumped to obey her mother's command, obviously posing as she opened the door for Tiffany's brother. Fortunately for Tiffany's peace of mind, Sebastian gave Louisa no more than a cursory greeting before looking past her.

His jaw dropped open.

"Tiff..." he sputtered. Actually sputtered, unable to form whatever words he was attempting.

Tiffany could not help but giggle, though she immediately suppressed it when her mother shot her a reproving look.

Sebastian gave himself a shake. "You look... there are no words. Gregory is going to swallow his tongue."

The way he stared at her, as if he did not recognize her, was the way she'd been staring at herself before the others had come in, so she did not take umbrage. She'd gone through a transformation. She'd had no idea that such small changes could make such a huge difference to how she looked, but it was not all in her imagination. Everyone's reactions proved that.

Tiffany found herself staring back at him. He looked so handsome in a dove grey morning jacket, a grey and forest green dapples waistcoat beneath it, and a matching forest green pocket square at his breast. The stiff white points of his starched shirt and the complicated knot of his cravat were snowy white, setting off his richly burnished brown hair as it waved away from his face.

He looked so much like their father, it made tears spring to her eyes. As much as she loved her brother and was so happy to see him, his presence was also a reminder of her father's absence. It was supposed to be her father walking her down the aisle to Gregory.

Her mother clapped her hands together, making them all jump, and smiled thinly.

"Enough of that. We do not want Tiffany to get a swelled head." She gave a light laugh that the other ladies joined as Sebastian chuckled. Tiffany smiled, though her chest felt tighter for some reason. "We must be on our way, so we are not late. It would not do to keep her bridegroom waiting."

"Of course," Sebastian said, turning to Tiffany and offering his arm. His expression changed again, his emotion rising in his eyes. Emotion matched by her own. They were both far too aware that the position he was currently taking was only because their father was dead. "I cannot believe I am about to give you away."

Reaching out to touch his cheek with her hand, Tiffany smiled at him through the tears in her eyes.

"I will still be your sister, no matter what. And now Gregory will be your brother in truth."

Sebastian huffed. "Don't remind me."

That made her laugh, washing away some of her sadness, as she slipped her arm through his. They were still family, no matter what happened, and she would not lose another family member. Not by any choice of her own.

The heartfelt moment buoyed her as they followed her mother and the other two ladies out the door. It was not until they were at the church and her mother had gone to be seated that Tiffany realized her mother was the only one who had not told her that she looked beautiful today.

TWENTY-FIVE

G*regory*

St. George's was packed, and there were more people outside, hoping to catch a glimpse of the high-ranking guests going in and out of the church. The day had dawned brightly sunny, the air warm enough that many a lady was idly waving her fan from her seat. The brightly colored dresses were dotted by grey morning suits, similar to Gregory's own, with some gentlemen popinjays adding more color to their attire to break up the grey.

Standing at the end of the aisle, trying to ignore the very full pews of guests and Father Patrick at his side, Gregory did his best not to jitter in place. Why he suddenly felt so nervy, he did not know, but he did.

Perhaps because marriage is a momentous occasion?

He glanced over his shoulder at Nathanial, who had agreed to be his best man. A position he'd always thought Sebastian would fulfill, but since he was marrying Sebastian's sister, his closest friend had a different duty today. Perhaps that was what was causing the sudden bout of nerves.

Could he be a good enough husband to Tiffany to satisfy his friend?

Oddly... the answer felt like yes. He truly enjoyed her company. He was far more attracted to her than he'd ever expected to be to his bride. After tasting her passion, he found he was no longer interested in seeking any others. Would that change after a few nights, the way it always had in the past?

Perhaps.

But there was a part of him that was already wondering whether he might be one of those husbands who cleaved to his wife rather than needing to be discreet. He supposed it would all depend on whether his new wife could satisfy all of his needs. If she could...

He certainly felt up to satisfying hers.

Ensuring her happiness felt of paramount importance to him. Therefore, he was not overly concerned with ensuring Sebastian was satisfied with his sister's lot as well since Gregory knew that would also be his primary concern.

His gaze skittered over the guests and landed on his mother, who was beaming at him from her seat in the front row. There was something smugly anticipatory in her expression that had been there from the moment she'd returned to the carriage after bringing Tiffany her jewels for the day. That might be the source of his consternation.

His mother knew something he did not. Something about Tiffany. Something she was anticipating seeing him react to.

Gregory did not like being kept in the dark, no matter how gleeful his mother was over the 'something'. He did not like waiting.

"She will be here soon enough; calm yourself," Nathanial muttered from behind him.

Taking in a deep breath, Gregory made his muscles relax. He had not even noticed the way he'd begun to shift from side to side.

The music continued as the doors at the back of the church opened, and Sebastian escorted his mother inside. Rather than sitting down with her, he would return up the side aisle while Lady

Louisa took center stage as Tiffany's maid of honor so he could escort his sister down the aisle as well.

Once the Duchess of Bolton was seated, Sebastian quickly moved away, and the doors at the back opened again to admit Lady Louisa before closing behind her again. She did look stunning, he had to admit, and a murmur of admiration swept the crowd. A trickle of unease slid through Gregory.

Though he had not been consulted on the matter of Tiffany's bridal party, he wondered how wise it was to have an acknowledged Diamond of the First Water as Tiffany's maid of honor, the lady who preceded her down the aisle. What unflattering comparisons would the *ton* make when Tiffany walked down mere moments later?

Tiffany had turned out quite a bit prettier than expected, but Lady Louisa was one of *the* elite debutantes of the entire Season. She smiled radiantly as she glided down the aisle, perfectly comfortable with all eyes on her, confident in her beauty. If Gregory heard a single unflattering comparison after this... he did not know what he was going to do, but he was determined to protect Tiffany from the cruelties of the *ton* to the best of his ability.

He grit his teeth, doing his best to keep a pleasant expression on his face, despite his displeasure at the inevitable contrasts between Lady Louisa's stunning beauty and Tiffany's more subtle appeal. The *ton* was not known for appreciating subtlety.

To Lady Louisa's credit, she did not milk the moment during her brief sojourn in the spotlight among the *haut ton*. The guests inside the church were the *crème de la crème* of the upper ten thousand by dint of Gregory and Sebastian's exalted rank. Another young lady might have been tempted to pose and preen, hoping to draw a gentleman's eye and make her own match, but Louisa quietly took her place across from him and Nathanial, then turned to face the back of the church.

The organ music paused, the silence hanging in the air for a dramatic moment, then it began again, this time playing the wedding march. The music swelled as the guests stood, turning to face the double doors as they opened at the back of the church.

Tiffany, on her brother's arm, stepped into the room, and it was like all the air had been sucked out of it.

She wore a veil that trailed out behind her, twice the length of the train of her dress as she walked down the aisle, but had left her face uncovered by it. The gasps of shock, the gaping open mouths as the *ton* got their first good look at the bride would have been amusing under other circumstances. Today, though, he was one of the afflicted.

Though Gregory had realized she was prettier than her brother had described her, though she'd been even prettier on the night of their engagement ball than he'd seen her before, that had not prepared him for today. She looked herself, yet so much more at the same time.

Her blushing cheeks were rosy against creamy skin that had often appeared sallow when against the oranges and yellows she favored. Even the mint green... even the blue ruffle... both had hinted at the possibilities, but neither had fully realized her beauty. The icy blue of the dress had somehow injected color into her where there had been little before. Her hair seemed brighter, richer, with blonde and red highlights glinting from the thick tresses of curls. The dress accentuated her curves, embracing and rejoicing in them. Gregory had not realized how much the lines of her dresses had made her appear unfashionable, how unflattering her previous silhouettes had been.

Something tugged on his jacket, and he realized that Nathanial was pulling him back into position.

He'd taken a step toward Tiffany without even realizing it, the sudden, primal instinct to leap forward and claim what was his before any of the encroaching males who had suddenly realized what a gem they'd missed out on could try to take his place.

But they could not because she was marrying *him*.

None of them had seen her. Not truly. Not until now.

He'd called her a swan because she reminded him of one, in her movements, in her grace. In this moment, the endearment felt almost prophetic. As a child, he'd been read the story of The Ugly Duckling, and now he felt as though he was watching it be played out right before his eyes.

Tiffany had blossomed into a beautiful swan, the likes of which easily rivaled Lady Louisa for the title Diamond of the First Water. Why she'd hidden her beauty so was a mystery, but the truth of it could not be denied.

Gregory stepped back into place, watching her come forward, a tremulous smile on her lips. As she came closer, he could see the anxiety in her hazel eyes, which helped him push his own nerves away completely, so he could be there for her to lean on. He smiled at her encouragingly as she and Sebastian came to a halt, waiting for Father Patrick to go through the ritual of Sebastian giving her away.

Giving her to Gregory.

Sebastian gave Gregory a glare as he placed Tiffany's hand in Gregory's. For once, Gregory had no desire to twit his friend. He gave Sebastian as reassuring a smile as he could, utterly sincere, and saw his friend's face relax.

Yes, Gregory could be unserious, perhaps the most so of their coterie of dukes, but that did not mean he was always flippant. When it came to this marriage, to Tiffany, he felt the weight of his responsibility to her in much the same way he felt the weight of his dukedom to the people under his care. He had no desire to jest or make light of either responsibility.

When his fingers closed around hers, he felt the oddest sense of possessive triumph.

Mine.

～

TIFFANY

From the moment she stepped into the church on Sebastian's

arm to the moment when she heard herself saying 'I do' as she stared into Gregory's dark eyes, Tiffany felt as though she was moving through a dream world. It did not seem real. It could not be real.

Then the ceremony was ending, and Gregory was pulling her forward for the kiss... their lips met and held. Clung. Tiffany shuddered as the memory of the way he'd kissed her before, the things he'd done to her, rolled through her. Her entire body quivered in memory.

It was no chaste kiss.

Then it was over.

Too quickly.

Except as soon as she remembered they had an audience, she realized it had likely not been over quickly enough. Father Patrick appeared slightly scandalized but also resigned.

Taking her arm, Gregory led her back down the aisle, and she caught a glimpse of her mother's disapproving scowl. Sebastian had the same expression of scandalized resignation Father Patrick had. A few of the more censorious elders of the *ton* were also frowning, but most of their guests were smiling in either amusement or complacent acceptance.

She breathed out a sigh of relief as they moved down the aisle, the weight of her train and veil dragging at her, yet she felt as light as a feather. It was done. She was married. To a duke.

To Gregory.

To most young ladies of her age and stature, marrying a duke was the pinnacle achievement. Any duke. That he might be one of the young and handsome 'tragic' dukes would be preferable but not a requirement.

For Tiffany, if she'd had a true choice, she would have picked Gregory.

The schoolgirl crush she'd had on her brother's handsome visiting friend had blossomed into so much more as she'd gotten to know him since that night in the library. Even now, knowing that he would eventually take a mistress, knowing it would break her heart when he did, she could not regret it.

For now, for however long it lasted, he was hers, and she was going to relish that time. Hopefully, by the time he lost interest in her, she would have at least one child to devote herself to and distract herself with. Perhaps, if he was discreet enough, she would not even know. That would be for the best if she could just pretend things were always as they were now.

Such thoughts were still depressing, and she pushed them to the back of her mind as she and Gregory stepped outside. The onlookers outside the church cheered even louder than they had for her arrival. She and Gregory paused at the top of the steps to wave before making their way down to the carriage bearing the Clarence coat of arms waiting first in line on the street.

Getting her dress and veil into the carriage with them was a process. The train could be cleverly detached, though it was not something she could do in front of such a large audience. Once they reached Bolton House for the wedding breakfast, certainly.

The carriage began to move, and they waved as they moved past the audience of people, who were looking between the carriage and the nobility beginning to exit the church.

At the end of the street, Gregory sighed with relief as the general audience was past.

"At last," he murmured, reaching over to draw the curtains on the carriage windows.

"What are you doing?" Tiffany asked, somewhat curious, somewhat alarmed as he reached over her to let down the curtains on her side of the carriage as well. The space—which would feel rather large if not for her voluminous skirts and train taking up so much of it—had suddenly become an intimate enclosure.

Eventually, she knew she and Gregory would be alone. She looked forward to it even, after their stolen moments at their engagement ball. But she was not prepared to do such things in a moving carriage... and they could not possibly have that much time...

"This," he said, putting his hands on her waist and hauling her onto his lap. Tiffany gasped in surprise as she found herself sitting on his hard thighs, something else hard digging into her bottom as he wrapped his hand around the back of her neck and pulled her down for a kiss.

It was a hot, needy kiss, far more passionate than the one they'd shared in the church, and Tiffany eagerly opened her mouth to be plundered. One hand caressed her neck as their tongues slid against each other in an intimate dance, then traced the lace of her gown down to where her breasts heaved. He cupped her over the fabric of her dress, and she whimpered, wriggling on his lap, as her gown suddenly felt horribly tight over her chest. His other hand was curved around her hip, holding her tight on his lap.

Her breasts ached as he squeezed, caressing her, touching her. She pressed her thighs together as the ache between them grew. The memory of his head beneath her skirts, the way his kisses were stealing her breath away, made her dizzy. She wondered if he was going to go beneath her skirts again, now, and whether she should attempt to stop him if he did. If she would even want to.

His mouth moved away from hers, moved over her jaw, down her throat until he was stymied by the necklace he'd given her to wear and the high neckline of her dress. Then his lips moved up again, working toward her ear. The hand on her breast moved up so he could tap his finger against the necklace.

"Do not forget," he murmured in her ear, his hot breath and low, rumbling voice sending another wave of aching need through her. "I want to see you wearing nothing but your jewels today while you are in my bed."

Heat flushed through her, embarrassment as much as desire. She was going to be naked in front of him. The very idea made her want to hide, yet... she wanted him to touch her again. More, she wanted to please him.

So, she nodded.

"Say 'yes, Gregory'," he ordered.

"Yes, Gregory," she whispered obediently.

"Good girl." The way he said it, combined with his teeth nipping at the soft skin on her throat, made her moan. His hands gripped her tighter. "We are going to spend as little time at this breakfast as possible."

"Yes, Gregory."

She was pretty sure he growled.

The carriage came to a halt, and they had to set themselves to rights… if Tiffany could be set to rights when her entire body was throbbing, aching for him to touch her again. To finish the concerto he'd begun on her senses.

If she was not so aroused, she would be furious at him for doing this to her right before she had to face all their guests. On the other hand, she no longer had room to be nervous about facing their guests when her body was so full of need for him.

As he helped her down from the carriage, she found that she was in complete accord with him. She, too, wanted to spend as little time at their wedding breakfast as possible.

TWENTY-SIX

Gregory

By Gregory's reckoning, after receiving their guests, they would need to stay for at least another half hour before he could shove Tiffany into the carriage again and make haste for Clarence House. There was a particularly memorable wedding breakfast some years ago where the Earl of Spencer threw his bride over his shoulder and carried her out of their wedding breakfast...

Unfortunately, as a duke marrying a duke's sister, Gregory had a feeling the *ton* would be more scandalized than amused. The higher one's place in Society, the more certain social mores had to be adhered to. Could he and Tiffany weather the *ton's* reaction? Of course. They were duke and duchess, after all.

But he did not want her to begin their marriage by weathering more scandalous behavior from him. Especially considering how their engagement had come about. However, he also refused to do the pretty for the *ton* for more than the bare minimum today.

Sebastian could not keep them apart now that they were married, and Gregory wanted to get his hands all over her. The taste he'd had in the carriage had not been nearly enough, as he'd known it would not be, but he had not been able to help himself, even knowing he was setting himself up for frustration.

There was plenty of time for passion to simmer and settle as their families arrived, then they got into the position for the receiving line. He was acutely aware of Tiffany by his side, smiling and greeting their guests with aplomb. He was even more aware of the way she sagged with relief once their duty was done, and he took her arm to lead her inside.

They took a moment for the train on Tiffany's dress to be removed—if he'd known that was possible, he might have tried to do that in the carriage; it would certainly have given him more room to maneuver—before entering their reception. Keeping her on his arm, they circulated among the guests.

Gregory was amused to see Matthew surreptitiously looking at young ladies and flipping his coin before brightening when it finally landed on heads, which had him approaching a young miss Gregory did not recognize. Mentally, he wished his friend good luck, though it was likely the Lord of Luck did not actually need it. Nathanial, of course, was already surrounded by young ladies with huge dowries, though from the hunted expression on his face, such a surplus was not actually assisting him in his search for the *right* bride for him.

Lady Louisa had immediately claimed Sebastian's attention, assisted by their mothers. Sebastian looked nearly as pained as Nathanial, despite only having one young lady to deal with. The addition of his mother's pressure was likely the cause of his strain.

"How long do we have to stay?" Tiffany asked in a whisper, clinging to his arm, making Gregory grin. His bride was as eager to decamp as he was.

"Another quarter of an hour... we should get something to eat." She was going to need her strength once he got her to himself.

She nodded and followed his lead over to the refreshments table. Christian was there, flirting with a small bevy of young ladies. He grinned rakishly and winked, causing a fluttering of fans from his admiring crowd. Their mamas were nearby, keeping close watch.

Christian was a duke, but he was also a rake, and his reputation was among the worst of their set. Especially since he had not bothered to hide his association with his actress.

As he and Tiffany filled their plates, Drake and Lady Astrid approached. They walked together, though she did not take his arm, which was causing some consternation among the gossips. Neither of them seemed to care. Lady Astrid smiled as she greeted Tiffany.

"The dress is perfection. You set the whole *ton* back on its heels," Lady Astrid said, her eyes alight with a kind of wicked enjoyment. "I look forward to seeing the rest of your trousseau in action."

"I am looking forward to wearing it," Tiffany admitted. Gregory frowned. If the rest of her trousseau showed her off as well as her wedding dress did...

Recently married, a purported love match, she should be safe from the wolves of the *ton*. At least until he stopped showing interest. Then they would descend *en masse*, a slavering horde ready to warm the bed her husband had left cold. Even if Tiffany was not the type to take a lover, that would not stop them from trying, and if temptation continued to beckon... The obvious solution was to never stop showing interest and keep the rakes and *roués* at bay by always warming her bed.

At the moment, he was certain that would be no hardship.

Drake gave him a look as the two ladies chatted, which made Gregory feel as though he knew exactly what his friend was thinking. He suddenly wondered if part of Drake's hesitation in going before the altar with Lady Astrid was for similar reasons. For now, Lady Astrid was spoken for and a virginal debutante. Once they were married, Drake would have to cleave to her or contend with the men who would come flocking to her beauty, wit, and charm.

"Where is Zachary?" he asked Drake, in part to distract himself and in part out of genuine curiosity, as he was the only one of their friends Gregory had not spotted.

"In the corner, brooding," Drake replied, nodding his head to the other side of the room. Gregory turned to see that Zachary was scowling, and his temper was likely being sorely tested because the current Northumberland had decided to join him there. Considering how close Zachary had been to his predecessor, the incumbent duke would do well to leave Zachary alone and cease his toadying. Unfortunately, the man did not seem to have the social savvy or self-preservation to realize the danger he was putting himself in.

"What happened?"

"The Baroness Ashfield left the Harrington's soiree last night with Conyngham."

Gregory shook his head. Poor Zachary.

Though, perhaps her moving on with a new lover would finally allow him to break free of his emotional attachment.

Personally, Gregory was rather enjoying his own attachment to his bride.

Speaking of which... he looked over as she finished eating the pastry that had been on her plate, her eyes sparkling brightly as she spoke with Lady Astrid. It seemed the two of them had become true friends, which he was glad to see. However, he could not wait any longer.

He turned back to Drake.

"Well, unfortunate as that is for Zachary, I have my own bride that needs tending, and I find I cannot wait any longer." He grinned as Drake raised his eyebrow.

What better way to confirm to the *ton* that they truly were a love match than whisking his bride away from their wedding breakfast as quickly as possible? Doing so also served his own purposes, his own needs. In truth of fact, he was feeling somewhat akin to Zachary and his obsession, but Gregory had had the good sense to marry the object of his.

Now, he would get to reap the reward.

~

TIFFANY

"There is something I need to tell you, before you go," Tiffany's mother said when Tiffany was finished with the necessary. Gregory had made it clear he wanted to go, and Tiffany had gone to the retiring room before they could leave. Her mother had followed her, to her surprise. She had not been sure what her mother wanted since she had waited silently until Tiffany was finished.

"Yes, mother?" Tiffany felt almost like going up on her toes, hopeful that her mother might finally acknowledge that Tiffany looked beautiful today. That she might finally repeat the compliment Tiffany had heard over and over again—how she'd blossomed, how she'd turned into a true beauty, how fashionably flattering her wedding gown was.

She knew her mother had been unhappy with the changes made, but she hoped the opinion of the rest of Society had softened the blow to her mother's unhappiness at having her own decisions upended.

"It is about your wedding night, or perhaps afternoon, as it seems your new husband is pressing for... though I suppose he is trying to ensure everyone truly believes you two are a love match." Her mother sniffed.

Tiffany's hopes dropped, though they did not entirely dissipate. Her chest squeezed at the reminder that the basis of her marriage was scandal, not love, and the second was just a shield to hide the first.

"So perhaps once you are alone, he will wait for tonight, but eventually, he will come to your bed, and you need to be prepared."

The way her mother said it sent alarm through Tiffany, as if her mother was trying to warn her against some portending doom. On the other side of that, she had the memory of Gregory in the library and the way he'd made her feel. She knew there would be more, though she was not entirely sure of the specifics or what it might be like, but she was rather eager to find out.

"Prepared?" she asked.

"For the pain." Her mother lifted her chin, hands smoothing over the front of her skirts. Her eyes flashed, and there was something in her voice, more than sincerity, almost as though she found satisfaction in bearing this news to Tiffany. "Bedding is a terrible pain, especially the first time, but you must do your duty to your husband and bear it."

"What kind of pain?" Tiffany did not bother to hide her alarm. She could hear the sincerity in her voice.

"A ripping kind of pain on your insides." Her mother put her hand on her lower stomach. "You will likely bleed as well. But it is necessary to the begetting of an heir. Men enjoy such things. If you are lucky, he will only do it a few times, then he will seek a mistress or lover to inflict his passions on."

That did not sound lucky to Tiffany.

Emotions warred within her. Her mother was too gleeful to be lying, yet... Gregory had never hurt Tiffany before. She could not imagine him enjoying her ripping pain or causing her to bleed. If anything, her pleasure had been at the center of how he'd touched her... though perhaps he was trying to prepare her for the worst.

Yet, even that did not make sense.

"Why does it not hurt mistresses or lovers?" she asked. Her mother's eyes flashed, angry that Tiffany was questioning her, and she quickly explained. "I am sorry, I just do not understand. Is there a difference?"

"You do not need to understand," her mother snapped. "It is inappropriate to speak of such things. You are lucky I cared enough to warn you; not every mother does. But I could not bear it if you went to your wedding bed unprepared, only to find agony waiting for you." She lifted her chin up. "That is all I will say on the matter."

True to her word, Tiffany's mother swept out of the room before Tiffany could retire, leaving Tiffany shaken, but...

Her mother had a lover. She knew her mother did. She might not be sure it was the Duke of Grafton's uncle, but she was certain her mother had one.

That meant that, at some point, the pain must end. She could not imagine her mother doing something that caused her painful agony on a regular basis when she did not have to.

There must be some benefit to it, at least, beyond bearing children.

Yet, her mother had also been very sure it would hurt. She could feel the certainty her mother had projected all the way down to her bones.

Obviously, she could not ask her mother to explain more. The idea of asking Sebastian made her blanch. Lady Astrid was not married, so she had no real experience. The Duchess—now Dowager Duchess—of Clarence? She might not tell Tiffany the truth since it was her own son who would be doing the deed... besides, Tiffany could not imagine approaching the older woman with such a delicate subject. If her own mother would not speak of it to her, she could not expect her husband's mother to do so.

She would have to ask Gregory and hope he told her the truth. Though she could not imagine what it would benefit him to lie when she would experience the truth for herself shortly. Besides, she trusted him.

If he told her it would hurt...

There was some part of her—the part that had dared to question her mother—that wondered if her mother was deliberately misleading her. The same way she had misled Tiffany about her clothing. She could not imagine why her mother would want to do such a thing, yet she could not forget the rage in her mother's eyes when Tiffany had appeared in her altered wedding gown this morning.

She could not shake loose the hurt that her mother was the only person to neglect to compliment her appearance today. Perhaps it was vain, as her mother would likely accuse her of being, but why could she not have one compliment from her own mother on her own wedding day? Lady Tremaine had been full of flattery. Gregory's mother had been effusive in her praise.

Why not her own mother?

Tiffany had devoted her life to trying to make her mother proud, and today, she had reached the pinnacle achievement and married a duke, yet her mother was still unhappy with her.

Was it just her mother's desire for control? Or... It was beginning to feel as though her mother was deliberately undermining her, though she could not understand why her mother would do such a thing. She did not even want to think about it, if she was being honest, because it hurt too much to think her mother would be so deliberately cruel. That her mother really did hate her, the way she sometimes feared. She always told herself she was imagining things, being too sensitive to the way her mother told her she was.

And yet...

The gleeful look in her mother's eye when she told Tiffany that being bedded would be painful would not disappear from Tiffany's memory, no matter how she wished it would.

Putting her hand on her own stomach, Tiffany tried to remember the pleasure that Gregory had given her. The light in his eyes when he said he wanted to see her wearing nothing but the sapphires and diamonds she now wore. Her body tingled at the memory, quivered in anticipation...

However, she could not entirely put away her consternation or her growing fear.

TWENTY-SEVEN

G*regory*

Something had happened between their carriage ride to Bolton House and this one. Something that had made his eager bride into a pensive one.

She had gone to the retiring room, and her mother had accompanied her... What had happened there between them? The Duchess of Bolton had sailed out several moments ahead of Tiffany, a wide smile on her face. Tiffany had followed, and, at the time, Gregory had not noticed anything amiss, but once they were alone in the carriage, she was not the same as she had been before. Instead of looking at him, her gaze was fixed out the window. Instead of quivering in breathless anticipation of what they might do in the carriage, she was trembling with nerves.

And she'd sat across from him rather than next to him.

Frowning inwardly, Gregory put a smile on his face and reached out his hand.

No, he was not imagining things. She hesitated before reaching back. And when their hands met, her fingers were stiff and cool against his.

"Come here," he said, closing his fingers about hers and pulling her toward him. She let out a shriek as she was lifted from her seat by motion, the carriage rattling along and assisting him with the change of seating. Gregory easily caught her with his other hand, twisting her body so she was seated on his lap, very much the same way he had before. "What is wrong, little swan?"

One hand round her back, the other dropped her hand onto her lap so he could lay his own hand against her stomach and begin to move it upwards toward her breast. He felt, as much as heard, her trembling breath in response.

"I..." Her voice trailed off, her gaze averting from his, as if she could not look at him.

"Look at me, Tiffany," he ordered. And it was an order, delivered in a tone of voice that he had not used with her before—in large part because he had not needed to. She was always so delightfully obliging, so easy to lead, it had not been required.

The order startled her, and she jerked her head up to meet his gaze, her eyes wide in surprise. Gregory knew he had that effect when he decided to take control of a situation or a woman. Many mistook his easygoing, charming nature to mean he was always that way. For a certain kind of woman, they were delighted when they discovered how incorrect their thinking was.

Gregory closed his hand around her breast, enjoying the way her pupils dilated, her lips dropping open in aroused shock. Whatever she was not telling him, it was difficult for her to put into words. Therefore, distracting her should help loosen her tongue.

"Tell me what is wrong, little swan." Rather than a question, this time, he phrased the query as an order, his hand kneading her breast, throwing her off physically while he pushed her verbally.

"I... my mother..." She stumbled over her words, a hot blush flushing across her cheeks. "When we... when you..." She heaved in a deep breath, her breast swelling against his palm, and met his gaze head-on. "When we bed, will it hurt me?"

His hand stilled on her breast. Ah. Her mother must have told her something of what the marriage bed was like. Enough to make her worry. Gregory realized that not all women had pleasant experiences with their husbands. He'd certainly bedded enough unsatisfied married ladies to know the truth of that. None of them had gone into the details of what their wedding nights had been like, but he could extrapolate.

Still, he felt the assumption that he would be so inept, so incompetent, as a blow to his pride. He was a rake, after all. An experienced one. Not some stripling youth blundering through his first time with a doxy.

Though he had never bedded a virgin before.

When he felt Tiffany start to tense, he realized he had not yet answered her question.

Still caressing her breast through the fabric of her gown, he rubbed his thumb over the bump where her nipple was, enjoying the way she gasped, shuddering against him. His cock was already rising again, eager to show her just how much pleasure he could give her.

"I have heard that it can be painful for a woman her first time," he admitted, not wanting to lie to her. "However, there are things one can do to ameliorate that pain. I have also heard that a great deal of horseback riding can mean that the lady experiences very little pain... do you ride much?"

"Yes." She gasped as he shifted her on his lap, releasing her breast so he could use that hand to tug her skirts up until he could slide his hand beneath the layers and touch the silk stockings she was wearing. Her hands came up to grip his jacket, holding onto the lapels for dear life as she stared at him in astonished arousal.

Gregory grinned at her. "Then it might not hurt at all. There is also a very thin line between pleasure and pain, something I would like to show you eventually, but today is not that day." His fingers moved higher on her leg, past the ribbons holding her stockings in place, and she gasped again as he touched soft, sensitive flesh. "Today, I am going to show you exactly how good I can make you feel."

With that, he leaned down to capture her lips, tipping her back against the seat of the carriage just as his fingers found the soft, wet folds of her pussy. And she was wet, aroused by his touch.

No, he was quite sure he could make it so she felt almost no pain at all.

~

TIFFANY

Oh, heavens...

Gregory was doing it to her again. Touching her in a manner that made thought and reason fly out of her head. The proprietary way he behaved with her body was both shocking and arousing, making her insides pulse, and when he touched her most private area, she felt as though she might melt back into the seat cushions of the carriage. In fact, she almost wanted to melt back into them, to forget... everything. To let Gregory take over and lead her where he wanted to go.

It was far more enjoyable than worrying about what her mother had said and why she'd said it.

Tiffany would much rather focus on what Gregory was doing to her. How he was touching her. How he was making her feel.

Even if it did hurt, even if there was pain, it might be worth it for the rest of this. For all the pleasure. Perhaps that was the tradeoff?

His fingers slid against her sensitive body, and Tiffany gasped against his mouth, the sound muffled by his lips, as she felt something actually slide inside of her. One long finger eased its way into her body, an utterly foreign feeling that was somehow both invasive and intimate. She felt him moving inside her, her body quivering around him, and his hand rocked against the sensitive spot he'd found before at the apex of her slippery folds, and Tiffany cried out.

The sensations were even more intense than when he'd put his mouth on her, leaving her trembling all over as the pleasure inside her tightened and began to whirl. His finger retreated, then pushed in again, thicker—joined by a second digit. The two pushed in deep, stretching her open as he kissed her, his tongue invading her mouth as thoroughly as he was invading her womanhood, the heel of his hand rocking against that sensitive spot as he stroked her from the inside.

Tiffany felt faint, as if there was not enough air in her lungs to breathe, and not only because he was kissing her breathless. She shuddered, gasping, her body clamping down around him as the pleasure swirled and grew. A sob rose in her throat as she teetered on the edge of ecstasy, then fell.

Gregory caught her. Held her through the tumult as she lost control of her wit and her body, the climax sending her soaring through the seas of passion while he anchored her to reality.

"Good girl," he murmured, releasing her lips and pulling her upright again to cradle against him. His fingers were still inside of her, stroking gently until the swells of pleasure slowed along with her breathing, leaving her spent and panting on his lap. Only once the last paroxysms of her body had dissipated did he pull his fingers from her, sliding his hand out from beneath her skirt. Tiffany watched in horrified fascination as he lifted the glossy digits to his mouth, inserting them and cleaning her juices from them with his tongue. Catching her watching him, he winked at her, his dark eyes glittering devilishly.

Goodness.

The carriage came to a halt, leaving her even more flustered than before as she realized she was now going to have to get *out* of the intimate space and walk in front of people. Not just people. Gregory's staff.

But there was no choice but to put on a stiff upper lip and bear it.

Obviously not as affected as her, Gregory exited the carriage first after the coachman opened the door for him, turning to help her down. She managed it, though her knees felt as though they might give any moment. The second her feet touched the ground, Gregory had a supportive arm about her waist, his other hand still holding hers across his body as he led her toward the house.

The door opened before they reached it, his butler obviously flustered, which was a feat. Tiffany stared in awe.

"Your Grace... Your Grace... we ah... the staff is not..." Paulson stammered, his eyes darting back and forth as though searching for an obvious solution.

"Do not fret. We are not ready to have the staff presented to us," Gregory replied cheerfully.

Tiffany's blush grew hotter as she realized what the problem was. As the new duchess, she would be expected to be formally introduced to the household, but as they had left the wedding breakfast early, the household was not ready to be introduced to *her*. She shrieked as Gregory suddenly let go of her hand and bent to sweep it under her legs, swinging her up into his arms.

"We left the breakfast precipitously. The household can meet her grace later."

"Very good, Your Grace." Paulson inclined his head, appearing torn between being scandalized and relieved.

"Oh God." Tiffany buried her face in Gregory's neck so she did not have to look anyone who might pass them in the eye.

The entire household was going to know what they were doing —and *she* did not even fully understand what they were going to be doing! But she knew that bedding in the middle of the day was not the done thing. The understairs gossip was going to be rife... which she supposed lent credence to their façade of a 'love match', but she felt fairly sure that was not Gregory's aim. From his ground-eating stride through the house, he was wholly focused on his destination, which ended up being his bedroom.

Despite the pleasure he'd brought her to in the carriage, the uncertainty of the unknown was creeping up on her again.

He did not give her much time to feel uncertain. As soon as they'd entered his room, she barely managed to look around to catch a glimpse—enough to realize they were unquestionably in the ducal apartment and not hers—before he kicked the door shut behind him, and his lips found hers again.

Tiffany kissed him back with all the passion, all the uncertainty, all the leftover tremors of pleasure she had going through her. Even if it hurt, even if it did feel like she was being ripped apart, she would do it. Whatever it was.

For him.

CHAPTER

TWENTY-EIGHT

regory

Distraction was the name of the game, Gregory had decided. He could feel his bride's hesitation where there had been none before and knew he had not entirely assuaged her fears. The only way to do that was to get through it so she could see that she did not need to be afraid, that he would not unduly cause her pain—though if it turned out she liked some bite with her pleasure, he would not be unhappy.

Perhaps he could even test the waters now to see how she responded and, hopefully, demonstrate that not all pain had to be bad.

If she could meet his needs, all his needs, he may not ever want for another lover. If he were being entirely truthful with himself, that was what he was hoping for because he already did not desire another lover. He wanted her.

Letting her legs drop so she could slowly slide down his front, Gregory kept their lips fused together as he began to move his hands over her body. Tiffany moaned against his lips, shuddering as his hands slid over the silky fabric of her wedding gown, caressing her

254

through the layers. He moved to the back of the dress and found the buttons and loops there.

He was an accomplished enough lover that he did not need to lift his head from the kiss to undo them. Though he did take his time with it, moving them slowly toward his bed. As her soft body rubbed against his, the thick length of his erection pushed against the front of his pants, pressing into her stomach as he kissed her breathless.

The initial impulse to take her to her rooms had been crushed under the desire to have her in *his* bed when he claimed her. He'd never shared his bed with another lady before. Their bed, not his. That was always the rule.

But Tiffany was his wife, and that already made her an exception. There was something powerfully possessive about using his bed to bed his bride.

She shivered against him as she felt her dress being undone.

More distraction was needed. And perhaps some balance in their positions.

Lifting his head from the kiss, he stared down at her.

"Untie my cravat," he commanded her, his voice husky with his need. Licking her swollen lips, Tiffany moved her hands up to tug at the ends of his cravat, loosening it from around his neck. "Now, my jacket."

Slim fingers slid over his chest, pushing under the fabric of his jacket, helping him shrug it from his shoulders. He let it fall to the floor, uncaring. Tiffany's gaze tracked down for a moment, as if she wanted to protest leaving it there, but he pulled her attention back to him with another command.

"My waistcoat, little swan."

Buttons, more buttons. His were far larger than the ones along the back of her dress, though. He finished undoing hers as she worked on the ones on his waistcoat, leaving a trail of kisses along her jawline and down her neck while she gasped.

"I cannot concentrate while you do that!" she protested, fumbling with the final button on his waistcoat.

"Good." He chuckled at the exasperated sound she made. "I do not want you to be able to concentrate." He'd reached the end of her buttons and tugged at the fabric, slipping the gown off her shoulder. It slid out from beneath the heavy necklace around her throat and down the side, baring part of her breast along with her shoulder.

Enjoying her gasp, he leaned down to kiss the newly exposed skin, and she made a sound in the back of her throat as she managed to pull the last button on his waistcoat free. The garment joined his jacket on the floor as he moved to the side, pulling Tiffany along with him, lifting his head long enough to lift her dress from her as well.

Her petticoats and bustle joined the clothing on the floor a few moments later, along with his shirt, then her stays, leaving her in her stockings, her chemise, and the shimmering Clarence sapphires. The chemise was a pale white trimmed with blue lace that allowed a glimpse of her creamy breasts and pink nipples as it moved against her.

"Gorgeous," he murmured.

She peeked up at him shyly, cheeks bright pink from her blush. She truly did not realize how beautiful she was, something which he was determined to change.

So as not to frighten her, he did not take off his breeches yet. Instead, he gently lifted her chemise over her head, baring her breasts and the furred cleft of her pussy to him completely. The jewels winking at her throat, her wrist, and her ears, the tiara still adorning her curls, made for a stunning contrast to her naked body.

Gregory's gaze roved over her in a shockingly blatant manner that made her insides tighten. She did not know what to think. Part of her wanted to hide because she was not supposed to be naked in front of a man... but he was her husband, which meant she was allowed to be in front of him. But it was so hard not to cover herself, even though he was obviously enjoying looking at her.

He did not seem to think that her breasts were excessive or her hips unsightly or her body unshapely. Tiffany's hand unconsciously drifted up, and she did not realize she was rubbing her arm on the spot where her mother would pinch her until Gregory gently put his hand atop her arm.

"Do not cover yourself," he said firmly, and she realized that by reaching across herself, she'd covered her breasts. She had not meant to do so, had not even realized what she was doing until he'd redirected her.

Stepping forward, Gregory claimed her lips again before she could decide whether or not to try to explain. His hands moved over her back, over her bottom, down to her thighs, and he bent slightly at the knee. Tiffany found herself being lifted against him, the soft fabric of his pants rubbing against her inner thighs. Her breasts pressed against his chest, the wiry hair adorning his hard muscles abrading the sensitive tips of her nipples as her breasts bounced.

She gasped as he tipped her back onto the bed, his hard body settling between the legs, his hands squeezing the backs of her sensitive thighs. She felt so small beneath him, so dainty, so helpless, yet, for some reason, she liked that. Because she trusted him. Because she knew that even if he did have to hurt her, he would do his best not to hurt her too much.

Lifting his lips from hers, he sat back against his heels, his hand entwining with hers and bringing her wrist up to his lips.

"You are still fearful," he murmured, pressing his mouth to the inside of her wrist, just above where her bracelet had slid down, sending a tremor through her body.

The cool, heavy necklace around her neck made her throat feel tight as she tried to catch her breath.

"I am trying not to be," she said.

His other hand slid from behind her thigh up to her hip, moving higher to her breast. He cupped the soft mound, his fingers caressing her, making her moan at the sensation of his touch against her bare skin.

"Not all pain has to be bad, you know," he said, nipping at her fingertips at the same time his closed around her nipple. She gasped as he pinched the little bud, her insides clenching at the shot of sensation that went through her.

It was pain, yes, but also pleasure. Arousal.

The bud throbbed in his grip as he rolled it between his finger and thumb, increasing the pressure until she cried out, her back arching. It did hurt. But she wanted more. Her other nipple ached in envy, its neglect leaving her feeling unbalanced.

"I... oh..." She could not find it in herself to form words as Gregory released her other hand so he could give her other breast and nipple the same treatment.

"Reach above you. Hold on to the headboard." The order was followed by a feeling of relief because she had not known what to do with her hands. Gregory's eyes gleamed as he filled his own palms with her breasts, squeezing and kneading, while Tiffany grasped the wooden headboard above her. The position stretched her out indecently, almost lewdly. Her breasts pushed up into the air, as if begging him for more. With the way he was positioned, kneeling between her legs with her thighs draped over his own, her entire body was open and vulnerable to him.

Gregory lowered his head to her breasts, and Tiffany cried out at the hot, wet sensation of his mouth closing over one aching bud. He did not give her any quarter there. While his hand pinched and twisted one nipple, his mouth suckled and nipped the other, his teeth scraping over the tender surface in a manner that had her writhing against him. She could not help herself, even as her cheeks heated in embarrassment at her reaction.

He was ravishing her senses as much as her body, and she had no defense against him.

He was the first man to have ever kissed her.

The first man to have ever touched her in such a manner.

To ignite the spark inside her.

A spark that had grown to a roaring conflagration she had no idea how to quell, other than through him.

"Gregory!" She cried out his name—a shocked protest, a heartfelt plea.

Rather than responding, he moved in one quick, smooth undulation so he was no longer supporting her lower body with his. Instead, his body was stretched out on the bed, and rather than his hips between her thighs, now his shoulders were. Tiffany stared down the length of her body at him.

She could see that her flush had gone far beyond her cheeks, down her neck to her chest, leaving patchy pink skin over the swells of her breasts. Her nipples were hard buds, pointing at the canopy of his bed, shiny from the ministrations of his lips and tongue. The furred triangle of hair atop her mound did nothing to protect her from his gaze as he draped her thighs over his shoulders, lowering himself to her most sensitive flesh.

Tiffany's breath caught in her throat as he looked up at her, their gazes meeting over her body, then he deliberately held her gaze as he pressed his mouth to her nether lips. She cried out, back arching to press herself more firmly against him, her head falling back as the strain of keeping it upright was no longer tenable.

It was the library all over again, except this time, she did not need to hold herself up, and he was not hindered by her skirts. Indeed, he was able to do so much more. Her heels dug into the rippling muscles on his back as his tongue went to work on her folds, licking and feasting on her arousal from the source rather than licking it from his fingers as he'd done before. With her legs draped over his shoulders, he bent her in half, his hands reaching up to close around her breasts, returning to massaging them, tweaking her nipples as she was overwhelmed by the sensual assault.

"Gregory! Oh, please... please..." She writhed, her head tossing back and forth as he drove her to her second climax of the day. By comparison, the one in the carriage had been rushed. Frenzied. This one went on and on, the tension bursting into pleasure that rippled through her like fireworks across her senses, waves of them going on and on as he did not stop suckling.

She could not bear it as her body became ultra-sensitive against the pull of his mouth. Releasing the headboard, she reached down to grip his hair and try to pull him away from her pulsing flesh. To her surprise, his head lifted immediately, and she panted for breath, her fingers wreathed through his dark locks, her heart pounding in her chest like a wild horse across the moors.

She stared back at him, dizzy from the pulsing sensations that still ricocheted through her body.

"Naughty, little swan. I told you to keep your hands on the headboard." Though he called her naughty and was clearly admonishing her, the way he said it did not feel like a critique.

"I'm sorry!" She immediately let go, stretching toward the headboard, but it was too late.

It happened so quickly that she was not entirely sure *how* it happened. One moment, she was on her back, reaching for the headboard; the next, the entire world was in motion, then she landed on her stomach with a soft *oof.* Her breasts were crushed beneath her, the sensitive nipples pressed against the fabric of the bedding, which felt far rougher against her front than it had her back. Her legs were still spread, with Gregory between them. She could feel his hard, hairy thighs against the tender insides of hers, so she could not close them.

"What—" she floundered, trying to get her bearings, but before she could, his hand came down on her bottom with a stinging swat. "Ow!"

The chuckle that drifted to her ears seemed entirely incongruous to the situation. She stared at the headboard, which was only inches away from her hands, somewhat aghast. If she had ever been spanked before, it was so long ago in her childhood that she did not remember. The sensation—and her reaction to it—were not what she would have expected if she'd ever thought about the possibility of it happening to her as an adult.

Gregory rubbed the spot where he'd just swatted her, almost as though he was rubbing the sensation into her skin. Her insides clenched. It had hurt, but not that much, and despite how satisfied she was already feeling, she felt her arousal prickling again from the bite of pain.

"Do not worry, little swan. Since it is our wedding day, this will only be a small punishment for disobedience... and in the future, you will remember to obey my commands." His voice was lower than normal, firmer, more in control, and he punctuated his statement with another swat to the other side of her bottom, so the stinging sensation matched in both cheeks.

Heat flushed through her at his words, which had as much of an effect on her as his hands. Before today, she would have described Gregory as charming, confident but free-wheeling, *laissez faire* even. The words *strict* or *dominating* would not have come to mind. Not until now.

Now, she was seeing an entirely different, unexpected side of her husband.

And, heaven help her, every part of her body thrilled in response.

TWENTY-NINE

Gregory

Spanking Tiffany on their wedding day had not been part of his initial plan, but he had not been able to help the impulse once he saw the opportunity. Especially after the way she'd responded to his commands, to his assault on her more tender parts... she liked a bit of pain with her pleasure. He'd seen her reactions. Gauged them. Now, he was testing her boundaries further.

Did she know they had moved beyond what another man might expect from his wife on their wedding night?

He could not imagine that she had expected to be spanked.

When he laid his hand down on the upturned curve of her bottom, leaving behind a pink mark where his palm met flesh, she moaned and shuddered. Her hips lifted her bottom as if asking for more, her arousal glistening on the plump lips of her pussy, framed by the fringe of dark curls. Her bottom hole winked at him as her cheeks clenched when he spanked her again, and his cock surged against his pants.

No, she could not possibly be ready for that yet.

Especially since she was already fearful of pain. He would have to prepare her carefully.

But he would prepare her because he was determined to claim *all* of her, eventually. The amount of possessiveness he felt over her was stunning, yet he accepted it as an inevitability not worth fighting.

"If it begins to hurt too much, just tell me to stop." This was an introduction to his perversions, after all, and her first night experiencing anything like it. His hand smacked her bottom again, causing the flesh to ripple, and his cock jerked. She gasped, wriggling in response, but she did not ask him to stop. Instead, her hips lifted again, offering her pink cheeks up for more. Her upper half remained down, her hands gripping the headboard once again, head bowed in supplication as she waited for his next move.

Bloody hell, she was perfect for him and so much more than he could have dreamed of.

He rubbed his hand over the pink spots where he'd spanked her, his other hand coming down on her lower back to keep her in position. Though spanking was not his favorite perversion, more like an occasional indulgence, he was certainly enjoying watching his wife's reactions to her first one at his hands.

"Four more, little swan, then I'll demonstrate how sweet the mix of pain and pleasure can be."

~

TIFFANY

How did pain become pleasure?

A question she had no answer to, though she was experiencing the possibilities.

Every time Gregory's hand smacked against her bottom, she felt the stinging response.

Four more.

His hand came down again, harder than before, yet her body lit with the same burst of arousal she'd experienced before. With his hand on her lower back, she did not jerk upright, and her hands clenched around the spindles on the headboard more tightly, maintaining her position. The swat still rocked her forward, and her breasts swayed beneath her, her nipples rubbing against the bedsheets with the movement, adding to the sensational mix.

The swat was repeated on her other cheek.

Then again. And again.

Tiffany panted for breath as he rubbed the two spots with his palms, his fingers digging into her soft flesh in a manner that was both pleasurable and painful. A sweet mix indeed. She wanted more. Craved it. Needed it. Despite the satisfaction he'd brought her, her body was already throbbing again, not entirely satiated from the earlier orgasms.

"Please," she begged as he massaged her cheeks, even though she did not truly know what she was begging for.

A moment later, she found herself on her back again, Gregory's mouth descending between her legs. She was becoming intimately familiar with the sensation of his tongue and mouth feasting on her there, and she eagerly pressed herself against his lips, seeking the pleasure she knew he would bring her. The sting from being spanked was already abating, swirling with the pleasure in a heady mix that was as sweet as he'd promised. Even as her bottom rubbed against the bedsheets, her cheeks far more sensitive than before, the slight sting only increased her pleasure.

He brought her to climax again, the wood creaking as her hands gripped it tightly.

He did not stop, the same as before, his mouth insistently suckling at her pleasure bud, sending wave after wave of ecstasy through her.

"Gregory, please! I cannot... it's too much..." she begged as she writhed for him, hanging onto the headboard for dear life, even as her muscles protested from the strain. Head thrashing back and forth, her entire body tensed, heels digging into his back as she was sent over the edge again.

The intensity was such that tears began to leak from her eyes, sliding down the sides of her temples and into her hair, as the pressure within her escaped by any means possible. She could not possibly take any more pleasure. It was too much.

She gasped with relief when his mouth lifted, releasing her from its demanding hold, and she was left quivering against the bedsheets, panting for breath. Eyes closed, body trembling from the physical exertions, she felt utterly limp, close to fainting.

"Beautiful," Gregory murmured, gliding his hands up her sides. Even that small touch made her shudder and gasp; she felt so exquisitely sensitive.

The bed shifted, then his lips were touching hers, his tongue sliding into her mouth, and she could taste the salty sweetness that coated both. The salty sweetness that came from her. And she did not know whether to be horrified or aroused.

Before she could veer either way, she felt something hard and strange prodding at her slick, swollen folds where Gregory's mouth had just been. Far larger than his fingers had been in the carriage, but just as insistent as it began to push inside her. His mouth swallowed her cry as she felt herself stretch open to accommodate the invasion. Her legs moved, finding his bare ones, and she realized that, at some point, he had removed his breeches without her noticing.

It did hurt, briefly, as he entered her, whereas his finger had not, but neither was it the pain her mother had warned her about.

Gregory's head lifted, ending the kiss, and he stared down at her, watching her face as his body shifted atop hers and the thing inside her moved deeper.

"Oh..." She gasped, clenching around it, but her soft, slick opening was no barrier to the hard thickness pushing into it. After all the climaxes he'd wrought upon her senses, she did not have the strength to do anything but lie beneath him, taking him within her.

"That's it, little swan," he murmured, studying her face. "Take my cock. I promise to make you feel good again." He retreated, then thrust forward again, sinking deeper into her, taking her breath away yet again as it felt as though it was being forced from her body for lack of room within her lungs.

Tiffany moaned at his words, not sure she could handle being made to feel good again. She was too drained. Too limp.

Yet, as he filled her, the sensation awakened new pleasures inside her. The initial sting of entry did not last long, but the stretch as he moved deeper did make her ache... but like the spanking, it was not unpleasurable.

"Let go of the headboard," he ordered, lowering his head to nuzzle against her neck as his body came to rest against hers.

She felt so incredibly, almost unbearably full. He rocked against her, rubbing himself against the bud of pleasure that he'd suckled so relentlessly, and Tiffany cried out again.

"Hold on to me."

With the little strength she had left, Tiffany obeyed, releasing the headboard and wrapping her arms around his neck. She hung on as he began to move atop her, move within her, sliding back and forth within her slick passageway and sending a jolt of hot pleasure through her with every thrust.

It did not hurt, or if it did, the pain was subsumed by the growing ecstasy, the incredible feeling of being filled by him, the passion that was sizzling through her. This was better than his mouth. Being beneath him, feeling him within her, she found herself holding on to him with legs and arms, wanting him closer to her, deeper within her. Her energy returned as she began to lift her hips to meet him, her eyelashes fluttering as the tension within her core wound tighter and tighter.

"Gregory... oh, Gregory..." She could not cry out; she did not have the voice, did not have the breath. All she could do was whisper his name as the most intense sensation grew larger and larger within her. When it burst over her, showering her with ecstasy, she could do little more than sob at the intensity of her erotic bliss, still holding him close as the waves of passion threatened to drown her.

Gregory

Feeling his wife's pussy clenching around his cock as she came for him again, Gregory lost control over his tightly reined passion. He pounded into her slick, hot warmth, his cock hardening to stone as he approached his own climax. His balls tightened, and he felt the tingles all up and down his spine before he thrust in hard, filling her completely.

He braced himself on his elbows to keep from crushing her as he shuddered above her, his cock pulsing within her as he pumped spurt after spurt of his seed deep within her pussy. Knowing that seed might take root. Hoping it would. Which was highly erotic in and of itself, feeling rather forbidden after so many years of trying to avoid unintentional by-blows.

Tiffany whimpered, shuddering, her soft body cradling his as his muscles slowly unwound, the tension leaking from them. He turned his head, pressing his lips to her temple. Wet, salty tears met his lips, and he flicked out his tongue to lick them away.

Delicious.

There was nothing Gregory loved more than bringing a woman to the utter brink from pleasure alone. There was a reason he was so popular among the ladies. They knew he was not only talented with his mouth but that he was going to make it his mission to leave them both depleted and satiated.

However, the ladies of the ton were going to have to find another nobleman with a penchant for using his tongue, someone else whose favorite perversion was leaving them spent from pleasure. Now that he had Tiffany, the idea of taking another woman to his bed felt more than wrong—it felt abhorrent.

"Gregory." She sighed out his name, her arms hanging loosely about his neck, fingers trailing through the edge of his hair, making all the hairs on the back of his neck stand up.

No, he certainly wanted no other woman. He moved his lips over the side of her face, gently kissing the remains of her tears away. Tears of passion, of pleasure. The only kind of tears he ever wanted to cause her. Her breasts heaved beneath him as she slowly calmed, coming up to meet his chest, then dipping back down again.

His cock was slowly shrinking inside her.

Time to see if she would accommodate another one of his... less common desires.

Drawing his hips back, he disengaged from her, making her shudder as he slid from within her. Her eyes fluttered open, dazed and hazy from pleasure—the look of a completely satisfied woman. Gregory smiled smugly, taking a brief moment to enjoy her expression before he got into position, sitting beside her. He did glance down to ensure there was no blood from her deflowering and was reassured to see that his dick was glossy with her arousal and streaked with the white of his culmination but nothing else.

"Come here, little swan," he murmured, sliding his hand beneath her head, cupping the back where it met her neck, and using it to turn her toward him. Her head was level with his lap. Her coiffure was now a mess of curls, tiara askew. The heavy weight of the sapphires dragged across the top of his thigh as he pulled her toward his softened cock. "Open your mouth. I want you to clean me with it."

She glanced up at him, startled, her body mostly limp in his, but then her head went down. Her cheek rested against his groin, and he felt her hot breath before she shifted downward and took him between her lips.

With a sigh of pleasure, he leaned back, his fingers massaging her neck above the necklace she was wearing, as she began to suckle the softened length of his cock. Her tongue laved over the sensitive tissues, cleaning him as he'd requested.

His sweet, submissive little swan.

CHAPTER

THIRTY

T*iffany.*

She'd fallen asleep suckling on his cock—and why it was called the same thing as a rooster, she did not understand. Strangely, doing so had been rather soothing, and combined with her frazzled nerves from the momentous occasion and her physical exhaustion from having so much pleasure wrung from her, she'd easily drifted into unconsciousness.

And woken with a slow growth of pleasure. It began as a dream, a dream about being with Gregory, about him putting his mouth between her legs... then as the sensations had intensified as she'd come up out of the dark of sleep rather than dissipating, she'd realized it was not a dream. Gregory was between her legs again, feasting.

She gasped, shuddering, reaching for him.

Hands entwined in his hair before she paused, but he did not admonish her.

Instead, he lifted his head, smiling.

"How do you feel, little swan?"

"I... good?" It came out as a question rather than a true answer.

269

She was not entirely sure how she felt. Whatever she had expected from her first day of marriage, it had not gone at all the way she'd thought it would. From leaving their wedding breakfast early, to her mother's warning, to the revelations within the bedroom, to the utterly indecent pleasures she and Gregory had indulged in...

Tiffany could not imagine trying to describe what they had done without dying of mortification on the spot. No wonder ladies did not discuss such things. No wonder her brother had not wanted to discuss such things with her.

Now, waking up like this... it was good. It was also strange. Part of her was unsure she was not still dreaming a very realistic dream.

But then he moved them around, rolling her over with experienced ease and shifting himself at the same time. Tiffany found herself on her hands and knees above him but with her face above his erect cock. Her knees straddled his head, his hands wrapped around the backs of her thighs.

"Put me in your mouth again," he ordered.

Tiffany did not obey right away, even as he pulled her down to meet his lips and tongue, swiping them through her swollen folds. She was sore there—she could feel the soreness—yet her growing pleasure almost made her not care. She wanted him inside her again.

Yet... this was also her first close-up look at a man's appendage. She had been too dazed, too discombobulated, to pay attention earlier. Also, from the brief glimpse she had seen, it looked very different soft than hard. Tiffany wrapped her hand around the shaft, pausing when Gregory shuddered beneath her at the touch. The head was like a blunt mushroom with a split dome, where a drop of pearly liquid had coalesced. She licked up the bit of liquid. It was salty. Familiar. She'd tasted it before when he'd had her clean him with her mouth.

To her fascination, it was also immediately replaced. She licked it again.

Gregory's hips lifted, pushing toward her, moving her hand

along the shaft, and she heard his growl and felt the rumble of his body beneath hers.

"Enough teasing. Put your mouth on me, little swan." A warning tap against her bottom threatened more substantial swats to punctuate his command. Though the idea of another spanking felt more intriguing than threatening, Tiffany did not want to disappoint him. So, she lowered her head, taking him in her mouth and suckling the same way she had before... except it was not the same at all. Before, he'd been soft in every way; now, the skin was velvety soft, but beneath, it was rock hard, inflexible as her lips traveled down the length of it.

He moaned, the sound muffled by his location, though she felt his hot breath and the vibrations along her slick folds.

There was something incredibly empowering about taking him in her mouth this way. Before, he'd been holding her neck, holding her in place, and she'd felt acutely pliable, helpless against his desires, in a way that had aroused her even when she'd been replete. Now, she was rather enjoying teasing him. Touching him. Finding the ways that made him moan or shift beneath her, the way he already knew how to do so well to her.

Knowing she could make him feel the same was intoxicating.

She moved her head up and down, doing her best to mimic the way he'd thrust into her earlier. It was not easy, especially with him at her backend, his mouth and tongue busily stoking her own passion, giving her an equal measure of pleasure. When she finally reached her pinnacle, she had to pull her mouth off of him entirely, holding the base of him in her hand as she cried out, gasping with ecstasy.

After that, he repositioned them again, so he could grip her hair and use it to move her mouth up and down his cock. Which, for some inexplicable reason, she loved even more than when she'd been able to explore on her own. There was something powerfully compelling about the way he took control of her, using her mouth for his own pleasure. And when he groaned, pushing her head down, making her gag as he hit the back of her throat, she swallowed all the salty fluid that came spurting from him.

They cuddled afterward, Gregory consenting to remove her jewels and assisting her in doing so, leaving her completely bare for the first time. Teasing the tiara out of her hair had required some work, and she did not want to even think about what her coiffure must look like now. She admitted that her mother had warned her about the pain that being bedded would bring, and exactly what her mother had said.

Somehow, being naked, being totally exposed physically, made it easier to tell him things that she had never told anyone else.

"I have no experience in bedding virgins… until now," Gregory admitted, winking at her, which made her smile even as her stomach twisted at the reminder that he was not inexperienced. Gentlemen were not expected to be, but she still did not like to think about it, so she pushed those thoughts aside. "I do know it can hurt, though, a great deal, in fact, which is always true if the lady in question is not aroused. I suppose it can be more difficult to arouse a virgin, especially if she is nervous or if there is no attraction between her and her husband."

"I felt a sting, but nothing more." She rubbed her cheek against his chest, amazed at how comfortable she felt with him, how natural it felt to be skin-to-skin. That he made her feel beautiful was one thing, but he also made her feel safe. Something she now realized she had not felt in years. "It did not pain me unnecessarily. Certainly, nothing like I feared or like my mother told me."

"It is possible that was how it was for her the first time."

Despite the reasonableness of his comment, even though she'd used many such explanations to herself in the past, Tiffany felt a surge of defensive anger coiling through her.

"Perhaps, but when I asked her why women take lovers or become mistresses, she had no answer for me. And she has a lover herself."

Gregory's fingertips, which had been idly making circles on her shoulder, stilled.

"She does?"

Tiffany nodded, knowing he would feel the movement even if he could not see it.

"Since before my father died. I think he must have had his own as well; they hardly ever lived in the same household." Tiffany sighed. As always, thinking of her father brought an ache to her heart, though, at least now, she would not be surrounded by the memories of him on a daily basis. She'd never hidden under the table in Gregory's library, reading, while her father sat in his chair and silently kept her company until she fell asleep. "As far as I know, when they were under the same roof, they lived wholly separate lives."

"My mother and father as well," Gregory replied, his fingers starting to draw little patterns on her skin again. "Though we were all relieved whenever he was away from us. Thankfully, he spent most of his time in London, where he could not torment my mother."

"I cannot imagine anyone tormenting her. She is so kind and thoughtful." Tiffany shook her head again. Though she missed her own father, she felt even more sad for Gregory, whose father had been more than lacking; he sounded awful. He sounded...

He sounded like her mother.

"She is, and unfortunately, she was saddled with my father. Though I am sorry for the loss of yours and the others, I have to admit, in many ways, my father's death was a relief."

Which was a horribly sad legacy to leave behind. His willingness to tell the truth spurred her to whisper her own, despite the fear of what he might say.

"Sometimes, I think the same about my mother." She whispered the words, barely more than a breath, and his arm tightened around her shoulder. He was silent for a long moment.

"I am sorry," he said finally, rather than remonstrating her.

Tiffany sagged against him in relief, turning her face toward his chest as tears pricked the corners of her eyes.

It was something she'd never been able to admit to anyone else. Most of the time, she could not even think about it herself because it made her feel so awful. But when they'd first learned of her father's death, her first thought was that she wished it had been her mother instead. And then she'd wondered how awful she could be to think such a thing.

But sometimes, the thought still popped up in her head.

"I have noticed she does not always seem as supportive of you as she is of Sebastian." Gregory's tone was hesitant, as if he was trying to say the truth in a way that did not hurt her feelings.

"He is the first-born son," Tiffany quipped, though it did not feel very funny. That was the reasoning she'd used over and over again, her entire life, when she could do nothing right, but Sebastian could do no wrong. At least not in their mother's eyes.

Gregory turned toward her, shifting their positions so he could look at her. Her head was still pillowed on his arm, but he cupped her face with his other hand. Reaching up, she wrapped her hands around his wrist, holding him there, savoring the comforting touch. Their legs moved, entwining together, and the tightness in her chest eased even more.

"You are the first-born daughter." His thumb stroked across her cheek. "That should mean something as well."

"Sometimes, I think it means my mother hates me," she whispered back before pressing her lips together against the sob that was rising in her throat.

GREGORY

The pain in Tiffany's eyes made Gregory want to punch something. Someone. Except, of course, he could not hit a woman. Not in that manner. Neither did he have any urge to spank her mother because that was far too intimate, but dammit, someone should.

Whether she'd meant to or not, she'd made Tiffany feel as though her own mother hated her.

He did not want to make Tiffany feel worse, but seeing how she felt, it was impossible not to think back through every interaction he'd witnessed between the two. Even the way her mother tended to focus her attention solely on Sebastian, he could imagine how that would be hurtful.

"My mother loves you," he said. It was the only thing he could think of to say, though he did not know whether that made things better or worse.

Tiffany sniffled, but she smiled, though her eyes were watery. He was glad he had not made it worse. She ducked her head, snuggling into his chest, and he wrapped his arms tighter around her. If holding her was what she wanted, then holding her was what she would get.

"I love your mother," she said, her voice only slightly muffled because of how she'd buried her face against his body. "She and Lady Astrid... I do not know what I would have done without them. My mother always dressed me in orange and yellow, and I never questioned why. But seeing how I looked in blue, seeing how I could look today, I do not understand why she kept insisting on anything but."

"Perhaps she is jealous," Gregory murmured because it was the only thing he could think of.

Tiffany moved her head back again so she could look at him, frowning in consternation.

"Why would she be jealous of me?"

"Because you are beautiful. Young." Gregory shrugged. "It happens within the *ton* when new beauties replace the previous Season's. Why not between mother and daughter?"

Tiffany worried her lower lip between her teeth for a moment, a furrow in the middle of her brow as she thought.

"I never felt beautiful. Not until I met you," she admitted.

Which made him want to go punch something again. Remembering the conversations he and Sebastian had had before the Season started, before he'd met her, he almost wanted to punch himself. His only excuse was that he had not known. Then again, it did seem as though Sebastian had been influenced by his mother as much as Tiffany had.

Well.

There was nothing Gregory could do about that, but going forward, he was going to do his best to protect her. From both her mother and her brother if need be. Sebastian might be his closest friend, but Tiffany was his wife, and who would protect her if not her husband?

"Trust me, you are very beautiful, and I am very glad I found you in the library so that I did not have to fight all of my friends for your hand." He kissed the tip of her nose, making her giggle. "You were always beautiful, little swan... though perhaps what you wore did not show you off to your best advantage. Such as, I had no idea that you had these beauties until today."

He hefted her breast with his hand, running his thumb over the nipple and teasing it to hardness as her eyes widened, and she let out a gasp. It was too soon to have her again, but he was going to enjoy teasing her, readying her for a return to his bed tonight.

"My mother always told me they were excessively large," she admitted, shuddering, her lower body moving closer to his. He felt his cock twitch with interest, despite his satiation.

"Which is proof that your mother has absolutely no idea how a gentleman thinks," Gregory said, shaking his head. He rolled his wife onto her back, cupping her breasts in each hand and lowering his mouth to shower them with kisses as he spoke. "These. Are. Perfect."

Tiffany was giggling again, her cheeks flushed with heat as he caressed her, and he might have gone for using his mouth again—or perhaps showing her what lovely things could be done with large breasts and a cock—when there was a knock at his bedroom door.

"Your food, Your Grace." That was Redding's voice. Gregory's lips twitched. Mrs. Bryant must have decided that his valet was the most appropriate choice to interrupt his and Tiffany's intimate celebrations. "Mrs. Bryant says the household will be ready to greet you in an hour."

"An hour!" Tiffany exclaimed, her hands automatically reaching up to shove Gregory off of her. He let her, sighing in resignation as he rolled onto his back. "Oh goodness, my hair!"

While he would have been perfectly content to spend the entire day in bed with her and damn the rest of the world, he did not want her to get off on the wrong foot with the household. Wrapping her up in one of his robes, he put on another before letting Redding in with their meal on a cart.

Redding obligingly kept his gaze averted from his new duchess while she was *dishabille*, which was good for Gregory's new sense of possessiveness. He thought she looked utterly delicious seated at the small table by his window, hair mussed from lovemaking, cheeks flushed pink, her hand clutching the top of the oversized robe closed at her neck.

He knew what he would rather be eating...

But they needed to keep their strength up and to get through the responsibilities of the day before he could feast again.

So, he behaved himself while they ate, ringing for Poppy, his mother's ladies' maid, to come assist her with her hair when he discovered that she did not have her own. He'd assumed... but when it came to what Tiffany should have, what she deserved, and what her mother should have provided her with, he was quickly learning not to assume.

An hour later, she was greeting the household, learning their names as Mrs. Bryant introduced her to them, stunning in a blue twill dress and undergarments that made the most of her 'excessive bosom'. Gregory could not help but snort and shake his head at the thought—quietly, so no one thought it was directed at Tiffany.

Well, his own mother was going to be happy to make up for the lack that Tiffany's mother had left, of that he was sure. She'd appeared for the introductions as well, happily beaming her approval as Tiffany was greeted by the household and greeted them.

It was a ceremony that would need to be repeated when they retired to Clarence Hall, their country estate, but that would not be for a while.

Not while there was still the mystery of their fathers' deaths to solve.

Gregory frowned.

He was going to need to have a word with Paulson and his footmen when his wife and mother were not within hearing distance. While there was no real proof of danger from Montblanc or his associates, it would be better to be safe than sorry. Paulson had been in charge of setting one footman to follow Gregory's mother ever since Gregory had found the threatening notes; he was going to set two on his wife.

Not because he loved his mother any less, but because...

Well, because.

He was not going to examine that impulse too closely because he was not sure he was ready to admit to what he might find.

THIRTY-ONE

Tiffany

Life in Clarence House was completely different from life in her old home.

To begin with, no one criticized her. Ever. Not her husband. Not his mother. While Sebastian had never been critical of her, exactly, he had hardly been beaming with approval all the time, either. He loved her, she knew that, but he did not light up when she walked into a room the way both Gregory and his mother did.

And the very idea of her own mother lighting up when she walked into a room was laughable. Her mother only did that for Sebastian.

Why not me?

A question she'd ceased asking herself long ago but which had begun popping up into her head again by her second day as the Duchess of Clarence.

Gregory's mother had reason to dislike her, if anyone did. Tiffany had taken over her rooms, supplanted her position in the household, taken on her title, and she was now the dowager duchess rather than the duchess. Yet, the dowager was delighted by the change in her position rather than resentful. She'd insisted that Tiffany call her 'mama.'

Tiffany felt as though she was living in a dream.

In some ways, she was. Newly wedded, they spent the first few days after their wedding eschewing events, which was wholly permissible. Though, since they were remaining in London, eventually, they would need to emerge from their intimate cocoon. At the moment, Gregory's mother was doing the rounds for them, but they could only stay away for so long.

Between learning the ropes of the household and the dowager duchess transferring duties to her, Tiffany found very little time to sit and reflect or think because her new husband seemed to want to take up all of her time. Not that she had any major objections, though she would have liked more time in the music room. Gregory did not have a harp there, but he assured her that he would buy her one and that he was having the music room at his estate prepared for when the Season was over.

At night, she slept in his bed after being thoroughly and wickedly pleasured. In the morning, she woke there to his head between her thighs. During the day, whenever she had a free moment, Gregory seemed to know of the break in her schedule, and he sought her out wherever she might be—the library, the conservatory, her own bedroom... He used his mouth as much as his cock, sometimes even more than.

The first time they used her bed was in the middle of the day, during which time he put her on top. Not that she was in control. No, he might have professed that he was teaching her to ride him, but in truth, his hands on her hips kept him in command of her body and senses.

It felt like her body was always buzzing from either arousal or satisfaction, which was a very distracting way to live. But she did not want to stop, either.

The only time she was in no danger of having her skirts tipped up, or removed, was when she was visiting his sisters, which she made a point to do every day. They were delightful and treated her as a favorite aunt, an attitude she was all too happy to encourage. Gregory visited as well, dealing extremely gently with Betty while he was there, though she looked to be coming out of her shell around him now that her uncle had disappeared, and she was not being held to blame.

Tiffany had done some gentle questioning of her own, but it was clear that Betty had no idea her uncle had been involved with the old duke's death, nor did she have any idea where he was now. Likely, that was because Montblanc was smart enough to know that keeping such knowledge from her was the best way to keep her safe. Unfortunately, it did very little toward solving the mystery surrounding her father's death.

On the fourth day of their marriage, Gregory's mother informed them that they would need to attend the Windham ball the following night.

"It is a major event. You cannot miss it with impunity," his mother said, giving him a stern look when he protested. "The Duke of Windham is firmly established in Society, as is his wife. You would not keep Tiffany from being acknowledged by a fellow duchess, would you?"

Tiffany blinked and looked at Gregory. She had not thought of it in such terms. Though the dowager had spent much of her time in the country prior to her husband's death, she had a discerning eye for how Society worked and what was expected. Far more discerning than Tiffany's own, she was realizing. She had only ever done what her mother told her to do. The dowager was greatly encouraging toward Tiffany making her own decisions, but she did not yet have nearly the length and breadth of knowledge the dowager possessed.

"Very well," Gregory scowled. "If we must."

"You must. And stay for at least an hour." The dowager paused, then amended her statement. "At least an hour, during which time everyone can *see* you. Do not think to sneak away for half of it."

The expression on Gregory's face was that of a put-upon,

aggrieved male, and Tiffany lifted her napkin to her lips to hide her giggle. She did not think Gregory would approve, and during several of their lovemaking sessions, he'd shown a distinct willingness to spank her over the smallest of infractions. Not that the spankings hurt very much, but it had become a bit of a game for her to see how far she could push him and what she could get away with before he swatted her bottom for it.

She was fairly certain that giggling at his masculine distress would qualify.

"Very well, mother."

The dowager glanced at Tiffany, who lowered her napkin and smiled.

"Of course, mama."

Beaming at her, the dowager nodded happily. She was beginning to become used to the dowager's constant approval, though she always looked at Gregory to be sure that he was not hurt by the turn in circumstances. This time, he happened to be looking at her. Catching her eye, he winked.

Happily, Tiffany returned her attention to her plate. She loved living at Clarence House. She loved being Gregory's wife.

She wished they could be like this all the time. But she supposed one must return to the real world, eventually.

Her stomach twisted, and she tried to ignore it, but she knew why. The Windham ball was going to be a major event. That meant that she would see her mother for the first time since her mother had tried to frighten her over being bedded. Unless, of course, she invited her mother to come visit her at-home either this afternoon or tomorrow.

But she did not want to.

Perhaps it would be better to face her mother at a ball. Her mother was often more pleasant in company.

Tiffany frowned down at her plate as the thought suddenly occurred to her that her mother might be more pleasant because she did not want others to know what she said to Tiffany. That she might not want witnesses to her more critical statements. Because she knew they would not agree.

Like with the color of Tiffany's dresses. Or her fashion. Or the fact that neither Gregory nor his mother had uttered a single reproach of her conversational choices, despite having been her constant companions for several days now. They were just as high on the instep as her own mother; they knew just as well what was and was not appropriate, yet...

Yes, perhaps seeing her mother with others around them was for the best. Not only to curb what her mother might say to her, but to curb some of the things Tiffany now wanted to say to her mother if she could only find the courage.

She took in a deep breath. Tonight, she would be wearing one of her new dresses. One that made her feel beautiful. The most beautiful.

❦

GREGORY

"My God..." Gregory murmured as his wife came down the stairs, frankly staring. He remembered telling Sebastian that she was a pretty girl when he'd kissed her.

That did not do her justice, not now that she knew what to wear to her advantage.

Hearing him, she looked up from where she was watching her feet as she walked, her dress lightly caressing the ground, despite her holding the silk skirts aloft. Her sapphires sparkled, matching the sapphire blue fabric of her gown to perfection, the gold setting glimmering like the gold embroidery decorating her gown.

The front of the dress dipped in a low V, revealing the tops of her creamy breasts. Gold scrollwork decorated the neckline and came down to her waist in the front. It also shimmered from her puffed sleeves and the bottom of her skirt. The gold embroidery started several inches above the hem of her skirt in an ornate pattern that was curved on the bottom like an upside-down heart, with the point elongated to reach halfway up her thighs. Just below the center of the upside-down hearts was another small burst of gold embroidery, like little tiaras decorating just above the hem of her gown, all the way around.

Her skin glowed in the lamplight, her cheeks flushed a fetching pink, and her hair revealed to be a rich mahogany when she wore colors that complimented her. The gold on her dress and around her jewels found matching gold glints in her hair, adding to the effect.

"Do you like it?" she asked nervously, reaching the bottom of the stairs.

Gregory came forward, taking her gloved hand in his and lifting it to his lips for a kiss as he stared into her eyes.

"You are Queen of the Swans, love," he said truthfully.

If he'd known how enjoyable marriage could be, Gregory would not have dreaded it so much. Though, in the lead-up to his wedding, his dread had grown less and less due to his bride. That was the largest contributing factor to his enjoyment. He doubted he would be so content with a woman other than Tiffany.

Walking into the Windham ball with her on his arm had filled him with a sense of quiet pride. She was everything he'd dreamed of in a duchess and so much more. He would not even mind fending off the many admirers he expected her to have trailing after her, as long as she remained his.

And he intended to ensure that she had no need to look to others to satisfy her needs. Not today, not tomorrow, not ever.

The Duke and Duchess of Windham greeted him and Tiffany into the fold with aplomb. They'd been married some years before, but Lydia, as the duchess asked Tiffany to call her, was not that much older than Tiffany. He could tell it meant a lot to Tiffany to have the other duchess welcome her so warmly.

His mother was just behind them, also exchanging greetings with the pair. Gregory waited for her to finish before escorting both of his ladies to the ballroom to be announced. Every eye turned to look at them, of course, seeing as they had been out of Society for several days now.

Gregory had no need to dissemble as he proudly led his new duchess into the room.

Murmurs, stares... some admiring, some ripe with envy, others in total shock at how Lady Tiffany had transformed from a duke's plain sister to a stunning duchess.

Gregory turned his head about, looking for any of his fellow dukes, but it was difficult to spot any singular person in the crowd. Tiffany pressed closer to his side as if nervous from all the attention, and he mentally cursed Society's strictures, which would cause tongues to wag if he did something as obvious as put his arm around her waist in support. He put his hand over hers where it rested on his arm, which was the best he could do for now.

Bending his head down, he whispered in her ear.

"Chin up, my Queen."

As he'd hoped, the soft encouragement helped to bolster her, and her chin lifted just as he'd wanted her to. She looked every inch a duchess.

"Oh, there is Mr. Little and his family," his mother said from his other side. "I wanted to introduce you."

Gregory caught Tiffany's eye, and she smiled and nodded. His mother had mentioned the Little family again recently. He had a feeling she was taking them on as a *cause célèbre* now that he was married and no longer needed her 'assistance'. He had no objection. Like his mother, he did not enjoy seeing anyone cut out of Society because of their family's disapprobation, especially when the reason was because a member dared to make their own choices about their own life.

If he could lend some ducal weight to the Little family's standing in Society, he was happy to do so, and he knew Tiffany agreed. Knowing more about her relationship with her own mother, he was sure she'd felt the threat of being cut out of the family if she stepped a foot wrong. Sebastian would have never allowed it, Gregory was fairly certain, but being ostracized by just her mother would be painful enough.

Personally, having seen the damage she'd caused to his wife, Gregory would be perfectly happy to give the Duchess of Bolton the cut direct, but without a visible reason, so soon after marrying her daughter, the repercussions within wider Society were unpredictable. And he did not want to cause Tiffany any further pain. The best they could likely do was avoid the woman as much as possible.

His mother led them over to the Littles, who were standing on the side of the ballroom. Gaining admittance to the events by dint of Mr. Little's relations did not guarantee acceptance. Despite the crush, there was a small space around them, as if no one dared get too close for fear of the Earl of Stilton's displeasure. As the Duke of Clarence, Gregory did not give a damn about the Earl of Stilton or his likely reaction to his outcast son and family being recognized and welcomed in front of the entire *ton*.

Mrs. Little's eyes lit up with relief and warmth as Gregory's mother came up to her, greeting her with cheek kisses as the surrounding members of the *ton* looked on with avid interest. She was a beautiful older woman, with two thin streaks of grey hair that started at her temples in a mass of gorgeous black locks that were pulled into a high coiffure decorated with cream and burgundy feathers that matched her dress.

"This is my son and his wife, the Duke and Duchess of Clarence. Gregory, this is Mrs. Little, her daughter, Miss Little, and her son, Mr. Ashwin Little. Have you met Mr. Little before?"

"If I did, it was eons ago," Gregory said with a smile to the man in question. "And, unfortunately, I do not remember."

"I do not believe we have, Your Grace," the man said, bowing deeply, an action which his son followed him in, though there was some consternation in the son's expression. Perhaps trying to decide what to make of being introduced by a duke while being eschewed by the rest of Society. His father's eyes had lit up with appreciation and also some calculation, which Gregory did not blame him for. He would understand exactly what was happening and why Gregory's acquaintance could be good for his family.

"Your Grace." Mrs. Little curtsied deeply, to the exact correct degree, at the same time as her daughter. Miss Kalina truly was a beauty, with her dark, fathomless eyes, straight nose, and black hair, all set off to perfection by the rose-pink dress trimmed with cream that she was wearing. Some of the *ton* would not welcome her due to her darker complexion, but she was beautiful enough that she would draw other, less tendentious admirers if she was given the chance to set herself up in Society.

Which was the point of speaking with them now, so formally, in front of so many eyes.

"A pleasure to make your acquaintance," Gregory said, bowing over Mrs. Little's hand and dropping a kiss on the back of it. "How are you enjoying the sights of London?"

A much safer question to ask about viewing the city at large than to ask how they were enjoying the events. Certainly, one that allowed for great conversation as Mr. and Mrs. Little began to recount the places they'd been visiting. The museums, the gardens, the shops, which allowed Gregory and Tiffany to suggest their own recommendations.

A few minutes later, Matthew and Christian joined them, which solidified the *ton*'s interest. Gregory scowled at Christian and shifted, so Tiffany moved a little farther away from him. He was used to seeing ladies' reactions when they got their first glimpse of Christian's handsome visage, but he did not like seeing it on his wife's face, even if she did recover quickly.

Very soon, Tiffany and Miss Little were in the midst of a group of admirers while Gregory and his fellow dukes had shifted to the side. A few of the other young men who were present at the ball had approached the younger Little, and they were now enthusiastically talking about the latest horse races. From what Gregory could overhear, Ashwin was not only interested, but already fairly knowledgeable.

He kept most of his attention on his friends and Tiffany, though, ensuring that none of the admirers now surrounding her and Miss Little were becoming too emboldened. As much as he wanted to step in and lay claim to what was his, he would wait for the first waltz.

She had not gone through her first Season as a debutante, which he could not regret. He would not want to risk her marrying anyone but him. It would not have gone the same, regardless. Along with her clothing, her entire demeanor had changed now that they were married. She would enjoy the Season far more as his duchess than as a debutante under her mother's wing... but he wanted her to feel the thrill of being admired and desired.

Even if he did have to grit his teeth against punching them in their moon-eyed faces and carrying her off over his shoulder to claim what was his. He could endure that... for her.

THIRTY-TWO

iffany

Dancing the cotillon with the Earl of Brighton's younger son, Tiffany tried not to pay attention to the way Lady Martin was simpering up at Gregory as he danced with her. She knew she could not dance every dance with her husband, so she accepted the younger Brighton when he asked, but she had not realized how it would make her feel to see her husband dancing with another woman.

A beautiful married woman who had already given her husband two children. Was she looking for a lover?

Tiffany ground her teeth as she moved through the steps, trying to pay attention to what she was doing and not what was happening across the floor. Trying to reassure herself that nothing of note was happening. He was dancing, that was all, just as she was.

She was somewhat reassured when the dance ended, and they returned to their respective circles; the two groups had been beside each other but not overlapping much before. As she was returned, she brightened when she saw Sebastian had joined the other dukes who had not taken to the dance floor.

"There you are." He was just as happy to see her as she was to see him. Though she appreciated the days she'd been able to settle into Gregory's house, she'd missed Sebastian. They exchanged greetings, and then Gregory came up beside her to greet Sebastian as well.

"Is Mother here?" she asked, steeling herself.

"Somewhere, about," Sebastian said, waving his hand at the throng. "I lost sight of her almost as soon as she found Lady Tremaine, and the two of them swanned off with Lady Louisa in tow."

Tiffany relaxed, only realizing how tense she'd become when it disappeared again. At some point, she would have to speak to her mother, but in the crush, she could hardly be blamed for not seeking her out.

A touch of a hand at her elbow had her turning. Gregory and Sebastian continued talking as she faced Lady Astrid, who was standing with a beautiful woman who looked vaguely familiar.

"Tiffany, I have a friend I would like you to meet. This is the Baroness of Ashfield, Delilah Voight."

"Your Grace." The baroness curtsied, spreading out her saffron skirts with grace. It was the topaz necklace around her throat, matching jewels scattered through her rich brown hair, that jogged Tiffany's memory. She'd seen the baroness at the modistes, though she had not known her at the time.

"Baroness." Tiffany inclined her head but also smiled and reached out her hands. As far as she was concerned, Astrid was her knight in shining armor, and she was happy to meet anyone Astrid wanted to introduce her to. "It is a pleasure to meet you."

"And you. Felicitations on your wedding." The baroness had a pleasant, throaty voice. Unlike some of the *ton*, she actually sounded as though she meant it, without even a hint of jealousy.

"How is being married?" Astrid asked, fanning herself idly. She was wearing a coppery-colored dress trimmed with tangerine and matching Cairngorm jewelry again. Her gaze scanned the crowd as much as she was able. Though, she was a bit taller than Tiffany, so perhaps it was easier for her. "Is your husband behaving himself?"

Tiffany had to laugh.

"I suppose it depends on what you mean by behaving himself," she said, turning her head to look at him. She caught herself before she frowned. Some bolder ladies had begun to insert themselves into her brother and husband's group of dukes. They were not debutantes. One of them was openly laughing at something Gregory had just said, her hand on his arm, and he was smiling at her with charm.

The insides of her chest squeezed, but there was nothing she could do about it. Married couples did not live in each other's pockets. Speaking to other women, charming them, even flirting with them, was just part of the social game. She understood that, she did.

But...

"May I suggest a glass of wine?" The baroness asked quietly, holding out her hand with her own glass, the red liquid shimmering in the light. Tiffany did not understand.

"I..." Was she supposed to drink it? Was the baroness offering to share? Somehow, that did not seem quite right. Her confusion must have shown.

"If you spill it on her, she'll have to leave." The baroness' lips quirked with amusement, but there was something else in her expression. "I picked up the trick from Lady Spencer, much good it does me now."

It was only then that Tiffany realized where else she'd heard the baroness' name—paired with Sebastian and Gregory's friend, the Duke of Grafton. They must have ended their... acquaintance. That was the something else Tiffany had seen—the hurt, the resignation from no longer needing to do anything to fend off the ladies.

Tiffany was not sure she could possibly be so bold. Gregory was not even doing anything wrong; neither was the lady.

"No, but thank you," she said quietly.

"If you change your mind, just say the word," the baroness said, pulling the wine glass back toward herself. The thin smile on her face was rather cynical. Tiffany's heart hurt, both for herself and the baroness. But if Gregory was going to find another woman, another lover, spilling a drink on the woman was hardly going to stop him.

They were married now. The need to trick the *ton* into thinking they were a love match in order to preserve her reputation was over. That had been the deal. Through the wedding, not more.

~

GREGORY

"I have heard you have an incredible collection of etchings, Your Grace," Lady Chisolm purred, leaning in to brush her breasts against his arm.

At one point in his life, he would have been all too happy to toy with her, then take her to bed, but he found himself repulsed rather than intrigued. Resisting her was no hardship because there was nothing to resist—he was not in the least bit tempted.

Gregory knew better than to deflect her too harshly. She was the type to turn vicious when bluntly denied. Playing the fool, as though he did not understand what she was hinting at, took longer, but the results would be more definitive and with fewer repercussions for him or for Tiffany. He would not like it if she took out her feelings on his wife, then there would be a scene that would keep the *ton* talking for weeks.

So, he blinked at her and smiled without any hint of awareness of her breast touching his arm or which collection of etchings she was referring to.

"Oh, yes, some lovely countryside scenes," he replied cheerfully. "I found them in Dorset. Lovely little set depicting different aspects of country life. They're really quite calming to look at."

He might have taken it a bit too far there. Lady Chisolm narrowed her eyes at him, as if she'd picked up on the fact that he was bamming her. Thankfully, before she could say anything else, there was a sudden commotion on the other side of the ballroom.

Everyone in their vicinity turned at the explosion of noise—the shouts, the shrieks, and a strange chittering.

"What is going on?" Sebastian asked from Gregory's side, drawn out of his own conversation with Nathanial. Nathanial had turned to look as well, frowning as he reached up to fiddle with the mauve pocket square, like he thought pulling it out might be helpful in some manner.

"Oh, it must be that awful monkey." Lady Chisolm wrinkled her nose and huffed, clearly put out by no longer having anyone's full attention.

"What monkey?" Three dukes chorused the question in unison, which made Gregory chuckle under his breath.

"Lady Hatchett's new pet. It seems a vicious little thing, but she insisted on bringing it tonight to show it off."

The noise was traveling through the ballroom, and Gregory caught a glimpse of a tiny blur of brown fur as it leaped from person to person. Shrieks and shouts followed in its wake.

"I'm going to kill that thing!" Lord Hatchett was clearly not as enamored with the monkey as his wife, following its path through the ballroom with a red face and a raised knife, which was causing even more alarm and shrieks. One woman fainted, hitting the floor before anyone could catch her because they were too distracted by the chaos.

The monkey seemed to know its life was in danger because it was fleeing from the man with all due haste. Out of the corner of his eye, Gregory saw Tiffany going forward, her gaze on Lord Hatchett as if she was going to intercept him.

Bloody hell.

He surged forward, catching her around the waist and pulling her back.

"We have to stop him!" Tiffany protested, pushing frantically at his hands.

"*I* will stop him," Gregory growled, turning to push her behind him firmly behind him, sending her brother a look. Grim faced,

Sebastian took hold of his sister's elbow, pulling her even farther away from Lord Hatchett's path.

A path had spread open for the lord, no one wanting to stand against him, and Gregory stepped deliberately into that pathway. Far better than risking his wife doing the same, and he was certain she would have if he had not pulled her back.

Hatchett glared at him but pulled up short. He might be a petty tyrant and a blowhard, but he was also wedded to his status, which meant he instinctively reacted to Gregory's.

"Clarence," Hatchett growled. "Excuse me, but I need to move past you."

"My apologies, but I cannot do that," Gregory said, shaking his head. "You are already distressing the ladies, Hatchett. They are going to become much more so if you actually harm the creature."

"It is mine. Therefore, I can do what I want with it. If it offends your sensibilities, I will take it outside before I chop off its filthy little head." Hatchett's voice boomed through the silent room as everyone watched the drama playing out in front of them, and Lady Hatchett let out a wail. Her husband did not even blink.

Even the monkey had fallen silent or perhaps escaped.

"Actually, Hatchett, I believe the monkey has chosen a new owner," a drawling voice said behind Gregory. Recognizing Zachary's sardonic tones, Gregory turned to look at his friend.

The monkey, which was barely bigger than a man's hand, was perched on Zachary's shoulder while Zachary stroked a finger down its back. Its tail was curled around Zachary's head. It was a very cute creature, now that it was not causing havoc through the ballroom, with fluffy dark brown fur, huge eyes, and a thin gold collar around its neck. The yellow ribbon that hung down from the collar had obviously been chewed through, about a foot from the monkey's neck, the tattered end standing out starkly against the black of Zachary's coat.

"Thank you for the gift." Zachary held Hatchett's gaze as he stopped petting the monkey long enough to reach down and take a grape from his other hand, lifting it up to the little pet to take. The monkey grasped it with both paws and immediately started nibbling on the round fruit. "Does he have a name?"

Hatchett paused, practically vibrating in place as he realized that his prey had escaped his grasp. He sucked in a breath through his nose, visibly grabbing hold of himself. Perhaps finally realizing exactly *what* a scene he'd created.

With two dukes opposing him, one of them thanking him for a *gift*, he really only had one choice that would allow him to save face.

"Name it as you please," he snapped out before giving them both a jerky bow. He was clearly seething but preferred his status and having a duke owe him a favor than his revenge on the little beast. "Excuse me."

The entire room tensed as he turned about, knife still in hand, and then blew a collective sigh of relief as he dropped the weapon onto the tray a nearby footman was holding. The footman was so pale, he looked like a stiff wind might knock him down, but he managed to hold himself upright as Hatchett passed.

Hatchett's wife, who Gregory had never met but seemed like an equal match to Hatchett's choleric temper, was fanning herself and ignoring her husband, intent on basking in all the attention now being heaped upon her. Ladies had already thronged toward Zachary, but the monkey on his shoulder screeched at their approach, and they immediately fell back, tittering nervously.

Gregory grinned and shifted his position so he could offer his arm to Tiffany. Immediately, she shook her brother loose and came to meet him.

"Let's go meet the monkey," he said wryly, and she beamed up at him.

It did not escape his notice that Lady Astrid and Baroness Voight had joined Tiffany's circle. The two were now speaking with Miss Little, the baroness' back definitively turned to where Zachary was standing. Which was quite the feat, seeing as all other eyes in the ballroom were still on him.

He now had the same little clearing of space around him that the Littles originally had, though for a very different reason. However, Gregory was not going to be put off by some screeching. He wisely plucked a strawberry tart from a passing footman's tray to offer to the monkey as they neared.

The monkey chittered, holding onto Zachary's ear, then slowly reached out to take the tart from Gregory.

"I am not sure that will be good for him," Zachary said with some amusement, still scratching the small creature on the back of its head.

"After his brush with death, he deserves a treat," Gregory argued. "What are you going to call him?"

"I was thinking I'd call him Sinclair." The other man's expression turned sheepish, and he shrugged the shoulder that was monkeyless.

Gregory's chest tightened and loosened at the reminder of their friend. In the whirl to find a bride and investigate the mystery of their fathers' deaths, his grief over Sinclair had been fairly well shunted aside. Then again, he had not been as close to Sinclair as Zachary. If Sebastian had been the one lost at sea, Zachary and Gregory would have switched shoes.

He looked at the tiny monkey, and his lips twitched.

"He would hate that."

"Which is what makes it perfect." The edges of Zachary's lips curved upward.

Tiffany shook her head.

"Do you think he would let me pet him?" she asked, peering up at the little creature. Apparently, she was going to ignore his and Zachary's exchange rather than comment on it.

"You can try." Zachary turned so his shoulder was tilted closer to Tiffany.

She slowly lifted her hand, but even that movement caused the monkey to eye her with suspicion, and it clambered up on top of Zachary's head, where she had no way of reaching it. Chuckling,

Zachary tried to pluck it off, but it shoved the remainder of the grape fully into its mouth and grabbed hold of his hair, refusing to let go.

"Apparently not." She sighed, letting her hand drop, and the monkey released Zachary's hair, returning to his shoulder. "Maybe I should have tried giving him a grape."

"At least he allowed you to approach," Gregory pointed out to console her.

They tried for a few more minutes without success. Sinclair, the monkey, wanted nothing to do with Tiffany, would tolerate Gregory petting him but refused to be coaxed into Gregory's hand, and kept his little tail firmly wrapped around Zachary's neck the whole time.

As the music started up the strains of a waltz, Gregory decided it was time to abandon the effort. He wanted to dance with his wife.

Unfortunately, as soon as he had her in his arms on the dance floor, he realized something was very wrong.

THIRTY-THREE

Tiffany

Spinning around the dance floor in her husband's arms, Tiffany found that she could not look up at him and meet his eyes. It was impossible to waltz with him without remembering their engagement ball; it was also impossible to dance with him tonight without remembering the ladies he'd been dancing with before.

She was stiff in his arms, and she could feel his gaze on her, knew that he realized something had happened... but she could not dissemble. The monkey had only provided a small distraction from her roiling emotions, her jealousy. Being back in his arms as he whirled her around, the urge to cry because she wanted to be the only woman in his arms, ever, confirmed her growing fear.

She was in love with her husband.

She did not want the normal *ton* marriage with him.

So, she could not look at him because if she looked at him, she would cry. It was not his fault that he did not return her feelings. That had not been part of their marriage bargain. He'd done everything he should as a true gentleman of the ton. Well, after he'd compromised her, but even that did not reflect poorly on him since he'd also done the honorable thing and offered for her.

She was the anomaly.

As a lady, it was her role not to burden him with the unwanted feelings she was experiencing.

Shoving her feelings down was not a new experience for her, but it had been years since she'd felt so raw. So vulnerable. And it was so much more difficult with him holding her, touching her, examining her so closely.

"What is wrong?" he asked in a murmur that she could barely hear over the music. "Sinclair the monkey will come around, I am sure. After being with Lady Hatchett, he is probably wary of the ladies, even if it was the lord who was chasing after him."

Tiffany shook her head, still avoiding eye contact with him, though she managed to put a smile on her face. Her heart was breaking because she'd realized she was in love with him, and he did not love her back. But he was concerned a monkey had hurt her feelings. So, at least, he cared for her in some small way. It was so very Gregory, and it just made her love him all the more.

He might not be in love with her, but he cared for her. Far more than some husbands cared for their wives. She would have to learn to be content with that and look the other way when ladies importuned him. At least now, she had a group of friends to help distract her. She'd enjoyed beginning a friendship with Miss Little, who had shyly given permission to be called Kalina when Baroness Ashfield insisted they call her Delilah.

She'd invited them over for tea on the morrow, all three ladies. Knowing she could invite them to visit her at home for a private gathering and that her mother-in-law would be nothing but supportive made her far bolder than she'd ever felt before.

Now, she was thankful she'd have them because if Gregory did not want her in his bed tonight or he went to visit another woman's... she was going to need all the distraction she could get.

His hand squeezed hers a little tighter, the hand on her waist pulled her in a little closer, and she felt the shift in his demeanor. Peeking up at him, she dropped her gaze immediately as she recognized the hard look on his face. The same one he'd had in the bedroom when he'd been ordering her about. The charming, flirtatious man he showed Society was no mask, she knew that, but the other side of his coin... and he had just flipped.

"Tiffany." His voice was low, demanding, the same way it had been in the bedroom.

Keeping her head ducked down, she shook it again.

Which... did not turn out the way she'd anticipated as the dance ended. Instead of letting her go or leading her back to her circle, she found herself being whisked away toward the exit. She glanced over her shoulder and saw Astrid looking after her—though she was no help; she winked and waved at Tiffany.

She supposed at least no one saw anything unusual in her and Gregory rushing away so quickly. Perhaps everyone else would attribute it to their 'love match' and their need to return to each other's company.

"Tiffany!" Her mother's sharp voice made her automatically wince, her head swiveling around.

But it did not matter. If Gregory had heard her mother calling out to her, it did not slow his pace at all. His hand remained firm on her back, propelling her forward. Tiffany only caught a glimpse of her mother's face, going from disapproving to shocked when Tiffany was unable to stop and go to her.

Relief made her nearly limp when she realized she was not going to have to face her mother yet.

The Duke and Duchess of Windham were just leaving their places at the front as Gregory and Tiffany went past them. Gregory barely paused, nodding and thanking them for their hospitality. The two smiled approvingly, seemingly not at all put out by the early departure of two of their more prominent guests.

"Remember when we could leave early?" the duke asked, watching Tiffany and Gregory as they passed.

"It is *our party*," the duchess responded reprovingly to which Tiffany heard the duke's sigh before the two were out of earshot completely.

Her chest ached in envy. The two of them were obviously a love match and had remained in love. She wished her path to happiness could be as easy as theirs, but she doubted that's what lay in her future.

Gregory got them out the door, and there was not a long wait before their carriage came round, but it felt like it took forever as they stood there in silence. The only blessing was that they were alone other than the footmen. None of the gossipmongers were there to see them standing silently for the minutes it took for the carriage to return.

He packed her into it in short order, and she had barely settled into her seat before he was across from her. Even in the dim interior, she could see his stern gaze in the moonlight.

"Tell me what is wrong." It was not a question; it was a command.

"Nothing is wrong." Nothing that he could do to fix. He could not help his feelings or lack of them, and she did not blame him. She was the problem. She was the one who had succumbed to an unlooked-for attachment. Somehow, some part of her had forgotten it was all pretense.

Or perhaps she would have fallen in love with him, anyway. Because, pretense of love or not, Gregory was her ideal man. Charming, kind, generous, attentive... that he was these things to everyone only showcased his character. That she yearned to be singled out, to have some things solely focused on her, that was her own failing.

Always so selfish. Her mother's voice whispered in her mind.

Tiffany pressed her lips together as the carriage began to roll forward, rocking them slightly in their seats.

"I can tell something is wrong, little swan." His voice had lowered, darkened. "You can tell me now, or you can tell me over my lap."

Over his lap? She did not understand, and her brow furrowed. She'd sat on his lap several times. Twice while they were naked. That had been very enjoyable. But she did not think that was what he meant.

It did not matter either way, she supposed, since she did not plan on telling him. She wracked her mind, trying to think of some explanation for what would be wrong, but other than realizing she was in love with her husband and he was not in love with her, the ball had been wonderful. Even being rejected by Sinclair the monkey had been amusing, not at all hurtful, though she'd wanted to pet the cute little thing.

Admitting her feelings was out of the question. Humiliating herself to admit to such a thing when he did not return them was bad enough, but worse would be if he felt sorry for her. If he was sympathetic. Or would it be worse if he pulled away so as to help save her?

She did not know. She did not want either... or, rather, she did not yet know what she wanted and needed some time to think about it. Time that she was not certain she was going to get because she had not been able to dissemble well enough to hide her consternation from him. He was able to read her emotions better than anyone, even better than her mother or Sebastian. Which made it all the more difficult.

"Last chance, little swan."

Tiffany metaphorically dug in her heels and shook her head. His lap was not a bad place to be, and she did not understand why he thought it would convince her to tell him anything.

Perhaps he was not being serious about questioning her? Perhaps he really had rushed her out of the Windham ball because he wanted to bed her? In which case... she could not mind. She would much rather have him in her bed—for as long as she could keep him there —than in another ladies'.

"Very well."

Tiffany was not surprised when he reached out and tugged her hand, pulling her toward him. She *was* surprised when he did not pull her straight across. Unable to anticipate his intentions, she indeed found herself over his lap. Head and arms on one side, legs on the other, bottom in the air with his hand tugging her skirts up.

Her protest was lost in a shriek when his hand came down on her bottom with a hard smack that burned. It was the hardest swat he'd ever delivered to her backside.

"Gregory!"

"Are you ready to talk, little swan?" He rested his hand on her bottom, rubbing the spot he'd just spanked. Tiffany hesitated.

The physical pain of a spanking or the emotional pain of admitting her feelings to someone who did not return them?

She hesitated too long, and Gregory made the decision for her, his hand going back up and coming down hard on the other side of her bottom.

"Let me know when you're ready to tell me what is wrong," he said, bringing his hand down over and over again in between his words. Tiffany covered her mouth with her hands to stifle her shrieks.

It *hurt.*

There was something very wrong with her because despite the sting, despite the growing burn, despite the fact that these were not playful swats, her body was reacting as if they were. She wriggled on his lap, her insides clenching, panting as both the pain and her arousal began to climb.

But even her growing desire did not stop the burn from growing, especially when his hand came down on the sensitive crease between her buttocks and her thighs. That burned like fire, and Tiffany jerked in place, trapped by his hand holding her side and her skirts hiding her upper body and head.

"Ow! Gregory, please!" She bucked against him, and he halted, rubbing her bottom, making her moan as he dipped his fingers into the slick heat of her pussy. Her sensitive tissues burned in an entirely different way, her body aching to have him inside her, but instead, his fingers moved up to her bottom hole. "Gregory!"

Squealing, she was unable to wriggle away as the slick length of his finger pushed against that tight little hole. It was a stark reminder of how vulnerable she was to him, how much of a command he had over her body and senses. He was pushing his finger into her in a most unnatural manner, yet it made her nerve endings sing as the discomfort of being stretched open mixed with the burn in her cheeks.

"Time to talk, little swan." His finger pumped gently, moving in deeper. "Or do not. I am happy to explore your tight little arse while I wait."

Oh, goodness... he meant to go deeper. Her face flushed hot and not just from the physical warmth of being trapped under her skirts. She knew he could not see her reaction, and she felt faint as he pushed his finger in deeper, invading a hole that had never been meant to have anything go into it.

In some ways, his inability to see her face was what finally made the decision easier.

He could not see her, and neither could she see him. She would not have to see his reaction.

And if she spoke up now, he would remove his finger from her bottom.

Taking a deep breath, she covered her eyes with her hands, even though she was well hidden beneath her skirts, and shouted out the truth.

"I have fallen in love with you!"

The words hung in the air, fraught and far too honest, and Tiffany wished she could die as she felt his finger halt its forward progress in her bottom. Her muscles clenched around it. She could only imagine the look of horror on his face.

The finger retreated, and she did not have time to rejoice over its disappearance nor quail over Gregory's reaction because he was pulling her up to face him. She was still on his lap but sitting on it now. The moonlight coming in from the window danced across a face completely lacking in horror, though he looked shocked down to his bones.

"What did you just say?"

She would have tried to look away, but the hand that had been holding her body in place for him came up, cupping her chin and forcing her to keep her gaze on him. His fingers were too strong for her to pull away, even if she wanted to.

The most awful feeling was rising in her breast.

Hope.

Such an ephemeral feeling. So fragile. So delicate. So easily broken, leaving devastation in its wake. And the stakes were far higher than they had ever been in the past.

But she could not help it. He did not look horrified. He looked as though he wanted to hear her words again. She could not find the breath to say them, though; she was too caught in her own fear, her own hope, the combining turmoil making it impossible to loosen her tongue and repeat herself.

His hand on her chin gentled, reaching up to brush a lock of hair out of her eyes.

"Did you say you've fallen in love with me?" he asked. His hand settled around the back of her neck, holding her head in place so she still could not look away. Not that she was sure she wanted to now.

Hope, that devilish little flame, actually wanted to see his reaction.

Just in case.

But her voice had fled the scene, so instead of saying it again, she nodded her confirmation.

Heat flared in his eyes, and he pulled her lips down to meet his.

"Oh, thank God."

At least, that's what she thought she heard him say, right before their lips touched, and pure joy flashed through her.

THIRTY-FOUR

regory

The moment he'd heard Tiffany's muffled declaration of love, something had fully settled inside Gregory's chest. Something he'd yearned for without knowing it. Something that had crept up on him, in small doses, until he heard her say it, and he could not deny it within himself any longer.

He was unfashionably, irrevocably in love with his wife.

And, thank hands of fate, she loved him back.

Why he could not admit it, even to himself, until he heard her confession, he did not know, but the truth of it was unavoidable.

Kissing her deeply, he held her as closely as possible, wondering exactly how much time they had before they arrived at Clarence House...

Not enough, it turned out, but that was for the best. He'd rather take her inside and take his time than an abbreviated interlude in the carriage. Though he could have gotten things started... still, some might say the spanking had done that. She was certainly wet enough by the end of it, despite the warmth that had been emanating from her chastised cheeks.

His little swan did like a small bite of pain with her pleasure. Maybe more than a small bite sometimes.

The carriage rocked to a stop, forcing him to end the kiss, but that was only the beginning. It only took them moments to depart the carriage, and he did not let Tiffany's feet touch the ground when they did, sweeping her into his arms from the step down and carrying her manfully to the door. Paulson obligingly opened it, turning a blind eye to Gregory's undignified antics by literally turning his head away from them and pretending not to see their entrance.

"We are retired for the evening, Paulson," Gregory said, sweeping past him as Tiffany giggled in his arms, burying her face in his shoulder to hide her blush from their stalwart butler.

"Very good, Your Grace," Paulson said to the ceiling, doing his best to ignore the impropriety happening under his watch.

Under other circumstances, Gregory would have snickered, but he was far too engaged in getting his wife up to his bedroom. Their bedroom, really, for they had not spent a night apart since their wedding, and he did not intend to any time in the future.

He paused on the first landing of the staircase to catch his breath, causing Tiffany to lift her head. Mischief danced in her eyes as she looked at him.

"Are you tired, husband? I can walk if you do not have the strength to carry me."

Gregory narrowed his eyes at her. He enjoyed her mouthiness, if only because it gave him an excuse to spank her now and then, but he did want to remind her who was in charge.

"Do not mock me, little swan. If I wanted to, I could strip you down naked and spank you right here on this staircase, and not a soul in this house would stop me." He growled the words, nipping her earlobe and enjoying her gasp of shock.

"You would not!"

"I would, and I would enjoy every second of it."

The house was mostly empty right now, and anyone who did

come by would immediately avert their eyes. Granted, it was a mostly empty threat, but if pushed, he would follow through.

Tiffany must have heard the seriousness in his voice because she squeaked and buried her face in his shoulder again. By now, he'd managed to catch his breath, and he continued up the stairs to the ducal suite.

Swinging her into the room, he kicked the door shut behind them.

Only then did he set her down, letting her body slide against his, her head slowly tipping back to keep their gazes locked as she was lowered to the floor. Her pink lips were slightly parted, her eyes bright with arousal, and her cheeks flushed nearly as pink as her lips from blushing.

"You are not upset?" she asked, only a hint of consternation in her voice.

"Upset? That you are in love with me?" He shook his head. "Why would I be upset that we share the same feelings?"

She brightened even more. "You love me? You... you did not actually say."

"Ah. An oversight on my part in my rush to get you upstairs." He grinned at her. "I love you." Bending his head, he caught her lips for a kiss before pulling away. "I love you." Another kiss and he had started heading them toward the bed, working to remove her clothing as they went. "I love you."

Laughing, she followed him, tipping her head back when he went to kiss her neck, giving him greater access to her throat. He nipped the soft skin, his hands full of her breasts, the fabric of her dress making a soft shushing sound as it was dropped to the floor. Tiffany moaned, arching her back and thrusting her breasts more fully into his hands.

"I love you, little swan." He picked her up and tossed her onto the bed, immediately following her. Her breasts bounced as she landed, but they were not his main objective. Pushing her legs apart, he dove into her pussy, using his tongue to slide up the slick seam and tease the little bud at the apex.

"Gregory!" Her hips lifted as his tongue circled her pleasure pearl, her legs draped over his shoulders, and he pushed her so she was folded basically in half. Pushing his hands into the crooks of her knees, he held her there, this position lifting her bottom so his tongue could move lower, exploring the same area his finger had in the carriage. This time, when Tiffany called out his name, it was as much a shriek of shock as of pleasure. "Gregory, stop! You cannot want..."

"I do want." He looked up at her between her legs, darting his tongue out to lave a long lick over the crinkled rosebud of her anus, making her gasp and quiver. "I want to taste every part of you. And, not tonight, but one day, I will slide my cock into this tight little hole and claim every part of you as well."

The pink color in her cheeks heightened further as he watched, her hazel eyes becoming glassy as she inhaled quickly, like she was imagining such a thing... and she did not protest against it. Gregory lowered his head again.

∼

TIFFANY

What her husband was doing to her was wicked... depraved... utterly indecent. She could not look at him with his head between her legs, licking her *there*. The very idea of him putting his cock there... yet she knew she would let him. Because the expression on his face when he'd told her what he wanted to do and the possessive way his eyes had gleamed made her want to give him that.

Made her want to let him do whatever he wanted to do to her.

No matter how it made her blush.

Reaching over, she pulled a pillow over her face, trying to hide her blush as his tongue licked and probed, sending pleasure fizzing up her spine. It was an entirely different kind of pleasure, an extremely naughty sensation, and it made her want to squeal and writhe, but she was pinned in place by his hands. The best she could do was hide her face in the pillow and muffle the sounds she was making.

When his mouth moved back up to her pussy, to the sensations she was more used to, she let the pillow fall away, gasping the cooler air in the room. Her cheeks were still hot, but this level of blushing she could contain.

Even when his finger began to push at her back entrance again, then began to push inside her. With his tongue working over her pussy, his finger moving deeper into her bottom, her pleasure was growing faster and faster. It tightened her insides, coiling her growing arousal around a spool in her core, making her tremble as the need for release grew stronger.

"Gregory, please..." She reached down, her fingers threading through his hair as she moved her pussy against his mouth, his finger moving back and forth inside her bottom as if it was a small cock. The sensation was uncomfortable yet arousing, filling her head with the image of him using her bottom the way he used her mouth and pussy, and instead of disgusting her, she found it shockingly arousing. "Oh, please... I need... I need..."

A second finger joined the first, and she groaned at the discomfort of being stretched farther open. The new sensation pushed her climax back, making her feel even needier. As if he sensed her growing frenzy, Gregory kept teasing her pearl, rather than stimulating it directly, so that she could not tip over the edge of ecstasy. His fingers moved inside her, stretching her, invading her, and his tongue danced around her sensitive lips, making her feel frantic for the release that hovered just on the edge of her senses.

Her legs bent, digging her heels into his shoulders and trying to bring him closer.

"Gregory!"

But instead of finishing her with his mouth, the way he so often liked to do, he lifted his head and moved, letting one of her legs slide away from his shoulder. The hand that had his fingers buried in her bottom stayed in place, that leg still lifted high as he got into position with his cock. His hand cupped her buttocks, his fingers knuckle deep in her tight hole as he began to thrust into her sopping pussy with his cock.

Tiffany cried out as he plunged into her, filling her with one hard thrust, her hips lifting to meet him.

She was full.

So incredibly full.

His cock, his fingers... she was tightly stretched around both, and it did not feel as though there was any room left in her body. Her breath had been pushed out of her because he was so deep inside her, taking up so much space within.

"Reach up," he murmured, leaning down to suck the tip of one pert nipple into his mouth. Tiffany whimpered as she obeyed. "Hold on to the headboard, and do not let go."

What followed was absolute erotic torment.

Rather than moving fast and hard, the way she'd expected him to, the way he often did by the time he buried himself inside her, Gregory did the opposite. For the first time, he was not looking to drown her in pleasure before finding his own. Instead, he moved slowly. Deliberately. His fingers moved inside her alongside his cock, taking turns moving in and out of her.

His mouth went back and forth between her nipples, suckling, nipping, adding to the growing sensations but not giving her enough direct stimulation to actually climax.

"Gregory, please..." she begged, her head thrashing back and forth, though she did not dare take her hands away from the headboard. If she did, he might stop what he was doing, might make her wait even longer. She felt wound so tightly, she thought she might snap.

"Tell me again."

"What?" She could barely think, much less try to piece together what he was talking about.

"Tell me you love me." His head lowered to her nipple again, sucking hard, and she cried out.

"I love you!"

He released her nipple with a nip and a pop that left the little bud throbbing in the cool air. Tiffany's entire body pulsed, her inner muscles clamping down around his cock and fingers as pleasure surged. His hips rocked, rubbing his body against hers, trapping her little bud between their bodies but not quite giving her enough stimulation to reach her pinnacle.

Again.

It was utter torture.

"Use my name," he demanded, moving his lips to her other nipple and sucking it into his mouth.

"I love you, Gregory!" She was all but sobbing out the words as the pressure of her need was becoming unbearable. "I love you, I love you, I love— Oh!"

He'd released her other nipple and his passion at the same time. Rough, hard thrusts buried inside her so fast, she lost her breath and could not catch it again as he pounded into her. Ecstasy keened, the suddenness of his passionate response sending her into a maelstrom of erotic rapture.

Golden starbursts exploded behind her eyes as she finally found the breath to cry out, the coiled spool at her core snapping open and releasing the tightly wound wire of pleasure.

Heat and bliss washed over her in waves, buffeting her about, and she clung to the headboard for dear life as Gregory rode her hard. The long buildup led to a long release, one that was so intense, she thought she might die from the initial burst, but then it kept going and going, and she had no option but to go with it. Her whole body trembled beneath him, soft and wet and open for his cock as he ravished her senses.

It was not until she finally went limp beneath him, delirious from the pleasure, that he thrust in hard again. Rubbing himself against her sensitive lips and bud, he drew one last cry from her as he began to pulse inside her, filling her with his seed.

She whimpered as his fingers slid from her bottom.

Gasped as his lips nuzzled over the skin of her neck. She shuddered, unable to stop the reaction because every part of her body felt so sensitive that the merest touch made her want to leap out of her skin.

"I love you, Tiffany," he murmured. "My little swan. My wife."

As exhausted as she was, it was the most gloriously satisfying moment of her life.

THIRTY-FIVE

Tiffany

"We will have the tea in here," Tiffany told Mrs. Bryant, leading the housekeeper into the back parlor. The light was overly bright at the moment, but by the time the other ladies arrived, it would be dimmer, softer, and more conducive to the atmosphere she was trying to arrange. She was nervous about hosting even such a small event without her mother's firm hand guiding her.

This morning, she had asked the dowager if she wanted to join them, but Gregory's mother had declined with some reluctance. She was spending the day making some arrangements for the dowager house back on his main estate, though she would be joining them for the Camden soiree that evening. Tiffany would have felt a bit surer of her footing with an older woman there to guide her, but the dowager's assertion that she had everything well in hand had helped a little.

She did know how to host. She had assisted her mother enough times, back in the country, several times during the little Season, then the events leading up to her and Gregory's wedding. Not that her mother had approved of most of Tiffany's suggestions. Mrs. Bryan's easy acceptance of all her directions, with approval in her eyes, was both gratifying and terrifying. She did not know if Mrs. Bryant was agreeing with her because she thought Tiffany was doing an adequate job or only because Tiffany was a duchess, and the housekeeper did not feel it was her place to correct her.

Lady Astrid was the first young lady to reach out a hand of friendship—true friendship, not the forced relationship that had been thrust upon Tiffany and Lady Louisa—and Tiffany wanted to impress her. Baroness Ashfield was also intimidating, a little older than Astrid, far more experienced in the ton. Friendly, but with more polish than Tiffany had.

She felt most comfortable with Miss Little, if she was being honest, who seemed as intimidated as she was by the social scene. Kalina had been thrilled when Tiffany invited her to tea, relief and gratitude shining in her dark eyes when she quietly accepted. It had been for more than the invitation when so many were tiptoeing around the Little family. It was also because a tea was so much more intimate and less intimidating than a major ball.

Well, unless one was hosting the tea in question.

Tiffany took a deep breath, frowning, when she heard the bell to the front door ring. Surely, it was too early for any of the ladies to arrive. Two of Gregory's friends were with him in his study—Christian and Nathanial—but she had not thought they were expecting anyone else to arrive.

Her understanding was that Gregory and the Duke of Montagu were advising Nathanial on financial matters. The whole *ton* knew that Hereford had reached *point non plus* and needed to marry immediately, but Gregory had told her that Nathanial was still doing what he could to shore up his finances.

"Who could that be," she murmured, looking at Mrs. Bryant, who shook her head in puzzlement. They both quit the parlor, and Tiffany moved quickly toward the front of the house, where she could hear voices. She winced when she recognized her mother's sharp voice set against Paulson's deeper one. Part of her had been hoping that perhaps Lady Astrid was running unexpectedly early.

She could hear Paulson trying to direct her mother into the drawing room while her mother insisted on being given free rein to seek Tiffany out. Immediately, Tiffany increased her pace, not wanting Paulson to have to face more of her mother's displeasure than necessary.

"I am here, Mother," she said, rushing into the foyer with an apologetic glance at Paulson. The butler was holding himself very stiffly, disapproving of her mother's refusal to follow the proprieties.

Her mother sniffed, eyeing her up and down. The dove-gray morning dress with thin blue stripes Tiffany had chosen to wear today was exactly the kind of gown her mother had never let her buy. It was part of her trousseau. The trousseau she had ordered after her mother had left the *modistes*, changing all the directions her mother had given Madame Allard.

Tiffany steeled herself against her mother's obvious disapproval.

"That is not how you greet guests," her mother snapped, shaking her head and apparently forgetting that she had just been insisting to Paulson that she was not a guest, that she was Tiffany's mother, and that was why she refused to be settled in the drawing room to wait. "Where are your manners?"

Tiffany took a deep breath, uncomfortable heat growing in her cheeks as she was aware of Paulson and Mrs. Bryant as their audience. The housekeeper had followed her to the foyer. At least there was no one else.

"I apologize, Mother. Good morning, welcome to my home." Tiffany did her best to smile, though it was not at all sincere. Her mother's presence in her home felt more like an invasion than a welcome visit. She gestured at the open door to the drawing room. "Please, come join me in the drawing room."

Her mother sniffed derisively and swanned past Paulson, who was still emanating his own disapproval. The fact that he was so patently obvious in his reaction to her mother made Tiffany wonder... if the butler thought her mother was in the wrong, perhaps she was. In Bolton House, no one would ever dare gainsay her mother. Paulson and Mrs. Bryant were held to no such strictures.

When she glanced at the housekeeper, she saw the older woman's lips were tightly pressed together. She was also watching Tiffany's mother move to the drawing room. She did not manage to emanate her remonstrance as comprehensively as Paulson, but it was there all the same.

"Mrs. Bryant, would you please send up a tray in case my mother is hungry?" Tiffany asked.

"Yes, Your Grace, and I will get started on the preparations for this afternoon immediately." Mrs. Bryant nodded her head with a decisiveness that had Tiffany blinking. She felt as though there was some undercurrent to the other woman's words, but she could not tell what the housekeeper was trying to express. She did feel reassured that the other woman had everything well in hand.

Taking a deep breath, Tiffany tried to settle her shaky nerves as she faced the open door of the drawing room. She could see her mother on the other side, standing in the middle of the room rather than sitting down, arms crossed over her chest. Though her skirts were too long for her feet to be visible, Tiffany had the distinct impression that her mother was impatiently tapping her foot. Bracing herself, Tiffany moved to face the dragon.

She pushed a smile onto her face, hoping that perhaps if she was more welcoming, her mother's disapprobation might be soothed.

"Hello, Mother, I did not expect you this morning," she said as she walked into the drawing room. "Are you hungry? Mrs. Bryant is going to send up some refreshments."

"I will not be staying long enough for that," her mother snapped, not relaxing one iota as she glared at Tiffany.

The urge to immediately apologize, even though she did not know what she had done wrong, was strong. It was strange, though, that the fear that she normally felt when facing her mother was not present.

"I want an explanation, miss."

"I... an explanation for what?" Tiffany asked, feeling at a loss. Her mother had a habit of catching her off guard. She was not sure what she was supposed to have done this time.

"For giving me the cut last evening! Do you have any idea how humiliating that was for me? It was the talk of the entire *ton* last night." Her mother uncrossed her arms so she could fan herself with her hand, as if she was so aghast that she needed more air. "Now that you are a duchess, I suppose you think you are too good to talk to your own mother."

"Of course not, Mother!" Tiffany protested. "I did not cut you—"

"You rushed right by me with barely an acknowledgment. You might as well have cut me!"

"But I did acknowledge you. I am sorry I could not—"

"Barely!" Her mother interrupted her again, starting to pace away from her, her tone going higher and shriller. Tiffany recognized the signs of impending hysterics. "You might as well have turned away from me completely. Well. Yesterday, all of Society was able to see what an ungrateful, ungracious little snob of a daughter I raised. Cutting her own mother! Bad enough that you trapped a duke into marriage. Now, you are using your position to act disgracefully, thinking there will be no repercussions. How do you think that made me feel, to have my own daughter act as though she did not know me? At best, like I was a stranger, not her own flesh and blood."

"I did not mean to cut you, Mother—" Tiffany felt herself shrinking inward as her mother harangued her.

"You never mean to. No matter how I've tried to train you, you have been utterly inept at comporting yourself with any kind of grace." Her mother threw her hands in the air. "Marrying a duke has not helped. Now, you think you are too high in the instep to even acknowledge your own family, much less all the others you cut."

Tiffany frantically thought back over her behavior in her head during the previous evening. It was true that she had been so wholly focused on Gregory that she'd had difficulty concentrating on anyone else. She'd been distracted by thinking he was arranging a rendezvous with another lady, by the revelation that she loved him, and thinking he did not return her feelings.

Had she been so preoccupied that she had inadvertently cut those around her? Not acknowledging them? Did they all think that she had married a duke and immediately presumed the rest of Society to be beneath her?

"Mother, I promise—"

Her mother held up her hand to stop her from speaking.

"You are to attend no more events without me by your side. I had my reservations about you marrying so quickly, but due to your scandalous behavior, there was no choice." Putting her hand up to her temple, her mother sighed. "Clearly, I was correct. Your ineptness will not be allowed to stain our family's honor—"

"Tiffany's behavior no longer reflects the Bolton family. She is the Duchess of Clarence and deserves to be treated with the respect due to her." The deep, censorious declaration was made from the doorway, and both Tiffany and her mother gasped as they turned to face it. Tiffany had forgotten that she had not closed the door behind her.

Her husband seemed to take up the whole space of the frame, his eyes flashing with anger.

"Your Grace, Gregory." Her mother was the most flustered Tiffany had ever seen her. "I... am not sure what you think you heard—"

"I heard everything." Gregory stalked into the room, moving to stand at Tiffany's side, prowling like a tiger about to pounce. "My wife is not a snob. My wife did not trap me into marriage—if anything, it was the other way around. My wife is not inept. And she is most definitely not in need of your guidance through the social scene. If, at any point, she desires your advice, she will ask for it."

Still glaring at her mother, he took Tiffany's hand and lifted it to his lips to give a kiss. Even though he was not looking at her, Tiffany could not help but stare at him in pure shock and adoration as he defended her—a knight in shining armor here to slay her own personal dragon.

No one had ever done so before. No one had been around to do so. But somehow, Gregory had known that she needed him, and he'd appeared.

"She is already an exemplary duchess, and I will not have it said otherwise."

Tiffany's heart soared in her chest at the compliment. She looked at her mother, who appeared a trifle paler than earlier and whose manner had completely changed from aggrieved to placating now that she was faced with Gregory rather than Tiffany.

"Oh, well, yes, of course... You must understand, I only wish for both of our families to be presented in the best possible manner," Tiffany's mother said in a rush.

"Of course," Gregory said coldly. "However, I believe it is time for you to leave now. My wife and I have a very busy day today. Next time, send a card ahead so that we can be properly prepared to receive you."

If Tiffany had not already been in love with her husband, this moment would have done it.

~

GREGORY

Quivering with rage that he could not express because he could not—would not—strike a woman, not even Tiffany's mother, Gregory stared down the duchess. He did not know what was wrong with her. He did not know why she saw Tiffany the way that she did, why she was so cruel to her, but he would not stand for it.

Not in his house.

Paulson had come to the study to let him know that the Duchess of Bolton had arrived to see her daughter. It was odd enough for him to let Gregory know such a thing, but his tone of voice when doing so had set off alarms in Gregory's head. He'd immediately excused himself from his friends and gone to the drawing room, where he'd listened outside the door, aghast.

He felt guilty he had not intervened sooner, but in his defense, he'd been shocked to his toes by the amount of vitriol the duchess had been heaping upon her own daughter. And that was what Tiffany had lived with for her whole life? Where the devil had Sebastian been to defend her?

"Well." The duchess sniffed, drawing herself up. She eyed him balefully, with calculation in her eyes that he had never seen before. Any semblance of her usual fawning demeanor toward him was gone. "I can see I have dropped by at an inopportune time. I will take my leave of you."

Nose still in the air, she whisked herself away at high speed, and Gregory felt Tiffany sag beside him as her mother exited the room. It suddenly felt as though there was a lot more air to breathe.

He turned his wife toward him, pulling her into his arms and tucking her head beneath his chin. Now that she was against him, he could feel the way she was trembling. Fear? Hurt? He was not sure. Grimly, he wished that he was *not* above striking a woman, for Tiffany's mother surely deserved it.

"Are you all right?" he murmured, stroking her back to comfort her as best he could.

"Yes." She sucked in a breath. "Thank you for coming. How did you know?"

"Paulson." He paused. "She is far worse than you told me."

Tiffany laughed, an abbreviated little laugh that bordered on hysteria.

"That was barely anything," she said, which made him tighten his arms about her. The idea of her living with that viper for a mother for all these years... "Normally, she only speaks to me like that where there is no one to overhear her. Father did hear her once, and I think he said something to her, but then he died not long after, and she was so much worse afterward."

Her voice was quiet, almost like she was speaking more to herself than to him. Gregory continued to stroke her back, encouraging her to lean on him.

"Did I cut anyone last night?" she asked him.

"Absolutely not." He shook his head even though she could not see him. "She made that up whole cloth. We can ask my mother, but I would be very surprised if anyone cared that I rushed you out of the ball... and everyone would know to blame me, not you, even if they did object to our hasty exit."

His wife let out a sigh of relief. The fact that she was still inclined to believe her mother's exaggerations made him frown, but at least she accepted his reassurance. Something was going to have to be done about the duchess' behavior. And Tiffany's. He did not like to think that she might have agreed to let her mother dictate her movements through Society if he had not interrupted.

"Excuse me, Your Graces?" The soft, hesitant voice had both of them lifting their heads, Tiffany pulling away. Gregory let her go with some reluctance. Such shows of affection in front of the staff were not the done thing, but he hardly cared about that. A maid stood in the doorway to the drawing room with a cart piled high with refreshments, an apologetic expression on her face. "Did you still want the cart?"

"No, thank you, Sally," Tiffany said, shaking her head. "I apologize for having you fetch it for nothing."

"Take it to my study, Sally," Gregory directed. "We certainly will not say no to some refreshments in there."

"Yes, Your Graces." Sally bobbed a curtsy before turning, pushing the cart away.

Tiffany and Gregory exchanged looks.

"I should return to Christian and Nathanial." He squeezed her hand. "If your mother returns, send Paulson for me."

"I will." She smiled wanly. "I doubt she will, though. At least she showed up now instead of after the other ladies arrived for tea."

Studying her face, which was still troubled, Gregory slid his hand around her waist and pulled her to him. Her eyes widened in surprise, then she melted against him as he leaned down to capture her lips with a kiss. Though he could not fully make her forget what had just happened, he could at least distract her somewhat.

When he lifted his head again, her cheeks were pink, her lips were swollen, and she was smiling. There. Much better.

"I look forward to hearing about your tea this evening," he said with a grin. He truly was, too. He was curious about who Lady Astrid's friends were, as she had a bit of a reputation for being friendly but not having actual friends in Society. That she had reached out to Tiffany to form a friendship was, he was sure, initially due to Tiffany's engagement to him, but Lady Astrid did not do anything she did not want to do.

Leaving his wife with a smile on her face, Gregory returned to the study, where Christian and Nathanial were waiting for him. They both looked up from their plates when he came in, having obviously taken a break from Nathanial's accounts when the food had arrived.

"Everything all right?" Christian asked from where he sat in an armchair, a tiny sandwich in hand, his boots resting on the ottoman in front of him.

Gregory hesitated, but he felt the need to vent, and he could hardly do that to Tiffany.

"The Duchess of Bolton came to see Tiffany... and harangue her. Was there any talk last night about Tiffany giving anyone the cut? Especially her mother?"

Both Christian and Nathanial exchanged a look of confusion, giving Gregory his answer even before they shook their heads. He sighed, helping himself to some food and drink while he shared the bare minimum of his wife's fraught relationship with her mother and what he'd overheard. Mostly what he'd overheard. He did not want to reveal too much of Tiffany's personal business, but it felt good to get it off his chest and witness Christian and Nathanial's shock. Their horrified reactions matched his own.

"First time I'm glad you married her and not me," Nathanial

muttered, shaking his head. "At least I escaped having to deal with her. I can still choose the mother-in-law I'm stuck with."

And choosing his bride was one of the few choices Nathanial had left to him, a fact that was becoming more and more clear as they worked through his finances. Christian and Gregory were able to offer some assistance and advice, as both of them had flourishing estates, and Christian was considered an expert when it came to investments, but there was only so much that could be done with next to nothing.

Nathanial was going to have to marry a lady with a large dowry this Season if he was ever to fully recover the dukedom during his lifetime, and certainly, if he was going to be able to settle his younger sisters into the kind of marriage they deserved. He did not want them to have to settle for title hunters the way he was going to have to. He wanted them to be able to pick *whoever* they wanted. Gregory thought it entirely reasonable and honorable, though now that he'd married Tiffany, he felt sorry that Nathanial was having to make such a decision in a cold, hard manner rather than allowing his feelings to have any kind of sway.

Gregory could only imagine what it would be like to have so little control over his own life. He might not have had a choice in his own bride in some ways, though he had made the choice to kiss a debutante in a deserted library, but he had control over everything else. Nathanial would be able to choose his bride, but he could not even control which ladies he would be able to choose from. Given his circumstances, he was bearing up admirably.

Once they'd finished eating, they got back to work. It could not have been more than two hours after the Duchess of Bolton had left in a snit before Paulson knocked on his door again. Gregory looked up as his butler entered the room, an expression of consternation on his face.

"The Duke of Bolton is here to see you, Your Grace," Paulson said. As Sebastian was not directly behind him, Gregory imagined his butler had left the duke cooling his heels in the foyer, unsure of whether to bring him in or not.

Gregory glanced at the other two, and both of them nodded. Christian's expression was openly curious. Ah, well. If Sebastian was here about Tiffany and his mother, perhaps some witnesses were not the worst idea in the world.

"Bring him here, Paulson," Gregory said, a pit growing in his stomach.

THIRTY-SIX

G*regory*

Watching Sebastian come up short as he stormed into Gregory's study, only to realize Gregory was not alone, was almost comical. The storm cloud on his brow did not abate, though.

"Sebastian," he said mildly, watching his friend warily. They had known each other for a long time, and though they rarely argued, much less fought, Gregory knew when Sebastian was angry. Right now, he was irate. "Did you come to help with Nathanial's accounts?"

Sebastian scowled at him, giving Nathanial and Christian curt nods of greeting. As Gregory had expected, the witnesses tempered some of Sebastian's demeanor. He was certainly calmer after seeing them than he had been when he'd come barreling through the door.

"No, I had no idea Nathanial was here," he said in a clipped tone. "I came to see why my mother was thrown out of her daughter's house."

"Is that how she's describing it?" Gregory asked, raising his eyebrow. Somehow, that did not surprise him. He was beginning to realize how manipulative the duchess was. She seemed to be deliberately destructive, too, rather than misguided or unintentional in her actions. Though he'd wanted to ascribe ignorance to her rather than malice, it was becoming more difficult to do.

"Are you saying you did not?" Sebastian asked the question stiffly, and Gregory paused before responding. He could tell Sebastian was now uncertain of his tack. Seeing Christian and Nathanial here had thrown him off guard.

"I certainly did not throw her out." Gregory shrugged. "I did make it clear that coming into my house and insulting my wife was unwelcome."

As expected, Sebastian goggled at him. Like Gregory himself, Sebastian had likely never looked too closely at his mother's behavior. And, as Tiffany had told him, the duchess was not as free with her viperish tongue when there were others about. Another sign that her intentions were malicious.

"Insulting Tiffany? How?" Sebastian was still stiffly demanding, immediately defensive, but not entirely disbelieving.

Gregory made short work of rehashing what he'd overheard between the two ladies in the drawing room, as well as the revelations that he'd felt he could share with Christian and Nathanial. Without their presence, he might have shared more, but upon further reflection, he was glad that they stymied his tongue. It was up to Tiffany whether she wanted to share with her brother what she'd shared with him.

As he spoke, Sebastian sat down, then slumped, one hand on his forehead, rubbing it as though he was getting a headache.

"I cannot believe she would so mispresent..." Sebastian started to say, then trailed off. He shook his head. "But then I cannot believe that you would fabricate..."

"When Gregory returned from speaking with your mother, he told us exactly what he just told you. I have also noted that your mother is not always... supportive of Tiffany," Nathanial said a bit hesitantly. No one liked to speak ill of their friend's mother, especially to their friend's face. Gregory was losing his hesitation over it, though. "She can be quite cutting, though she does it in such a way that she says it as a jest or in a manner than could be taken more than one way."

Sebastian scrubbed his hand over his face, leaning forward to rest his elbows on his knees. He did not respond.

Huffing, Christian groaned.

"I did not want to have to tell either of you this, but it now seems it is necessary." That confession meant all eyes immediately went to him, Sebastian lifting his head with an unhappy look on his face. Christian avoided looking at him, focusing on Gregory instead. "During your wedding brunch, I happened to be speaking with Lady Monmouth when you and Tiffany departed so precipitously. She commented that the Duchess of Bolton must be wrong, and you truly were a love match after all."

Both Sebastian and Gregory stiffened. Tiffany's mother had told Lady Monmouth that they were not? If she had told Lady Monmouth, had she told others? How much damage had she been trying to do to her daughter's reputation and standing by using the truth as gossip?

Coming from her, it was far more likely to be believed.

"We *are* a love match," Gregory said immediately. It was the only defense he had against the truth about the original arrangement. Sebastian had been opening his mouth, but he snapped it shut, looking at Gregory in shock. Gregory looked back at him with all the sincerity he could, silently sending him a message, and Sebastian slowly nodded. The look in his eyes changed from surprise to gratified relief.

"Of course, you are. Even a blind man could see that," Nathanial reassured him, to his surprise. "What would she get out of saying differently?"

That was the question. They all turned to Sebastian for the answer, but he shook his head helplessly.

"I do not know. I will have to talk to her. I do not know what she is thinking. She's been having a hard time this Season; constant megrims, she's been more out of sorts than usual. Perhaps Lady Monmouth misheard something she said or... I do not know."

It was the kind of excuses Gregory had made in his head for the duchess in the past, but no more. Still, he could hardly demand that Sebastian turn on his own mother. But he would not countenance her upsetting Tiffany in the future, either.

Christian reached over, patting Sebastian on the shoulder.

"Perhaps she did mishear. It will work itself out, old chap, do not worry." Not particularly encouraging coming from Christian, who rarely worried about anything, but it was well meant.

Obviously not eager to return home to his mother, Sebastian offered his services to look at Nathanial's accounts. Unfortunately, he was not able to find any more advice to give than Gregory and Christian already had. Nathanial was as stuck as they feared.

"You should let me give you a loan," Christian insisted, but Nathanial shook his head, his stubborn pride showing through.

"I can fix this on my own."

"By getting married."

Nathanial raised a sardonic eyebrow. "Is that not the usual way for our set?"

"Yes, but you should have a choice in who you marry," Christian argued stubbornly.

Gregory and Sebastian watched silently. He was not sure why Sebastian was silent, but he knew that for himself, he could see both of their points. Nathanial was all stubborn pride, wanting to be seen as equal to his peers, wanting to solve the problem on his own. Christian was the type to put practicality above pride... but he also had never been in Nathanial's position before. He might feel differently if pride was all that he had left to him.

Gregory had never been in Nathanial's position before, either, but he was far more empathetic than Christian. Hell, a worm was probably more empathetic than Christian, when it came down to it.

He was a good man, but understanding perspectives other than his own had never been his strong suit.

"I have a choice. I can choose whether to let my friends fund my life or I can marry. I choose to marry." Nathanial's eyes blazed, his grim tone reflected in the set of his jaw. "And I will choose my bride. After that, many more choices will open up to me. You should stop worrying about who I am going to marry and start worrying about choosing your own wife."

Waving an indolent hand, Christian made a face. "There is time enough for that yet."

As they'd rather exhausted the topic, Gregory suggested that they move their gathering to Tattersalls. Some of his anger at his mother-in-law was still simmering and admiring the recent arrivals of horseflesh sounded just the thing. It would also give them all something else to focus on and Sebastian a reason to avoid returning home for a while. Unsurprisingly, the others immediately agreed, with varying amounts of relief.

Making their way to the front of the house, Gregory heard the sound of feminine laughter echoing up the stairs. When they reached the landing, it was clear that it was time for Tiffany's tea to start—the foyer was full of ladies in varying hues. Seeing his wife's happy expression, he felt his own heart lighten a bit.

Of course, Lady Astrid and Baroness Ashfield were known to all of them. They had not spent as much time with Lady Astrid because Drake did not spend much time with her, but they had all been introduced. The baroness they were all on far more friendly terms, which made this meeting rather fraught since Zachary had ended their relationship.

All the gentlemen were relieved when she greeted them without a hint of censure. Whatever her current feelings about Zachary, she was not painting them with the same brush.

Which left Miss Little. Sebastian had been introduced to her last night and greeted her with the same friendly smile that he had both Lady Astrid and the baroness.

"Hereford, Montagu, this is Miss Kalina Little. Miss Little, these are my friends, the Dukes of Hereford and Montagu." His mother would certainly approve of him introducing the young woman to more dukes.

Dark eyes wide, Miss Little sank into a deep curtsy, bowing her head as she did so. To Gregory's bemusement, Nathanial was the one who stepped forward, beating Christian to take her hand. It was odd not because Christian was overly eager when introduced to a lady but because Nathanial had the tendency to hang back, observing before acting. That he moved quickly to be the first to make his bow was not exactly in character for him.

"Miss Little. A pleasure to meet your acquaintance." Nathanial bowed over her hand, smiling. She smiled back at him, a small smile, but there was something between them. It reminded Gregory of the little sizzle of attraction he'd felt when he'd first seen Tiffany in the library.

Gregory could not help but wonder if Nathanial knew the gossip around her family.

As far as the size of her dowry, she would be a good match for him. Gregory had learned that her father had a stake in a rose diamond mine, one of the rarest diamonds. The pink jewels she currently wore were a stunning example of her wealth and were perfectly set off against the cream and mauve gown she wore, both of which made the most of her dark skin, hair, and eyes.

Unfortunately, her current standing with the *ton* and the Stilton's lack of welcome to her family were a mark against them. Nathanial had three sisters who would need guidance through Society as they made their come-outs over the next few years. Someone like Christian, with no younger sister, or Sebastian, whose only sister was now married, would be far more suitable on that front.

But from the way Nathanial was looking at her as Christian took his turn bowing over her hand... well, Gregory would have to have a word with him to be sure he knew the current imbroglio around her family.

He would need to keep one eye on that situation and another on Tiffany and Sebastian. Tiffany knew her brother had not been expected this morning, and she was currently frowning at him in consternation, and Sebastian was studiously avoiding her gaze. Probably because he still did not know how to handle this morning's revelations.

Right now was not the time to have the siblings finally talk about their mother, though.

"We are off to Tattersall's." He took Tiffany's hand and squeezed her fingers. "Enjoy your tea, ladies."

"We intend to," Lady Astrid said, causing the baroness to laugh. Tiffany lifted her free hand to cover her giggle while Miss Little blinked in surprise. Gregory led the gentlemen out, noting Nathanial's last glance at the dark beauty he'd just met.

Yes, he was definitely going to need to have a word with the other man.

~

TIFFANY

It became quickly apparent to Tiffany that she much preferred a small social gathering with a select group of friends over the nerve-wracking crush of the balls or the socially significant at-homes and larger teas. It was not difficult to relax with these three ladies, their social mores falling one by one as they chatted. Baroness Ashfield was now Delilah, Lady Astrid had already told Tiffany to call her Astrid but now it felt easier to, and Miss Little was Kalina.

Tiffany, as a reining duchess, was the highest ranking among them, but she did not want to be treated as such, and the others followed her lead.

Although the most exciting moment from last night was centered around the rescue of the monkey Sinclair, they barely touched on that topic out of deference to Delilah's feelings. Kalina was the only one who was confused when they did not discuss it further. Tiffany would have to inform her of Delilah's prior relationship with the Duke of Grafton and why dwelling on anything involving him was unwelcome.

It did not hurt that, of course, they all wanted to know all about Kalina and her family's decision to relocate to England—a less-than-triumphant return for her father. Despite Kalina's inherent shyness, as they questioned her about her home and how she grew up, comparing it to their own upbringing, she became more verbose. Like Tiffany, she seemed far more comfortable in this setting than in larger social situations—likely because no one here was pretending she and her family did not exist.

Tiffany was happy to hear her speak more, and not just because she wanted to get to know her better. Kalina's English was flawless, but her accent was unlike anyone else in the *ton*, and she found it beautiful to listen to. Far more melodic than even the usual *tonnish* way of speaking. She wondered if Kalina sang.

"Papa missed England," she explained when they reached this Season on the timeline of their lives. "He wanted us to see it, and he hoped if we appeared in person, his family would not be able to ignore us anymore. Especially because... well..." Her fingers lifted to the stunning rose diamond necklace she was wearing.

It was smaller, less showy, than the one she'd worn the night before, delicate rather than grand. That she had two such pieces was an indication of the wealth her father had amassed while away from his family. For some families, that would be enough. Unfortunately, the Stilton family had their own deep pockets and were far too priggish to be swayed by their youngest son's financial success.

Lady Astrid snorted indelicately.

"Never underestimate the English's penchant for snobbery," she said. "Even if they needed your father's wealth, they would take it while looking down their noses at him and your family the entire time."

"Sadly accurate," Delilah murmured, lifting her teacup to take a sip. Despite the lightness of her tone, there was bitterness laced through it. "Everything must be done a certain way, to certain social strictures, or else the sky would fall down." The last part of her statement was heavy with sarcastic mockery.

It was the closest she'd come to referring to her own relationship with Zachary, and Tiffany's heart hurt for the woman. She had clearly loved him, only to be given a dismissal when it was time for him to marry, and all because gentlemen were supposed to marry virgins rather than their lovers. No matter their feelings.

"Have we crossed the line on any?" Kalina asked, appearing worried that something in Delilah's statement referred to her.

"No, dear, I was talking about my own situation." Delilah sighed and frowned. "I am not sure how much I can tell you without offending your sensibilities or, at the very least, saying something I should not in front of young, unmarried ladies. Astrid does not count, of course. She already knows far more than she should."

"About what married ladies and mistresses do?" Kalina asked. Everyone looked at her. With her dark complexion it was impossible to tell if she was blushing or not, but Tiffany felt that she was. "My mother has explained, in detail, what passes between a man and a woman and that it is not always necessary to be married for, ah, intimacies."

"Really?" Tiffany could not help but ask, mentally comparing such a statement to her own experience with her mother. "My mother would have rather died than talk about such things." Well, at least until she had to talk about Tiffany's wedding night. And then her description had been both terrifying and erroneous. Tiffany was glad her mother had not spoken about it to her before.

"English snobbery," Astrid said darkly. "It is so important to keep us young virgins in the dark so we do not know our fates because, with knowledge, we might actually find a way to control some of our own lives." Quite a statement from someone who had been betrothed since nearly birth.

"My mother did not want me caught unawares and to be very careful of any gentlemen with nefarious intentions. She wanted me to know what they might try to do." Kalina frowned, brushing imaginary crumbs off her pink and cream skirt.

"Your mother is very wise," Delilah told her. "There are far too many so-called gentlemen in our set who are happy to take advantage of a young woman's naivete. Especially one who is new to Society and without the support of her family."

They all knew that Delilah meant the broader family of the Earl of Stilton, not Kalina's immediate family.

"Well, you have our support now, and that is no small thing," Tiffany said, rather delighted as she realized the truth of her words. As a duchess, there was a good deal she could do to advance Kalina's interests. The same for Astrid, as a future duchess. Delilah might not have their rank, but she did have more connections due to her status as a widow and being a bit older than the rest of them. She'd had more time to make those connections.

"Not small at all," Astrid agreed, a little glint in her eye, exchanging a look with Delilah. "In fact, we know a matchmaker of exceptional skill. That is if you truly want a husband."

"I do," Kalina said immediately, nodding earnestly. "One that will make Papa happy."

"But what do you want?" Delilah asked gently. "Other than your father's happiness? Do you even want to marry an Englishman?"

Kalina paused. Her mouth opened. Closed. Tiffany could not help but wonder if she'd ever considered the question before.

"I do not mind marrying an Englishman. I find your country very different from my own, very exotic. The tea is... perhaps not as strong as I enjoy, and the food not as spiced as I prefer, but I do like it here. Or I think I would if Papa were happier." She smiled. "This is very nice, being here today."

That made Tiffany's heart warm. Kalina wanted friends as much as she did. She was amused to hear Britain described as exotic especially with the mania for items from India, which the British thought of as exotic, but she supposed that was the point. "Exotic" was whatever one was not used to.

"What kind of Englishman would you like to marry?"

"Ah… someone kind. Who will not be upset if Papa's family never comes around to our presence here." She paused again. They waited. But it appeared that was it. Astrid and Delilah exchanged another glance. Tiffany would have felt a bit left out, but Kalina met her gaze at the same time, and she realized that the two of them were closer in temperament.

She understood Kalina's impulse to do what was best for her family, putting her own considerations to the side. Not even bothering to have considerations. In that, she and Kalina were very much alike.

Astrid cleared her throat.

"Well, we can certainly introduce you to some gentlemen who will fulfill that description. We also know a very talented matchmaker, another friend of ours, if none of the gentlemen we introduce you to suit." Astrid nodded her head, as if she'd made a decision, the gleam in her eye very much like the one she'd had when she'd taken over Tiffany's dress fitting at Madame Allard's.

Which had worked out very well for Tiffany in the end. She could only hope fate would step in and do the same for Kalina. Though, if fate did not, she felt sure that Lady Astrid would.

THIRTY-SEVEN

G*regory*

To Gregory's surprise, after her tea, Tiffany was far more excited about their evening—she'd chosen to attend the Chesterham soiree, one of the smaller balls, rather than the larger event at Donning House. When he'd inquired why, she'd tipped her chin up in a move rather reminiscent of Lady Astrid and informed him that she would only be attending events where her friends were welcome, and the Littles had not been invited to Donning House.

Gregory had grinned, given her a kiss on the tip of her upturned nose, and agreed. His mother would certainly approve as well. He had a feeling that Lady Astrid had already been making such decisions. Adding two more duchesses to the cause would very likely tip the *ton's* hostesses in favor of sending invitations to the Little's least-favorite son and his family.

He decided to add his own ducal weight by sending messages to his friends about where he would be that evening and encouraging them to join him there. When one had six other dukes to throw, might as well chuck them at a good cause. Whether or not they chose to attend was up to them, but he'd made the effort.

Nathanial may or may not. Upon hearing the whole story about Miss Little's father and his family, he had turned very thoughtful and rather resigned. Gregory had felt bad, but Nathanial had more considerations than just a lady's dowry to his choice. He had the right to make a fully informed one, and Gregory would not be a good friend if he had not ensured his friend was in possession of all the pertinent facts.

To his and Tiffany's delight, upon arriving at the Chesterham soiree, they found that Zachary, Matthew, and Christian had already arrived before them. Lady Chesterham was also delighted when she greeted them, *in alt* to have such an august crowd on a night when the majority of the *haut ton* were gathered elsewhere. Monkey Sinclair had also accompanied Zachary and was currently seated on his shoulder, warily watching those around them.

"I say, good idea to attend one of the smaller events for a breather," Christian said when he greeted them. "And if we all do it together, the larger hostesses cannot complain. Strength in numbers and all that."

"Well, that's not the reason why," Gregory admitted and explained the situation in a quiet voice. Tiffany was too enthralled with monkey Sinclair, trying to tempt him into accepting a small piece of fruit from her to overhear, which allowed him to be blunt and quick.

Unsurprisingly, Christian was all too happy to take up the cause as well. Setting a cat amongst the pigeons was very much suited to his personality, and he seemed eager to enjoy the invariable squawking that would occur. Matthew was less enthusiastic, but, of course, he'd flipped his coin, and it had directed him to follow Gregory's request.

"Do you know if the others are coming?" Gregory asked, and they all shook their heads.

Still, four dukes and two duchesses present was a goodly

number. His mother, being a dowager duchess, did not take anything away from her rank. And when the Little family arrived shortly after, they all made it clear that the family's attendance was why they had chosen to appear. Gregory was more than a little gratified when the rest of those present followed their lead.

Likely, Lady Chesterham had invited the Littles for the same reason they'd received invitations elsewhere—a little bit of scandal present always added spice to an event. Or perhaps he was not giving her enough credit, and she had sent the invitation after noticing his mother's interest in the family and wanted to show her support as well. She had a reputation for being very kind-hearted. Regardless, it was very clear that even if the Earl of Stilton and his heir were giving the youngest son and his family the cut, they had even higher-ranking connections.

Mrs. Little brightened when she saw Gregory's mother, and the two immediately began talking as Miss Little joined Tiffany's circle of gentlemen. They stayed close by to chaperone, of course, but it was clear to everyone watching that both ladies were friends with the Duchess and Dowager Duchess of Clarence. Not only that, but the Dukes of Clarence, Montagu, and Grafton all asked for Miss Little's dance card.

The Duke of St. Albans did not immediately ask Miss Little to dance, but no one would make much of that. The Lord of Luck's erratic behavior was common knowledge, even if the reason for it was not. Gregory's lips quirked when a surreptitious coin flip had Matthew engaging her younger brother in conversation instead.

Mr. Little had puffed up his chest, watching everything with understandable relief and calculation. He knew what was happening, and when he turned his gaze to Gregory, his abject gratitude shone in his eyes. Gregory just smiled and nodded his head in silent acknowledgment.

Those present were agog, Lady Chesterham's ballroom fair buzzing with the gossip that would be flying the next day.

The only minor hiccup was when Baroness Ashfield arrived in

the company of Lady Astrid and her mother. Lady Blackstone imme-diately joined Gregory's mother and Mrs. Little, and Lady Astrid and the baroness went to join Tiffany and Miss Little… which made Zachary go stiff as a board.

Up to that point, monkey Sinclair had been remarkably well-behaved, but almost as soon as the baroness joined the group, the monkey finally jumped from Zachary's shoulder to Tiffany's arm. His wife was thrilled, but the monkey was not there for the fruit she was holding. It ran up her arm to her shoulder and then launched itself at the baroness… who caught it against her chest, wide-eyed with shock.

It appeared that there were only two people in the world who monkey Sinclair was prepared to like on sight—Zachary and his former mistress. The awkwardness was… astounding. Gregory was quite sure that retrieving the monkey was the closest the two had physically come to each other since the baroness had been given her *congé*.

Drake came through the crowd, his gaze focused on Gregory, who straightened. While Drake was not the most expressive man, his face was not normally so blank.

"I have news," he said as soon as he reached Gregory. "From Bow Street." His gaze shifted to where Tiffany was standing beside him. She'd straightened as well, as she was standing close enough that she could not help but hear Drake's statement, no matter how low he'd kept his voice.

"You can speak in front of her," Gregory said quietly. "Her father was there, too. Besides, Sebastian and I have already told her everything."

From the expression on Drake's face, he did not approve, but neither did he quibble.

"The runners have been seeking out all the servants who were there and survived that night. Two of them have confirmed that it was your father's steward, Montblanc, who directed the shipment of gunpowder and was insistent on where it should be stored in the house. However, they all also reported that he left the lodge long before the accident happened."

A chill went through Gregory as he was metaphorically rocked back on his heels, his whole body tensing at the realization that his steward had been far more involved than he'd realized. It sounded as though he was directly responsible. Tiffany leaned in closer to him, taking his hand where her skirts would cover the movement and squeezing his fingers hard enough to hurt.

"This is *not your fault,*" she said fiercely. "It is the fault of whoever planned it. I am not going to say that your father brought it on himself, but if he had not behaved in such a manner that he was so hated by his staff, if he had left Betty alone, Montblanc would likely have never acted. Absolutely none of that can be laid at your feet."

The bands around his chest loosened. If *she* could say that, she who had lost a father she actually loved, maybe it was true.

Maybe his friends would not blame him.

He gathered his courage and looked back up at Drake, whose blank expression had softened a touch.

"She is correct. No one in their right mind would blame you," Drake said softly. As he was one who had been particularly close to his father, that was incredibly reassuring to hear. "There is still a lot we do not know. I do not think Montblanc was the force behind the plot... I think he might have been a pawn, used to set things into place. Someone used his rage, his sense of justice, to push him into such a heinous act."

"I think you are right." Gregory rubbed his forehead with his free hand, holding tight to Tiffany's fingers with his other. "I still have trouble believing he was capable of it... of my father, yes, but not of so many. Not with such risk to innocents. I cannot see that."

Yet, Montblanc had done just that.

"I am going to tell the others," Drake said quietly. Gregory nodded his understanding. He kept watch as Drake moved from one of their friends to the next. Each of them reacted differently... none of them looked up to glare at him the way he was afraid they would.

Matthew and Zachary both shot him sympathetic looks. Not long after, Christian came over to reassure Gregory that he did not blame him in the slightest.

All of which was a relief, even though it left so many more questions.

The ballroom had been filling up and was enough of a crush that when he heard the Duke and Duchess of Bolton announced, Gregory could not immediately see where they went as they descended the stairs. Hopefully, Sebastian had been able to see them... and hopefully, he would lead his mother elsewhere before joining them.

Gregory sidled closer to his wife. It appeared as though tonight they would be supporting each other.

$\sim$

TIFFANY

Spending the ball with her friends, having a purpose in helping to establish Miss Little, was making the entire evening one of the most enjoyable Tiffany had experienced. The only fly in the ointment was Drake's news, but she had become very good at pushing aside her emotions so she could still enjoy the moment she was in. As much as she wanted to know more, like who else had been involved in her father's death, it was not as though she could go out hunting them now.

Though she did quietly update Lady Astrid, whose narrow-eyed gaze immediately went to her betrothed. It seemed the Duke of Ormonde did not see fit to tell her the latest revelation. That did not matter because Tiffany would. It was all she *could* do for now. Later, she would talk to more of the servants, see if there was more she could find out now that she knew Montblanc had been present at the hunting lodge for a period of time.

But right now, she needed to focus on what was happening around her currently. Her father would not want her to mourn forever. He would want her to find her joy where she could, she was sure of it. That she was happily married would make him happy. She wanted to live her life in honor of him, not mourning him.

And she truly was happy. Knowing her husband loved her, that Gregory had no eyes for any woman but her, made the evening far more enjoyable than previous ones where she had been so unsure of him.

It was easier to watch him and truly see how he interacted with the other ladies. They might flirt, but he did not reciprocate. He might be charming, but it was his natural charm, without any deeper intention. Now that they had said the words to each other, now that they both knew their pretend love match had turned into one for truth, the jealousy that had been gnawing at her was gone.

Which was why she felt no compunction about slipping away when she needed to use the retiring room. Alerting Astrid to her direction, Tiffany moved to the doors that led to the hallway. She felt as though she was walking on air, smiling and nodding as she made her way through the crowd, acknowledging those she passed. Her head was so in the clouds, she did not realize her mother had followed her out to the hallway until she was already there, alone, and a sharp grip on her upper arm made her yelp.

"Where do you think you are going?"

Spinning, wrenching her arm away from her mother, Tiffany lifted her hand to rub the spot where her mother had dug her nails in. She frankly stared. Though her mother looked as fashionable, as beautiful, as she always did, there was something very off about her. Something in the eyes, a kind of glassiness, which showed through even when her mother narrowed them.

Tiffany's heart fluttered in her chest, but even as she felt the fear and trepidation that always came when facing her mother's displeasure, there was a new emotion rising with it as well.

Anger.

For the first time she could remember, she felt truly angry with her mother. She lifted her chin in the air.

"To the retiring room, Mother, but I do not require your

assistance." Turning again, she began to sweep down the hallway, taking long, quick steps to try to get away from her own mother. It felt like fleeing, but Tiffany tried to tell herself this was the direction she would have been walking, anyway.

"Do not walk away from me, you haughty miss!" Her mother's voice came closer, and she grabbed a painful hold of Tiffany's arm again, in the exact place she had before. Tiffany bit her lip against yelping, once again, turning to pull her arm free.

"I am not being haughty. I am trying to get away from you." She could not remember ever speaking to her mother in such a manner, and the look of shock on her mother's face was exceedingly gratifying. Knowing she was going home to Clarence House, that her mother could no longer lock her in her room without supper, destroy her sheet music, or tear up her favorite things, made her far bolder than she could have countenanced.

Perhaps it was also the way Gregory had defended her earlier.

"You ungrateful little bitch," her mother stepped closer, and Tiffany held her ground by sheer force of will. She and her mother were about the same height, but somehow, her mother managed to make it seem as though she was looming over Tiffany. Her mother's hot breath wafted across her face, the odor of alcohol hanging heavy on it. Staring into her mother's glassy eyes, Tiffany realized she was drunk. "Now that you're a duchess, you think you are so much better than me."

"No, I do not, but I also do not want to be around you, not when you keep saying things like that to me." Tiffany shook her head, her anger rising up again. Why? That was the question she had for her mother, and she could hold it back no longer. "Why did you treat me so differently from Sebastian? Why are you so cruel to me? Why did you deliberately dress me in unflattering dresses?" She felt a sob rising up in her throat as the unfairness of it all threatened to swamp her emotions, to drench the flame of her anger.

"You think you are equal to your brother?" Her mother's laugh was high and cruel, mocking her for daring to think such a thing. "He is a *duke*. He was born to be a duke. You are nothing compared to him. You never were."

Tears sparked in Tiffany's eyes. She sucked in a deep breath against the pain, doing her best to bolster her courage.

"I am a duchess now. Same as you."

The rage that filled her mother's eyes made Tiffany step back in shock, a new kind of fear gripping her. She had never seen her mother look at her so hatefully, loathing emanating from every fiber of her being. It was as if a mask had been ripped off, and the truth was finally allowed to surface.

"You are not the same as me." Spittle flew from her mother's mouth, tiny droplets dotting Tiffany's face. She raised her hand to block it, backing away even more, but it did not matter because her mother was still coming toward her. "You will never be the same as me. You were not supposed to marry a duke!"

Her mother's voice had risen to a shriek. Tiffany did not understand.

"You wanted me to marry well!"

"But not above me."

Her mother had backed Tiffany up against the wall so she could not retreat any farther. An odd kind of anguish had arisen in her body. It felt like her heart was being torn asunder as she realized how much her own mother—the mother she'd tried so hard to please—hated her. That her mother had not wanted the best for her.

That her mother was angry that her daughter was a duchess because it meant they were societally equal in rank.

"You are a terrible mother," Tiffany said through the tears that were beginning to slide down her face. It both hurt to say the words and felt like relief to finally be able to say them. "I am so glad I have Gregory's mother because she is five times the mother you are."

"I gave you everything, you ungrateful little harlot!" Her mother's hand rose in the air and was descending downward when Sebastian appeared out of nowhere behind her, grabbing their mother by the wrist and pulling her away from Tiffany. The expression on his face was terrible to behold. The same pain Tiffany felt. His utter disillusionment. Fury he directed at their mother, who was staring up at him in shock. A grim kind of determination.

As he pulled her away, Gregory inserted himself in front of Tiffany, his broad shoulders easily blocking her view of her mother. Using his body as a shield between them. He looked down at Tiffany with pride, compassion, and concern.

"Are you all right?" he asked.

She nodded, stepping forward into his arms and burying her face in his chest. She was all right, now that he was there. She might have spoken in the heat of the moment, but what she'd said was true.

His mother was a hundred times the mother of her own, and henceforth, she was going to be the only mother Tiffany acknowledged. How her mother could be so awful, why she would care so much about her rank that she was willing to undermine her own daughter, she did not understand. Could not understand.

"Sebastian! What are you doing here?"

Now that her ear was attuned to it, Tiffany could fully appreciate how differently her mother spoke to her and Sebastian. Her entire tone was softer, more loving. Sebastian was her golden boy, her duke... and Tiffany was, in her mother's eyes, some sort of rival. Even though she'd never wanted to compete with her mother; all she'd ever wanted was her approval.

"Gregory and I followed you to see why you were following Tiffany," Sebastian replied grimly. "I wanted to know if they were telling the truth about the way you behaved to Tiffany after you claimed that she and Gregory had you thrown out of their house."

"That was all lies! I told you. That's why I'm so upset. I saw Tiffany here, and I could not help but confront her." Her mother sniffled, sounding distraught. How she'd managed to change her emotions so quickly, Tiffany had no idea. "She said such awful things to me, I lashed out. I was so hurt, just like before. What kind of daughter is so disrespectful to her own mother?"

Tiffany felt Gregory stiffen and start to turn, but she held fast to him. It did not matter what her mother said. She knew he did not believe a word, and that was what mattered most to her. She hoped Sebastian knew her mother was telling falsehoods, but the far more important opinion belonged to her husband.

"I overheard quite a bit more than you apparently realized," Sebastian said coldly. Tiffany had never heard him sound like that before, certainly not when speaking to their mother. "You and I are going home. Right now. We're going to have a very long discussion about how things will be going forward."

Moving to the side, so Tiffany could see her brother, she watched in utter shock as he gave her a grim nod of apology, then bodily began dragging their mother down the hall, despite her protests. Gregory's arm tightened around her as they watched the pair go.

"I am sorry we did not intervene sooner," Gregory murmured in her ear. "But I wanted him to see the fullness of her behavior."

"How much did you hear?" she asked. She had been so caught up in the confrontation, she had not even noticed them there.

"We walked into the hall early enough to hear her call you a bitch." The menacing rage that thrummed through his voice made Tiffany shiver. Her mother might be lucky that Gregory had let Sebastian hustle her out of there. "It was not easy to stay back, but your brother needed to know the whole of it. Needed to see and hear it for himself."

Otherwise, it would be too difficult to believe, especially as her mother had been a very different person in his presence. Because his mother had never treated him that way.

"I understand." Turning back into his arms, she rested her forehead against his shoulder and took in a deep breath before letting out a shuddering sigh. Part of her might have wished she had not had to hear her mother say those things, but in some ways, she was also glad she knew. She hurt for Sebastian, but she was also relieved.

While she would not have wanted him to feel the same way she did about their mother, it also felt so good not to be alone. To see him come to her defense. To know that he did not take their mother's side.

Tilting her head back, she looked up at her husband.

"I want to go home."

Gregory's fathomless dark eyes met hers. He bent his head, giving her a gentle kiss that filled with warmth some of the cold spaces her mother had opened within her. She sighed, leaning against him. Her stalwart protector. Her anchor in the storm.

Her love.

His lips lifted from hers.

"Then let's go home."

THIRTY-EIGHT

G<u>*regory*</u>

"We have been invited to a house party," his wife informed him when he joined her and his mother for breakfast. The two of them made quite the pair. Tiffany was dressed in a morning gown of sprigged blue and cream muslin, which set off her coloring just as well as the sapphire dress she'd worn the night before. Meanwhile, his mother had opted for a gown of sunny yellow decorated with green and violet ruffles. Tiffany beamed at him as he walked into the room while he scowled back at her.

When he'd woken this morning, he'd reached for her, only to find the spot beside him empty. It had left him feeling disgruntled and aroused. For all that he'd pleasured her to satiation last night, he'd been looking for another taste this morning. But he could hardly complain about that with his mother sitting right there.

At least he was feeling more himself this morning. More even-keeled.

"You woke up early," he responded, which was the closest he could come to expressing his feelings about her absence from their bed this morning. The amused smile on her lips and the little twinkle in her eye made it clear she knew exactly why he was feeling out of sorts. For some reason, she'd decided to purposefully push his bounds this morning.

Well, if the little minx wanted a spanking, a spanking was what she would get.

Truthfully, he was happy to see her so relaxed this morning. Despite his best efforts after they'd returned home from the Chesterhams, he'd been uncertain how she would handle the revelations from her mother. He wished he could have throttled the woman while she'd been abusing Tiffany, but his wife seemed no worse for the wear, so perhaps he'd done the right thing.

It had been important to him that Sebastian knew, that he would believe the things Tiffany told him if she ever chose to open up to her brother.

"Good morning to you too, Gregory," his mother said reprovingly, looking up from her kippers with a frown on her face.

"Good morning, Mother." He leaned down to buss her cheek before taking his own seat between them. Tiffany took a smug sip of her tea, the expression on her face making his hand itch. She did delight in needling him. He narrowed his eyes at her. "Good morning, wife."

"Good morning, husband. We've been invited to Lady Blackstone's house party." She smiled serenely at him. "This upcoming weekend."

"A jaunt out of the capital sounds nice," he replied, reaching for the toast and butter. As he began to spread the butter, one of the footmen arrived with his cup of coffee, and he shot the man a look of abject gratitude. "Do you know who else has been invited?"

"I am sure we will find out," his mother answered airily, waving a piece of toast in the air. "I would not be surprised if some of your friends were invited. Likely the Littles. I know Lady Astrid is also good friends with Baroness Ashfield. Perhaps some of her neighbors. Her mother and I were discussing it last night. My impression is that it will be a very select event."

Which meant Zachary would likely be left to his own devices in the capital. Ah, well. He'd rather brought that on himself. Even though it was technically Lady Blackstone's house party, Gregory was certainly receiving the impression that Lady Astrid's hand was guiding things. If he was not misreading things, it seemed she wanted to give Miss Little a tilt at multiple dukes at once. He was sure other debutantes would be present as well; it would not do to be too obvious, but everyone would know.

Doubtless, none of his friends would mind, as they were on a determined hunt for brides. Hell, Christian might just make an offer for no reason other than to send the *ton* into a tizzy.

Paulson appeared in the door to the dining room, stiffly upright and slightly disapproving.

"The Duke of Bolton is here to see you, Your Graces." The slight disapproval was threaded through his voice as well. It was far too early to be calling, after all, but Sebastian *was* family, so Paulson's ire was not as great as it could be.

All three of them immediately sat up. Gregory could only assume that Tiffany had told his own mother about the contretemps from last night before he'd joined them at the table.

"See him in, please, Paulson." Whatever had Sebastian on their doorstep this early in the morning, it would have to do with the Duchess of Bolton. There was no other reason for him to come by so early. Paulson nodded and disappeared from the doorway, and Gregory slanted his gaze toward his wife.

Tiffany was sitting up straight as a poker in her seat, her white-knuckled grip on her fork and her clenched jaw practically shouting her tension to the world. Reaching over, Gregory put his fingers atop hers, breaking through that tension. She started before looking back at him and relaxing slightly.

"Everything will be all right," he murmured.

Hearing the rumble of his voice, his mother looked over at them as well and nodded sharply.

"You have our full support," she said, not bothering to lower her voice. "And that is no small thing."

His mother might not have quite as many connections as the Duchess of Bolton because she had not been as active in the *ton* while his father was still alive, but she was still a dowager duchess and had her own influence. Not to mention Tiffany's friendship with Lady Astrid. The exclusive invite to her mother's house party was appearing more and more serendipitous.

Paulson returned a moment later to announce the Duke of Bolton. Sebastian strode into the room, appearing rather haggard. There were dark bags under his reddened eyes, his jaw was set in a way that said he'd been clenching it for a good long time, and his appearance was most kindly described as 'disheveled'. He'd clearly had a rough night.

Immediately, Tiffany jumped to her feet, releasing Gregory's hand.

"Sebastian! Are you all right?" She rushed around the table to meet her brother as Gregory got more slowly to his feet, his mother joining him with an expression of concern on her face. While Tiffany might be her priority, she cared about Sebastian as well.

"As well as I can be, I suppose," Sebastian replied, his voice hollow, as he folded his arms around his sister. Though he was taller and wider than her, his hug enveloping her completely, when he turned and rested his cheek on the top of her head, it was clear that she was the one providing support for him. Coming around the table to stand beside them, Gregory clapped his hand on Sebastian's shoulder.

"Come eat, and you can tell us all," he said.

Sebastian opened his tired eyes and nodded. "Thank you."

Though, of course, he did not make it to the table without also being hugged by Gregory's mother, her eyes full of concern. For a moment, Gregory thought his friend might break down, but Sebastian kept his stiff upper lip by the skin of his teeth. As he straightened up, there was a gleam of liquid in his eyes that he rapidly blinked back.

"Sit." Gregory pointed at the chair beside Tiffany. Sebastian practically collapsed into it, his knees folding as if he'd been struggling to hold himself up. "Have you broken your fast yet?"

"No." Sebastian sighed, leaning back in the chair as he was served coffee, then leaning forward again to reach for the toast. "I do not know how much I will be able to eat. My stomach is…" His voice trailed off, and he grimaced.

Tiffany reached out a hand, touching his shoulder gently. He turned to look at her, covering her hand with his own, his gaze full of remorse.

"I am so sorry," he said, tightening his fingers around his sister's. "I had no idea…"

"I know. She was always worse when you and Father were not around. I thought it was because she was trying to spare me the embarrassment of sharp correction in front of you." Tiffany shook her head. "It was not until Father overheard her and intervened that I realized it was because he might not approve. And I did not know what you would think. Or what you would say if I tried to tell you. Most of the time, I thought she was right, that if I could just do better… but I no longer think there is anything I could have done to make her happy."

"I do not think I would have believed you if you had told me, and I am even sorrier for that." He dropped his head down for a moment, then lifted it again, looking up at Gregory. "I know I already apologized to you before, but I feel as though I should again. Even after you told me how my mother spoke to Tiffany, part of me did not fully believe you."

Gregory shrugged.

"She was your mother. I never saw that side of her until now, either. There were many things she said to Tiffany that, looking back, I can see were malicious rather than thoughtless. She said them in front of me, and I still dismissed it, still gave her the benefit of the doubt, and came up with reasonable explanations for why she would say such a thing, and she was not even *my* mother." He shot an apologetic look at his own mother, who had disliked the other duchess almost from the beginning.

He should have listened to her instead of dismissing it as feminine squabbling. Especially since his mother was not exactly the type to indulge in unnecessary disputes.

Now, he knew better for the future.

Tiffany

Chest aching, Tiffany wrestled with her internal emotions. Part of her wanted to hug her brother and reassure him. Another part of her wanted to scream because she could not help but wonder if she'd been invisible to him until now. Why had he not noticed the difference in how their mother treated them?

Her mother had manipulated them both. She knew that. Deep down, she knew that. Sebastian's haggard face and obvious guilt helped soothe some of her resentment. He was castigating himself far more effectively than she would likely be able to. The only reason he would do that was because he truly did love her. Which helped quite a bit.

Knowing her husband had defended her to her brother also warmed her. She had not realized... it must have been when Sebastian joined the others while she was preparing for her tea. Gregory had not mentioned it. Likely trying to protect her again. They were going to need to discuss that, eventually.

"I always wanted to believe she said the things she did because she was trying to help me," Tiffany said, some of the tightness loosening in her chest. It was a little easier to forgive her brother when she realized she had also tried to explain away her mother's little cruelties. She'd always blamed herself.

She had wanted to believe her mother loved her.

How could she blame Sebastian for the same thing? Especially because their mother doted on him.

"Well, you do not have to worry about her trying to *help* you anymore." Sebastian let go of her hand and began buttering his toast. His voice had hardened, his posture stiffening as he moved from apologetic to angered. "I've sent her to the Grange. I put her in the carriage myself this morning before I came over here."

Tiffany's jaw dropped open. The Grange was the smallest and most far-flung of Sebastian's estates. The one time Tiffany could remember visiting there was when her father was alive, and the entire family had been invited to the former Duke of Grafton's sister's wedding. The Grange was close to Grafton lands and allowed them to attend without needing to be hosted by the Duke of Grafton, as Sommerset Chase was already full of wedding guests who'd had to travel farther distances.

Her mother had hated every minute of it, from what she remembered, complaining about the smallness of the house and the shabbiness of the furniture and décor.

"The Grange?" she squeaked. She could only imagine her mother's rage.

"Yes. The Grange. She can stay there until she learns how to behave herself. I also told her that I would start removing servants from the household for each unflattering rumor I heard about you or your marriage," Sebastian said darkly. "I might be able to banish her to the country and keep a tight grip on her funds, but she'll still be able to write letters to her friends. I will not have her doing further damage."

Tiffany stared at him. Of all the outcomes she might have expected, she was utterly taken aback. At most, she'd hoped Sebastian might be able to curb their mother's tongue a bit or influence her to be kinder to Tiffany. He loved their mother. For good reason.

"You did not have to do that for me," she said quietly.

"Yes, I did. You did not hear the way she ranted on the way home or after we got there. There's something very wrong with her. She vacillated back and forth between cajoling me and demanding I cut you off from the family entirely." He shook his head. "Something about you becoming a duchess has her completely unhinged. I spoke with Harleen. She sends her apologies as well for not being able to do more to protect you. She has gone with mother to the Grange to keep an eye on her."

Eyes filling up with tears, Tiffany pressed her fingertips to her lips.

"I wish I could have said goodbye to her," she said sadly. Harleen had not always been able to champion Tiffany, but she had done her best to make life more bearable for her. That she would still be watching over Tiffany from afar made her even sadder that she had not been able to say farewell.

"You can write to her if you wish. She would be happy to hear from you. Once I got her away from mother and started asking questions, I was able to learn a lot more." He shook his head. "She had not asked to speak with me in the past because she could not be sure she would be heard. But she told me that mother deliberately dressed you to appear unfashionable and plain. Her opinion was that mother was torn between jealousy of you and wanting you to shine enough to reflect well on her and the family."

"Jealous of me?" Tiffany could hardly countenance such a thing.

"It must have been quite the pebble in her shoe when Tiffany married Gregory then," Gregory's mother said. She'd been so quiet, and when Tiffany looked at her, she appeared more sad than smug. Mama met her gaze, nothing but affection and sorrow for both her and Sebastian apparent in her eyes. "I am so sorry, darling. You deserved so much better from her."

The truth of her words struck a chord in Tiffany's chest that ached unbearably. As if he sensed it, Gregory reached out to take her hand again, offering her his silent support. She smiled at him through the ache.

"My understanding is that the combination of Tiffany becoming a duchess and her new appearance was taken by mother as being some kind of insult to her." Sebastian shook his head, scrubbing his hand over his face. "I confess, despite Harleen's explanations, I do not entirely understand it."

"Because you are a sensible young man." The older woman's lips twisted. "Your mother is not behaving sensibly. My own opinion is that she saw Tiffany as an extension of herself, not as her own person. She wanted Tiffany to be controlled by her and to reflect well on her, but certainly never to outshine her." Now, some smugness came through as Gregory's mother beamed at Tiffany. "Unfortunately for her, despite all her efforts, Tiffany turned out to shine as brightly as the North Star."

"Thank you, Mama," Tiffany replied. There was pain that she would never hear such words from her own mother, but she was still surrounded by love. Her mother-in-law seemed determined to make up for the lack of her own, and Tiffany was happy to reciprocate.

"Trust me, my dear, you are most welcome. As are you, Sebastian. I hope you will join us for all family gatherings in the future." The dowager gave him a look that turned the 'hope' into more of a 'demand'. A glimmer of a smile played on Sebastian's lips.

"Thank you, I would love to," her brother replied.

As awful as she felt about being relieved that her mother had been sent away, not just from Tiffany herself but from Society, and that she would not need to worry about her anymore, she had to admit this was far better than if her mother stayed in town. That Sebastian had threatened her with lessening some of her creature comforts if she tried to undermine them from afar relieved her even more.

Gregory's hand lifted hers to his lips, and she turned her head to smile at him. Her brother might have been the one to take action, but she knew she would not be where she was right now without Gregory. Without his support. Without his love.

She was very much looking forward to being able to show him her gratitude.

THIRTY-NINE

Tiffany.

"Ow!" Wriggling her bottom, Tiffany pushed her hips back toward her husband, despite the stinging slap he'd landed on her upturned cheek. No, not despite. Because of.

She wanted another.

Gregory obliged almost immediately, his hand coming down with a sharp smacking noise against the other side of her buttocks to give her a matching red, throbbing spot. Moaning, Tiffany shuddered, rocking slightly to drag the tight nubs of her nipples across the bedsheets, stimulating the sensitive buds.

"Is there a reason you left our bed without waking me this morning?" he asked, his hand coming down again, this time on her right sit spot where the curve of her bottom met her thigh. She squealed as the hot sting flared through her.

"Ah... I thought you looked like you needed more sleep?" It was not a very strong excuse because it was not meant to be.

She'd left him lying there for the exact reason she was now kneeling on the bolster at the foot of their bed, breasts hanging beneath her. Both of them naked as jaybirds, with her in a position of supplication. Because she'd hoped to earn a spanking from him.

Gregory snorted at her weak reason.

"Do you know what I think, little swan?"

His hand came down on her other sit spot, and she squealed again, jerking forward, then shuddering as her breasts swayed beneath her, nipples rubbing against the bedsheets. Between her thighs, her pussy pulsed eagerly.

"What do you think, husband?" she asked breathlessly.

Rather than his hand coming down hard again, he gripped her inner thigh, moving his hand up the center until his fingers found the wet folds of her arousal. She moaned as he rubbed the tips of his fingers over the swollen pearl of her clitoris, making her insides clench as her body hummed with need.

"I think you left me lying in bed this morning because this is what you wanted for our afternoon," he purred, his other hand coming down and squeezing her bottom cheek where he'd spanked her while his fingers toyed with her slick pussy before plunging in up to his knuckle. He twisted them inside her. Tiffany made a little moaning sound and did not deny his words. "Which means I need to teach you a little lesson about who is in charge."

She was so lost in the haze of growing pleasure that she did not immediately comprehend his words. They floated around her, outside of her, only making their way into her consciousness when his fingers pulled out of her slick hole and began to press against the tighter, higher, drier one.

"Oh! Gregory!"

"Stay still, little swan," he ordered in a growling voice as his fingers forced their way past the tight ring around her entrance, making her gasp. It stung far more than any of the swats to her bottom had. "I need to stretch this little hole out, or I might hurt you more than I mean to when I use my cock."

More than I mean to.

The sentiment made her thoughts fuzz and her heart pound in her chest, her muscles feeling suddenly watery and weak. If she'd been standing, she was not sure her knees would have held her up. As it was, she bent her head down, whimpering as he plundered her bottom with his fingers, pressing her forehead against her arms in front of her.

"Good girl, that's it. Take my fingers up your tight little arse. Bigger things will be there yet." The anticipation in his voice was impossible to deny, and it sent a shiver up her spine.

Tiffany was breathless with aroused fear as he continued to push his fingers back and forth, stretching her out. It did not hurt unbearably, but it was not comfortable either. Still, she would bear the discomfort if it pleased him. She also knew that she had put herself in this position, taking action to tease him, knowing she was playing with fire. Was it any wonder she was about to be burned?

His fingers withdrew, and he started spanking her again, making her gasp and rock as heat bloomed in her cheeks. She felt suddenly so very empty, even though she was not sure she wanted him inside her again... at least not there. Neither was she sure she did not want him there. If he ended up sliding into her pussy, rather than her arse, she might even be disappointed.

Though the thought of taking his thick length into her tighter back entrance was intimidating. How could he possibly fit?

His hand came down again and again, distracting her from her worries as the skin of her bottom heated. It was turning pink under his hard hand; she was sure of it. Tiffany moaned, wriggling back and forth as he peppered the swats over the entire swatch of her curves, up and down, and occasionally landing a blow right between her legs on her throbbing pussy.

"Gregory!" She shrieked his name when his fingers snapped against her clitoris, making the little bud pulse.

"Soon, little swan. I want your cheeks nice and red hot for me before I slide my cock between them." His voice was dark, growly, the tone one she had become accustomed to thinking of as his 'bedroom voice'. Not that he only used it in the bedroom. He used it whenever he was taking charge of her.

The visual he painted as he spanked her, his hand returning to the same spots now because there was no fresh skin to abuse, made her body throb in excited anticipation. Surely, by now, her bottom had to be red. It certainly felt hot, especially when he paused to caress her chastened skin before lifting his hand to spank her again.

She had no idea how long it went on. All she knew was that she was hot and ready by the time he slid his cock into her pussy. But he did not begin to thrust. Instead, he held himself inside the warm clasp of her body as something slick dripped into the crease of her bottom, coating the outside of her hole.

Tiffany gasped as his fingers pushed against her. The slickness of her arousal might have eased his fingers way before, but that was nothing compared to whatever oil he was now using on her tight hole. The lubrication made it impossible for her clenching muscles to get any sort of purchase on his digits—and pleasured him as she inadvertently clenched around his cock simultaneously.

With his fingers in her bottom and his cock in her pussy, she felt so full, she could barely breathe, as if there was no more room left in her body for air. Even the heat on her cheeks from her spanking seemed to subside when set against such overwhelming sensations. His fingers moved, probing, twisting, setting off the little nerve endings around the rim of her entrance.

Then they pulled out, and his cock retreated a moment later, only to shift upward, the blunt head pressing against her bottom hole. Tiffany whimpered, shuddering as Gregory gripped her hips tightly, holding her in place as he began to thrust forward between her heated cheeks. The slow, steady intrusion was shockingly intimate, even more so than his fingers somehow.

He was thicker, stretching her even more than she'd already been, making her pant from the exertion. Harder. There was less bend to his cock than to his fingers. She moaned as she felt herself being pressed open, her little hole clenching around him. The combined lubrication meant her muscles spasmed in vain, unable to slow the inexorable assault. He just kept going deeper and deeper in one excruciatingly long movement.

Tiffany wriggled, but there was only so much she could move. The bolster she was kneeling on was at such a height that it benefited him completely—her lower body basically trapped between the bed and him. She felt him getting closer, his knees sliding between hers, keeping her legs spread open as his weight pressed into her from behind.

He groaned as he slid in deeper, his fingers gripping and relaxing on her hips as he plundered her virgin depths. Tiffany closed her eyes as she felt his groin come to rest against her hot cheeks.

"That's it, little swan. Your tight arse feels so good around my cock." He caressed her hips, and she shuddered, her tight ring squeezing the base of his cock. It hurt, but not unbearably. It hurt in that way that made her pulse race faster, her pussy throb with need, and her nipples tighten as they rubbed against the bedsheets. The sensation was wickedly indecent and made her feel all the more aroused. "How does it feel to you?"

"Full." Tiffany felt as though she could barely gasp out the word. "Hot."

He chuckled, a darkly erotic noise. "Well, you are certainly both."

Rather than giving her a chance to respond, he began to withdraw, his cock sliding along her sensitive tissues as it moved. Somehow, it felt even more raw, even more unsettling than the sensation of him sliding in. Tiffany cried out, her fingers clutching the bed as if it could hold her in place.

Then, before he could completely remove himself from her tight hole, he reversed directions and began to thrust in again. The effect on her body was dizzying. Her entire existence seemed to narrow into herself, to the assault on her senses, to the almost unbearable intimacy of having him move inside her in such a manner. She cried out, rocking with him, pushing back against him, as her pleasure began to grow, drowning out the discomfort.

She felt him moving harder, faster, his thrusts causing him to reignite the sting from her spanking as his body smacked against her chastised cheeks. The relentless strokes back and forth in her tight hole, eased by the oil, were making her feel quite wild. A strange kind of ecstasy was building inside her, a deep well of wicked rapture that felt far more encompassing than her previous climaxes.

The throbbing in her clit was almost painful, and she reached down, sliding her fingers between the bed and her body to curve over her mound, trying to find some relief. Almost the moment she touched the little bud, she felt the fireworks explode in her, that tiny bit of stimulation being all she needed to push herself over the edge.

She cried out, her fingers rubbing against her clit as Gregory kept thrusting, kept moving, sending wave after pulsing wave of pure bliss through her. The grip on her hips tightened as she spasmed around him, her muscles clenching and massaging his cock as he filled her over and over. As she cried out again, she heard his lower groan and felt him slam home inside her, burying himself completely in her and flooding her bowels with his seed.

~

Gregory

Claiming his wife's final virginity brought with it a sense of possessive satisfaction Gregory had never experienced. He was her first, and he intended to be her last, which was something he'd never been able to say about any woman before. He'd also wanted all of her.

Now, she was lounging on the bed, thoroughly cleaned, and he'd just finished wiping himself off so he could crawl onto the bed and curl around her. Luxuriating in the ability to hold her and touch her as much as he wanted. He pressed a kiss to her brow.

"You are perfection," he murmured, making her giggle.

Then he felt her shift a bit.

"I do not feel perfect," she confessed with a little sigh, nuzzling her nose against his chest hair. The sensation was distracting, but he was not going to ask her to stop. He liked the closeness. He stroked his fingers down her back, sliding his legs between hers, enjoying the twining of her silken limb about his.

"How are you not perfect?"

"I am glad Sebastian sent my mother to the country." She nuzzled closer, her movements akin to trying to bury her face in his chest.

"Well, then I am not perfect, either, because I am also glad Sebastian sent your mother to the country."

Tiffany snorted, the little noise making him grin. She slapped his chest lightly, and he reached down to squeeze her sore bottom in retaliation, making her squeak.

"It is not the same. She is not *your* mother."

"I think that you feeling guilt about not feeling bad shows what a pure heart you have," he replied, taking the hand she had smacked his chest with and holding it against his heart. "She does not deserve your consideration."

"Even though she is my mother?"

"*Especially* because she is your mother. You should have been *her* consideration, not the other way around. Can you imagine treating our children the way your mother treated you?" He already knew the answer because Tiffany did not have a cruel bone in her body.

"Absolutely not." Tiffany shook her head, her body recoiling at the very notion of such a thing. Then she stilled, as if realizing what that meant about the way her mother had treated her. She shook her head again, her voice going even quieter. "I still feel guilty that I like your mother better than I like my own."

"My mother likes you. 'The blood of the covenant is thicker than the water of the womb.' Just because your mother birthed you does not mean you have to cleave to her for the rest of your life. If she ever changes and you want to try to build a better relationship with her, that is understandable. But in the meantime, do you want to be around her? Do you want her around our children?"

Tiffany shook her head again, even more emphatically.

"No. I do hope that maybe she will change, that being separated from everything and having some time to reflect will help her see…" Her voice trailed off, and she sighed. "I do not have any great hopes, though."

Gregory did not either. His mother-in-law did not strike him as the kind of woman given to self-reflection or admitting her failings. He hugged Tiffany tighter. How she had turned out so sweet and kind with a mother like that… it just went to show her strength of character.

"I wish my father was still alive," she whispered, making his heart pang.

"I do, too." He felt the usual surge of guilt. Not so much over Montblanc's involvement in their fathers' deaths but over his relief that his own father was gone. Still, he'd rather them both alive than both gone. Though, if their fathers were not dead, he might not have been looking for a wife this Season. He might not have seen Tiffany in the library. They would not be married right now.

Sometimes, fate worked in mysterious ways.

There was one thing he could do, though.

"We will find out who did it, and we will get justice for your father." He had already vowed to do so, along with his friends, but he wanted her to hear the words, too. "I will keep you informed of everything we discover."

"And I will help as I can."

"As you can," he agreed. He kissed the top of her head, his chest filled with the warmth of his emotions. "I am here for you. Always. No matter what. I love you, my little swan."

Tipping her head back against his arm so she could look at him, her legs wound around his, hand caressing his back, his wife smiled at him.

"I love you, my indecent duke."

He raised his eyebrow at her.

"Indecent, am I?"

"From the moment you kissed me in the library to right now." She narrowed her eyes at him. "My bottom is still throbbing."

Well, he could hardly argue with that. Rather than try, he lowered his lips to hers, claiming them in a searing kiss. She was his little swan, but she was also his indecent duchess.

EPILOGUE

Nathanial

Wife. Money. Wife. Money. Wife. Money.

His family needed the second, which meant he needed the former.

If only there were another way...

That thought flittered through his head at least ten times a day, but he had been over it and over it and over it again, by himself, with his man of finances, and with his friends. They all came to the same conclusion. Most avenues of increasing his wealth would either take far too long or need an influx of capital to be viable in any manner.

Capital he did not have unless he agreed to a loan from one of his friends—a good deal of his family's debt was to the very banks he'd originally gone to—or married a woman with a large dowry. A very large one would cover his debts and allow him to make some moves to turn things around, though it would still take time to bring the coffers back to what they should have been.

Sometimes, he wondered if he should thank whoever had murdered his father, whose profligate ways had gone far beyond squandering the estates for which he was responsible. Even his position as a duke might not have been able to keep him from Newgate prison if he'd kept going on the way he had been. Nathanial's mother's family did not have the means to bail them out, either.

"Which means I need to marry. Soon." Saying the statement out loud always felt like he was giving it more weight, as if the load was not heavy enough already. Which was why he forced himself to do it. To remember why he was putting himself through the torture of a search for a bride. Why he was at a house party this weekend.

He stared out the window of Blackstone Abbey, down at the courtyard where another carriage was pulling up. Another guest for the house party he'd been invited to this weekend. Lady Astrid had assured him that almost all the ladies in attendance would have dowries more than sufficient to cover his debts and that she would be sure to point him in their direction.

A knock on his door had him turning away from the window.

"Come in." He waited only long enough for the door to open and nodded his greeting at Matthew, Duke of St. Albans. The Lord of Luck nodded back, grinning as he stepped inside, closing the door behind him.

"Watching the arrivals of our brides-to-be?" he asked, chuckling.

Nathanial pushed a smile that he did not feel onto his face. Matthew was one of his friends who had offered him money. Not even a loan. Matthew did not need to be repaid. Unlike Nathanial's father, everything Matthew touched turned to gold. The gambling hell owners groaned when they saw him coming.

There was a part of Nathanial that wanted to just take Matthew's offer and relieve himself of the burden his father had placed on him, but his pride would not allow it. And pride was one of the few things he had left in his possession, other than the entailed estates the family literally could not sell. Everyone would know that he had taken money from one of his friends. His family's reputation would take another hit. With his sisters all nearing their debuts into Society, he could not do that to them. They deserved to be able to marry *whoever* they wanted, and he could make that happen for them.

He just had to take the only honorable way forward and marry a young lady with a large dowry from a family of good reputation and a multitude of connections.

"You were not?" he asked in return, moving his attention back to the family disembarking from their carriage. A little jolt went through him. Even at this distance, it was impossible not to recognize the Little family. Mrs. Little, Miss Little, and the younger Mr. Little all had skin far darker complexioned than the rest of the *ton*.

Nathanial did not care about that, though he knew some did. From the moment he'd met Miss Little, he'd felt a spark, an immediate attraction... and he'd had to bury it.

"Ah, Miss Little." Matthew peered over his shoulder before coming around him. "Very pretty. Dowry is certainly large enough for you. Smart of Mr. Little to capitalize on the rose diamond mines in India. Too bad it did not do anything to help convince his pater to accept his marriage and children."

"Her dowry is more than large enough, but..." Nathanial let the thought hang.

"But what?" Matthew blinked owlishly, turning to look at him in confusion. Though he was a wonderful friend, sometimes Matthew was very obtuse, especially when it came to navigating the *ton*. Everything always worked out well enough for him.

Unfortunately, unlike Matthew's Midas touch, everything Nathanial's family touched seemed to turn to pure shit.

"I have my sisters to consider."

"You think they would not like her?"

"I think that she would not be able to help them navigate their own Seasons. With the way she and her family are being ostracized this Season, I cannot risk marrying her and hope that the *ton* changes their collective mind by the time Juliana debuts next year."

"Juliana debuts next year?" Matthew was genuinely horrified, which was exactly how Nathanial felt. "When did she get old enough for that?"

"Time creeps up on us, does it not?" Nathanial chuckled grimly.

"Another reason why my own wedding needs to happen as soon as possible. To a bride with connections, who can help guide her and who will help bolster our family's reputation after what my father did to it." He took in a huge breath and sighed, his gaze lowering back down to the family in the courtyard. He had to give his sisters the best chance he could to find good matches to honorable men who would treat them well and care for them.

Miss Little's pink traveling dress set off her dark hair and skin to perfection, her matching bonnet hiding most of her features. Just looking at her made him want to throw his responsibilities to the wind and do something for himself. Truly choose for himself.

He consoled himself with the knowledge that it was nothing more than an initial attraction, and it would fade. Perhaps getting to know her better during the house party would help it fade faster. Instant attraction rarely lasted beyond true interaction.

Matthew's hand came up to Nathanial's shoulder to give him a comforting squeeze.

"We will find the right bride for you." He gave Nathanial's shoulder another pat, then reached into his pocket, pulling out his lucky coin. "Maybe she's the right bride for me."

Though he refused to show it on his face, Nathanial's entire gut clenched when Matthew flipped his coin in the air. He had the most unnerving desire to reach out and grab it so it could not land.

Matthew caught it and opened his hand, sighing as he shook his head. The tension immediately unraveled from Nathanial's body as he let out the breath he had not known he'd been holding.

"Still says no," Matthew said cheerfully.

"You have flipped for her before?" Nathanial asked. He had not realized.

"Of course. She's pretty, she's quiet, she's sweet. I need to marry someone." Matthew leaned forward, squinting in the distance. "There is another carriage coming."

"Are you flipping to marry them or just to court them?"

"Court them. Mostly." Matthew shrugged. "Sometimes just a dance. It depends on my mood."

Wonderful. Whether or not Miss Little married his closest friend was dependent on the coin landing correctly. Maybe for once, *he* would get lucky, and the coin would point Matthew at some other young lady for the duration of the party.

The Littles moved out of view. The carriage coming up the lane was approaching the house.

Out of the corner of his eye, he could see Matthew slanting a glance at him. His friend turned away slightly, flipping the coin again.

"What did you just flip for?" It was not a question; it was a demand for an answer. Something about the way Matthew had looked at him made him suspicious.

"For you and Miss Little." Matthew shrugged, sheepishly tucking the coin into his pocket so Nathanial could not see how it had landed.

"What did it say?"

"I do not know if it works for anyone but me." Matthew shrugged, leaning forward to watch the carriage stop in front of the house.

Nathanial thought about pressing him but decided against it. Not that it mattered. Unlike Matthew, he did not live his life by the flip of a coin. He made his own decisions, and Miss Little was not for him.

~

NATHANIAL FINDS *his bride in The Duke's Indecent Match.*

All About That Harp

Tiffany

The music room in the manor on Gregory's estate was glorious. She had a suspicion that he'd made sure of it, before they removed from the capital to the country, and that it had not looked this way before. But she loved it.

The location of the room meant it was lit with sunshine for the majority of the day, a soft golden glow that played off the gold tassels holding the navy blue curtains in place. The view from the windows overlooked the gardens and an expanse of rolling hills that ended in forest in the distance. Sometimes she came in here just to look out the window.

Today, though, her fingers were itching to play.

Crossing the room, passing the pianoforte and the various stringed instruments that were in place should she decide to use them, she went straight for the harp. Running her fingers over the strings to check that they were in tune before she sat down, she was startled when she turned and saw Gregory standing in the doorway as if he'd appeared from nowhere.

"I thought you were working on your accounts," she said,

bemused. His study was not far from the music room, but she hadn't expected his company this morning.

"Are you going to play the harp?" he asked, rather than answering her.

"I planned to."

"Then the accounts can wait." Stepping inside, he closed the door behind him and locked it, which made her raise her eyebrow at him. With his mother now happily ensconced in the Dower House and no visitors currently staying with them, the odds of someone else coming to listen to her play were very low. If he was locking the door, it was to ensure that none of the servants interrupted them.

Suspicion as to intentions roused and were quickly confirmed as he strode towards her with a particularly intent gaze. She knew what that meant.

"Gregory! I came in here to play," she said, laughing as he pulled her into his arms, before he could bend his head to kiss her.

"Oh, you are going to play," he replied firmly. "I have a very particular fantasy about you playing this harp for me."

Before she could question what kind of fantasy, his lips were on hers, cutting off her opportunity to speak. Laughter bubbled up in her chest, but she leaned into his kiss, because she knew he was not going to be put off till later. Though what kind of fantasy he could have that included her playing the harp, she had no idea.

Her body roused as his hands moved over her, his tongue delving between her lips to dance with hers.

Finding out what his fantasy was certainly didn't sound like a hardship. Tiffany moaned, shuddering as he cupped her breast through her morning dress, his other hand moving to undo the buttons that had only been done up an hour ago by her maid. Her body came alive at his touch, desire surging in anticipation of pleasure.

It did not take him long to get her down to nothing but her corset and stockings, tossing her clothing to the side. His hands moved over the stays of her corset and up to the fabric covering her breasts.

Lifting them out of their cups, he massaged the soft flesh, his lips clinging to hers despite the necessary space between them for his movements.

Then his lips lifted and he moved around behind her, shucking off his jacket as he did so. Tiffany turned her head to see him sitting down on the chair she was going to use, undoing the placket of his pants for his cock to spring free. Unlike her, he remained fully dressed, other than his jacket, and he grinned up at her, dark eyes sparkling.

"Come here, little swan," he said, reaching out to grasp her hips and move her back towards him, facing away from him – facing her harp. "Come sit on my cock."

"Oh!" He guided her down, her hands automatically going to hold onto the frame of her harp as she found herself being seated upon his cock.

Her pussy was already wet with anticipation and arousal, and she felt the blunt head part her folds and then begin to sink into her. The position of trying to hold herself up while he was seated behind her was impossible. She sank quickly down on him, gasping as he filled her. The fabric of his clothing rubbed against her skin as she parted her thighs to make it easier for her to balance atop him, draping one leg on either side of his.

Gregory rubbed his hands over her bottom, groaning with pleasure as she impaled herself on him. Then he ran his hands up the sides of her body, over her corset, and to her breasts so he could cup them from behind.

Pressing a kiss to the nape of her neck, his fingers found her nipples and gave them a rough pinch that made her clench around him.

"Play for me, little swan," he murmured, dropping hot, wet kisses over the back of her shoulders as his hands squeezed her breasts. "I want to listen to you play while you sit on my cock."

Tiffany shuddered as his words went through her, her body squeezing down on him again. Her wits had fled, along with her clothing, and his hands moving on her breasts did nothing to help them return. Nor did the stiff cock throbbing inside her, making her squirm in distraction.

"What should I play?"

He squeezed her nipples again, making her mewl.

"Whatever you want."

Beethoven, she decided impulsively, the variations. She had them memorized, she didn't need to focus as much to play them. They were short and she could play them over and over without needing to look at any sheet music.

Which was just as well, because as her fingers began to dance over the harp strings, the music flowing through the room, Gregory began doing his best to thoroughly distract her. He wasn't intentionally trying to, she was sure of it, but the music seemed to make it impossible for him to sit still.

He rocked beneath her, not quite thrusting, but making her move along to the tempo of the music. His hands plumped her breasts, fingers pulling and tugging on her nipples, making the tiny buds ache and throb along with the clenching of her pussy. It was not lovemaking exactly, and yet it was wildly intimate as she played, no longer trying to follow any composition, but letting her fingers move as they willed.

Pushing back against him, she was now rocking on top of him, his cock held deeply inside her. There was no thrusting, no friction, and yet her pleasure was growing anyway.

How long they stayed like that, the sunlight warming her bare skin, her fingers pulling music from the harp while his elicited soft moans from her, his cock throbbing deep inside her, she could not say. It could have lasted mere minutes or an hour as she squirmed atop him, the slow crescendo of pleasure winding about her senses like a tightly drawn harp string.

She was going to snap at any moment.

Breathlessly, she ground down atop him, trying to get the stimulation that she needed to reach her pinnacle. Not quite able to find it.

With a groan, Gregory shuddered beneath her, releasing one of her breasts to reach down between her legs and begin to rub her clit.

Tiffany's breath caught in her throat as her muscles spasmed around him. Her fingers lost their place on the strings, but it didn't matter anymore. She dragged them over the strings, the rippling notes ringing in the air as Gregory's fingers circled the tiny nub of pleasure and sent her soaring.

She cried out, back arching, pussy clamping down on his cock, muscle memory prompting her to play a glissando over the harp again and again as she and Gregory rocked in simultaneous ecstasy. The music was somehow a part of her climax, the sound adding to the sensations spiraling through her.

Gasping, she came to a shuddering halt, clinging to the harp frame as the last tremors of her orgasm were wrung from her by Gregory's fingers. She could feel him pulsing inside her, the wet head of his seed filling her with his own climax. A final shudder from her husband and then his hands relaxed.

Closing her eyes, Tiffany shook her head, though a small smile played about her lips. She was never going to be able to look at her harp the same way again.

A BONUS FOR YOU

What's next is the original intended bonus content for the book - an entry from Isabella's diary. I intend to include one for each book so that we can watch her story progress as she will not be marrying one of my seven dukes, but I don't want to leave her hanging completely.

Thank you so much and happy reading!

~Golden Angel

ISABELLA'S DIARY – ENTRY #1

Sinclair is dead but not buried.

His funeral service was today.

To grieve without a body, without a last look upon his face, seems somehow worse than if he were there before me. William told me of his last glimpse of Sinclair, the waves pulling him away from the ship during the storm. I understand that they could not recover him from the middle of the Atlantic.

Sometimes I dream of him, myself standing in William's place, running to the rail of the ship and trying to throw myself overboard after him. Trying to save him.

But the waves pull him under before I can touch the water.

I wonder how he felt, as he watched the distance between himself and the ship grow. If he felt dread.

If he felt fear.

If he thought of me.

Selfish creature that I am, I hope he thought of me because I think of him daily.

I believe I will do so for the rest of my life.

It has been years since I kept a diary, but today I felt compelled to write. To remember. Because it feels as though otherwise he will be completely lost to me. I do not want to forget a thing about him, and yet already it is difficult to recall things.

The mind does not retain memories of him the way I wish they would.

I can remember the touch of his hand, the way his lips would brush over mine, gently at first and then more firmly, deepening the kiss.

Yet I cannot remember exactly where each of our kisses happened.

I remember the first one, two years ago on my birthday. I remember the dress I was wearing. I remember his crisp white of his shirt against the sharp black of his jacket, the way his dark hair waved back from his face. I remember the way my nose bumped against his, how I gasped when his tongue slid between my lips and into my mouth to touch mine. I remember the way my body tightened against his and how he held me as my head whirled and my knees weakened.

But what about the second kiss? The third? The fourth?

My mind strains but I do not know.

And I weep not only for the loss of him, but for the memories I have already forgotten. That I did not anticipate would be important holding onto. Because I thought we had forever ahead of us.

William has assured me that as Sinclair's heir, he will take care of everything. He has offered to allow me to go through Sinclair's things, if there is anything I want to keep to remember Sinclair by - that is not entailed to the estate or part of the family's heirlooms of course. He has reassured me that I need not return the engagement ring, as Sinclair bought it for me specifically.

Looking down at the opals and diamonds still adorning my finger, I almost wish that he had demanded its return, because how shall I ever bear to make the decision of when to remove it myself?

I cannot imagine ever doing so and yet I know that eventually I must. My parents expect me to marry. They will not push me while I'm in mourning, but unless I plan to become the spinster aunt, forever supported by my brother or his heir, I know I have no other choice.

My heart grows heavy with these thoughts, even knowing that it is a necessity that I think of my own future. Sinclair would want me to. He would want me to take care of myself and secure my future - in truth, he would be quite angry with me if I did not.

But for now, at least I have six months of full mourning before I have to entertain any such notions.

Six months to gather myself and think about what I shall do next. What I want from a life without Sinclair.

Today, though, I am going to sit and dream of the life we would have had together.

The life we should have had together.

As ever,

Isabella

About the Author

Golden Angel is a USA Today best-selling author of heart and bottom warming romance.

She is happily married, old enough to know better but still too young to care, and a big fan of happily-ever-afters, strong heroes and heroines, and sizzling chemistry.

When she's not writing, she can often be found on the couch reading, in front of her sewing machine making a new cosplay, hanging out with her friends, or wandering the Maryland Renaissance Fair.

www.goldenangelromance.com

BB bookbub.com/authors/golden-angel
g goodreads.com/goldeniangel
f facebook.com/GoldenAngelAuthor
instagram.com/goldeniangel

ACKNOWLEDGMENTS

I have a lot of people to thank for helping me with this book.

My amazing beta readers, who are invaluable in helping me catch mistakes, doing the initial grammar and word checks, identifying continuity issues, and working through problems with me. Marie, Candida, Marta, Rara, Piper, and Katherine – you all make these books so much better!

My Patreon subscribers, whose comments and assistance keep me motivated and bring me so much joy.

Another extra special thank you to Katherine, who got me started down this career path and has been by my metaphorical side ever since.

Thank you to my husband for his continued loved and support. I could not do this without you.

And, as always, a big thank you to all of you for buying and reading my work... if you love it, please leave a review!

OTHER TITLES BY GOLDEN ANGEL

HISTORICAL SPANKING ROMANCE

Domestic Discipline Quartet

Birching His Bride

Dealing With Discipline

Punishing His Ward

Claiming His Wife

The Domestic Discipline Quartet Box Set

Bridal Discipline Series

Philip's Rules

Gabrielle's Discipline

Lydia's Penance

Benedict's Commands

Arabella's Taming

Pride and Punishment Box Set

Commands and Consequences Box Set

Deception and Discipline

A Season for Treason

A Season for Scandal

A Season for Smugglers

A Season for Spies

Desire and Discipline

A Season for Bliss

A Season for Desire

A Season for Christmas

Indecent Dukes

The Duke's Indecent Scandal

The Duke's Indecent Match

The Duke's Indecent Purchase

The Duke's Indecent Desire

The Duke's Indecent Proposal

The Duke's Indecent Betrothal

The Duke's Indecent Courtship

Bridgewater Brides

Their Harlot Bride

Standalone

Marriage Training

The Duke's Pursuit

Rogue Booty

CONTEMPORARY BDSM ROMANCE

Venus Rising Series (MFM Romance)

The Venus School

Venus Aspiring

Venus Desiring

Venus Transcendent

Venus Wedding

Venus Rising Box Set

Stronghold Doms Series

The Sassy Submissive

Taming the Tease

Mastering Lexie

Pieces of Stronghold

Breaking the Chain

Bound to the Past

Stripping the Sub

Tempting the Domme

Hardcore Vanilla

Steamy Stocking Stuffers

A Sassy Christmas

Entering Stronghold Box Set

Nights at Stronghold Box Set

Stronghold: Closing Time Box Set

Masters of Marquis Series

Bondage Buddies

Master Chef

Law & Disorder

Switch Play

Legally Bound

Shallow Submission

Hidden Away

Secret Submission

Third Wheel

Black Fox Security Doms

Danger and Dominance

Cuffs and Cupcakes

Security and Submission

Whips and Weddings

Rescue and Ropes

Bondage and Bad Guys

Dungeons & Doms Series

Dungeon Master

Dungeon Daddy

Dungeon Showdown

Dungeons & Doms Boxset

Daddies Everywhere

Chef Daddy

Foosball Daddies

Taco Daddy

Cheese Daddy

Garden Daddy

SCI-FI ROMANCE

Tsenturion Masters Series with Lee Savino

Alien Captive

Alien Tribute

Alien Abduction

Standalone

Mated on Hades

SHIFTER ROMANCE

Big Bad Bunnies Series

Chasing His Bunny

Chasing His Squirrel

Chasing His Puma

Chasing His Polar Bear

Chasing His Honey Badger

Chasing Her Lion

Night of the Wild Stags

Chasing Tail Box Set

Chasing Tail... Again Box Set